THE ENLIGHTENMENT ADVENTURES * BOOK TWO

I0586708

VINCENT
AND THE DISSIDENTS

Christopher Locke

Edited by Jaya Bhumitra

Published by Fathoming Press

ISBN 978-0-9904197-2-3 (paperback)
ISBN 978-0-9904197-5-4 (ebook)

Fathoming Press
www.Christopher-Locke.com

PRAISE FOR *THE ENLIGHTENMENT ADVENTURES: BOOK ONE PERSIMMON TAKES ON HUMANITY*

"Not only is *Persimmon Takes On Humanity* a riveting read, but it also tackles one of the most important issues of our time with poignancy and heart."

—Gene Baur, President and Co-Founder of Farm Sanctuary

"Rarely has a book so powerfully combined lovable characters, gripping adventure, and a profound message of compassion. This story will make you laugh, cry, and wish you were one of the team."

—Katie Cantrell, Executive Director and Founder, Factory Farming Awareness Coalition

"In taking on industries that exploit animals head on, Christopher Locke is as courageous as his indelible heroine, Persimmon, and has created a memorable novel that's a searing expose of some of the most oppressive, yet seemingly benign industries on the planet. People who have never explored these issues will, quite simply, have their minds blown, and even the most seasoned animal advocates will find themselves re-galvanized by this little raccoon and her big heart."

—Marisa Miller Wolfson, Writer, Director, Editor, *Vegucated*

"With a deep passion for his subject and a wonderful skill in storytelling, Christopher Locke opens an enlightening window onto the little-seen world of animals raised to serve human wants. Sometimes uplifting, at other times disquieting, it's a thoughtful novel that teaches as it entertains. The adventures and tribulations of this unlikely band of raccoons, squirrels and other animals make for an engaging, page-turning read that is hard to put down."

—David Robinson Simon, Author, *Meatonomics*

"With colorful characters and an enthralling story, *Persimmon Takes On Humanity* is not only enjoyable to read, but it might just change your view of humankind, and of the world that we have created."

—Mark Devries, Director, *Speciesism: The Movie*

"The story of Persimmon, a raccoon on a mission, is at times magical and at times a searing view of the abuses animals endure, told from their own perspective. I'll never look at animals the same way after reading Christopher Locke's poignant portrayal."

—E. Van Lowe, Bestselling Author, *Boyfriend From Hell*

For my brilliant wife, Jaya Bhumitra.
Thank you for continuing to believe in this story and me.
Though I know your heart is with Team Rawly,
I will always be grateful that you were the very
first person to join Team Persimmon.

For all my family and friends who donated to my
crowdfunding campaign. This novel would not be
possible without your generous support.

CAST OF CHARACTERS

PERSIMMON – A clever and compassionate female raccoon who has mostly brown fur with sprinkles of gray. After a failed attempt to rescue a group of calves who were trapped in a veal farm, Persimmon was inspired to form a team that goes on adventures rescuing any animal they find suffering at the hands of humans. The team was originally called The Uncaged Alliance, but when they split apart at the end of Book One, Persimmon named her new team The Enlighteners.

DERPOKE – PERSIMMON'S opossum best friend, who is her closest confidante in The Enlighteners. He's analytical and cautious, and he would follow Persimmon anywhere.

SCRAPS – PERSIMMON'S younger brother who is unusually tiny because he was the runt. At the end of Book One, he left Persimmon's team to join Rawly's team.

RAWLY – A male raccoon who means well but often gets on Persimmon's nerves because of his arrogance. At first, he was reluctant to join Persimmon's team, but soon he became a dedicated activist. During the circus mission, his sweetheart, Claudette, and his friend, Fisher, were killed by humans, causing him to lose his temper and release tigers to attack the humans. This prompted Persimmon to suggest he leave the team, which he did, taking Scraps, Apricot, and Drig with him.

Persimmon said that he could keep the original name of the team, The Uncaged Alliance.

VINCENT – A cunning mink whose fur is mostly black with a hint of blue. He lived a hellish life on a fur farm before he finally escaped. He then vowed to himself that he would rescue the minks who were still trapped on the farm. A few months later, he was lucky enough to meet Persimmon and her team. They joined forces and successfully rescued most of the minks. Little did Persimmon know that after she and her team had moved on to their next mission, Vincent began gathering his own army of animals who would rescue other animals.

BRUISER – A Doberman pinscher who looks intimidating on the outside but really has a gentle heart. His fur is mostly black with a few patches of caramel around his face and legs. Persimmon rescued Bruiser from a backyard where his humans had abandoned him to die. Bruiser is one of Persimmon's most loyal friends, so when the team split, he stayed on Persimmon's team.

CHLOE AND TUCKER – A squirrel couple who lived near the veal farm. After seeing the calves suffer for so long, they were inspired to join Persimmon's team, although Chloe is more the activist of the two. Chloe has proved to possess great leadership qualities during the rescue missions. The couple also stayed with Persimmon to join The Enlighteners at the end of Book One.

DRIG – A strong, large raccoon who is Rawly's best buddy. He switched to Rawly's team at the end of Book One.

APRICOT – A sassy and sarcastic orange tabby cat. She led The Uncaged Alliance to the circus (mostly because she thought it would be entertaining to watch them attempt—and fail—to storm the building), but soon she was moved by the plight of the animals abused in the circus, so she ended up joining the team. At the end of Book One, she switched to Rawly's team.

NIBBIN – A young male mink who has brown fur. Persimmon and her team rescued him from the fur farm and he asked to join The Uncaged Alliance. At the end of Book One, he rallied behind Persimmon and joined The Enlighteners. Since he's an orphan, he sees Persimmon as a mother figure.

DUSTY AND LINDER – Raccoon friends of Rawly. After Persimmon's team conducted the rescue at the fur farm, the mink Vincent recruited Dusty and Linder to join his army.

SYNOPSIS OF
THE ENLIGHTENMENT ADVENTURES:
BOOK ONE
PERSIMMON TAKES ON HUMANITY

AT THE BEGINNING of Book One, Persimmon, her opossum best friend, Derpoke, and her younger brother, Scraps, were leading idle lives in the woods. That all changed one night when they were approached by the arrogant raccoon Rawly, who dared them to follow him deep into a dangerous part of the woods to see a mysterious creature. Persimmon and Scraps couldn't resist the lure of an adventure (Derpoke could, but he's not fond of leaving Persimmon's side), so the four of them trekked through the woods and came upon a large building.

They soon discovered that inside the building were animals called calves—the babies of cows and bulls—and to the friends' horror, these animals were suffering. Unbeknownst to Persimmon and her companions, they had stumbled across a veal farm and the calves were doomed to be killed so that humans could eat them.

Because of their deep compassion, Persimmon, Derpoke, and Scraps planned a daring mission to rescue the calves (Rawly joined at the last minute), but to everyone's great disappointment, the humans discovered the team in the middle of the mission and recaptured all the calves. Persimmon's tail was even shot off during the scuffle.

Even worse, soon thereafter, the humans shipped the calves off to a slaughterhouse. Persimmon was the only one of the friends able to sneak onto the transport truck, and despite her best efforts, all the calves were tragically slaughtered right before her eyes.

On Persimmon's journey back home, she came upon a Doberman pinscher named Bruiser who had been left to die in a backyard by his humans when they moved to a new house. Persimmon freed Bruiser and they returned to the forest where they met with Derpoke, Scraps, and a squirrel couple, Chloe and Tucker (these two lived by the veal farm and were also disturbed by the humans' mistreatment of the calves).

Persimmon told her friends that the tragic death of the calves had inspired her to form a team (The Uncaged Alliance) that would go on missions rescuing any animal that they saw suffering at the hands of humans. Her friends loved the idea and were excited about the adventures ahead. They were a little more reluctant about Persimmon's second idea, though, which was never to eat any other animals again. Once she explained that in order to be truly compassionate to all living beings they must not harm other animals for any reason, the team jumped on board. The only one who didn't join the team was Rawly, who refused to be anywhere near Bruiser (there's a long-standing tension between dogs and forest critters).

The friends headed off on their next rescue attempt at a fur farm where minks were imprisoned. There, they met a cunning mink named Vincent, who had escaped the farm the winter before. Vincent had led a hellish life in the fur farm, witnessing the deaths of many friends and family, including his dear brother Frestin, so now he was trying to find a way to rescue the other minks trapped inside.

Before the rescue began, Rawly joined The Uncaged Alliance, bringing with him a new crew of raccoons (including his sweetheart, Claudette, and friends Drig, Linder, and Dusty).

The rescue mission of the minks was a grand success. They were able to save all the surviving minks without being accosted by the humans that ran the fur farm. After that, a young mink, Nibbin, asked to join The Uncaged Alliance since he was in awe of these heroes who had saved his life (he was an orphan, so he wanted a new family).

Little did Persimmon know, though, that while she and the rest of the team were rescuing the minks, Vincent had sent another secret team of minks (led by his brother Trenton) to kill the owners of the fur farm, the Petersons.

After the rescue effort was over, Persimmon and her team went searching for their next mission, never discovering that the Petersons had been killed and that Vincent was now setting his sights on leading his team to rescue all the minks at other nearby fur farms.

On The Uncaged Alliance's next expedition they came across a sassy tabby cat, Apricot, who led them to another location where animals needed rescuing: the circus. There, the team met all the animals trapped and brutalized in the circus (elephants, tigers, camels, horse, and more). The team also heard the heartbreaking story of two elephants, Nayana and Shey. Nayana and Shey were best friends, but after years of abuse, Shey eventually died from tuberculosis. This left Nayana devastated. She was hopeless until Persimmon and her team came to rescue them.

Unfortunately, the mission went horribly awry. The animals in the circus were too big and conspicuous to rescue and a massive battle between Persimmon's team and the humans erupted. By the end, humans had killed Claudette, Fisher, and all the elephants and tigers, and many humans had been killed as well. In a moment of vindication, Nayana was able to get her revenge on the human who had abused Shey and her their entire lives. Unfortunately, Nayana was shot and killed in the process.

Persimmon and the team were shocked by the violent outcome of their latest mission. Persimmon was also perturbed at Rawly, who had released tigers to murder the humans (to retaliate against the humans for killing Claudette and Fisher), so Persimmon suggested that Rawly leave the team.

Rawly snapped back by extending an offer to other team members to form a new team with him. Drig, Apricot, and Scraps all joined Rawly.

Persimmon was devastated that the team had split apart (and especially that her brother had joined the other side). Before Rawly left, Persimmon told him that he could keep the name, The Uncaged Alliance. She was so upset when the team parted ways that she wanted to start fresh with a new name—one that truly represented her goals in starting the rescue missions in the first place.

She finally came up with the name The Enlighteners and exclaimed to the remaining team members that despite the recent setbacks, they would continue the brave missions to rescue any animals they found suffering at the hands of humans—no matter the cost. Teammates Derpoke, Bruiser, Chloe, Tucker, and Nibbin were excited to resume their adventures, which brings us to Book Two...

1

PERSIMMON OPENS HER eyes. The room is pitch black. *Where am I?* The confused raccoon starts to sit up, but suddenly the room begins to spin. Dizziness overcomes her, and nausea hits her hard. She closes her eyes to collect herself. She takes a deep breath. *Breathe. Breathe.* With her eyes closed, her hearing becomes more acute. She can hear other animals in the room—weeping, moaning. She quickly pops her eyes back open. *They're in pain. I need to help them.*

Persimmon goes to hop up, but she realizes there's metal wire all around her. She's in a cage! She attempts to stand up to claw her way out but stumbles when she tries to stand on her right front leg. It's missing! Her right front leg has been hacked off. In its place is a white bandage stained with blood.

Panic sets in. *What happened to my leg?!* She falls against the mesh wire of her tiny cage and peers out over the dark room at all the other animals trapped in cages just like hers. The creatures whimper desperately. Whoever hurt her has hurt them, too.

Persimmon frantically scans the cages to see if any contain her friends. Part of her hopes to see the friendly face of Derpoke, Bruiser, Chloe, Tucker, or Nibbin, but mostly she hopes that whoever captured her did not capture them as well. There are opossums, skunks, squirrels, a few birds, and other raccoons—none of the cages has any of her friends, though. She's relieved yet saddened. *Where is everyone? Are they okay?* A sickening thought hits her. *Am I the only one left? Is everyone that I love in this world gone?*

Dizziness consumes Persimmon again. Even when she's sitting down she feels like her cage is spinning around her. Losing her leg pales in comparison with the thought of losing her friends. *Please let them be okay. Please.*

2

PERSIMMON; HER OPOSSUM best friend, Derpoke; and her Doberman Pinscher pal, Bruiser, trek through the woods at a brisk pace with the squirrel couple, Chloe and Tucker, following in the trees above. The little brown mink Nibbin rides on Persimmon's back—not because he's tired but because it's fun.

As they walk, Persimmon proudly looks over her team: The Enlighteners. *What would I ever do without each of them by my side? We've been through so much together. When Gilby and the other calves were killed, I never thought I'd feel happiness again, but having this group come together to save other animals is what kept me going. Our whole team shared in the triumph of freeing so many minks—one of whom was sweet Nibbin—from the Peterson fur farm. And despite the overwhelming danger of trying to rescue those poor animals trapped in the circus, this courageous crew didn't hesitate to risk their lives. On top of that, these wonderful friends stuck with me* instead of joining foolhardy Rawly's team.

Immediately, thoughts of Apricot, Drig, and Scraps flash through Persimmon's mind. She clenches her jaw in frustration. She's tried to make peace with that painful situation in the past few weeks, but it still stings—not because of some silly pride over feeling like those three deemed Rawly a better leader but because she misses them. Even though Apricot was as sassy a cat as Persimmon had ever met, the feline revealed her true bravery when she joined the team after witnessing the callous abuse of the animals in the circus. The brawny raccoon Drig was also a great help to the rescue missions with his strength and matter-of-fact nature. Then there's Scraps. *My little brother. For the first time since you were born, I have no idea where you are, and I can't be sure that you're safe. How am I supposed to come to terms with that?*

"Persimmon?" Derpoke wheezes as he struggles to keep up with his friends.

Persimmon snaps out of her daydream to find Derpoke panting as he walks alongside her.

"Are we almost there? I…" Derpoke sucks in a deep breath. "I think… I'm going to… collapse."

Persimmon slows to a stop. "My poor Derpoke. I'm so sorry. I was lost in thought, and I'm excited about getting to our next rescue mission, so I didn't even notice how fast we were going."

"You can ride on my back, if ya want, Derpoke," Bruiser offers.

"I'm fine. Thank you." Derpoke drops to the forest floor with a thud. "I just need… to catch…" He doesn't finish his sentence; he's too wiped out.

Persimmon calls up to Chloe and Tucker in the tree. "We're taking a quick break."

Chloe and Tucker cease their hopping between branches. Tucker calls down, "Again? I thought you said we were almost there." Tucker sees his opossum companion sprawled out on the ground, gasping for air. "Oh." Tucker turns to Chloe. "Aren't you glad we don't have stubby legs?"

"I can hear you," Derpoke complains.

Tucker lets out an embarrassed chuckle. Chloe shakes her head and bats her partner's tail. "Way to go, pupsy."

Persimmon peers up at the night sky. She can faintly see the stars fading away and the sunlight filling the sky. "Darn. I was really hoping we'd finally get there tonight, but we may have to rest here."

"Well, maybe we can—" Bruiser begins to reply, but at just that moment, the young and energetic Nibbin, who is still perched on Persimmon's back, interrupts them by tickling Persimmon's sides.

"Tickle, tickle!" Nibbin giggles.

To Nibbin's surprise—and disappointment—Persimmon does not break into a fit of laughter.

"Boo, you're not ticklish," Nibbin says.

"Nope." Persimmon grins. "But you know who *is*?"

The raccoon twists around and grabs Nibbin off her back. She kisses him and tickles his belly with all four paws, throwing him into hysterics. In fact, Nibbin is laughing so hard he can barely breathe, so Persimmon finally lets go, and the brown mink darts down the path as if he were a wind-up toy.

Bruiser watches Nibbin race through the woods. "Sure is a sprightly lil' feller. Sad to think he mighta been stuck in a cage his whole life."

Persimmon nods. "If those vicious humans had had their way, it wouldn't have been a very long life either." The raccoon pats Bruiser on the leg. "But then we came along and saved him. When he's old enough, he'll certainly be a great asset to The Enlighteners. My hope—"

"Persimmon!" From off in the distance an exuberant female voice calls.

The team braces themselves for trouble, but Persimmon instantly recognizes that voice.

"Aunty Adelaide!" Persimmon skips gleefully down the path in the direction of the voice.

The Enlighteners have arrived at their destination.

3

PERSIMMON RUSHES UP to her aunt and uncle. The three nuzzle and lick one another to say hello. Her aunt and uncle have white hairs sprinkled throughout their fur. They look much older than when Persimmon last saw them, but they haven't lost their chipper spirit. They smile warmly as Nibbin runs circles around them.

"My dear Persimmon, what a lovely surprise!" Aunty Adelaide is so overjoyed to see her beloved niece that she can't stop cuddling her. "I can't wait to tell you about all the latest gossip in our part of the woods. I have some outrageous stories!"

Uncle Bennett is all smiles, too, until he notices the stump where Persimmon's tail once was. "My goodness, Persimmon, what happened to your tail?!"

"Oh my. Oh my." Aunty Adelaide is immediately concerned.

"I'm fine," Persimmon replies. "It's a long story, but I promise to tell you later."

"You poor thing. What a fright that must have been," Aunty Adelaide says. "Goodness, where are our manners? You must be exhausted after your long journey from home. Oh, that reminds me, where is our favorite nephew, Scraps?"

Persimmon's smile fades away over being reminded of her absent brother. There's an uncomfortable silence. Persimmon doesn't want to say that they parted ways, because she's not ready to admit that they've really said goodbye forever.

Before Persimmon has a chance to gather her thoughts, her aunt and uncle spot Derpoke, Bruiser, Chloe, and Tucker walking toward them. "Persimmon, there's a giant dog behind you, and he's holding Derpoke and two squirrels captive," Aunty Adelaide quickly warns.

"It's a dog! Run for your lives!" Uncle Bennett zips up the closest tree as fast as his old legs will take him.

Persimmon looks back to see her four smiling companions skipping happily toward them. "No, Aunty, that's Bruiser. He's my dear friend."

"I get it," Aunty Adelaide leans in and whispers. "He can hear us. Just give me the signal, and we'll run into the woods to safety."

"Aunty, he's a snuggle bug. You're going to adore him."

"A dog?! I highly doubt it."

"Get up in the tree, crazyheads! He's going to eat you!" Uncle Bennett screams frantically from high in the tree.

Bruiser, Derpoke, Chloe, and Tucker walk over to Persimmon and her aunt. Aunty Adelaide steps protectively in front of Persimmon to shield her from the "ferocious" Doberman. Bruiser frowns at the gesture. "Guess ya don't think too kindly of dogs, eh?"

Aunty Adelaide looks to Persimmon for the signal to rush into the woods.

Persimmon, of course, does not give the signal. "She's just kidding, Bruiser. That's my aunty for you. Always joking." Persimmon nudges her aunt to be polite.

As if someone flipped a switch, Aunty Adelaide smiles widely with a welcoming warmth. "Dearest Bruiser, I was just having a laugh. Any friend of my niece's is, of course, a friend of mine. Speaking of which, it's a great pleasure to see you again, darling Derpoke." Aunty Adelaide caresses Derpoke's cheek. "Such a handsome opossum."

Derpoke blushes and giggles awkwardly.

Aunty Adelaide turns to look into the tree at her panic-stricken partner. "Dear, he's Persimmon's friend and he's perfectly cordial."

"But he's a dog!" Uncle Bennett grips the tree tighter, staring at Aunty Adelaide and Persimmon as if they have lost their minds. For all the times that dogs have terrorized him and other raccoons, he can't imagine ever trusting a canine, especially one who looks as intimidating as Bruiser.

"If he were such a ferocious dog, would he let me do this?" Persimmon lovingly hugs Bruiser's front left leg, and Derpoke and Chloe follow suit by hugging Bruiser's other legs. The Doberman plays along by affectionately licking Tucker. Tucker harrumphs, not expecting a glob of dog saliva on his head. Chloe motions for Tucker to act happy, so Tucker forces a smile.

"See, a real snuggle bug." Persimmon beams at Uncle Bennett.

Uncle Bennett stares down at Aunty Adelaide, hoping for some support. He is so frightened his paws shake as he struggles to keep hold of the tree trunk.

"Okay, calm down, dear." Aunty Adelaide crawls up the tree to Uncle Bennett and pats him on the belly. "You'll upset your stomach if you keep up like this. I have an idea. Why don't you get Persimmon and her friends some food?"

Aunty Adelaide whispers down to Persimmon. "It will calm him down if we distract him with a task." Aunty Adelaide—oblivious to the fact that Uncle Bennett could clearly hear her—turns back to him and says, "Go see if you can catch some fresh fish for them."

"No! No fish." Persimmon immediately climbs up the tree, blocking her uncle from hopping down. "We don't eat fish."

Aunty Adelaide almost falls out of the tree, she's so flabbergasted by this statement. "What respectable raccoon doesn't like fish?"

"Actually, we *do* like fish," Persimmon explains. "That's why we don't eat them."

"You're speaking in riddles, dear. I can't understand you."

"All of us have vowed to be compassionate toward other animals, which includes not eating them," Persimmon says.

"But you'll die of starvation if you don't eat other animals," Uncle Bennett says.

Persimmon points to her team. "None of us except Nibbin has eaten animals in a long time, and we're clearly still alive and healthy. As for Nibbin, he only eats animals who are already dead, such as leftovers from a human's trash can."

"That's foolish, Persimmon," Uncle Bennett says. "You have to eat at least *some* animals to survive. Not even this dog can stop me from getting you some fish immediately."

Persimmon grabs her uncle's fur as he tries to pass her. "I said no."

Uncle Bennett stops in his tracks, stunned by her forcefulness.

"My friends and I formed a team that saves any animal who is suffering," Persimmon explains. "That's actually why we came here, because I thought you two could help us."

Aunty Adelaide's eyes light up. "Wait a second, are *you* The Uncaged Alliance?"

The team's jaws drop.

"You've heard of us?!" Chloe asks, smiling widely.

Nibbin hops up and down. "We're The Enlighteners, not The Uncaged Alliance."

"Yes, Nibbin." Persimmon turns to her aunt. "We changed our name to The Enlighteners, which I'll explain later, but how did you hear about The Uncaged Alliance?"

"You're the talk of the forest. Everyone's going on and on about this group of animals that rescues other animals from humans."

"Really?!" Persimmon looks down at her crew and gives them a clenched-paw victory salute.

"Oh yes, you're heroes," Aunty Adelaide says. "We heard that you rescued minks who were going to be killed for their fur. I'm assuming Nibbin is one of the lucky survivors."

Nibbin hops up and down in celebration of his rescue.

"We also heard that you tried to release the exotic animals trapped in a circus," Aunty Adelaide continues. "We never even knew what a circus was—or an elephant, for that matter—until we heard the exciting story of your rescue attempt. Everyone in the forest was furious when we found out what those humans did to those innocent creatures. So heartbreaking."

Aunty Adelaide looks sorrowful for a moment, thinking about the animals being shot and killed. She perks back up. "I'm so proud that you're the ones who bravely attempted to save them. We'd be honored to assist you, but what could *we* possibly do? We're not exactly as sprightly as we used to be, as you may have noticed."

"You two always seem to know what's going on in the forest, so I thought maybe you'd be able to direct us to any animals who might need some help."

Aunty Adelaide and Uncle Bennett ponder this for a moment. The team waits eagerly to hear what its next rescue mission might be.

"You know, we do know of these animals at the other edge of the forest," Uncle Bennett finally says. "Maybe—"

"No, dear, it's too dangerous," Aunty Adelaide interjects.

"But they're in such pain," Uncle Bennett says. "I hear those animals crying out every time I go near there."

"I thought we agreed it was too dangerous to go there. Those humans will snatch you up and hurt you, too."

Persimmon cuts into their bickering. "Our team is very capable at this point. We'd at least like to scope out this location to see if we can help. To which type of animal are you referring?"

"Have you ever heard of chickens?" Uncle Bennett asks.

4

"ARE YOU SURE Persimmon isn't going to come looking for you, Scraps?" Rawly asks. He, Scraps, Drig, and Apricot are climbing through the thick brush deep in the dark forest, miles away from Persimmon and her team.

"I already told you, she understands why I left her team. Why do you keep asking? Are you afraid she's going to come thrash you?" Scraps razzes him.

"No," Rawly snaps back, clearly annoyed. "I just don't feel like listening to another one of her condescending lectures."

"I like Persimmon and all," Drig chimes in. "But I will not miss those lectures of hers."

Drig and Rawly guffaw and nod.

"Hey, that's my sister," Scraps retorts. "Watch it."

Apricot perks up. "Oh good, are you three going to fight? Finally, something interesting will happen on this journey."

"We're not going to fight," Rawly says. "Scraps, I admire your sister, but unlike on *her* team, we're not going to be so judgmental on mine."

"Boring," Apricot declares. "Scraps, why don't you run around and I'll chase after you."

Apricot bats Scraps on the head to get the game going. Scraps just looks at her, surprised.

"What?" Apricot asks. "Isn't that what you and Bruiser used to do?"

"Yes, but I wasn't afraid Bruiser would actually bite me if he caught me."

"Afraid of a cat, are we?" Apricot's eyes widen with predatory glee. "Ooh, that makes things all the *more* interesting."

Just then, the team hears gunshots off in the distance. They abruptly stop walking. Then they hear a small animal screaming in fear.

The team immediately rushes toward the sounds of the gun shots, crashing through brush as fast as they can to rescue this creature.

Rawly stops the team as they step into a pathway. There, in the distance, they see two minks rushing feverishly toward them. Close behind is a man wielding a shotgun.

Just as Rawly is about to direct the team toward the petrified minks, a voice calls out impatiently from behind a tree on the other side of the path. "Get out of the way!"

Rawly peers into the woods and sees a third mink, motioning for him to step off the path, clearly agitated. Another voice forcefully calls from behind him. "Get off the path NOW!"

Rawly, Scraps, Drig, and Apricot are thoroughly confused, but they hop behind one of the trees lining the pathway. Three minks are hiding there already.

"Shh." One of the minks warns the team.

Rawly, Scraps, Drig, and Apricot look around the forest and realize they're surrounded by minks hiding everywhere—even some raccoons are scattered throughout the concealed crowd.

The two minks dart down the path past the spot where the team is hiding and jump over a pile of leaves and branches. The human aims his gun as he runs. "I'll get you, little bastards!"

Just before the man shoots his weapon, he steps on the pile and, to his horror, crashes into a deep pit. His torso rams into the side as he digs his fists and elbows into the ground to avoid falling all the way in. You can hear his ribs crack. The gun goes off, shooting bullets into nearby tree trunks, narrowly missing a few minks.

To the great surprise of Rawly and his team, suddenly thousands of minks and a few dozen raccoons come running out from behind trees and pounce on the screaming human, knocking him all the way down the hole. His wailing can be heard as he's torn to shreds.

Then everything goes quiet. The minks and raccoons cheer as they climb back out. Three minks push the man's gun into the hole, and then all the minks quickly kick dirt into the hole, filling it up. Just as fast, raccoons scatter leaves on top of the dirt. Miraculously, in a matter of moments, no one would have any idea that a still-warm human body was underfoot.

Rawly, Scraps, and Drig stare at the crowd of minks and raccoons, horrified. These animals killed that human with such speed and skill— it was eerie. The three team members feel ill over witnessing so much brutality at such close range, but Apricot doesn't. She's awestruck. The precision of the hunt was impressive. She's going to like these minks and raccoons very much.

Out from the swarm of fearsome creatures, the mink Vincent appears—blood dripping from his nails and smeared on his black fur. He saunters over to Rawly and his team with a satisfied smirk. "Welcome back, Uncaged Alliance. We've been expecting you."

5

"SO THE HUMANS shot and killed all those animals just as you were finally freeing them from that wretched life in the circus?" Vincent grits his teeth. A wave of rage crashes through him. He slashes the tree trunk beside him with his claws, tearing a deep gash. He slices over and over, furiously ripping at the bark. Rawly waits awkwardly while the mink vents his wrath.

Vincent and Rawly are inside a hollowed-out tree while the rest of Rawly's team, the minks, and raccoons wait for the two leaders to instruct them on their next mission.

The eye-catching blue tinge of Vincent's fur shines in the moonlight. He sucks in a deep breath, calming himself, and turns around to face Rawly. "I had heard rumblings about The Uncaged Alliance's courageous but failed rescue attempt, but I didn't know all the details until now. Those animals were so close to freedom. To have it taken away at just that moment..."

Vincent looks right at Rawly—his glare so intense that the raccoon looks away, uncomfortable. "I assure you, Rawly, as soon as we can, we will put a stop to these barbaric circuses. I also want you to know I'm impressed that you released the tigers to attack the humans. Those tigers deserved to be free and those humans deserved to die. I only wish

I could have been there to see the looks on those humans' faces as the animals they had abused for so long bit into their flesh. Releasing those tigers is the type of creative thinking we need if we're going to succeed in our mission."

Rawly stands up taller. It's incredibly gratifying to have Vincent compliment him for the exact reason Persimmon kicked him off her team.

Vincent continues. "I am sorry you lost your friend Fisher and your love Claudette. As you know, I am no stranger to great loss."

Vincent sighs, thinking about his family, friends, and all the other minks who were murdered at the Peterson fur farm. He thinks about his brother Frestin being skinned alive right in front of him. So many memories have faded with time, but that one—that horrifying experience—never fades.

Vincent stomps the dirt to knock the memory from his mind. "And you're telling me that Persimmon still thinks humans are redeemable despite the fact that they murdered all those animals, including two members of your team?"

Rawly nods.

"How dangerously naïve." Vincent shakes his head, bewildered. "I was hoping she might come to her senses and join forces with me."

"*I* came back," Rawly blurts out. He instantly feels embarrassed for so clearly seeking approval from the mink.

"Yes, you did, and you brought a valuable crew with you. The cat Apricot is an interesting new addition. Like their cousins, the tigers, I've heard these smaller cats are very cunning and excellent hunters. That will be beneficial as we take on these humans. Speaking of which, that human you just saw my troops pushing into that hole was the last of the mink murderers in this area. You just witnessed history being made. And the best part? Now we can move on to the next stage of my plan."

Rawly's fur bristles over hearing this promising news. "What's the *next* stage?"

Vincent licks his chipped tooth. He's just as excited as Rawly to begin this next part and can't wait to see the raccoon's reaction to how ingenious it is. "We need to be strategic here. We're not going to be able to defend ourselves against humans with just minks and raccoons on our side. We need strength."

Rawly hops into the air as an idea pops into his head. "What about releasing more tigers? You should have seen how fierce they were. I swear some of those humans died from the mere sight of them."

"An intriguing idea… for later. But for now it's too conspicuous and who knows how many tigers we can find? We need animals who are much more abundant and won't draw so much attention from humans."

"Do you have a creature in mind?" Rawly asks.

"Dogs." Vincent grins. "They're powerful and capable of great ferocity. But their real asset is that humans consider them friends, even part of their families. Just wait until the dogs turn on them."

"Adding dogs is a brilliant move, but how are you going to get them to turn on their humans? They're super loyal and—"

"Don't worry." Vincent cuts him off, uninterested in any negative feedback. "I have that figured out."

"Okay, I think it's a great idea. For a while now, I've thought we needed more dogs in The Uncaged Alliance."

"Not The Uncaged Alliance, Rawly." Vincent turns to walk out of the tree trunk. "Forget teams. Think bigger. I'm building an army. And I'm doing it right under the humans' noses. They won't suspect a thing before it's too late."

The minks and raccoons stir outside in the woods as they see their fearless leader stepping toward them.

Rawly watches, slightly shocked, as Vincent walks away. That wasn't how he planned this conversation at all. Ever since Vincent revealed his plans to conduct more aggressive rescue missions, Rawly secretly wanted in. And when Persimmon humiliated Rawly by kicking him off her team, his very first thought was to head back to Vincent and join forces. But Vincent clearly has more specific and calculating plans than Rawly is clever enough to dream up. The raccoon suddenly feels left out again. He thought he was going to be a leader alongside Vincent, but instead he just watched The Uncaged Alliance dissolve before his eyes.

Rawly calls out to Vincent in disbelief. "What are we even called?"

Vincent stops just before exiting the tree trunk. He looks back at the confused raccoon. "We're The Dissidents."

PERSIMMON, DERPOKE, BRUISER, Chloe, Tucker, and Nibbin follow Aunty Adelaide and Uncle Bennett as they lead the team to the place where these animals called chickens are being held against their will.

The team rested during the day, but the moment night fell, Persimmon urged her aunt and uncle to immediately take her and her friends to where the animals were trapped. Persimmon didn't sleep well knowing that there were animals nearby who needed rescuing, but Aunty Adelaide insisted that it was too dangerous during the day to venture near the facility.

As the team treks through the forest, Aunty Adelaide motions for Persimmon to step back from the group. The two of them walk out of earshot of anyone else.

"It's been so long since I last saw you, my dear," Aunty Adelaide says. "I thought maybe we could catch up while we have a moment."

"Sure," Persimmon replies. "Sorry it's been so long. You know I adore you and Uncle Bennett, but time just flew—"

"No need for niceties," Aunty Adelaide says. "I know why you didn't come around. You were avoiding the chance you might run into your mother."

Persimmon's stomach drops. The mere mention of her mother upsets her. The only thing she wants to talk about less than Scraps leaving her team is her mother.

Aunty Adelaide continues. "Now I know you don't want to talk about her, but—"

"You're right. I don't." Persimmon quickens her pace to rejoin the team. She crawls through some thick brush to make it difficult for her aunt to follow.

"She does ask about you." Aunty Adelaide maneuvers through the brush with some difficulty but presses on. "She also worries about you. And she has a new litter, which—"

"What a surprise," Persimmon cuts in, annoyed. "Has she abandoned any of them or were none of them runts? Not that she cared to look after her healthy babies either since she's so busy having new ones all the time."

"Persimmon," Aunty Adelaide chides. "I want you to stop right now and talk to me."

Persimmon huffs loudly. She comes to a halt next to some purple flowers glistening in the moonlight and quickly looks away from them. She's not in the mood to see something so beautiful.

Aunty Adelaide steps around Persimmon to face her. "Dear, I know you don't like to dredge up all this past unpleasantness, but it's not healthy to keep it all tucked inside. I'm not asking you to forgive your mother, or even like her, but harboring all this anger toward her is only harming *you*."

Persimmon looks her aunt directly in the eye. She's not going to avoid this issue any longer. "Aunty, do you know what my mother said when I told her that she couldn't just leave Scraps in that tree to die?"

Aunty Adelaide shakes her head no.

"She said, 'We have to let nature take its course.' Just writing it off, as if she had no control over it. As if it's natural to sentence a pup to his or her death."

"Most runts don't survive very long, Persimmon. Either they die because they're not fully formed or if they do live past the first month, they're easy prey and get killed. For a momma with a new litter, it takes too much extra effort to nurse one pup to health when you're so busy trying to raise your other little ones. It's not an easy decision for a mother, but it's for survival. She was just following the way of the forest."

"You're too smart to say something so archaic, Aunty. Just because something has been done one way for generations doesn't mean you should continue to do it."

Persimmon sighs. She doesn't want to argue with her aunt.

"Aunty, I love you. It's clearly a sore subject for me, especially with Scraps leaving. I know you mean well, but there's no changing my opinion of my mother. I don't respect her, and I would be perfectly fine if I never saw her again. I have an important purpose now. I'm saving other animals' lives."

"That's a whole other issue. I already said that saving other animals is a very noble cause, but I think you're going to be extremely shocked at how massive this farm is and how many chickens there are. I'm worried it's going to be really dangerous to try to save them."

"These missions are always dangerous, but if you were held captive somewhere, in terrible pain—fearing that every day was the day you would be killed—you'd want someone to come rescue you too, right?"

"Well... yes. But you also look so exhausted, Persimmon. I'm concerned about you. How can you rescue these animals safely if you're so fatigued? I don't understand why you and your friends couldn't rest for a few days before your next mission."

"It's hard to rest when I know there are animals out there suffering, Aunty," Persimmon says.

"But there will *always* be animals suffering somewhere."

"Well, then it looks like I won't be relaxing any time soon, eh?" Persimmon smiles and heads in the direction of her team members.

"You're getting me off topic." Aunty Adelaide runs in front of her niece again to head her off. "Persimmon, I know you said that the reason you came to see me and your uncle is because we're busybodies and you thought we'd know where there were animals suffering. But I think there's another reason you came. I think now that Scraps has left, you want to reconnect with family."

Persimmon ponders this. She nods. "I hadn't thought of that, but what does that have to do with my mother?"

"We've never discussed this before because you always shut down the moment I bring up the issue, but I want you to know that I admire you for taking on the responsibility of looking after Scraps at such a young age. You were still so young yourself and yet you stepped up and raised him all by yourself. You're a remarkable raccoon."

Persimmon looks away. She doesn't want to get emotional, but this is such a painful subject for her, and she's especially raw because Scraps left so recently.

"Before your mother abandoned Scraps, you were very close with her, so I know how hard that was to turn your back on her. And whether you want to admit it or not, I don't think you really never want to see her again. Maybe, somehow, you both can find peace someday. Not for her, because I agree that she's irresponsible at times, but for you."

Persimmon closes her eyes and thinks. *Make peace with Mom? Isn't it just better to never see her again? Nothing my mother says will change what she did. And hearing her try to defend her decision to leave Scraps—one more time—will just make me despise her more. I don't—*

"Persimmon!" Derpoke is faintly heard hollering for his raccoon friend from far off. There's a mixture of excitement and anxiety in his voice.

Immediately, Persimmon snaps out of reflecting about her mother and dashes toward her team. *These chickens are counting on me with their lives. Who cares about my irresponsible mother? My work with The Enlighteners supersedes everything else.*

Aunty Adelaide frowns, realizing she didn't get through to her headstrong niece. She quickens her pace to catch up to the team.

7

PERSIMMON RUSHES UP to the team members who are sitting at the edge of the woods. They're all peering at the expanse of the farm in front of them, filled with anticipation and trepidation—the same feeling they get every time they come across a new site for one of their missions.

The smell of the farm hits Persimmon first, as is always the case. It's that pungent odor of urine and feces that they find at all these places animals are imprisoned. Looming large before the team are three massive metal sheds that stretch almost as far as the eye can see. The ends nearest to the team are about 40 feet wide, while each building's length is around 450 feet. The stadium where The Enlighteners attempted to rescue the animals from the circus was the tallest building they had ever seen, but these sheds are certainly the longest.

Everyone listens intently. They barely hear a sound from inside the sheds—only a faint chirp every now and then.

"It's so quiet," Persimmon says. "Are you sure these buildings are filled with these creatures, Uncle?"

"They're in there all right," Uncle Bennett says. "Maybe they're sleeping or the walls are really thick. Maybe they're too scared to make any noise. I don't know."

Chloe sighs as she surveys the three massive sheds towering before them. "I just got this unsettling feeling as if I were sitting back in my tree with Tucker, listening to the calves calling out for their mothers. Gosh, we just got here and my heart's already breaking."

Tucker leans in closer to his sweet pea to comfort her.

"Don't worry, Chloe," Persimmon says. "We're here to rescue them. Soon they'll be chirping for joy when we release them and they fly high into the sky. Come on. Let's take a closer look."

"This isn't close enough?" Aunty Adelaide says as she reaches for Persimmon's fur to hold her back. "This is the farm, and the chickens are in those sheds. What else do you need to see?"

"Everything," Persimmon explains. "We need to know every inch of this place if we're going to rescue these chickens safely. You can stay here, if you'd prefer."

With that, Persimmon steps into the open grass before her and the rest of the team follows. Aunty Adelaide and Uncle Bennett reluctantly trail behind.

On the far side of the last shed on the left there is a huge cornfield and another cornfield can be seen a ways off to the right. Between the sheds are dirt roads. Persimmon leads the team between the last shed on the left and the cornfield.

She whispers back to the team. "If there is any sign of humans, everyone should quickly dart into the cornfield. We'll meet back at Aunty Adelaide and Uncle Bennett's tree."

The team nods.

As they walk along the side of the shed, Persimmon turns to Derpoke. "I don't know if you noticed, but I haven't seen any windows on these sheds so far."

"Huh," Derpoke says. "You're right. Maybe they're on the other side."

It takes a while for the team to walk the 450 feet to the other end of the shed. Derpoke begins to huff from exhaustion. Of course, Nibbin bounds around without any trouble. He darts ahead of Persimmon to take the lead—he can't contain his enthusiasm for exploring.

"Nibbin, wait for us!" Persimmon calls after him. "Don't get too far from the group."

Nibbin doesn't listen to Persimmon and peers around the corner of the building.

"There's a house!" Nibbin yells. "There's a giant human house!"

"Wait there, Nibbin. Don't go any further." Persimmon quickens her pace to catch up to the little guy, but he disappears around the corner.

"Nibbin!" Persimmon hollers as she runs at full speed.

She turns the corner to see Nibbin gazing at a two-story blue house off in the distance beyond the third shed on the right.

"That's where the nasty humans are!" Nibbin says as he hops up and down.

"Yes, Nibbin," Persimmon steps over to the small brown mink, breathing in a sigh of relief that he is okay.

Bruiser comes bounding around the corner, ready to take on any human threat that might be waiting for him. "He okay?"

"He's fine," Persimmon says. There are large fans on the side of the shed blowing air out of the building, so she has to talk over them. "He just got a little carried away with the adventure." Persimmon turns Nibbin around to face her. "I know you're excited, but you have to stay with the group. What if there had been a human hiding on the other side of this shed? I'd crumble to pieces if you got injured."

"Sorry." Nibbin puts his head down.

"Lil' troublemaker," Bruiser says as he licks him affectionately.

The rest of the team rushes around the corner and is happy to see that everyone is fine.

Persimmon motions to the house and addresses the team. "That's going to pose a problem. Just like where Nibbin and the minks were held captive, the humans live on the property. That means there's a viable chance they'll wake up if we're not able to keep our rescue attempt as quiet as possible."

"I saw what looked like doors on the other side of the sheds facing the forest," Chloe notes. "That seems like a safer way to release the chickens without the humans seeing from the house."

"I completely agree, Chloe," Persimmon says. "All these sheds look the same from this end, but I want to double-check. I don't want all of us venturing too far from the cornfield in case we need to make a quick getaway, so why doesn't everyone else stay here? Bruiser, if you can join me for safety, I'd appreciate it."

The team nods, although Nibbin quietly pouts over not being able to join in on the expedition.

Persimmon and Bruiser gallop through the grass scanning the sheds. She's happy to see that there aren't any humans milling about at this time of night. That bodes well for a successful mission. She looks down the lengthy road between the sheds and is surprised that there still aren't any windows in sight. *If I think it's frustrating that I can't see what's happening inside, I can only imagine how disheartening it is for the chickens who would want to see what's going on outside.*

She and Bruiser walk along three gigantic metal tanks on the sides of the buildings and see water dripping out. *This must be where their water is stored.* She can still barely hear any noise coming from inside the sheds, though, so she presses her furry ear against the side of the building. Bruiser does the same.

The raccoon and dog listen as intently as they can. They hear a little more chirping on this end of the shed, so it seems the chickens must all be congregating on this side for some reason.

"They sound like babies, right?" Persimmon says.

"Yeah," Bruiser says as he does his best to listen again. "But I can't make out what they're sayin'. They definitely sound sad, though. I feel all sick inside worryin' what's happenin' to 'em in there."

Persimmon nods solemnly. Her stomach's been in knots since they arrived, too.

She and Bruiser quickly finish their exploration and run back over to the team.

"Okay, everyone, let's return to the other side," Persimmon says. "We'll enter the shed from there."

"Wait, what?!" Aunty Adelaide asks. "What do you mean 'enter'?"

"Aunty, we're investigating the property," Persimmon says. "How else are we supposed to figure out the best plan to get these chickens out of there?"

"What if the humans hear you opening the shed? Or worse, what if there are humans waiting for you *inside*? They could shoot you. They could shoot us all!" Aunty Adelaide starts to hyperventilate.

"Aunty, calm down." Persimmon steps over to her and strokes her neck to soothe her. "The only way to get these chickens *out* of there is to see exactly how they're trapped *in* there. Are they chained up like the calves or the elephants were? If so, we'll need some way to unfetter them. Are they trapped in tiny cages like the minks were? If they are, we'll need more raccoons on the team to open the cage doors. This is vital information, and I'm not leaving here until I know these things."

Aunty Adelaide looks as distressed as Persimmon has ever seen her.

Uncle Bennett can't take seeing his dear Adelaide so upset any longer. "Okay, okay. I'll tell you everything I know about this farm. Just promise me you won't go inside those sheds."

The whole team turns to Uncle Bennett. Apparently, he knows a lot more about this place than he was letting on.

8

"SO, WHAT DO you know about the farm, Uncle Bennett?" Persimmon asks.

"Yes, Bennett," Aunty Adelaide adds sternly. "Please do tell us what you know about this farm that you and I agreed was too dangerous to visit."

Uncle Bennett squirms. The whole team has moved to the side of the shed out of view of the humans' house, and he's now surrounded by everyone staring at him. Persimmon, Derpoke, Chloe, Tucker, Bruiser, and Nibbin are all quite eager to hear his insight, but he's not sure how much he should reveal—the look in Aunty Adelaide's eyes already tells him that it's going to be a long night when they get back to their tree.

"Well, I know the chickens are normally on this farm only for about a moon and a half. Then big trucks come and take them away. I asked the other animals in the area and they said that they believe the chickens are taken somewhere to be killed for human food."

"So they're raised to be eaten just like the calves," Persimmon says. "And that happens when they're only six weeks old? But that means they're only babies."

"That's just like the calves," Derpoke adds. "I guess humans like the taste of babies."

Derpoke shudders. Everyone does.

"Do you know how long this particular flock of chickens has been in these sheds?" Persimmon asks.

"I think maybe they arrived around half a moon ago," Uncle Bennett says. "To my recollection, that's when I saw the truck arriving and the humans tossing them in the sheds."

"Excuse me, mister," Aunty Adelaide cuts in angrily. "Exactly how many times have you snooped around here?"

Uncle Bennett gets very quiet. He looks like he wants to shrink into the ground. "A few," he says very quietly.

"What if you had been captured and killed by the humans, and then I sat in the tree waiting for a partner who would never come home?"

"If you must know, Adelaide, I came here looking for a treat for us. I didn't want to say anything that would upset our niece and her non-animal-eating friends. I thought the humans might leave a few chicken scraps around, but every time I've come, the dead chicken bodies are infected all over. Not appetizing in the least. Anyway, now my niece hates me. Happy?"

"These two bicker more than we do," Tucker whispers to Chloe.

"I think it's cuter when *we* argue." Chloe winks.

"Hush, Aunty and Uncle," Persimmon says. "This is supposed to be a stealth mission, and you two are yelling loud enough to wake the humans."

Aunty Adelaide and Uncle Bennett hunker down, embarrassed.

"Aunty, if Uncle Bennett has information that may help us save these chickens, my team needs to know. He already gave us a very helpful timeline for how long these chickens are in the sheds before they're taken to be killed. Earlier you said that you were proud of us for saving other animals. Well, this is how we do it. Now, Uncle Bennett, do you have anything else to add?"

Uncle Bennett looks at Aunty Adelaide to see if she'll yell at him again. She rolls her eyes and looks away.

"Well, I guess the only other thing is that there are thousands and thousands of chickens in those sheds. I have no idea how you could possibly get them all out of there without alerting the humans. Even if you do get them out, the humans are just going to come looking for them. Then what are you going to do?"

"Leave that to us," Persimmon replies confidently. "We'll figure it out like we always do. The good thing is that they're birds, so the majority of them can just fly away. The big question is, how many of them are too injured to fly? This is one of the reasons I'm going into that shed right now."

Persimmon heads toward the other end of the shed.

"Wait," Uncle Bennett yells in shock. "You promised you wouldn't go in the shed if I told you everything."

"I promised no such thing. Besides, Uncle Bennett, as you should know by now, I'm not so fond of others telling me what to do."

Persimmon grins and trots down the dirt path between the cornfield and the shed. The rest of the team follows, leaving Uncle Bennett and Aunty Adelaide behind.

"She takes after your side of the family," Uncle Bennett says.

"That she does," Aunty Adelaide replies.

9

CHLOE, TUCKER, NIBBIN, Uncle Bennett, and Aunty Adelaide wait anxiously outside the shed door. Ostensibly, they're keeping a lookout for any humans, but they're way more interested in—and nervous about—what's going on inside the shed. Persimmon, Bruiser, and Derpoke disappeared into the shed for what feels like forever ago, and the rest of the team is concerned about what's taking so long.

Aunty Adelaide taps Uncle Bennett's claws that are tightly clenched around her front leg. "Dear, you're hurting me."

"Oh, sorry." Uncle Bennett loosens his grip. "I never thought I'd say this, but I really wish we had more dogs around. I'd feel a lot safer in case anything bad happens."

Chloe smiles and pats him on the back. "I knew you'd warm up to dogs eventually. They're the best!"

Suddenly, a great deal of noise reverberates inside the shed. The team tenses up.

The chickens are heard squawking with even more distress than when the team first opened the shed door.

Chloe, Tucker, Nibbin, Uncle Bennett, and Aunty Adelaide rush forward.

"Help me open it! They're being attacked!" Uncle Bennett yells.

"Persimmon said not to open it until they gave us the signal from inside," Chloe says, although she herself is questioning whether to follow Persimmon's request.

"Quiet, quiet! You'll wake the humans!" Bruiser is heard barking at the chickens from inside the shed.

"They're being attacked!" Uncle Bennett pulls at the door with his front legs. "Help me open it!"

Chloe, Tucker, Aunty Adelaide, and Nibbin all grab hold of the metal door and slide it open.

There's another tiny room just inside the doorway and through a second door the team sees Bruiser, Persimmon, and Derpoke darting toward them from inside the shed.

As Chloe, Tucker, Nibbin, Uncle Bennett, and Aunty Adelaide stand in the doorway, their eyes begin to burn from the disgusting air wafting out from the shed. They have to look away.

Moments later, Persimmon, Derpoke, and Bruiser come dashing out of the shed, closing the first door behind them and then Uncle Bennett and Aunty Adelaide slide the second door shut.

Persimmon, Derpoke, and Bruiser crumble to the ground, coughing and scratching at their watering eyes. They can barely breathe.

But that's not the biggest surprise. The team stares with amazement at the two white birds who just toppled off of Persimmon's and Derpoke's backs. The birds are filthy and they have a few bald spots where the skin looks bruised and raw.

The two chickens—one male, one female—stare right back at the team, completely bewildered. They've never seen creatures like these in their entire lives. In fact, this is the first time that they've ever walked freely outside that shed.

Persimmon can't open her eyes, they sting so badly, but she finally manages to blurt out: "We have to get them out of there... NOW!"

10

ELSIE THE KINDHEARTED

(TWO WEEKS AGO)

DAY 1

THE GIANTS ARE hurting them! Elsie watches in horror as three men hastily toss two-day-old chicks onto the shed floor. She's trapped in a cramped crate with fifty other chicks, awaiting her turn to be thrown onto the floor.

Just two days ago, Elsie and these other chicks hatched from their eggs, bright-eyed and eager to start their lives, but since that moment, they've been thrown around as if they were mere objects, not fragile babies. First was the rough handling in the hatchery—being tossed from one container to the next and banging around on conveyor belts. Next, Elsie and the other chicks were packed into overcrowded crates and shoved into the back of trucks where they've been stuck for two days without food and water. Elsie is thirsty and famished, so she's more than ready to get out, but she's afraid of how roughly these humans are handling this process.

The men are dumping the fragile birds so rapidly that some chicks hit the floor and cry out in pain from injuries—a broken wing, a twisted leg. She is determined not to meet the same fate, so she gets ready to flap her wings as hard as possible the moment she's tossed out.

A man grabs her crate. *Here we go.* Elsie begins flapping her wings wildly. The man chucks the chicks onto the wood shavings that cover the floor. She hits the ground on her stomach, but luckily bounces back up without a scratch. No thanks to her wings, though—they did nothing to keep her airborne. *I need to work on this flying thing.*

A male bird who was trapped in the container beside her during the truck ride didn't fare so well. He landed right on his wing, snapping it. He squawks loudly and cries.

Elsie doesn't notice, though. She's too busy dashing off with the other yellow fuzzballs in search of water and food.

There are so many chicks that they bang into one another as they run. Elsie makes it to a large, shallow dish filled with brown pellets. There are thin metal dividers all around this circular feeder allowing multiple chicks to stick their heads through at the same time to peck for food. Elsie dives her head in, gorging herself. The food isn't all that appetizing, but she'll eat anything, she's so hungry.

There are rows and rows of these feeders, which extend to the ground from metal bars that can be raised to the roof after feeding time. Chicks who were just tossed onto the floor come running up from behind and bang into her, pushing for their place at one of the feeding stations.

Elsie steps back to allow the other chicks to eat. She's had enough for now. They deserve a turn, too.

She rushes over to a drinking station next. Similarly, there are multiple rows of long metal bars throughout the shed that bear dispensers, but in this case there are metal knobs from which the chicks can drink. Elsie knocks her beak into one of the knobs, drinking heartily. It feels so refreshing. Again though, she's shoved away from the drinking station by other chicks fighting for their turn.

She walks a few feet away and stops. She looks down at her orange feet and observes the wood shavings below. There's a gross odor emanating from them. *What is that smell?!* Little does she know that the shavings are soaked with the urine and feces of the countless flocks of chickens who were trapped in this shed before her. She also has no idea what happened to all those chickens. She will find out soon enough, though, that she and the other chicks are intended for the same dreadful fate.

"Mommy?!" A frantic chick darts past her desperately searching for a mother she will never find.

There are no mommies—just scared babies and mean Giants. The fact that their mothers were nowhere to be found is the first thing Elsie noticed when the truck pulled up to the shed. Like all the chicks, she had been hoping they'd get to meet their mothers when they arrived at wherever they were going. Instinctively, the chicks crave nurturing, but this shed was not built for maternal solace.

Elsie walks around, surveying the shed. It's massive and yet suffocating at the same time. Every minute, more and more chicks are tossed onto the ground. *How many of us are they going to stick in here? Why are we here at all? When can we leave?*

She watches the other chicks dart around the room, crying, searching for food, searching for comfort—each yellow fluffball more miserable and confused than the last.

"Help me! Someone please help me!" A tiny voice is heard calling out, back where Elsie was tossed on the ground.

She steps over to the male chick lying on the ground—the one who was pressed against her during the long truck ride. His wing is bent the wrong way.

"It's okay," Elsie says. "I can help you. I'll be right back."

Elsie rushes to one of the feeders and pushes her way through the other chicks. She fills her beak with pellets and darts back to where the male chick is lying in pain.

Elsie tries to put the pellets in the bird's mouth, but he just keeps crying in pain. She finally places the food beside him.

"It's here if you want it," Elsie says.

"It hurts so much," the bird says.

"I know. What can I do to help you?"

"I want my mommy," he cries uncontrollably.

Elsie pauses. There are no mothers in this place, and she has no idea if there ever will be. But she can't say that to him. It will only upset him more.

"Our mommies aren't here right now. But I'm here. I'll stay with you."

Elsie nestles down close to the male bird. She gently rubs her head against his and coos softly, "My name is Elsie. I won't leave you. You are not alone."

The male bird sniffles and ceases crying for the first time. "I'm Jasper."

Elsie and Jasper snuggle in close. They peer around the shed, noticing other injured birds—even some chicks who aren't moving. *Are they dead?*

The rest of the chicks run all around them, every which way, frantically crying. What a terrible introduction to the world. From the moment she was born, she's felt so lost—being banged around at the hatchery, being tossed around by the humans. She just wants to find some peace, and sitting here with Jasper is the closest she's felt to any type of calmness. Sitting here comforting this frightened chick feels like something she was meant to do. She can't fix his wing, but she *can* make him feel less alone. In turn, it makes *her* feel less alone. In this shed filled with chaos and desperation, that's the best for which they can hope right now.

DAY 2

Elsie awakens with a jolt. There's a thunderous pounding at the door. It suddenly swings open and a human steps into the shed. Immediately, the chicks near the entryway scatter, screaming. Elsie shudders. *The Giants are back.*

She and Jasper fell asleep for a few hours when the lights went dark late last night. For the most part, the lights have been on a dim setting the entire time she's been in the shed, but they went out for a few hours so the birds could rest.

The human who entered is wearing a flashlight on his helmet, which makes him look like a cyclops with one bright eye. He's holding a white bucket and Elsie sees that he's picking up the chickens who are lying motionless on the ground. *Oh no! Those chicks are dead, and there are even more now than the last time I counted yesterday.*

"Jasper, wake up." Elsie nudges him with her head.

Jasper opens his eyes. He winces as he remembers how much his broken wing hurts.

Elsie points her beak at the farmer walking through the shed. Wherever the man goes, chicks rush away and he leans down and picks up a lifeless bird.

Jasper is overcome with sorrow. "They're dead."

Elsie nods solemnly.

The man takes a sudden turn in their direction. The chicks around Elsie and Jasper begin to scatter, but Jasper struggles to get up. He realizes that he has internal injuries in addition to the broken wing.

"Come on!" Elsie calls out.

The man's flashlight shines directly on Jasper. He squawks and attempts to run away, but the man is on him faster than he expected.

The farmer scoops up the incapacitated bird with his free hand. Jasper shrieks.

"Be careful! He's injured!" Elsie yells at the human.

The man holds Jasper's neck down against the edge of the bucket and presses firmly. Jasper squawks helplessly as his neck snaps. He goes limp.

Elsie lets out a soft yelp. The man drops Jasper's body into the bucket and moves on through the shed, searching for other severely injured or dead birds.

Elsie doesn't move. She can't. She's in shock. *How can Jasper be dead? He was just alive. He was so sweet. Why would the Giant kill him?*

The man picks up the last dead bird and exits the shed. The rest of the birds squawk loudly—some cry, some yell angrily, all of them are frightened. Is that their fate—to die and be thrown into a bucket?

Elsie's heart is racing so fast that her whole body is shaking. She lets out a quiet, sad moan. From everything she'd experienced so far, she knew that humans were mean, but now she is sure they are evil.

She can't get the sound out of her head of Jasper shrieking as his neck was snapped. Every part of her is scared—scared that she'll die the same grisly death; scared that the worst is yet to come.

*   *   *

DAY 4

Why is the Giant so hateful toward us? Elsie wonders. She's been too depressed to move much ever since Jasper was killed. For the last day and a half she's sat in the same area, not eating or drinking, just thinking. Whenever the man enters the shed, she observes his behavior toward the other chicks. He kicks them out of his way as he searches for injured or dead birds. If he finds an injured chick, he'll brutally snap the baby's neck. He even pulled so hard on one chick that he pulled her head right off. Elsie nearly fainted when she witnessed that.

She grieves deeply for the other birds. *Everyone is so scared all the time.* Some birds sit and cry all day. She wants to comfort them, but she's felt so disconsolate herself that she can barely move her wings, much less walk around.

Someone help us. Please. I can't bear to see everyone suffering so much.

As she looks around the room at the other chicks, it occurs to her that they don't call out for their mothers any longer. The first two days they were running around panicked, crying for their moms, but eventually they stopped. They realized it was hopeless.

"Leave me alone! Please stop!"

Elsie hears a chick crying out in distress. She turns around to see three chicks violently pecking at a male chick. He's struggling to defend himself and not one other chick in the area is coming to his defense—fearful of getting assaulted themselves or too depressed with their own problems to be bothered.

Without even thinking about it, Elsie springs into action and rushes over to the melee.

"Stop! Don't hurt him!" Elsie hollers. She steps between the male chick and the three attacking birds. They turn on her and peck her head and back.

"Stop!" Elsie pleads. "You're better than this."

The three chicks cease pecking and stare at her, perplexed.

"We're all frustrated in here," Elsie says. "But we can't take it out on one another. We must treat each other with kindness. That's the only way we'll survive in here."

The three chicks look at one another. They're not quite sure what to say. They've spent the past few days focusing so much on their own survival that they've lost sight of their empathy for anyone else. Her heartfelt plea, though, promptly reawakens their thoughtfulness.

The three chicks walk back to the feeders and commence eating.

Elsie turns to the male chick beside her. "Are you okay?"

"Yes." The chick preens his feathers. "They were pecking at this poor chick on the ground. I tried to stop them and then they pounced on *me*."

Elsie notices the female chick lying huddled on the wood shavings and is immediately reminded of Jasper. Her heart sinks. This female chick is in bad shape. There are bald spots where other birds have clearly pecked out her feathers, leaving raw flesh underneath, and her breathing is labored.

Elsie steps over to her. "You poor thing. What have they done to you?" Elsie rubs her head on the female chick's back soothingly. "They're not going to hurt you anymore. I promise."

The chick looks up at Elsie with weary eyes and sighs. "Thank you." It seems to take every ounce of energy she has left to talk. She rests her head back on the wood shavings. Elsie fears this chick has very little time left to live.

Elsie turns to the male chick. "Do you know her?"

"No," he says. "I just saw them pecking her, so I had to help."

"You have a good heart. What's your name?"

"Hop."

"I'm Elsie. Stay here with her for a few moments. I'll bring some food and water for her."

Hop sits down beside the sickly bird to protect her from any other attacks. Elsie picks up food with her beak and brings it back to the female bird, but the ailing chick doesn't eat. Then Elsie collects water in her mouth and the bird takes a few sips. After that, Elsie sits down on the other side of the female bird.

Dread comes over Elsie. She knows where this is leading. Eventually, that man will pound on that door and then come over and snatch up this innocent chick and crush her spine.

What can I do to help her? I don't even know how she's injured. She's just... dying. If only I could take away her pain, but things are only going to get worse for her. Do I tell her what's to come? How will that help? She's already frightened beyond belief. That will just make it worse.

The realization hits Elsie. *I have to warn Hop. He may have no idea what the Giant will do to her. He's probably seen the Giant pick up dead chicks, but he may not have seen him snap their necks. Hop seems so compassionate. He'll be devastated. Worse, maybe he'll try to fight back and get hurt. I can't risk that happening, but how can I break the news to him with her right here? What a horrible thing for her to hear. What do I do?*

Elsie sits quietly, full of anxiety. To make matters worse, the ammonia in the air has reached unbearable limits. Ammonia forms in the air because uric acid in the chickens' droppings decomposes from bacteria in the litter. The fact that the farmers never clean the litter between flocks only compounds the problem.

The burning in Elsie's eyes is so agonizing it feels like the pungent gas is eating into her brain. She wants to rub her eyes against her feathers so badly, but the feces caked all over her just makes it worse. She hopes to clean herself one day, but that's not possible within these walls—all the wood shavings are filthy with urine and poo—the excrement of 20,000 chicks. Elsie knows the number of birds in the shed because she counted the chicks in one section and then multiplied that by how many total sections are in the shed, a detail she knew from looking at the way the ceiling was divided into sections by metal bars.

Sometimes Elsie will do math to keep her mind occupied. There's nothing to do in the shed—no grass to rummage through, no dirt in which to dust-bathe, no hay bales to peck or on which to climb. The birds aren't in a playful mood for obvious reasons. She's surrounded by 20,000 despondent chicks, and they're getting more hopeless by the day.

Elsie looks down at the frail bird who has laid her head against Elsie's wing. A short while ago this chick was being viciously attacked by other birds and now she's sleeping on Elsie's wing with the most peaceful expression. It melts Elsie's heart. *This poor bird. No one should die alone and unloved. If all I can do is provide her comfort, then here I will sit.*

Now that the bird is finally resting, Elsie sees her moment to warn Hop about the murderous human.

"Hop," Elsie whispers.

He looks over at her.

"At some point that Giant will come through that door. When he does... what will happen... It's going to be awful... He's going to..."

"I know." Hop nods. There's pain in his eyes. He's seen the chicks killed. He knows what's coming. "I just don't want to leave her alone until then."

Elsie sighs deeply. She's met a kindred spirit. "I'm glad I met you, Hop."

"And I you, Elsie."

*   *   *

DAY 8

"It will never work," Hops says.

"It *has* to work or we're going to die in here," Elsie explains as she and Hop stand near the wall staring at the door.

"The Giant will see us. It's too dangerous."

"No, he won't. That's why we're standing on *this* side of the door. When he opens it, he'll be facing forward and the swinging door will conceal us. Then we'll run behind him. He doesn't have eyes in the back of his head. I looked. We'll slip through the doorway without him being the wiser."

"Then what?" Hop asks. "There's just darkness beyond that door. There could be ten other Giants hiding in there waiting to snap our necks."

"It's a chance I'm willing to take. We're all dying in here. How many chicks have died right next to us? We sit by them for hours, comforting them, and then either the Giant crushes their necks or before he can get to them, they just stop breathing. We don't even know why they're dying. They don't have any noticeable injuries, just like that first female chick didn't. We're clearly running out of time. I need to get everyone out of here, and the only idea I can think of is to find someone to help us."

"Who will help us? Giants?"

"Of course not, but someone will. After we tell them what's happening to us in here, how could anyone *not* want to help us?"

Hop sits down in the wood shavings. It's not that he isn't brave; he just has no idea what's beyond that door. Those two days stuck on the back of that truck feel like such a blur now. He had just hatched, so he can't remember anything about what he saw as the truck barreled down the road. Plus, he and Elsie have an important purpose in this shed. How can they abandon that?

"Can't we just stay here and keep consoling everyone? If we run through that door and get lost or killed, who will keep all the other chicks company as they live out their last moments? It seems to bring them such peace."

Elsie crouches beside him. She points her wing at the other chicks pushing and shoving their way around in the warehouse. "Look at them. Something is happening to us. Look how many chicks' legs are twisted the wrong way. They didn't trip and break their legs. Their bodies are *growing* that way."

They study all the birds whose legs are deformed. The chicks flap their wings wildly as they struggle to maintain balance with their misshapen limbs dragging behind them.

"Look how plump we are," Elsie continues. "I can feel it. I can feel myself growing… large. My body aches even sitting still. Why are we becoming so big so fast?"

Elsie holds up one of her orange feet, revealing festering open wounds underneath. "Our feet are covered with sores. Our skin burns from sitting on this dirty ground. Being stuck inside this place is eating away at our bodies. If we don't find someone to help us, we will all die just like the birds we've sat beside."

Hop's breathing quickens. He knows she's right, but how will they ever pull this off? Where will they go even if they get out of here? There's no easy answer, and every path seems to lead to imminent death.

BOOM! BOOM! BOOM! The farmer bangs on the door from the other side. Both Elsie and Hop jump in fear. Hop actually falls onto his side.

"Get ready!" Elsie blurts out.

All the other chicks dash away from the door, squawking and terrified. The door opens and the man steps into the room with his blood-smeared white bucket. Elsie jolts into gear and runs behind the man toward the open doorway.

"Come on! Follow me!" she yells back at Hop.

Against his better judgment, he rushes after her. The door is swiftly swinging closed. They both dart as fast as their thin legs will take them.

"You can make it! You can make it!" she yells to herself.

The door is almost shut, so she quickly turns around to see if Hop is close behind. No. He's too far back. Should she go in by herself? The door is shutting. She must make a choice.

Elsie jumps through the door just as it closes. Hop is not by her side. She's alone and enveloped by darkness.

11

ELSIE THE KINDHEARTED, PART 2

DAY 8, PART 2

"ELSIE?!" HOP SMACKS right into the door and falls back on the ground. *She's gone.* How will he survive in here without her? Panic starts to overtake over him, but then it hits him: *Maybe she's free! Maybe she'll find someone to rescue us after all!*

Hop stands up and turns around. A group of chicks is staring at him in amazement. They can't believe they just witnessed a chick escape through the door.

Further in the shed, the man stomps through the wood shavings doing his usual rounds picking up injured and dead birds. As always, everywhere he goes, chicks dart in the opposite direction.

The man gets to one chick in particular and picks up her lifeless body. He examines her plump chest and shakes his head in disappointment. "What a shame. You were growing so nice. I might have eaten you myself if you had made it."

Every single chick within hearing distance instantly goes silent. What did the man say—that he would *eat* her?!

Fear rumbles throughout the shed. Chicks shriek as loudly as they can.

"He's going to eat us!"

"The Giants eat us! We're going to be eaten!"

The man is taken aback by all the sudden squawking. Chicks climb over one another, running in no particular direction, just to get away from the fear of being devoured.

"Shut up!" The man hollers. He kicks at the birds nearest to him. "What the hell has gotten into you?"

His kicking just causes more mayhem. The birds flutter about the room, but since they can't fly any real distance, they simply flap their wings erratically. They want out, but there's nowhere to go.

The man gives up collecting dead chickens for the day. It's too chaotic and noisy to think straight. He rushes for the door, kicking at birds to get out of his way.

Hop stands by the door to see if he can run through and join Elsie. All the other birds scatter when the man nears, but Hop stays right where he is, staring down the towering figure coming his way. The man swings his boot at Hop, but the small chick dodges him and stays near the door.

"Get outta here!" The man yells as he kicks at Hop again.

Hop jumps out of the way and positions himself further from the door. He glares at the man and the man glares right back.

"Don't even think about it," the man warns Hop.

The small chick stands right where he is, glowering at the large human looming over him. The man shakes his head in disbelief at how bold this small bird is.

The farmer opens the door and Hop quickly yells, "Elsie, the Giants—"

Before Hop can get the full sentence out, the man slams the door behind him.

Elsie doesn't make a sound. She's hiding behind a piece of farm equipment in the corner. When she first walked into the room, she stepped into a web. She can feel a spider crawling on her back, but she doesn't want to alert the human by moving, so she sits deathly still.

This is it. Get ready. The room is pitch black. She can't even see her own feet.

She hears the farmer cuss, frustrated by the insolence of the chickens.

Focus. You can do this.

The farmer opens the outside door. The sun blasts into the room! Elsie steps forward and is immediately blinded.

I can't see! She stumbles over her own feet. The lights in the shed were always so dim; she's never seen light as bright as the sun.

She can hear the door closing shut. *Go! Just believe. You will make it.*

Elsie dashes toward the light with gusto. Bam! She slams into the back of the man's shoe. If she had run even an inch to the right, she would have made it.

"What the—" The man looks back to see Elsie flapping her wings to swivel upright. He leans down and angrily picks her up by her legs.

"What the hell is wrong with you damn birds today?"

"Don't hurt me! Please!" Elsie begs. She still can't see anything. She covers her head with her wings in case he swats at her.

The man pries open the outer door, yanks open the inner door and tosses Elsie back into the shed. She lands with a thud. All the other birds turn to the door to see what the fracas is about.

"Now shut up! The whole lot of you, just shut up!" With that, the man slams the door closed.

Hop and the other chicks crowd around Elsie. Hop is disappointed that Elsie wasn't able to escape, but he's also elated to see her again.

"Are you hurt?" Hop asks.

Elsie doesn't answer at first. She's startled from the frightening experience. She examines her body. No noticeable breaks. If only that could bring her comfort.

"I was so close." Elsie sighs. "The light was so bright, though. I couldn't see anything. I failed, Hop."

"You're alive. That's all that matters. Elsie, I have to tell you something. The—"

Another chick jumps in. "What was it like out there?"

"Beyond the door?" Elsie thinks about it for a moment. She was outside—only for a second, but she was outside the shed. "The air was so fresh," she says wistfully. "I wish we could live out there. I tried—"

"Elsie." Hop cuts in. "The Giants… they're going to eat us."

Elsie is stunned. *What did he just say?*

"Did you hear me?" Hop asks. "When the Giant picked up one of the dead chicks, he said that he was disappointed he wouldn't be able to eat her."

Elsie looks at the other chicks. Everyone has a panicked expression. Elsie feels dizzy. This is real. It's so grotesque, though, how could it be real? But it is. With all the appalling things that have happened to them thus far, this is a perfectly plausible outcome.

Of course we'll be eaten. That's the most gruesome thing imaginable. Of course that's why we're here.

Elsie goes to say something, but nothing comes out. Instead, she closes her eyes and cries. What else is there to do?

12

ELSIE THE KINDHEARTED, PART 3

DAY 15

"I'M RIGHT HERE," Elsie says softly to the frail chick beside her. "You are not alone." She has done this so many times—sat by sickly birds who have mere hours to live. It shatters her heart every time. It's even more tragic that the chicks are always incredibly grateful. This life is so utterly miserable, they can't believe someone is showing them kindness.

This female chick, Clover, is more alert than some of the others, which is not a good thing. It means she'll most likely survive until the man comes and snaps her neck. There's a slight chance that she will die before he comes—he's been entering the shed every few days now instead of every single day—but either way Clover will be dead very soon.

There's nothing Elsie can do to prevent that. The only thing that's made these experiences any easier is that at this point all the chicks are aware of their grim fate. Before, Elsie had to tell them, and it was sickening to see their reactions to discovering that they would be killed—and not just killed, but violently murdered. Two chicks actually became so distressed over the news that they had panic attacks and died on the spot. Elsie was shocked, but also relieved. Now they were spared.

After Elsie and Hop's failed escape, they did a thorough search of the shed for another possible way out, but they found nothing. Their best hope was somehow getting over the metal gate that divides the shed in half, but the chicks are much heavier now, so their flying capabilities are even more limited.

The chicks have always been curious about that metal gate. *Why did the Giants put up this barrier keeping us from going on that end? Are they planning to trap more chicks over there?*

The chicks have grown so large that they've mostly filled up this entire side of the shed. *We could really use that space over there.*

The metal gate is just one of the thousands of questions that Elsie feels they'll never get answered, and in terms of importance, it's low on her list. She's preoccupied by the impending doom she and the other chicks face. After two weeks in the shed, Elsie and Hop can tell that they're not as vibrant as they once were. They are weighed down not only physically but emotionally. She and the other chicks used to run around more, but everyone's slowed to a gloomy gait, if they walk at all.

She warned the other chicks not to eat so much—knowing that the man is fattening them up to eat them—but no one other than Hop listened. There's nothing else for them to do but eat. Besides, they feel hungry all the time from growing so much.

Hop steps up to Elsie. His eyes are filled with tears.

"Are you okay?" Elsie asks.

Hop looks at Clover and motions for Elsie to step away with him. It's impossible to get any privacy in the shed. There are chicks smashed side by side everywhere they go, but he wants to be away from any dying birds for what he has to say.

Elsie and Hop maneuver their way closer to the metal gate at the center of the shed so they aren't surrounded on all sides by birds.

Hop turns around. "The chick I was just sitting with, Salvatore… he died."

Elsie nods. "I know it's hard, Hop. You should take a break. Sitting with our injured friends is important, but we need time to recuperate, too."

"That's not it. When we were sitting there, do you know what he asked me? He said, 'Does the Giant despise us?' He couldn't understand why the Giant was putting us through all this misery just to eat us. And I don't either. Do we taste that good that our suffering is unimportant?"

Elsie knows that Hop is a sensitive soul—that's the reason he sits with these other birds—but these experiences tear at him. He isn't able to compartmentalize his emotions as well as Elsie.

Elsie snuggles up to him, putting her wing over his back. "I think about these things, too, Hop. When that Giant walks in here, it would be impossible not to see that we're all suffering. Sometimes I wish that I could talk to him, plead with him not to hurt us. But I think when he looks at us he doesn't see living beings; he just sees food."

"But I'm not food. I want to live."

Elsie doesn't say a word. She normally tries to be strong to give others hope, but he hit a nerve. *I want to live, too. I don't want to be eaten. Why does this mean Giant get to decide how and when we die? Why don't we have a say in the matter?*

Usually she's so good at finding comforting words to assuage the other chicks, but right now she feels angry, helpless, hopeless.

That's when they hear a loud creak at the far end of the shed—the side on which they've never been. Elsie and Hop peer through the metal gate, deep into the dimly lit shed. They can just make out the door opening.

In walk three furry animals. Elsie and Hop have never seen such creatures. Instead of feathers, they're covered in hair, similar to what the Giant has on top of his head but way more.

One by one, the other chicks notice two of the furry critters making their way toward the metal gate. The third one stands back by the door. A hush comes over the shed. Who are these creatures? *What* are these creatures?

Elsie, Hop, and the other chicks are mesmerized as the two animals step toward the barrier. The other chicks step back, but Elsie and Hop stay right where they are.

"Hello?" The one furry animal calls out. She has brown fur with sprinkles of gray and a striking black mask. "It's okay. We're here to help you."

Elsie and Hop stare at the furry animals wide-eyed, not sure what to say. They're here to help?

The critter with brown fur steps slowly up to the gate. "It's okay, sweet one. My name's Persimmon and—"

"What *are* you?" Elsie asks.

"You mean what type of animal am I? I'm a raccoon. This is my best friend Derpoke. He's an opossum. And our other best friend back at the door, Bruiser, is a dog."

Persimmon coughs from the dust in the air. "My friends and I are The Enlighteners. We rescue animals who are suffering, and from the looks of things, you poor chickens are definitely in need of help."

A wave of elation comes over Elsie. There's so much kindness in Persimmon's eyes. Elsie is used to seeing so much fear in the eyes of other birds and so much disdain in the eyes of humans, but this animal is brimming with compassion.

"I knew you'd come," Elsie says. "I knew it all along."

Persimmon is touched. She has to hold back tears. It sounds hopeful, but with the look in this chicken's eyes, she can tell it really comes from deep despair.

Elsie almost collapses. She is so overcome with emotion. She didn't want to admit it to herself before, but she had begun to think that they were all going to die. She was staying strong for all the other chicks in their darkest moments, but secretly, she was losing hope that anyone would ever save them. But now… she's looking into the eyes of her savior, an animal she didn't even know existed. It's the most powerful moment of her life.

Persimmon puts her front paw against the gate. "We're going to do everything we can to get you out of here." The raccoon coughs again. Her eyes are watering from the burning ammonia in the air. She goes to rub them.

"No, don't rub your eyes," Hop warns. "It will only make it worse."

Derpoke steps nearer, coughing. His eyes are red and watering. "I already rubbed my eyes. They sting so much. We need to get the chickens out of here as soon as possible. This place is revolting."

The other chicks gather nearer to the gate, hearing that Persimmon and Derpoke are possibly there to free them.

"Can you get us out of here?" a chick asks.

"Please! The Giants are going to eat us!" another chick yells out.

The chicks shove each other to get closer to these animals who are promising escape.

"Yes," Persimmon calls out. "We'll do everything we can to get you out of here, but we can't start a panic. We don't want to wake the humans."

"What are humans?" Hop asks.

"They're the ones keeping you here," Persimmon says.

"Oh, the Giants," Elsie says. "Yes, there's one Giant who comes in here and hurts us terribly. When can you free us?"

Persimmon leans in closer to the gate and whispers. "We need to come up with a plan first. There are two other sheds full of chickens right next to yours. It will be morning soon, so there's no time—"

"There are two more sheds like this one full of other chicks?" Elsie can't believe it. It's worse than she thought.

"Yes…" Persimmon coughs again. She can barely see through her watering eyes. They sting unbearably. She whispers even more quietly. "I can't breathe. We should talk outside. You can tell us everything you know about this place so that we can rescue all of you. I'm worried that the moment you fly by our side, everyone will fly over and it will be chaos."

"We can't fly," Elsie says.

"You can't?!" Persimmon asks.

"But you're birds, right?" Derpoke says.

"All we've ever been able to do is flap around a little and fly short distances, but now our bodies are too heavy to do even that."

Persimmon feels like she was punched in the stomach. That's a huge setback. The chickens' ability to fly was going to make this the easiest rescue mission yet. *What will we do now? There look to be thousands of birds in this shed. How will we carry thousands of birds?*

Persimmon continues to whisper. "Derpoke and I can carry two of you right now, but that's all we can manage."

She climbs up the gate. The chicks squawk with excitement and anxiety. They couldn't hear what Persimmon and Elsie were saying, so they're filled with anticipation over what this animal is planning to do.

"Persimmon!" Derpoke calls up at her. "Be careful. You could get trampled in there."

Persimmon ignores him and drops onto the wood shavings. The ground is wet with urine and feces. Persimmon is disgusted, and when she looks up, she sees that she's surrounded by a mass of white feathers.

As politely as possible, she moves through the chickens searching for Elsie. She finally comes upon her. Persimmon is worried about upsetting the crowd of birds when they realize that they're not all being carried out at once, so she stealthily motions for Elsie to cling to her back. Elsie just stares at her.

Persimmon motions to Elsie again and says quietly, "Ready?"

Elsie looks over at Hop. He nods.

Elsie turns back to Persimmon. "Hop and I need to stay here and take care of the other chicks. You should take two other birds."

Persimmon can't believe what she has just heard. No animal in all the rescue missions has ever turned down the chance at freedom. It's a beautiful, selfless act. *Who is this altruistic chicken?*

"Are you sure?" Persimmon asks.

The other chicks who are pushed up against Persimmon and Elsie start shoving now that they understand what is going on.

"Take me!"

"No, take me!"

Persimmon gets jostled around and squashed between desperate birds.

"Be patient. Please," Persimmon pleads. "Someone is going to get hurt."

The frenzy has already begun, though. Persimmon falls to the ground as a wave of chicks rushes toward the gate. Talons dig into her flesh. Her nose gets slammed into the excrement-drenched wood shavings. The filth hits her eyes, burning them.

Persimmon crawls toward the gate. Derpoke screams from the other side. "Persimmon!"

He crawls to the top of the gate, peering into the flurry of white feathers, searching frantically for his best friend. Then right below him, Persimmon crawls up through a crowd of chicks, holding one in her mouth.

Birds far back in the shed are completely baffled by the commotion at the gate, but when they see Persimmon holding the chick in her mouth, they begin to scream. "They're trying to eat us! They're going to eat us!"

This causes even more mayhem. Chicks jump on top of one another, squawking. Some are trampled to death.

Persimmon drops the chick over the fence as gently as she can and then twists around and picks up the nearest chick with her teeth and carries him over the fence.

"Come on!" Persimmon yells to Derpoke.

The two chicks hop onto Persimmon's and Derpoke's backs and the two friends rush as fast as they can toward the shed door.

Bruiser, who is standing guard, barks at the chickens. "Quiet, quiet! You'll wake the humans!"

Chicks holler through the gate. "Don't leave us! Please! The Giants are going to eat us!"

Elsie and Hop push their way to the side of the shed. They want to get as far away from the chaos as possible. Their hearts race as they press against the wall. Chicks continue to bang into them. Elsie looks through the gate and catches Persimmon and Derpoke carrying the birds through the entryway. The shed door closes. They're gone.

Elsie's heart sinks. She wants so badly to go outside into the fresh air, where her eyes don't sting, where there's not death all around.

She surveys the panicked chicks. *What kind of bird would I be if I left everyone else in here? Who would watch after them as they died in the filth, feeling lonely and unloved? I couldn't live with myself. I won't leave this place until every one of us does.*

She and Hop nestle closer to each another. "We're going to be free, Hop."

Hop nods—excited and anxious. "You were right. We just had to believe."

Their miracle came in the form of two compassionate critters. Now Elsie and Hop just have to wait for their return.

13

RAWLY RUNS ALONGSIDE the other Dissidents through the brush. He's amazed at how silent and focused everyone is. When he was with Persimmon's team, between rescue attempts, they walked leisurely, joked around, and took snack breaks. Not The Dissidents. They dash stealthily through the woods directly to their next mission—no joking, no snacking, no fun. It's certainly efficient, but it's a little more intense than he had anticipated.

Rawly treks beside Drig and their old friends Dusty and Linder—the two raccoons who joined Vincent's army right after they liberated the minks from the Peterson fur farm. The four buddies had joyfully reunited, but only briefly. The army immediately began the journey to their next mission, so the four friends didn't get a chance to catch up. Rawly has so many questions about their missions at the other fur farms, so despite everyone's silence, he finally whispers to Linder. "Jeez, you'd think we were running *away* from something instead of *to* something."

"Ha. Better get used to it," Linder whispers back. "No matter where we go, Vincent wants our entrance to be a surprise. It works. We raided a ton of fur farms—just stormed right in—and we rescued every single mink without one team member getting killed or even hurt."

"Yeah, much better than when we were with Persimmon," Dusty adds as he hops over a fallen branch. "I'm still in shock that Claudette and Fisher were killed. What the heck went wrong?"

Rawly pauses for a moment. He pretends to catch his breath as he sprints into some thick brush, but really, he's stalling. The truth is that *he's* the one who made the call to rush the humans, which directly led to Claudette's and Fisher's deaths, but Rawly still blames Persimmon for not being more aggressive against the humans sooner.

"The mission wasn't planned properly from the start," Rawly explains. "Persimmon was worried some of the creatures, like the tigers and elephants, would be too dangerous or too large to free successfully. She wasn't bold enough to admit that in order to free all the animals, some humans might get hurt—even killed. Those tigers and elephants deserved a chance at freedom as much as any of the other animals. I don't regret the decision I made."

"What decision?" Linder asks.

Rawly realizes he may have revealed too much. He corrects himself. "The decision we *all* made to run into the middle of those humans so that we could free the elephants. Helping them was the right thing to do, but it—"

"Keep it down!" a nearby female mink hisses at the raccoons. "Are you *trying* to announce to the humans that we're coming?"

Rawly glares at the mink but keeps quiet—no need for him to make enemies when he only just joined the team. The four raccoons don't talk for the next hour until The Dissidents finally come to a halt.

Rawly sighs in relief. He's out of breath, so this break is more than welcome. All the soldiers quickly disperse into hiding spots in the forest—in trees, under logs, and so on. Rawly is amazed by how secretive everything feels.

He sees a tree trunk with a rotted interior and motions for Drig, Linder, and Dusty to follow. The four of them crawl into the trunk. Spider webs fill the inside, but at least it's private enough that they can talk.

Rawly has been aching to ask about one topic in particular, so he jumps right in. "So Vincent and his team kill humans—as in every single one you come across?"

Dusty nods. "That's one of the first things we do when we arrive at the fur farms. We kill all the humans in their sleep, and then we're able to rescue the minks trapped there without fear of being attacked. After what you told us about how dangerous and chaotic that mission at the circus was, I really don't know how else we could have accomplished all these missions and not had any casualties on our side."

"Yeah, that's so great that you all haven't had anyone get hurt, but..." Rawly leans in. *This* is the question he's really interested in asking. "Have you two *personally* killed humans?"

Linder looks down, solemnly. Clearly this issue has weighed on him. "It's tough... I mean, it's gruesome. But we have to protect everyone in The Dissidents, right? And all those poor minks were suffering so much. These humans... what they did to those minks. It's evil."

"Of course those humans are evil," Dusty jumps in, defensively. "We're not doing anything wrong—*humans* are. We all know that if humans catch us trying to rescue these other animals, they'll kill us, so killing the humans first is merely the smartest way to protect ourselves. It's also the only way to ensure they'll never hurt another animal."

Rawly pats Dusty's back. "No judgment, my friend. There's no excuse for what these humans are doing. They must be stopped. I just... I was just curious about your previous missions."

Rawly quickly changes the subject since things are getting a bit tense. "What do you all think about recruiting these dogs? No offense to Vincent, but dogs hate all of us forest creatures. Plus, they're notoriously loyal to humans. Do you really think they're going to join our team that attacks humans?"

"I wouldn't underestimate Vincent," Dusty says. "We've been on many missions with him now. He's really something to watch. He convinced all these raccoons to join The Dissidents. With the minks, it makes sense that they'd join the fight, but you know how we raccoons are. We're ambivalent about humans. No raccoon wants to get shot and killed for our fur, but it's a nice treat that humans waste so much tasty food that we can nab from their trash cans. That's why I think it was so hard for Persimmon to convince other raccoons to join her team. But gosh, everywhere we go, Vincent is so persuasive, he recruits new team members in a flash."

"And you should see how we conduct the missions," Linder cuts in, excitedly. "Vincent doesn't wait around for days trying to conjure up some quiet plan to sneak in and release the other animals. No way. He briefly scopes out the location and then bam…" He whacks the moss-covered trunk with his paw. "… He storms in and releases everyone. It's thrilling!"

"Shh!" The same irritated mink leans her head into the tree trunk and shushes them. The four friends are startled.

The mink looks right at Rawly and whispers with pure contempt. "You're new, so I'm going to make this really clear. Our lives depend on going into these locations as focused and quiet as possible. I won't have you putting me and the other soldiers at risk. Do you understand?"

Rawly is stunned. *No one* talks to him like that, especially in front of his friends. He can't have them seeing him as weak, so he marches up to the mink who's peering into the trunk from above. "Who do you think you are, talking to me like that?"

The mink hops down gracefully and stares right into Rawly's eyes. Her fur is such a dark black that she almost blends into the night, and it's not until she's in his face that Rawly realizes that though she's smaller than he is, she's much fiercer.

"The name's Ember, and if I have to tell you again to keep it down, you'll be kicked out of The Dissidents."

Rawly's blood is boiling. "*You're* gonna kick *me* out? I'm one of the leaders."

Ember's whole demeanor changes. She chuckles and turns to a group of minks nearby. "Did you hear him?"

The other minks laugh.

Ember turns back to Rawly and calmly proclaims, "There is one—and only one—leader of The Dissidents, and that's Vincent."

Rawly notices that a few minks have gathered around—and none seems too fond of someone new coming in and usurping Vincent's leadership. Rawly glances over at Drig, Dusty, and Linder to make sure they have his back if a fight ensues. Drig holds up his paw and shakes his head; this isn't worth a row.

Never one to give in, Rawly stands on his hind legs and snaps back. "Oh yeah? Well, I'm going up front where a leader belongs. Try and stop me."

Ember grins. "You're going to bother Vincent when he's trying to secretly scope out the new location?"

Ember looks over at the other minks as if to say, "Is this raccoon really that much of an idiot?" Then she looks back at Rawly. "I'll join you. I want to see your expression when Vincent gives you a mouthful."

Rawly clenches his jaw. For a moment, he's actually worried that he has sealed his own fate. But it's too late to back down, so he harrumphs and hops out of the tree trunk.

Drig sighs. He respects Rawly, but he also knows that his friend doesn't quite know when to keep his mouth shut. He watches as Rawly walks through the woods toward the front of the line and worries that their time in The Dissidents is about to come to an abrupt and awkward end—just like it did with Persimmon's team.

14

RAWLY JOURNEYS THROUGH the woods, searching for the front of the line where Vincent is. Ember follows a few paces behind, but the two refrain from speaking to each other.

Rawly can feel the raccoons and minks who are hiding in the brush staring at him as he passes by. *Is this a dumb idea? Will Vincent really be upset that I'm coming to the front?... Why should he be? I have a right to scope out the location just as much as he does. Besides, I've done multiple rescue operations. I know what I'm doing.*

A few trees ahead, Rawly notices Scraps and Apricot sitting on some leaves. Apricot bats at the young raccoon's gray-and-black striped tail.

"I said, stop." Scraps swats her paw.

"But your tail is so fluffy!" Apricot says. "It's asking to be hit."

"We're supposed to be quiet," Scraps explains—not used to being the mature one in any situation. "If *I* can sit still, *you* can sit still."

Apricot rolls onto the ground and groans. "I hate waiting. This is boring!"

Rawly walks by his two companions but doesn't look at them. He doesn't want to have to explain himself.

"Where are you going?" Scraps asks.

Rawly ignores him and keeps walking.

Scraps scurries to catch up with Rawly. "Hey, where are you going? Is everything okay?"

Rawly quickens his pace to try to shake the small raccoon. "I have something important to do. I'm going to the front. It's too dangerous for you. Just stay here."

Scraps keeps following alongside the agitated raccoon. Rawly doesn't want to make any more of a scene, so he walks even faster, hoping that Scraps will eventually tire and stop trailing him. Of course, Scraps is a ball of energy, so he won't be tiring any time soon.

Apricot saunters over to Ember. "Why are you stalking Rawly?" Her eyes light up. "Ooh, is he your prisoner?"

"What is the problem with you new soldiers?" Ember hisses. "You need to learn to be quiet. This isn't a game. We're saving lives here."

"Whoa!" Apricot says. "Somebody's got an attitude. Never mind."

The orange tabby sprints forward and joins Rawly and Scraps. Rawly mutters under his breath, but he knows that Apricot is even more difficult to deal with than Scraps, so he holds back from lecturing.

Soon after, Rawly, Scraps, Apricot, and Ember hear barking up ahead. The barking is so intense that they're actually nervous to keep moving forward, but they're also curious to see what's going on.

About a dozen minks and raccoons stand near a large wooden fence. The fence has no holes, so the team isn't able to see through to the other side. This barrier is clearly not meant to protect the property from intruders; it's meant to hide what's going on within those walls.

From the barking on the other side of the fence, the group can tell that there are dozens of dogs.

Rawly is as stunned as everyone else. *Why would a human have so many dogs? Do they kill the dogs for their fur like they do the minks? Or maybe they eat them. Wait, do humans eat dogs?* The thought had never occurred to him since most humans seem so fond of dogs, but with the abuse he's seen on these missions, he realizes anything is possible.

Vincent is sitting atop the fence, deep in thought. When Rawly and the others arrive, the minks and raccoons motion for them to stay quiet.

Vincent senses the new arrivals and turns around. Rawly motions to see if he can have a look as well. Vincent nods.

Before Rawly steps up to the fence, he glances at Ember and gives her a smug smirk. Ember is surprised by this turn of events but fantasizes that perhaps Vincent will push Rawly into the dogs' area to teach him a lesson.

Rawly climbs the tall fence. His heart is pounding. It's not just the number of dogs that worries him; it's the ferocity of their growls. These are clearly no everyday dogs found at your average human dwelling. These dogs can definitely back up their growls with force.

Rawly peeks over the fence. The yard is filled with pit bulls, each chained by the neck. The chains, driven deep into the ground, are only a few feet long, which means their entire span of movement for most of their lives is mere feet. It reminds Rawly of how the elephants were chained up in the circus.

Each pit bull has a station set up so that no dog can step into another's area. The dogs are far enough apart that they can't do damage to one another but close enough that their personal space feels invaded. This creates a constant state of agitation in the dogs, which is exactly how the humans want them to feel.

Their small areas are mostly bare—just dirt on the ground with excrement smattered here and there. No food or water is in sight. Each dog has a broken-down shelter—some are old, large plastic barrels and others are wooden doghouses poorly slapped together.

The dog stations near the fence are positioned among trees, but the dog stations closer to the human's house are out in the open.

Rawly can't believe how many dogs are crammed in the yard, and he's very concerned that all of them are now staring at him.

"There's another one!" a dog yells.

"You want some food, little critters?" another dog barks. "We don't have any, so *you're* the food."

Rawly sees a few dogs lick their lips and laugh. Others are so uncomfortable and miserable, they're not in a laughing mood.

"Get out of here or we'll kill you!" another dog hollers.

Rawly looks at Vincent for reassurance, but Vincent is busy examining the pit bulls one by one. He doesn't seem to notice that the dogs are threatening their lives. Rawly decides to attempt to calm the creatures down.

"Wait, listen," Rawly pleads. "We're here to help you."

"You think you can come here and trick us?" a dog close to the fence growls. "You think we're stupid?! We told you, we don't have food. If you say one more word, I'll break this chain and eat you alive."

"Get him, Krait!" another dog goads him.

Rawly accidentally locks eyes with the dog. Krait is growling so viciously that Rawly's paws begin to shake. He feels dizzy and starts to teeter. The thought of hurling into the mouth of that dog frightens him even more, so his shaking worsens.

Vincent grabs a hold of Rawly's fur, keeping him from falling. "Don't waste your breath. They're trying to show off to one another who's the toughest. I have another idea, but first, I want to scope out that shed."

What shed? Rawly looks to the far left and realizes there is, in fact, a shed. He was so focused on all the menacing dogs, he didn't even notice it. Light is pouring through the rickety building's walls and he can hear humans inside cheering.

Vincent digs his nails into the fence and slides down. Rawly is more than happy to follow.

The two trek along the edge of the fence with Scraps, Apricot, Ember, and the small group of minks and raccoons trailing after.

Rawly catches up to Vincent. "Just so you know, I wasn't actually scared. I just lost my balance a little."

Vincent nods. No need to embarrass the raccoon.

"But on that note," Rawly continues. "I could see how the dogs might frighten the other team members. I've never seen dogs who looked so ferocious. It's like they were pure muscle and teeth. I don't know how you're going to convince all those dogs not to eat us much less join our fight."

"Ah, but I don't need to convince *all* of them," Vincent explains. "I just need one dog all the others respect and *that* dog will convince them. When I see him or her, I will know."

"Huh." Rawly smiles. "That's a really smart idea."

"Yes," Vincent says confidently, as if it were already established that his plan was brilliant.

As The Dissidents approach the shed, the sounds from inside get louder. The team suddenly feels sick to their stomachs as the ghastly sounds become more pronounced. The most prominent is the humans' cheering, but it's not joyful like they're celebrating—it's a menacing cheer. That's not the worst sound, though. When the team listens more closely, there's an even more disturbing one: the dogs'. Two dogs are heard violently fighting, but they're also yelping.

What's happening inside that shed? Each member of the team is sure that after they look, they will always wish they hadn't.

15

THE MOONLIGHT SHINES on Vincent's black fur—bringing out the blue tint—as he and Rawly stealthily crawl onto the roof of the shed. It would be too conspicuous if everyone climbed up there, so the rest of the group anxiously waits on the ground.

The mink and raccoon search for a hole so they can see into the building. Vincent notices a large beam of yellow light shining through the wood, so he motions for Rawly to follow him. Vincent is eager to see what is happening inside, but Rawly is dreading it.

They peer into the hole, and what they see is as revolting as they had imagined. In the center of the room is a large circular pit with dirt covering the ground. The pit is enclosed with wooden walls that are a few feet high. Surrounding the wall is a crowd of bloodthirsty humans ravenously enjoying a heartbreaking sight: In the pit are two dogs ripping at each other's flesh. Rawly instantly loses his breath as if someone has just kicked him in the stomach, but Vincent just grits his teeth. The mink is too jaded to be shocked anymore by the abuse humans inflict on other animals. This is exactly what he expected to see.

The two pit bulls are covered in blood with deep gashes in their skin, and they're panting heavily—clearly fatigued from being forced to fight for over four hours. Three humans are in the pit with the dogs—two of which are coaching the dogs to tear each other apart.

"Come on, Chopper!" One human wearing a shirt and tie yells at the brown pit bull. "Bite your way out! Get out from under him!"

Chopper is pinned down by the other dog who is biting painful holes into the back of his neck. Chopper is so exhausted, he can't move to escape these blows.

The man gets on his knees in the dirt right next to Chopper and hollers at him. "You're a damn grand champion. Act like one!"

That's true. Chopper has "won" five fights ("won" according to the human; "survived" according to the dog), which in the dogfighting world warrants the title grand champion. Chopper had actually been retired from fighting before this bout. Coach—the human yelling at him—was using Chopper to breed new fighting dogs and since Chopper had survived so many fights, his puppies were selling for a substantial sum, which pleased Coach immensely.

Chopper was appalled that Coach was selling his babies into the fighting life, but the only good thing was that he wasn't being forced to fight any longer. Unfortunately, that retirement ended when another dogfighter offered Coach a great deal of money to have Chopper take on an up-and-coming fighting dog. Coach, being who he is, could not pass up an opportunity to cash in big, so he agreed to the challenge.

That's how Coach runs his dogfighting operation, Beast Dog Kennels. The only worth these dogs have to him is to make him as much money as possible. He sees himself as a savvy businessman and the dogs' well-being doesn't factor into that equation. If you asked him to his face, he'd say that he loves the dogs in his yard, but only so long as they keep winning. The moment they lose, he has his 19-year-old nephew, Dale, dispose of them with a bullet to the head.

Coach's dogfighting isn't exactly a secret in town, yet he's a well-regarded member of the community. He's in his early forties and coaches the local high school football team but acts like he's in charge of some all-star professional team. All the townsfolk adore him for running one of the best teams in the state. They figure: What's a little dogfighting when you keep leading the football team to state championships?

Chopper was mortified when he heard the news that he'd have to fight again. He had let himself believe that he was finally free from ever having to enter that pit again—to hurt another dog or be hurt himself—but here he was being forced to fight for his life one more time. He's over seven years old, which is a long time to survive in the dogfighting world since each match leads either to death or to grave injury, and he's completely burned out. It had also been a year since his last fight, so he's out of practice. More importantly, he doesn't have any fight left in him. He never wanted to fight, but at least when he was starting out he felt a fire to survive. Now he feels broken. So here pinned to the ground, he just wants it all to end. Everything. He doesn't want to hurt any more dogs. He doesn't want to feel the sting of another dog's teeth tearing into his flesh.

"Get up, you damn dog!" Coach hollers. "Fight!"

Vincent and Rawly watch in horror.

"We have to stop this!" Rawly says frantically. "We have to help them."

Rawly hops up and paces around.

"Calm yourself," Vincent says coolly. "There are too many humans, and they have weapons."

Rawly hadn't noticed the guns on the men's belts, but that was one of the first things Vincent had searched for when they looked into the shed. Rawly is too worked up to let the guns deter him, though. "We'll run in there so fast, we'll kill all the humans before they have time to grab their weapons. That's what your army does, right?"

"It is not yet time to strike," Vincent says, keeping his composure. "Be patient. I have a plan."

"But these humans are making these dogs kill each other," Rawly says, throwing his paws up in frustration. "How can we just sit here?"

"Look out in that yard." Vincent points his nose toward the backyard filled with dogs. The dogs' eyes glow in the moonlight. Now that they've stopped barking, it is easy to see how miserable they are—all chained up, scars covering their bodies, and living in squalor. "We're here to save *all* of them. If we rush into this shed right now, it will jeopardize their chance at freedom. You're too smart to let that happen."

Rawly slumps onto the roof in defeat.

Vincent looks back into the hole. He's just as upset as Rawly over this disgusting spectacle, but he's not impulsive like Rawly, and he knows that it would be absolute chaos if The Dissidents stormed the shed at this moment. Team members would get killed, and some humans would surely escape, which would be a disaster for his grander plan. It pains him to admit it, but they cannot save these two dogs. One of them is about to die.

Blood trickles from Chopper's neck into the dirt around him. *It will all be over soon.* But just then, the thought of Rasha pops into his head.

Who will protect young Rasha if I'm gone? He instantly feels guilty. *I can't abandon her.*

Suddenly, with all the force Chopper can muster, he twists around and bites hard into the other dog's cheek. He slams the dog onto his side. It happens so swiftly, the other dog doesn't have time to react. Chopper chomps down into the back of the other dog's neck and bites with such force that it cracks his spine. The dog cries out in pain as the referee quickly puts a metal breaking stick in Chopper's mouth to pull him off the dog.

"It's over," the referee declares.

The humans stand there stunned. They had thought the fight was finished. Most of them had bet on Chopper's opponent, who is now lying in the dirt, spasming.

Coach hugs his nephew, Dale, who is in the crowd. "Grand champion, baby! Take that, Maxwell!"

Maxwell, the man who had been standing alongside the other dog in the pit, is speechless. He just lost a lot of money as well as a promising new fighting dog. He's furious at his dog for losing, but he's even more furious at himself for making the bet so high.

Vincent watches the losing dog as he convulses in the dirt. Chopper has also collapsed on the ground and looks like he has little chance of surviving these injuries.

Vincent grinds his teeth and scratches the roof in anger, ripping marks in the wood. He hasn't been this enraged since his brother Frestin was murdered right in front of him. *How can these humans be entertained by something so hideous?* He didn't think it was possible, but he may have just found humans crueler than the ones who imprisoned him and the other minks in that fur farm.

Vincent looks up to see Rawly facing the other way. He couldn't bear to watch any more of the fight. "It's over, Rawly."

The raccoon turns around slowly. His furry face is wet with tears, so he quickly tries to wipe them away, hoping Vincent won't notice.

Vincent steps over to the despondent raccoon and looks directly into his eyes. "We will avenge these dogs. I promise you."

Vincent sprints to the edge of the roof. The time to strike is drawing near.

16

"YOU PROMISE YOU'RE not going to eat us?" the female chick, Hazel, asks meekly as she stares up at Persimmon, Derpoke, Bruiser, Chloe, Tucker, Nibbin, Aunty Adelaide, and Uncle Bennett. She and the male chick, Arden, stare at the group of animals standing before them—three raccoons, a dog, two squirrels, an opossum, and a mink—creatures they never even knew existed before an hour ago when they were rescued from that shed. These animals are all smiling, and they have kind eyes, but each of them also has claws and sharp teeth. From their appearance, some of them are even scarier than the humans.

"Oh no," Persimmon says. "We would never harm you, and no human will ever harm you again, either. You're free."

"Forever?" Arden asks.

Persimmon smiles warmly and nods. "Forever."

"Will you make the other chicks free, too?" Hazel asks.

"We're going to do everything we can to rescue all the other chickens as well," Persimmon assures. "But I don't want you two worrying yourselves about that. You've been through enough."

Persimmon steps toward Hazel and Arden. She does it slowly so as not to scare them. She gently rubs Hazel's neck and wings with her paw. "This is your new home—the forest."

The two birds gaze up at the sky. There's no dim light fixtures above them—the sky is a gorgeous purple as the dawn approaches. The trees make a comforting, soft sound as they rustle in the breeze. The air is so fresh. The dirt and leaves under their feet feel so smooth. There are no birds smashed against them, shoving for space. They actually have room to move around. Freedom—what bliss.

The male chick tears up. "It's so beautiful out here. I never knew it could be so beautiful."

The team gets choked up, too, seeing these two birds experience liberty for the first time—Bruiser and Nibbin can especially relate to those first few euphoric moments when they realized that no one would ever have power over them again.

Nibbin excitedly bounds over to the two emotional birds. "Don't cry, chickens. We're going to help you just like The Enlighteners helped *me*! When I'm sad, eating always cheers me up. What do you eat?"

"Umm… they're brown pellets," Hazel says. "I don't know what they are, but they don't taste good."

Chloe's eyes light up. "There's so much delicious food that we're going to introduce to you. Nibbin, Tucker, why don't you help me gather some food?"

"I'll help, too," Derpoke chimes in.

Aunty Adelaide taps her niece on the back. "Persimmon, can your uncle and I talk to you privately?"

Persimmon almost protests since she wants to make the new additions to their team feel welcome, but then she sees the serious look on her aunt's and uncle's faces. Persimmon nods, quite aware that she's about to get a lecture.

Chloe, Tucker, Derpoke, and Nibbin begin sniffing through the foliage to find anything edible, while Bruiser stays beside the chickens to keep them safe. He even begins to lick them clean. At first, the chicks are frozen in fear, but then the grooming starts to tickle and feel good, so they nudge in closer to the large dog.

Persimmon follows Aunty Adelaide and Uncle Bennett out of earshot of the team.

"What's so urgent?" Persimmon asks.

"We are concerned about your mission," Aunty Adelaide says. "You come running out of that building with all these scratches. You have two chickens that the humans could come searching for. It's quite unsettling."

"There were thousands and thousands of birds in there," Persimmon says. "The humans won't even notice that they're gone. As for my scratches, the chickens were so desperate to break out of the shed that they panicked for fear they wouldn't be rescued. You should have seen the filth inside that building. What these chickens are going through is appalling."

"I'm sure it was upsetting," Uncle Bennett says. "But your aunt and I don't think you and your friends should get mixed up in this one. There's no way you'll be able to get all those chickens out of there, especially since we now know they can't fly."

"You really think we're going to give up that easily?" Persimmon asks. "Yes, it's going to be difficult... *and* dangerous—all these missions are—but in a matter of a few weeks all those chickens will be slaughtered unless we do something. How can you possibly suggest we not help them?"

"To be quite honest, your uncle and I aren't so sure how we feel about this mission. The chickens are the humans' food. The humans have to eat, right?"

Persimmon's mouth drops open. "I can't believe you just said that. Yes, humans have to eat, but they don't *have* to eat chickens. I thought you two were proud of our team for saving other animals."

"We are," Uncle Bennett says. "The minks were being killed for their fur, and the animals stuck in that circus were being abused to entertain humans. That's wrong. But the chickens... well, they're food. I mean, your aunt and I eat fish and so many animals eat other animals. Are you going to tell us that we're wrong for doing that?"

"I get it." Persimmon shakes her head. "This isn't because the mission is too dangerous. It's because you feel vilified for doing the very thing for which we're condemning the humans. That's pretty selfish, don't you think?"

"I don't appreciate your tone, young lady," Aunty Adelaide chides. "I also ask that you keep your voice down."

Aunty Adelaide notices that some team members are pricking up their ears to listen to the conversation as they search for food. She's embarrassed, feeling like they're all judging her.

Persimmon lowers her voice. "Do you see those two chickens over there—how scared they are? Do you see all the sores on their bodies? All the bald spots where feathers are missing? Are you really going to sit here and tell me that you're okay with letting them be killed?"

"You have no respect for your elders," Uncle Bennett says. "Where do you get off being so self-righteous?"

"You know who doesn't think I'm self-righteous? All those birds stuck in that shed, living in pure fear over the day that they are going to die."

"I found food! I found food!" Nibbin calls out from a nearby tree. He hops up and down gleefully.

Persimmon sees Nibbin celebrating. She notices the pile of meat and the pieces of apple and carrots next to him.

That's odd. Persimmon's stomach suddenly drops. "Nibbin, don't! Don't touch it!"

Nibbin keeps jumping up and down, not listening.

Persimmon dashes as fast as her legs will take her. Nibbin leans down to pick up a piece of fruit. Persimmon grabs him with her mouth and tosses him aside, but unfortunately, she keeps hurling toward the pile of food. SNAP! The sharp metal teeth of a spring trap violently clamp down on her right front leg, shattering her bone into fragments.

Persimmon howls in pain. She writhes around screaming and the more she moves, the more it shreds her skin. Her shrieks fill the forest. Animals within hearing distance know instantly that some other animal is dying a horrible death. They have no idea that this is the one animal who was trying the most to save them all.

17

THE WHOLE TEAM rushes up to Persimmon frantically as she flails around, yelping in agony with her right front paw clamped tightly in the razor-like teeth of the trap.

Bruiser leaps at the trap, biting at it to break Persimmon free.

"Don't," Persimmon begs, gritting through the pain. "Ow. Don't move it. Please."

Bruiser stops biting at the trap. The metal is so thick, it's useless anyway.

Derpoke is crying uncontrollably. He knows there's no way out of this one. He's going to lose his best friend.

Persimmon weeps as well. The throbbing in her crushed leg is so intense that she feels like she might black out.

Chloe leans in to her ensnared friend. "Persimmon, I've seen these traps before. I know there's a way to open it. Humans trap animals in them all the time and then somehow release them to take them home."

"No, no," Persimmon begs. "Please don't touch it. It hurts too much."

Chloe, Tucker, Derpoke, Bruiser, Aunty Adelaide, and Uncle Bennett look drearily at the blood pouring out of Persimmon's leg onto the leaves below.

"But you'll die," Chloe says as her heart sinks.

"Persimmon, let us help," Aunty Adelaide pleads. "We can undo the trap somehow."

"Please, everyone, give me a minute," Persimmon says. "It hurts to talk. I need to be quiet."

Everyone goes silent. All that can be heard is sniffling and crying.

The team watches mournfully as Persimmon moans. She tries not to move, but it's difficult. The trap closed upright, so she's forced to stand on her two hind legs, and it's nearly impossible when she's weak from the pain.

Derpoke crawls toward her sheepishly. He knows that she said not to bother her, but he can't just sit by while she staggers in distress. He crouches down. "Rest on my back."

Persimmon lays her body across his. Luckily, his body is just the right height for her to lean on, taking some of the pressure off her leg.

"Thank you," Persimmon says, breathing heavily.

Persimmon closes her eyes. Her leg feels like it's on fire. The anguish is unbearable. *Please let this end. Just make the pain end... I don't want to die. There are so many animals to save. All those chickens will die... Oh no, the chickens!*

"Where are Hazel and Arden?" Persimmon blurts out.

The team turns back to the spot where the chickens were last sitting by Bruiser. They're not there. Everyone on the team loses their breath.

"There," Chloe says. "Behind that tree!" She sprints over to where they're hiding and attempts to coax them out.

"And where's Nibbin?" Persimmon asks.

The team feels embarrassed. Their friend is dying in a trap and she still has to run things. They didn't even notice Nibbin's absence, they were so caught up in Persimmon's predicament.

"He ain't here," Bruiser says. "Probably ran away due to the commotion."

"Can you look for him, Bruiser?" Persimmon asks.

"And leave *you*? There could be wolves or mountain lions around. If they heard ya screamin', they'll be showin' up soon lookin' to cause some trouble. I ain't leavin' ya."

"It's okay. I doubt Nibbin is far, and you're the best tracker we've got. Nibbin probably thinks we're mad at him because I got caught in the trap. Please, he's just a baby."

Bruiser grumbles but knows she's too stubborn to let it go. He sniffs the surrounding area, searching for Nibbin's scent.

The rest of the team hadn't thought of predators coming to attack Persimmon. What a nightmare. The thought of seeing her bleed to death was horrifying enough, but to watch her eaten alive? They can't even begin to stomach the thought.

Persimmon's head sways. She's overcome with dizziness and losing a lot of blood. She yelps from pulling on her broken limb. "I can't do this. It hurts too much. Please, I want it to stop!"

"Let us look at the trap, Persimmon," Aunty Adelaide insists again. "We might be able to open it."

Persimmon nods—anything to stop this pain.

Aunty Adelaide and Uncle Bennett crawl over to the trap and begin inspecting it. They push on different metal prongs and pull on anything that looks like a lever, but the trap doesn't budge. As carefully as possible, Uncle Bennett attempts to pry open the teeth, but it doesn't give in the least. He pulls harder, grinding his teeth.

"Come on!" Uncle Bennett hollers.

"Careful, dear," Aunty Adelaide warns. "You'll chop your paws off."

"We have to open it somehow, Adelaide!" Uncle Bennett yells, more angrily than he intended. "I'm sorry. I'm upset."

"It's okay, Uncle," Persimmon says. "Aunty is right. Humans built this thing so we animals can't escape. It's no use."

"Then we just sit here and watch you…" Uncle Bennett can't bring himself to say what everyone is thinking. "There *has* to be a way. Besides, Bruiser's right, a mountain lion may come, or worse, the humans who set this trap will return. Then they'll take you away and do who knows what to you."

"Uncle… calm," Persimmon says. "We have to stay calm. Let me think."

Persimmon's dizziness consumes her. She takes in deep breaths to ward off the nausea. She tries to come up with a plan, but she's too distracted between faintness and her aching leg. There's a deep throbbing, as if the metal teeth were continuously biting down on her bone, but she knows it's not moving. It just feels that way.

Bruiser races back to the team. "Nibbin's out there. I could see 'im, but every time I neared 'im, he ran away further. You're right. I bet he thinks we're mad at 'im. He'll come back when he's ready."

Persimmon sighs. *It's not his fault. He didn't know.* She rests her head on Derpoke's back—his soft gray fur is comforting. She hears his muffled crying.

"It's okay, my sweet Derpoke," Persimmon says. She closes her eyes again. She feels so fatigued. Fighting through the incessant pain is so exhausting. She wants to sleep. *What if I never open my eyes again? What if these are my last moments alive? There was so much more I wanted to do—so many animals I intended to save. I'll never see Scraps again. My baby brother… I don't want to die. I'm not ready yet.*

Persimmon's friends and family watch, helpless. It's a disturbing scene: the mighty Persimmon bleeding to death with her leg grasped firmly in the jaws of this barbaric metal contraption.

The team stands there in shock. With all the perilous missions they've gone on, is this really how she's going to die? It's such an absurd accident… and yet it's not. A human set this trap for this very purpose. A human will come here and get excited upon seeing a dead raccoon. The human will be thrilled to skin Persimmon and wear her fur as a hat or as trim on a jacket.

Never! No matter what, this team will not let that happen.

18

BRUISER, CHLOE, TUCKER, Aunty Adelaide, Uncle Bennett, Hazel, and Arden are huddled together a few trees away from where Persimmon lies on Derpoke's back, out of earshot. It's midday. The sun is shining brightly. Normally, they'd all be resting peacefully at this time, curled up together. Instead, they're anxious that any minute the human who set that trap will gallivant over here to collect the "prize." The team is desperate to figure out how to flee from this place before that happens.

"I tried," says Uncle Bennett. "That trap is too complicated for me. Humans are pretty dumb in general, but if they're clever about one thing, it's about concocting deadly devices for us other animals."

"We all know she's going to bleed to death if she's left in that trap," Chloe says. "I know this is hard to hear, but the only way I can think of getting her out is if she or one of us bites through the skin and bone."

The team shudders and gasps. It's too grotesque to imagine.

"Absolutely not!" Aunty Adelaide says. "I will not subject my niece to that horror."

"I've seen other animals with missing legs," Chloe says. "They got hit by a car. They got stuck in a trap. I don't know how they lost it, but they were alive. That's the important part. This is an extreme situation. We have to make extreme choices."

Chloe looks at Tucker for reassurance. He pats her on the back.

"Persimmon's tough," Tucker says. "If anyone can survive something like that, it's her. I mean, what else is there to do?"

"I got an idea," Bruiser speaks up. "It's dangerous... real dangerous, but it might just work."

∗   ∗   ∗

As the rest of the team huddles a few trees away, Derpoke sits as still as possible, not wanting to disturb Persimmon who is passed out on his back. He can feel her breathing, so he knows she's still alive—and that is, quite frankly, the only thing keeping him from falling apart. *If only I were stronger or cleverer I could open that trap. I could save her life. But I'm useless. All I can do is sit here and give her a place to rest as her life pours out of her leg. Is she really dying? Is this really the last time that I'll ever be near her?*

Derpoke's face is wet with tears—the leaves below him are even soaked through. He's never cried so much in his life. He wishes he could hug her, but he can't turn around. He has to stay in this position to keep her stable, so he will.

"Derpoke?" Persimmon says weakly. She is clearly more enfeebled as time passes.

"Yes?" Derpoke says. "Is there something I can do for you?"

"I was just thinking," Persimmon says. She talks slowly and has to take breaks as she speaks. She's normally so quick and alert; it's upsetting to see her so drained. "I think I'm being punished."

"What?!" Derpoke exclaims. "For what?"

"I need to tell you something. Something I've never told anyone because I was so ashamed."

Derpoke's heart starts to race. What could she possibly have to reveal?

"You can tell me anything, Persimmon. I would never judge you."

"I know," Persimmon says. "That's why you're my favorite."

Persimmon has to take a break to muster the courage to admit this. She looks at her mangled, blood-soaked leg, dangling limply in the trap. She then sucks in a deep breath and continues. "Remember how I told you when I was really young I found a fox with her head caught in a trap? How I said she growled at me, so I was too afraid to help her?"

Derpoke nods.

"That's not the whole story. She wasn't alone. She was a mother, Derpoke. She had two pups with her." Persimmon tears up. She's harbored this secret for so long. She's felt so guilty about this, she never thought she'd tell anyone. But now, as she lies here dying, she feels that she must confess.

"I knew a human would come eventually and take her away. I didn't want the babies to be harmed, so I tried to get them to follow me to safety. But they wouldn't leave their mother. Her head was clamped in the trap, so she couldn't warn them... Ow!" Persimmon yelps as she accidentally pulls on her leg. A lightning bolt of pain shoots up her leg straight into her chest.

"I thought maybe I could lure them away with fish, so I ran to the river. When I came back... a man was there. He had tied ropes around the pups' necks, and he was stomping on the mother's head. The babies were crying and crying as they watched him repeatedly ram his heel into her skull. And I did nothing. I was a coward."

Persimmon buries her face in his fur, crying. She accidentally pulls on her leg again. "Ow!" Every time she yanks on her leg it feels like someone is shocking her with a thousand volts of electricity.

"Persimmon, stay still. You're hurting yourself. It wasn't your fault. You were a baby, too. And you tried to help, but what could you do?"

"I think about that day all the time. I think about the mother. How she probably thought I'd abandoned her. How petrified she must have been when that human showed up, realizing her babies were going to be killed. How helpless she must have felt not being able to save them. Why didn't I do more to help? I cowered in those bushes while he killed her and hauled her body away with her pups dragging after. I just wept, doing nothing. How do you forgive yourself for something like that?"

Persimmon pauses, sighing deeply and sorrowfully. "You don't, Derpoke. You can't."

"Persimmon, stop!" Derpoke chides. "I will not have you blame yourself for that. What happened to them is not your fault. You're the bravest, most compassionate animal I know. How many creatures have you rescued? How many times have you risked your life to save so many other animals' lives? And not just on these missions, but before that. You saved your brother's life, denouncing your own mother. What a brave, selfless act. *That's* the kind of caring raccoon you are."

Derpoke looks over his shoulder. "Are you listening? I can't see you properly behind my back."

"Yes, I'm listening," Persimmon says quietly.

"It's my turn to tell *you* a story. It's about a young opossum. He was trying to eat a giant cob of corn—one that was larger than his entire body. Then out of nowhere an adult male raccoon—a huge one—stormed over and snatched that corn right out of his mouth. The opossum tried to pull it back, but the raccoon just bared his teeth and swatted his claws at him. That little opossum cried and cried, and you know who came bounding up?"

"Me," Persimmon says shyly.

"Yes, *you*. You were small yourself, but you hissed at the raccoon and fearlessly swung your claws in his face. He was bigger than you, so he just pulled the corn away, but you were so courageous attempting to fight him off. I couldn't believe that you—this raccoon I had never met before—was standing up for me. Even back then, when you were so young, you were saving other animals."

Persimmon smiles for the first time since her leg got caught in the trap. "I guess I was. You were just so cute, all tiny, proudly dragging that humongous corn."

"Of course I was proud. That corn was almost completely uneaten. I was so excited to show it to my mom. Do you remember what you did after the mean raccoon ran off with the corn?"

"I gave you my pear."

"Yes, you did. Not only did you fight to defend me, but you gave me *your* food. Right then, I knew..." Derpoke tries to hold back tears. He clears his throat. "I knew that for the rest of my life, I would love you."

He said it. After all this time, he finally revealed how he really feels. He's dreamed about this moment for so long, wondering if he'd ever get the courage, but in all those fantasies, he never imagined it would be like *this*—with her dying, without a hint of romance. He instantly feels vulnerable and humiliated.

Derpoke closes his eyes and puts his head down on the wet leaves below him. Come to think of it, this is exactly how he knew it would be when he revealed his feelings for her—awkward and pointless.

Persimmon lays her head on his back and hugs him with her left front paw as warmly as she can. "I love you, too, Derpoke. There is no me without you. You know that, right?"

Derpoke nods, but he knows she doesn't mean it—not the way he does. He has known that all along, though. He didn't admit his feelings because he thought she might confess her secret love for him. He told her because very soon she'll breathe her last breath, and he needed her to know that she's the great love of his life.

Persimmon feels terrible for Derpoke. She's known forever that he had a crush on her, but she never quite knew how to handle it. Better to avoid bringing it up, she thought. But now he has, and this could be the last thing they discuss. *My poor sweet Derpoke. It must have been so hard for him to finally say that to me. What do I say in return? I* do *love him—as*

*much as I love Scraps. He's the best friend I could ever have hoped for, but I
don't love him the way he wants... This can't be the way we're going to say
goodbye. He deserves to feel loved. He deserves to be loved. If only I could feel
that way for him, but I...*

Persimmon starts to black out again. She begins to feel sick to her
stomach as stars cloud her vision. "I feel so..."

She faints without finishing her thought.

"Persimmon?" Derpoke yells frantically. "Persimmon?!"

The team runs over, scared that she'd died before they could put
their plan in place to save her. Bruiser listens very closely and is relieved
to announce that she's still breathing.

Persimmon passes out hard for hours. Night comes on. No humans
arrive. The team fears what will happen when the human who set the
trap comes back. How long will it be?

Persimmon drifts in and out of consciousness all night. Then, very
early the next morning, she awakens. Everyone is sitting around her,
anxiously waiting—all except Nibbin, who is still hiding in the woods
nearby, hating himself for causing the death of the kind raccoon who
had saved his life and taken him in as her own.

Some of the team members are crying—Derpoke, Aunty Adelaide,
and Uncle Bennett. All are an emotional mess. She's dying and they
feel helpless.

When the team sees her stirring awake, they watch intently.

"You're still here... Don't cry, my friends." Persimmon slurs her
words. She's almost incoherent. But she has something to say. Whenever
she's awakened into consciousness, she's wanted to say it, but she hasn't
had the strength. Now, she finally has the energy to get it out. It will
be the most difficult thing she's ever asked them to do. They're going to
protest, but it's for their own safety.

Every word takes everything she has left, but she finally reveals the
last request—a shocking plea—that she will ever make of them. They

listen and disagree as she had expected, but they finally give in—or so she thinks. Secretly, their plan is already in place—a very different plan from her own.

If only they had followed her plan. Things wouldn't have gone so awry. Of course, if they had followed it, Persimmon wouldn't still be alive.

19

HOURS HAVE PASSED since Vincent and Rawly witnessed the humans forcing the two dogs to fight. All the people have left except Coach and Dale, who live in the house on the property. Coach's wife is in the house, too, but she wasn't at the fight since Coach considers fights "men-only" events. It's past midnight, so all three humans are fast asleep. Little do they know that right in their backyard a raid has begun.

Vincent steps up to the chained dogs in the yard who furiously bark and lunge at him—only the shackles around their necks holding them back.

"I'll kill you, rat!" a dog hollers. "Get out of our yard!"

Behind Vincent is a sea of minks, raccoons, and one cat—all filled with unease as their fearless leader stands far too close for comfort to these menacing dogs. They trust that Vincent has a solid strategy for convincing these dogs to join The Dissidents, but that doesn't abate their anxiety over his safety.

Vincent is concerned that all the barking will awaken the humans, but he's searching for the right dog. He needs a visionary dog who understands the importance of joining forces to rebel against the humans and who commands the respect to easily convince the other dogs of that importance. But all the dogs are lashing out so fiercely, he's beginning to think that they may have been so gravely mistreated here that they're unable to trust anyone.

Then he sees *her*: Rasha, the one dog who isn't barking. She's just staring at him curiously. And not just curiously—she looks concerned for him. *She's* the one. That's exactly the type of dog who will be reasonable to talk to. He just has to get through these other dogs to have a word with her.

Vincent steps closer to the barking dogs. There's an audible gasp from some of The Dissidents behind him.

"Vincent, they'll eat you alive!" Rawly warns.

Most of the minks and raccoons are so scared of these vicious-looking canines that their fur is standing on end. Despite their fear, they're ready to pounce on the dogs if any of them lays a paw on Vincent.

Vincent holds up his paw. "Do not follow me. It is too dangerous. I will return shortly."

Rawly, Scraps, and Drig can't believe the audacity of this small creature, but Linder and Dusty have come to expect this daring behavior. Apricot is, of course, beside herself with excitement. She loves death-defying feats.

Vincent weaves through the deadly obstacle course of pit bulls. Some dogs bark so close that their spit sprays onto his fur, but he doesn't flinch. The Dissidents, on the other hand, nervously hold their breath.

Vincent steps up to Rasha. He now sees how disfigured her face is from her many fights—a missing ear, chipped teeth, a nose chewed so badly it's almost unrecognizable as a nose. Vincent is overcome with heartbreak and anger to see her so torn apart. He is reminded of his traumatic experience imprisoned in the cage at the fur farm. He knows the hell she has endured.

He can also see the anguish in her eyes. He then notices Chopper lying on the ground a few feet back, chained up in his own area. Vincent realizes that the two dogs must be friends. Chopper has been amateurishly stitched up by Coach as he does all the dogs after the fights—at least the ones he hopes will survive. This dog still has value to him as a breeder, but the wounds look deep, and some are still bleeding. Chopper most likely won't live to see another sunrise.

Rasha stares at Vincent, perplexed, realizing that this tiny creature has risked his life to talk to her.

"I know it must be odd to—" Vincent begins to say but he's drowned out by all the barking around him.

"Quiet!" The female dog barks with such force at the other dogs that one by one they quickly fall silent.

Vincent peers up at her. He's not frightened, but his heart is racing. She's not only compassionate but also fearsome when she wants to be. He has definitely found just the right dog.

Rasha looks back down at the tiny creature. "It isn't safe for you here, rat. A dog—dear to us all—has been terribly hurt tonight. Life in this yard is difficult, but this..."

Rasha's face scrunches with grief as she looks back at Chopper. These humans have put her through so much, it's unbearable. She collects herself as best she can and continues, hoping to send this visitor away as fast as possible. "Please don't bother us for food. We don't have any."

"I'm not looking for food. I'm looking for *you*."

Rasha stares at this curious creature, puzzled. The last thing she wants is to be bothered right now, but how could a comment like that not pique her interest?

"We're not rats," Vincent explains. "We're minks. We were rescued by a group of animals who saw how the humans were murdering us for our fur. We know all too well how it is to suffer at the hands of humans. That's why we have come to help you."

"You mean set us free?!" Rasha can't believe what she's hearing.

"Yes, but not just that." Vincent steps closer and looks up at this battered dog. "We've seen how these humans are mistreating you, and we're going to help you kill them."

Rasha stiffens, unable to move. She's speechless. Relief rushes through her, followed by rage. Considering what these humans have put her and the other dogs through, she can't imagine more fitting justice— to have the humans killed by the very dogs they forced to be killers.

But how can this troop of forest creatures pull this off? It seems so fantastical. One minute she was devastated over Chopper—at this very moment, he lies next her, butchered and dying—and the next minute she's hit with the news that she may actually escape this place. Vincent has no idea what this means to her. Not just because of the hell the humans have already inflicted on her, but because of what they were *about* to do to her.

20

RASHA'S FIGHT
(MORE THAN TWO AND A HALF YEARS AGO)

RASHA WRESTLES HER brother Minton to the ground. She's only three months old with the sweetest puppy-dog face you ever saw. Her fur is dark gray with one white line cascading down from her forehead to her nose. Her gentle playfulness deeply contrasts with the world into which she was born.

She, Minton, and a handful of other pit bull puppies—some her other siblings—are being held in a small area surrounded by welded wire fencing. They've been here ever since they were torn from their mother at eight weeks old. At the time, they didn't understand that they'd never be close to her again. Their mother did her best to warn them about the hard life ahead, about being forced to fight, but they were too young to grasp the severity of their fate.

Today, Rasha and Minton are having a ball rolling around in the grass and pinning each other to the ground. Rasha's favorite move—and Minton's least favorite—is to slather his brown face with sloppy kisses until he begs for mercy. It doesn't occur to them how ominous this game is.

As Rasha holds Minton to the ground, Coach walks through the yard with a few humans pointing at the various dogs chained up in their dirt stations.

"This dog's superfast," Coach says. "He'll bite the balls off his opponent before the other dog even has time to get out of his corner."

The two men grin.

Coach moves over to the pen holding Rasha and the other puppies. "This is my crown jewel. Every one of these puppies was bred from champions."

Coach notices Rasha and Minton wrestling. "Look at 'em. Born fighters."

Coach reaches into the pen and Rasha licks his hand. She's always happy to let someone join playtime, but this good-natured gesture is something she will always regret.

"Don't worry," Coach laughs. "They'll toughen up with some work. So whad'ya say? You know I got the best fighters around. Let's talk money."

Rasha and Minton go back to running around and playing until a very shocking thing occurs. One of the humans reaches into the pen and picks up Minton.

Rasha stands on her back legs and leans against the wire fencing. "Hey, put my brother down!"

The humans ignore Rasha's barking. Coach shakes the hands of the two humans, and they all walk toward the fence.

"Rasha?!" Minton calls down to his sister, not sure what to do.

"Hey!" Rasha barks at the humans. "I said let him go!"

All the puppies, including Rasha's three other siblings—Remington, Jax, and Afilia—run to the side of the pen alongside Rasha.

"Where are they taking him?" Afilia asks.

Rasha frantically tries to crawl up the wire fencing, but her paws just keep slipping. "Minton!"

"Rasha!" Minton calls out one last time just as he's being carried out of the yard.

The gate slams shut. Minton is gone.

All the puppies immediately start howling. The other dogs in the yard watch with sympathy. They remember the day that they were split from their siblings. At the time, they thought it was the worst experience of their lives, but they were wrong. It only got worse from there.

Dale storms over to the pen. As always, he's wearing his favorite hat with the Beast Dog Kennels logo on it. "Shut up! You're giving me a headache."

The puppies instantly quiet down. Even though it's clear that Coach runs the yard, Dale is the more menacing of the two. Dale is the proud protégé of his uncle's dogfighting operation, and one day he expects to run this place. What Rasha will soon find out is that unlike his uncle, Dale is less interested in the money-making aspects of dogfighting and more interested in the sadistic "sport" of watching two dogs viciously attack each other.

Rasha slumps down in the pen. *Is Minton coming back? Of course he is... right?*

Rasha can't believe that today will be the last time she'll ever see her brother. She didn't even get to say goodbye. Then another scary thought hits her: Which one of us is next?

$$* \quad * \quad *$$

Two weeks have passed since Minton was kidnapped by the humans. Every day, Rasha, Remington, Afilia, Jax, and the other puppies wait earnestly, hoping the humans will open that gate carrying Minton in their arms, but it never occurs. They're saddened by the loss of Minton, but they're also terrified that they'll be the next one ripped away from their little pack.

Rasha decides that she will not let that happen. *No human's filthy hands are reaching in here and taking away my friends and family!*

Whenever Coach or Dale walks near the pen, Rasha rushes out front, ready to sink her teeth into the humans' flesh. Coach and Dale don't even notice the defiance since they're too busy focused on other tasks in the yard.

On top of being petrified of abduction, the puppies experienced one of the scariest nights of their lives last weekend. The first dog fight since they were born happened on the property. They couldn't see into the shed to witness the fight firsthand, but they heard the screaming and hollering of the humans inside and the sounds of two dogs tearing at each other's flesh. The puppies were so frightened, they didn't even cry. They just sat huddled together, feeling sick. They now know without a doubt that they were born into a sinister place.

It's early morning and the puppies are curled up beside one another sleeping. Suddenly, they're awakened by the sound of the gate creaking open. As they feared, Coach walks in with another human they've never seen before. The day has come. Another one of them will be kidnapped.

"I'm scared, Rasha!" Remington cries.

"It's okay," Rasha says. "Stay behind me. They're not taking any of us."

Coach leads the man through the dogs chained in the yard, spouting his usual spiel. "This one is so tough, she'd keep fighting even if her eyeball had popped out."

The human seems pleased. When he smiles, the dogs see that some of his teeth are green and rotten.

Coach then leads the man to the puppy pen. "And these are my crown jewels. Each puppy is bred from champions."

The two humans look at the puppies huddled together behind Rasha. "They're looking a little timid to me."

"They're still puppies, you know that," Coach says. "You gotta put 'em on a chain and show 'em who's boss."

Coach walks to the other side of the pen and reaches in to grab a puppy.

"Get away!" Rasha barks as the puppies run to the other side of the pen behind her.

"That's some neat trick," the man says with a laugh.

Coach clenches his teeth, getting embarrassed. "Dale! Come over here and help me grab one of these dogs for Mr. Thornton."

Dale puts down the dog food he was carrying and rushes over to the puppy pen. He can tell from his uncle's voice that he's getting irritated, and he knows better than to dawdle when Coach is in one of his moods.

Dale reaches into the pen, and Rasha and the puppies dash to the middle. If it were only one or two of them, they could huddle in the middle, out of arm's reach, but there are too many puppies to pull that off.

Coach grabs for Remington, and Rasha quickly lunges at the man's hand and chomps down.

"What the—" Coach grabs his hand as droplets of blood appear on the skin. "She bit me."

"Whoa," Dale says. "Coach, we gotta put her down. Hand me your .38."

"Hold on," Coach says as he stares at Rasha.

Rasha glares right back at him. "That's what happens when you hurt anyone in our pack."

"But boss," Dale whines. "You said that if a dog is too aggressive against humans it's too dangerous to train. You told me we gotta get rid of 'em."

"I know what I said," Coach replies, even more aggravated. "You don't need to tell *me* about how to raise fighters, boy. I got a good feeling about this one. You see that dog I was grabbing for? That's her brother, Remington. Loyalty. I respect that."

The puppies are still huddled in the middle of the pen. Rasha can't stand in front of all of them for protection, so she runs around them in a circle, keeping watch.

"This one's feisty!" Coach yells jubilantly. "Love it!"

"How much do you want for her?" The man asks Coach.

"Oh no," Coach says. "She's mine. I got big plans for this one. But I'll give you a discount on one of the other ones due to the commotion today. We're all about customer service here at Beast Dog Kennels."

"Deal," the man says. "Now we just gotta catch one of 'em."

The three humans close in around the pen. Rasha barks as she tries to keep an eye on her three siblings and the other puppies. It's not in their nature to be aggressive, so the other pit bulls crouch as low as they can, hoping they won't be picked up by the humans.

Dale reaches for Jax, so Rasha jumps at him. At that exact moment, Coach grabs Afilia's scruff and lifts her off the ground.

"Rasha!" Afilia cries out.

But it's too late. Coach hands Rasha's sister to the man with the green teeth, and he carries her through the gate.

The puppies are all stunned. Any uncertainty they'd had about whether they'd be separated has officially been quashed. These are their last days together.

As they predicted, in the next few months, one by one, all the puppies are sold to strangers. Rasha fights back every time, and Coach and Dale laugh. Coach loves her persistence. Now that he knows she's combative, he playfully swats her around when she gets near. Rasha falls onto her back in the grass, and every time she instantly gets up to rush at him again.

"See that?" Coach beams. "She doesn't give up. I'm telling you. We got a real fighter on our hands."

Rasha is incensed. *This is a fun game for you?! You're kidnapping my friends, sisters, and brothers. You're a monster!*

Then one day it's just Rasha and Remington. Her last brother.

They sleep on top of the other in the middle of the pen.

Rasha licks his forehead. "If they take you, I'll break free from this place, and I'll come find you, okay?"

"Not before I break free from wherever they take *me*. Then I'll come back here, and I'll rescue all of *you*. Mom too! And then we'll search for Jax, Afilia, Minton, everyone. I promise!"

"I promise, too. They're messing with the wrong dogs!"

That afternoon, Coach escorts a man through the yard, and the man takes Remington. Rasha puts up the biggest fight she ever has, but it's no use. She's so tiny and Coach and Dale are so large. With one swat, they just knock her down.

Then she's left all alone. There's no cuddling or talking. She'll learn quickly that the dogfighting world is a cold, solitary place. Taking away her last sibling wasn't the worst thing that Coach will ever do to her, but it's certainly one of the things that hurt the most.

21

RASHA'S FIGHT, PART 2

DREAD

(A YEAR LATER)

AT ONLY A year and three months old, Rasha is still a puppy, and unlike when The Dissidents meet her a year and a half later, she still has that sweet puppy face—a very different look from the other pit bulls in her vicinity.

Rasha is now stuck on a chain, which is connected to a car axle buried underground, just like the 50 other dogs—who are mostly males—around her in the yard. Right now, they are all staring through the black of night at the large shed thirty feet away, fear rumbling through them. A yellow glow shines through the cracks in the wood panels, and the sounds of humans cheering and hollering crash through the walls. Inside, two dogs are being forced to rip each other to shreds as entertainment for these humans, and all Rasha can think is: *Very soon, that will be me.*

Each dog in the yard is covered with scars—torn lips, shredded ears, gashed necks, and faces—all from fights that they've won. Yes, *won.*

Their opponents looked worse and are now buried underground some-where—a lot of them in the surrounding woods just outside the fence. In the dogfighting world, you're either covered with hideous wounds or you're dead.

But Rasha has yet to be forced to fight, so she's scar-free. She knows, though, that her first fight will come any day now. A nearby brown pit bull, Chopper, tipped her off. He told her that, according to the humans, she looks "ripe for fighting."

Ripe for fighting?! There's no way anyone would see me and think I look ready to fight for my life against another dog. I'm trembling right now hearing the screams of the humans coming out of that shed.

She thinks about this for a moment. *You rarely hear the dogs as they fight. It's always the humans hooting with excitement. The dogs are too busy trying not to die.*

The other dogs in the yard are also quiet, listening to the hysteria. They sit in the darkness, feeling sick to their stomachs and yet relieved that they're not the ones in that shed.

Soon after Rasha was moved to the chain, Chopper warned her not to be aggressive toward Coach and Dale.

"You were protecting your pack," Chopper said. "I admire that, youngin', but you gotta know, these humans won't put up with us dogs standing up to 'em. They're trying to train us to be killers of other *dogs*—not humans. If they think we're a danger to them or the other humans that will be in that pit when you're fightin', they'll shoot you dead without thinking twice about it. I don't wanna see that, so that's why I'm warnin' ya."

Rasha's anger toward Coach and Dale for taking away her siblings runs deep, but she heeds Chopper's advice. No need getting killed when it's better to escape. *Escape. It seems impossible, but am I really going to just be trapped here my entire life fighting other dogs? No way! This can't be my life.*

Rasha imagines the violence that must be playing out inside that shed right now. At some point, a group of humans normally yells angrily and curses. That's when she knows a fight has ended. Rasha's never seen a fight, so she's not sure exactly how a winner is chosen. Sometimes it seems a dog must die during the fight, meaning the other dog is a clear "winner," but most of the time one dog is carried outside alive—a bloody mess, but still alive. Not for long, though. Dale kills any losing dog from Beast Dog Kennels, and dogs brought in from different locations are killed by the humans who brought that dog in.

Rasha shudders thinking about all the times she's seen other canines murdered only thirty feet away. Normally, the person shoots the dog in the head, but sometimes a human will be so irate that the dog lost, the human will beat the dog to death. In those instances, Rasha would give anything to run over and stop the human, but it's useless. She must look away and hope it ends as quickly as possible.

She can barely move, though. All day and night she's stuck on this thick logging chain that gives her only five feet in any direction. The chain itself is heavy enough, but the humans added a ten-pound weight to her collar. It's so heavy, she struggles to lift her head.

At first, she had no idea why the humans would put more weight on her shoulders, but one day as she was standing up, it all made sense. She felt the muscles in her neck and legs tighten and she realized: *The extra weight is there to make me stronger. It's all part of this plan to make me a fighter. It's the same as putting us dogs in this yard just close enough together to feel threatened without actually being able to fight one another. Everything these humans do to us dogs is intended to make us fighting machines. I've got these humans all figured out. They're trying to make us hateful. But as long as we know that, it won't work.*

Rasha wants to share these revelations with the dogs around her, but for the most part, the other dogs refuse to talk to her. There's so much distrust among them. *Am I going to be forced to fight any of these dogs? Is that why they won't talk to me? But I have no hostility toward them. I don't want to hurt them any more than I want them to hurt me. So why can't we be civil to one another? We're in this together... But they've all been here longer than I have, and they've all been forced to fight. Maybe that experience changed them. It made them hate life, become suspicious of other dogs. If they would just listen to me, I could get them to understand it's all a trick. The humans are our enemies, not one another.*

She's gone over this so many times in the past few months. It never gets her anywhere. It just feels odd to be surrounded by so many dogs and yet feel so isolated. The only dog who talks to Rasha is Chopper.

At first, Chopper was intimidating. His personality is gruff, and he's clearly been in numerous fights. His face is covered with scars; he's missing an ear; and his lip on the left side was ripped off, leaving his teeth permanently bared. All this makes him look downright ferocious.

When the two first started talking, Chopper acted tough about all the fights he had been in, but something in his eyes made it clear he'd prefer never to be in another. That's what endeared him to Rasha. Unfortunately, Rasha knows that his wish to never fight again will never be granted. If she's learned one thing, it's that these humans don't keep you around unless you're a fighter who wins.

In Rasha's vicinity, there's only one other female dog, Sadie, who's stationed across from Rasha on the side closer to Coach's home. Rasha thought maybe Sadie would be more open to conversing since they're the only females in this area. But Sadie ignored her, so Rasha let it go.

Rasha is knocked out of her daydream by the sound of humans in the shed cursing. *It's over. The fight has ended. Who survived? The dog from our yard or the other dog?*

All the dogs in the yard tense up. They don't want either dog to be hurt or killed, but they feel a special kinship to the dogs in their own yard, so even though it feels sickening, they root for them.

The shed door swings open and Dale drags a bloody dog out by his scruff. Rasha gasps as she sees that it's the dog from their yard.

"How much time did I waste on you?" Dale hollers. "You get bit a few times and you give up?"

"I'm sorry," the dog howls. "Please don't hurt me!"

Dale pulls out his handgun, drops the dog on the ground, and fires. The dog goes limp. Dale then opens the fence and lugs the dog's body out into the woods. Coach has him bury all the dogs in the woods so that if the police come snooping around, they won't be able to find any dead dogs on his property.

Nausea swirls through Rasha. She rests her head on her paws in the dirt. *If I lose a fight, I die. But there's no part of me that wants to fight. I don't feel hatred toward other dogs. Quite the opposite. I spend so much of my time wishing I could curl up beside them. I don't want to hurt them. I want them to be my friend… That said, if I don't fight, I die. The other dog will chew me to pieces or Dale will shoot me in the head.*

Panic rushes through Rasha. *Why is this my life? Why can't I be on the other side of that fence?*

Rasha looks over at the fence. She's imagined herself jumping over it so many times, but she knows there's no escape. The fence is too tall to jump over, and besides, she's never off this chain. It's hopeless. Her future lies in that shed.

22

"GOOD MORNING, SLEEPY!"

Persimmon opens her eyes to find a female raccoon staring at her through the cage with a big smile. Persimmon has been in this cage for a week, but she's been in and out of consciousness the entire time and is only now remembering how she got her leg caught in that fur trap. *What happened after I blacked out? How did I get here and where are my friends?* Her best bet for answers is this raccoon, but Persimmon is still too groggy to speak.

The raccoon outside the cage is plumper than Persimmon, and she has a purple collar with a fancy purple bow. A tag on the collar shows the name "Laurel" on one side and a phone number on the other.

On the floor, a male skunk looks up at Persimmon's cage. He also has a tag—his is turquoise—with a name and number on it, although Persimmon can't make out the name. When he sees Persimmon rousing, he cheerfully shakes his black-and-white tail.

"She awakens!" the skunk declares theatrically.

On top of being surprised that these two animals are gawking at her, Persimmon is amazed that neither the female raccoon nor the skunk is in a cage. *Are they here to rescue me?*

Along the walls of the room are tables with multiple cages, and when Persimmon arrived a week ago, the enclosures were filled with moaning and injured forest critters. But now only a few animals are left—another raccoon, an opossum, and some type of mysterious animal in a cage with a blanket over it at the far end of the room.

An alarming thought hits Persimmon: *I have to save the chickens!*

"How long have I been here?" Persimmon asks.

"Um, maybe a week," the female raccoon says.

"Oh no!" Persimmon stands up with her three good legs and stumbles to the edge of the cage. It's very hard to move with a missing leg, but she has bigger things to worry about. "You have to help me get out of here. I need to save the chickens."

"The chickens?!" The skunk shakes his head. "Laurel, I thought we would finally be able to talk to her, but she's clearly still out of it—talking nonsense about some chickens."

"It's not nonsense," Persimmon insists. "I am perfectly coherent. My friends and I found chickens who need our help. They had only a few weeks before they were going to be slaughtered to be eaten. Please open my cage and let me out."

"Hold on there," Laurel says. "You're in no state to walk. You lost a lot of blood, and it could be weeks before your leg is healed."

"Weeks?! Thousands of chickens are counting on me to save their lives." Persimmon rattles the cage door with her remaining front leg. "I need to save them *now*!"

"Golly, are you always this intense?" the skunk asks.

"Yes, when animals need rescuing."

"Well, right now," Laurel says. "*You're* the animal who needs rescuing, so hold on a second. What's your name?"

"Persimmon. Look, I'm not trying to be rude, but there—"

"Okay, Persimmon. Listen for a second. My name is Laurel, and this is my best friend Lyric."

Lyric shakes his bushy tail playfully.

"Just a few days ago, we didn't know if you would even survive. You have been severely injured, if you haven't noticed." Laurel motions to Persimmon's missing leg. "If you ran into the forest right now, your wound would open up again, and you'd bleed to death. You wouldn't be much help to these chickens if that happened, right?"

Persimmon nods reluctantly.

"Oh," Lyric hops up gleefully. "Tell her about the blood, Laurel!"

"What *about* the blood?" Persimmon asks warily.

Laurel grins widely. She's been waiting all week to tell Persimmon about this. "You lost so much blood that Dr. Misra used my blood to nurse you back to health. You have *my* blood inside you!"

Persimmon is baffled by this boisterous raccoon and skunk. She's not sure what to say about the blood. Heck, she doesn't even understand what Laurel means by "you have my blood inside you." Persimmon is more interested in the human Laurel mentioned. "Who is Dr. Misra? Is that the woman who's been bringing me food all week?"

"Yes, she saved your life," Laurel says. "She used to be a veterinarian. That's a human who heals other animals. She saved the lives of all the animals in this room."

Persimmon is dumbstruck. *What is going on? A human who saves other animals' lives? So this Dr. Misra didn't set that trap? Then why am I here and who did set the trap? More importantly, where are my friends?!*

"Do you know what happened to my friends?" Persimmon asks. "The group is comprised of an opossum, two raccoons, two squirrels, a mink, and a dog. Have you seen any of them?"

"Did you say an opossum?" Laurel asks. "So he's your friend? When you came in here, there was an opossum clinging to you for dear life. Dr. Misra had the hardest time pulling him off you. He seemed like a bit of a creepo."

"That's Derpoke!" Persimmon stands up. "Where is he now? Is he okay?"

"He didn't have any injuries," Laurel says. "So Dr. Misra released him outside. She doesn't like to keep wild animals in the house after she heals them. Lyric and I are exceptions, of course. She couldn't get rid of us when she tried."

Laurel and Lyric laugh and shake their tails in joy.

"What's all the chatter in here, troublemakers?" Dr. Misra enters through the doorway. She's in her late sixties, and when she smiles, the whole room lights up. She's carrying three plates of fish and assorted fruit.

The opossum and raccoon in the other cages perk up at the sight of the food, but Persimmon crouches down. Laurel and Lyric may vouch for this woman, but she's not taking any chances with a human.

"Treats! Treats!" Lyric trots over to the woman and scratches gently at her legs, begging for a snack.

"Not right now, Lyric," Dr. Misra says. "You know the routine. Our guests eat first."

Dr. Misra puts the plates of food in the opossum's and raccoon's cages. Then she turns to Persimmon's cage and sees that the raccoon is sitting up. "Oh good, you're awake!" She looks at Laurel and Lyric. "Is this who you two were chatting up? I hope you were being nice."

Dr. Misra motions for Laurel to step away from Persimmon's cage. "Give her space, Laurel. She's badly hurt, which is why I have a little surprise for her hidden in the fish, but don't tell her I said so."

Dr. Misra puts her hand on the door to Persimmon's cage. "You're not going to run out of there, are you?"

"Persimmon, remember what I said about bleeding to death in the woods," Laurel warns.

"I'll behave," Persimmon says.

Dr. Misra opens the cage, quickly puts the plate of food inside and closes the door again. "Success!"

Dr. Misra steps back to give Persimmon space but stays to watch her eat. "Eat up, chickadee. It's super tasty."

Persimmon turns to Laurel. "What does she mean, 'a little surprise' in the fish?"

"It's medicine," Laurel explains. "It will heal you faster."

"Hmm. I want to heal, but I'm not eating the fish." Persimmon moves toward the plate. "I don't eat other animals."

"What?!" Lyric exclaims from the floor. But then he realizes…"Wait a second, then maybe Dr. Misra will give the fish to *me*. Good idea! Don't eat the fish."

Laurel leans against the edge of Persimmon's cage, peering in at this curious raccoon. "But it's fish. All of us raccoons love fish."

Persimmon munches on slices of banana. "My friends and I don't want to do any harm to other animals, so we pledged not to eat them."

"Persimmon!" Derpoke shouts joyously.

Persimmon swivels around to see Derpoke pressed against the window screen by her table. He has the biggest smile.

"Derpoke!" Persimmon bangs against the side of her cage. She reaches her paw through the cage. "You're alive!"

"*You're* alive!" Derpoke is standing on his hind legs, exuberantly pounding on the screen.

"Shoo!" Dr. Misra rushes over to the window, swatting at Derpoke. "This pesky opossum just won't go away. You're free now! Go run in the forest."

Derpoke quickly jumps out of view.

"No!" Persimmon protests. "He's my friend!"

Persimmon angrily strikes the side of her cage, knocking over the plate of food.

"Okay, okay," Dr. Misra says. "Wow, somebody has a temper. We'll leave you be. Come on, Laurel. Come on, Lyric. Our patient is getting agitated by our presence. Let's leave her alone to eat in peace. Now it's *your* turn for some lunch."

Lyric scampers out of the room immediately. Laurel sits and stares at this peculiar raccoon. She can't quite figure Persimmon out. She doesn't eat fish; she's really intense; and she's ranting about saving chickens when her own leg was recently severed.

"Laurel!" Dr. Misra calls out sternly. "Leave the raccoon alone. She's not like you. She's wild, so she doesn't like all this hoopla."

Laurel climbs down from the table with ease and exits the room with Lyric and Dr. Misra.

Persimmon waits a few moments and then whispers, "Derpoke, are you there?"

Derpoke peeks over the windowsill. "Are they gone?"

"For now," Persimmon says. "Oh, Derpoke, it's so good to see you! Where's the rest of the team? I can't remember much other than I got my leg stuck in a trap."

Derpoke's demeanor changes drastically. The vibrancy in his face turns instantly to gloom.

Persimmon's heart sinks. "What's wrong, Derpoke? Is everyone okay?"

But from the expression on his face it is very clear that everyone is, in fact, *not* okay.

23

(OVER A WEEK AGO)

"I GOT A raccoon, Dad!" Gavin, an eleven-year-old boy, yells in celebration.

Gavin stands beside his thirty-two-year-old father—they are wearing matching camouflage pants and hats. The father holds a .22 rifle and the boy wields a shotgun—the weapon even more eerie in such a young boy's hands.

The father and son have just come upon Persimmon's limp body in the trap. She's blacked out and doesn't look to be breathing. The leaves below her are caked in blood, and there's a rotten smell from the meat, apples, and carrots beside her. No other animals are in sight, just the helpless raccoon teetering dangerously close to death.

"You got your first coon, son!" The father proudly pats his boy on the back.

Gavin skips gleefully toward the trap. "I'm gonna make a hat out of it!"

"Be careful," the father warns. "Mind your gun, boy."

Gavin slows his pace. He lays his shotgun on the ground near the trap. "Aw, man. It's missing the tail. What good's a raccoon without a tail?"

"Some vermin must have come by and eaten it off." The father steps over to the trap. "No matter. You can still use the fur for a cap and the paws for good luck charms. Do you remember how to unhinge the trap?"

"Yes, sir." Gavin puts one foot down on a lever and the other foot down on another lever.

"Okay, I'm gonna pry it open and I want you to do the honor of pulling out the body, but don't be an idiot and reach into the trap. Got it?"

"Got it."

The father pries open the trap and Gavin quickly pulls Persimmon's body away from the teeth. The boy struggles to hold her up, though, and he drops her in the dirt. "Whoa, it's heavier than I thought it would be."

"They're heavier when they're dead. Grab—"

"Now!" Bruiser barks.

Suddenly, Chloe and Tucker leap down from the tree onto the father's and son's heads and start scratching and biting their ears. Bruiser, Derpoke, Aunty Adelaide, and Uncle Bennett come charging from all sides, screaming and chomping on the legs and backs of the two humans.

The father and son flail around and shriek at the top of their lungs. Bruiser picks up Persimmon's body and starts to dart away.

BAM! The boy wildly shoots his gun in no particular direction, sending most of the team scattering behind nearby trees. Luckily, no one was hit. Unfortunately, not everyone got away.

Bruiser stares into the barrel of the father's gun. Before the Doberman could run to safety, the father picked up his weapon and aimed it at Bruiser, who is holding Persimmon's limp body in his mouth. Derpoke sits defiantly on the ground beside the dog. They're not leaving Persimmon, gun be damned.

Gavin swats at the air—so frantic that he's fighting off animals who are no longer attacking him.

"Son, get a grip!" the father yells. "They're gone. Stop it!"

The boy pants as he tries to cool down.

The father stares Bruiser down. "Thought you were gonna get away with our pelt, huh?"

Bruiser growls as he holds firm to Persimmon.

"You're a tough one, aren't you?" The father keeps his rifle aimed right at Bruiser's head.

"Hey, that dog's got my raccoon," Gavin whines.

"Boy, that was some amateur crap, discharging your weapon like that. I taught you better. You could have shot me or yourself, but we'll discuss that later. For now, reload your weapon. I'm gonna teach you an important lesson today. You're gonna shoot this dog."

The Enlighteners all freeze. Bruiser, Derpoke, Chloe, Tucker, Aunty Adelaide, Uncle Bennett, Hazel, and Arden (the two chickens are hiding nearby) and Nibbin (also hiding in the woods)—all stop breathing. This can't be happening. First Persimmon is near death and now these humans are going to shoot Bruiser?

Gavin's mouth drops open. "What?! Why?"

"That canine tried to steal what is rightfully yours."

Gavin just sits there, not picking up his gun. "But he's a dog, Dad."

"What's the difference between a raccoon and a dog? Nothing. You need to be ready to shoot whatever comes your way out here, and this dog is trying to steal your pelt. Now reload your weapon and aim it at this dog."

Chloe, who is hiding behind a tree with Tucker, calls out. "Bruiser, you have to let Persimmon go. We tried, but it didn't work. Just put her down, and they'll let you walk away. She wouldn't want this to happen. She told us to leave her."

Bruiser holds his grip on Persimmon. There is no way that he will let her go. She saved his life. She bravely walked up to a "vicious" Doberman, undid his collar, and gave him freedom. He could have chewed her to pieces, but she was more concerned about *his* well-being. Every second of his life was utterly miserable until that moment she rescued him. Now it's his job to rescue *her*. No matter what, there must be another way out of this.

Gavin whistles at Bruiser in a friendly manner. "It's okay, boy. Just put the raccoon down. We're not gonna hurt you."

"Gavin Cooper!" the father yells furiously. "If I have to tell you again, you're gonna get the worst whooping of your life."

Gavin's face turns red. His lip quivers. He reaches into his backpack and reloads his shotgun.

Bruiser looks down at Derpoke, who is positioned by his leg. He whispers to the opossum from the side of his mouth. "Derpoke, get outta here. They'll shoot ya and skin ya, too. Get away while they're focused on me."

"I can't, Bruiser," Derpoke cries. "I can't leave Persimmon."

Gavin looks at his father to see if he'll really make him do this. The father gives the boy the evil eye, threatening him.

Gavin slowly lifts his gun and aims it at Bruiser. Tears stream down the boy's face.

Bruiser looks at the boy and whimpers. *Come on, kid. Don't pull that trigger. You're better than this.*

Aunty Adelaide and Uncle Bennett hold each other tightly as they watch from a tree. This is too much for them to take.

A few trees away, Chloe turns to Tucker. "We have to do something, pupsy."

"Yes, we do, sweet pea," Tucker says. "You have a plan?"

Chloe nods and darts off with Tucker following.

"That's right," the father says. "Aim it at the body. You don't want to shoot the coon in the dog's mouth and ruin the fur."

Gavin's hands shake. He sniffles, trying to hold back the tears. He puts his finger on the trigger.

Bruiser whimpers again. He looks the boy in the eye and he's suddenly reminded of Aidan—the little boy of the family who left Bruiser chained up in their backyard. Bruiser loved Aidan—he was the only being in the entire world who showed him any kindness. The boy used to sneak him leftovers, and he'd even pet him until his dad came out to yell at him that they needed to keep Bruiser mean to attack intruders.

This boy, Gavin, has the same demeanor as Aidan—rowdy, maybe even reckless—but there's still an innocence about him. Even though this boy has a gun pointed right at him, Bruiser doesn't see hate in the boy's eyes; he sees fear.

Tears stream down Gavin's face. This isn't why he came hunting today. He always wanted a dog. His dad said they're too much work, but Gavin loves dogs.

"I can't, Dad," Gavin cries.

"Damn it!" The father storms over to Gavin and grabs the back of his neck, squeezing hard.

"Ow, you're hurting me," Gavin shrieks.

"Boy, pull that trigger or it'll hurt worse."

Right then, a barrage of small sticks hits the father in the face. "What the—"

He looks up to see Chloe chattering angrily and throwing tiny branches at him. Simultaneously, from behind, he suddenly hears a rustling. Quick as lightning, Aunty Adelaide, Uncle Bennett, and Tucker come charging toward him, hollering at the top of their lungs.

The father swings his gun around and the three animals quickly split up and dash into separate directions. The man aims his gun at the fleeing critters, trying to find one to focus on.

Bruiser sees his moment. "Derpoke, go! Go!"

Bruiser and Derpoke dart toward the nearest trees and BAM!

Bruiser howls from the bullet piercing his back and collapses to the ground, dropping Persimmon in the leaves.

The father secures his rifle on his shoulder, pleased with his quick aim, and snatches his son's gun from his hands. "Give me that. You didn't earn this today."

The boy cowers, fearing he might get a slap to the head, but instead his father heads toward the injured dog.

Bruiser tries to stand up, but the pain is too severe. He calls out to his opossum friend, who's frozen in the leaves close by. "Run, Derpoke!"

Derpoke's whole body shakes. He's panting uncontrollably as he sees the large man coming their way. He attempts to warn Bruiser, but no words come out.

Bruiser looks back at the man marching toward them. "Don't watch, Derpoke."

The Doberman gazes at his dear raccoon friend, who is unconscious and vulnerable sprawled out in the open. "I'm sorry, Persimmon. I failed ya."

The father steps up to Bruiser, and the dog barks at him ferociously and bites at his legs.

"You are one tough son of a gun," the father says. "I'll give ya that." He raises Gavin's shotgun at Bruiser's head and fires.

The Enlighteners gasp and turn away.

How did things go so wrong? What were they thinking, taking on two humans that have guns? But they couldn't have lived with themselves if they had just left Persimmon to be skinned for her fur. Even if she can't survive this injury, the thought of the humans making a hat out of her was too much for them to bear. But this is the outcome of their heroism. Now, not just one but *two* team members are dead, and a third—Derpoke—is out there now, frozen in fear, ready to be snatched up any minute. They dare not run out again, though, or else more of them could be killed. But are they about to watch Derpoke get shot to death, too?

The father turns around, looking for Persimmon's body. He sees it a few feet away and then notices the opossum, huddled in the leaves, shaking.

Derpoke looks at him—first with fear, then with hatred. *Bruiser! My poor friend. You killed him!*

The man glares at Derpoke. "Well, well, well. Still trying to eat my raccoon, are we?"

"Run, Derpoke! He's going to kill you!" Chloe yells frantically.

Derpoke looks at Persimmon and then peers back up at the giant man. To everyone's surprise, instead of running in the opposite direction, Derpoke waddles as swiftly as he can over to Persimmon and latches tightly onto her body, shielding her from the human.

"What in the hell?" The man steps over to Derpoke, who is holding onto his best friend for dear life, and flicks him in the head. "You are one stupid possum, you know that? You could have run away but instead you're gonna be chopped up and put into stew. Serves you right for trying to eat my raccoon."

Right then Gavin comes rushing up and punches his father really hard in the back. The dad grabs his back in pain. "Ow, you little…"

The boy screams at his dad. "I hate you!"

Gavin kneels next to Bruiser's body, crying, still yelling at his father. "I'll never forgive you! You didn't have to shoot him."

"You little idiot." The father stands up and shakes his head. "You're embarrassing yourself, crying like a baby over a dead dog. I raised you to be a man, not a girl."

The father takes a pair of gloves out of his back pocket, puts them on and lifts up Persimmon and Derpoke. The opossum closes his eyes and holds tight to Persimmon. No use in fighting off the man now.

He needs to think of a plan to get him and Persimmon far away from this monster.

The man starts back down the path and calls to his son. "I'm gonna put this raccoon and possum in the truck and put our guns away, and if you aren't standing by the side of the vehicle by the time I do all that, I'll whoop you out here in these woods. See if I don't."

The father walks out of sight. Gavin kneels by Bruiser's side—nose running, face wet with tears. "I'm sorry, boy."

He looks at the blood-soaked body. He puts his hand on the Doberman's back and strokes his black fur. *How could he shoot a dog?*

Gavin thinks about the whimpering sound Bruiser made when he pointed the gun at him. Anger soars through the boy. He thinks of his shotgun. *I have more bullets in my backpack. I could pretend I'm fixing the gun on the rack, secretly reload it and wham, shoot Dad right in the head. Bam! Right in his temple and watch the blood pour out.*

He imagines the frightened look on his father's face as he pulls the trigger and the bullet pierces his father's skin. *Then he'd know what it was like to be hunted.*

But Gavin's not a murderer. He only wanted to go hunting and trapping in the first place to impress his father. But why would he want to impress the man who has beaten him numerous times? Over what— spilling his cereal, not cleaning his bedroom?

I'll never hunt again. Never. His father was right about one thing: There is no difference between a dog and a raccoon. These animals don't want to die. They're not evil. The only evil one in these woods is his father. Gavin understands this now.

Gavin pats Bruiser on his side one last time, then stands up and heads back to the truck.

The father has already started the truck, and Gavin sits down without saying a word. The dad hits the gas and drives off.

In the back of the pickup, Derpoke and Persimmon are in a small cage. The opossum bawls as he holds his friend's limp body. It's unbelievable that she still has a heartbeat. After all that she's been through since her leg first got stuck in that trap, somehow she's still holding on.

If only he could feel joy over this. Instead he feels numb. He has no desire to live—Bruiser's dead, and now he and Persimmon are on their way to be hacked apart. Derpoke is afraid of how much it's going to hurt, but he's already decided that no matter how much pain these humans inflict on him, he will never let go of Persimmon.

He's resigned to his death. How could they possibly escape now? He can't take on these two humans by himself and even if he did somehow manage to slip past them and carry her body back into the woods—which is impossible—there's no way she'll survive this injury. Too much blood has drained from her leg.

All is lost… and yet it isn't.

In a million years, Derpoke would never have guessed that he and Persimmon would be saved by a human. Not just *any* human, but the little boy sitting at the front of that truck. Gavin, who set the trap that started this whole disaster, had an awakening that day. Seeing Bruiser—a dog he would have loved to call his best friend—killed right in front of him stirred compassion in him that his father was doing everything in his power to suppress.

Unbeknownst to his dad, late that night, Gavin sneaks out of his house to take the dying raccoon and her devoted opossum companion to a woman in his town that the locals call "that crazy animal lady." Gavin has never met her before, but he knows she used to be a vet, and deep down he has to believe that she can save these two critters. He's racked with guilt over Bruiser's death, and the only thing that will make him feel like he's not a completely terrible person is saving these two other animals.

If only Gavin had been able to tap into his compassion before Bruiser died, the world wouldn't have lost such a wonderful being. With a heartless parent like Gavin's, though, it's a miracle he had the revelation at all. Gavin proves to be a special kid, however, and Persimmon, Derpoke, and the whole team are hoping there are more humans out there just like him.

24

(PRESENT)

AFTER HEARING DERPOKE recount the events surrounding Bruiser's death, Persimmon crawls under the blanket in her cage and sobs.

"Bruiser. Bruiser." She calls out his name over and over as she wails. He's dead. One of her dearest friends is dead, and he died protecting *her*, so it hurts all the more.

Derpoke, Laurel, Lyric, and the other raccoon and opossum in the nearby cages peer into Persimmon's enclosure, feeling awful for her and not knowing what to do.

"Persimmon?" Derpoke leans against the window screen, calling out to his friend. "I'm sorry. I know you wanted us to leave you in that trap, but we couldn't. How could we let some human drag you away and skin you? We wouldn't be able to live with ourselves."

Persimmon doesn't even hear him, she's crying so hard.

Laurel steps over to the window and whispers to Derpoke. "I think we should just let her be for now."

Derpoke looks at her, surprised. He feels so helpless stuck on the other side of this window screen. All he wants to do is hug Persimmon and comfort her. *He* needs comforting, too. Bruiser was also his dear friend, and he hasn't had a chance to grieve since he's been so worried about whether Persimmon would survive.

He knows Laurel is right, though. There's no comforting Persimmon now. He slumps down on the porch chair and curls up in a ball. *Is this the end of The Enlighteners? Maybe it should be before any more of us gets injured or killed. We tried. We tried to bring peace to all animals, but too many humans are filled with too much hate. It's an unwinnable battle. We must end our quest now, before it's too late.*

25

VINCENT, EMBER, AND Scraps make their way through the dark woods. All around them are dogs and minks digging holes in the forest floor. One by one, the pit bulls climb into the holes and pull out the bodies of dead dogs. These are the mass graves of all the pit bulls who were unlucky enough to be born in Coach's yard. Dogs are everywhere among the trees, dragging the bodies along the ground toward Coach's house.

Vincent is pleased with the dogs' progress. Everything is moving forward as he had planned. The first step was convincing Rasha to help him and The Dissidents fight back against humans, and once Vincent had accomplished that, Rasha easily persuaded the other pit bulls to join in. Then The Dissidents unbuckled the heavy collars from the pit bulls' necks, giving them their first taste of freedom in their lives. The dogs immediately began assisting Vincent in his next elaborate scheme.

Vincent, Ember, and Scraps stop before a hole where Krait and two other pit bulls are scratching through the leaves and dirt, revealing a dog's body.

Krait gets a hold of the carcass and pulls it onto the leaves near Vincent.

"Thank you for doing this, Krait," Vincent says. "I understand how difficult this must be for you to see your fallen friends."

"They'd understand if they knew it was gonna keep us safe," Krait says.

Soon after the excavation began, Vincent noticed something that would interfere with his plan. It's not an easy thing to bring up, but if his plan is going to succeed, he needs to mention it to The Dissidents and get it resolved.

"Krait, this is a sensitive topic," Vincent says. "So I want you to know I am aware of that as I pose this issue. I noticed that the dogs' bodies are badly decomposed. That will surely look suspicious to the humans who find them. But if we can mask how long they've been dead, then I believe we'll be in the clear."

"Mask?" Krait asks. "What'd you have in mind?"

"Fire," Vincent says.

All the animals in the vicinity tense up. Fire is one of the most dangerous elements on Earth. From birth, they've known that if they detect fire, they must quickly dart in the opposite direction. What could Vincent possibly want to do with fire?

"I know this sounds grotesque," Vincent says, "but if we burn the bodies enough to mask how much they've decomposed, the humans will assume the dogs were killed tonight without looking into it further. Meanwhile, all of us Dissidents will be miles away without any humans searching for us."

Krait contemplates this plan for a moment. Vincent waits patiently, hoping he hasn't offended the canine.

"It *is* grotesque." Krait nods. "But so is everything these humans have done to us our entire lives. There isn't much you can do to shock us dogs. We've seen Dale and other humans burn dogs alive. At least this time, the dogs won't be screamin'."

Vincent, Ember, and Scraps shudder.

"Before this night is through," Vincent says, "these humans will be the ones screaming for mercy. I assure you of that. Then they'll never be able to hurt another creature again."

"I'm countin' on it," Krait says.

Vincent turns to Scraps. "How much do you and the raccoons know about starting a fire?"

Scraps wanted to tag along with Vincent to observe how he leads. Because of Vincent's devious nature, Scraps had a feeling something like this would come up—he was even counting on it—but he's still nervous being on the spot. "Persimmon always told me to stay away from fires, so I don't know anything about how to start one. Sorry."

"Normally smart advice," Vincent says, "but we're going to need your help on this one."

"I know there's some gasoline and matches in the shed," Krait says. "If the raccoons can use their paws to light the matches, I can walk you through everything else, including making sure we don't light the whole darn forest on fire."

"Good," Vincent says. "It's settled then. Once we've taken care of the humans, we'll start."

Krait nods. He then grabs the dog's carcass with his teeth and begins the long journey to the yard.

Vincent watches Krait drag away the body. He surveys all the dogs as they dig in the dirt, unearthing carcass after carcass. There are so many dead dogs; it's overwhelming.

Vincent grinds his teeth. Anger shoots through him with waves of sadness. Images of his own brutal past flash into his mind. The torment these animals endured before they were tossed into these shallow graves… he can only imagine.

26

RASHA'S FIGHT, PART 3

SURVIVAL

(OVER A YEAR AGO)

RASHA HIDES INSIDE her dilapidated doghouse. Actually, it's not a house as much as a pile of wood haphazardly nailed together. Early on, she learned the hard way that it wasn't wise to scratch against the sides or she'd get impaled by an errant nail or splinters.

The sun bakes the yard with ferocity. Rasha looks out her doorway and sees that most of the other dogs are curled up in their shelters, too. Some of the dogs have large, empty barrels to sleep in and others have wooden contraptions like Rasha's. The shelters are far from luxurious, but they come in handy when there's intense sun, rain, or snow.

The fleas are biting angrily today—maybe they're grumpy and overheated, too. Rasha scratches incessantly at her neck, then at her stomach, then back at her neck. On days like this, she wishes she was stationed further back in the yard among the trees, so she'd be better protected from the sun. She'd be closer to her mother that way as well, but the dogs don't get to choose anything in this place, so she just lies in the doghouse overheating.

Rasha thinks about her mother often. She knows that her mother is stationed farther in the yard at this moment, but she's not exactly sure where. For a short window of about a month, Rasha could actually see her mother in the whelping pen. She was stationed there with a new litter of pups, and if Rasha stood in one particular spot near her doghouse, she could see into the pen through the other dog areas. What Rasha saw broke her heart.

Her mother looked to be in a constant daze. Her nipples dangling flabbily from her belly from so many years of being forced to breed. Her left ear was missing. Her eyes were dull and milky, as if the life had been drained out of them. Her mother looked similar when Rasha was a pup, but Rasha was so young that she didn't understand *why* she looked that way. Now Rasha knows. The hellish life in this yard beat her mother into a haggard shell.

Rasha would stand there for hours trying to get her mother's attention. She'd give anything to cuddle up to her mother, but all she could hope for now was at least to make eye contact—to try to connect with her in some small way even from such a distance.

At first, Rasha would call out to her mother, but Coach and Dale got on her really quickly about making so much noise. So then she just stood there, wishing and hoping her mother would look her way.

Finally, one day Rasha's mother locked eyes with her. Rasha was so elated, she hopped up and down in the dirt. But that quickly fizzled when she realized that her mother's face did not light up the same way. Her mother stared at her. She didn't cry, but her mouth began to quiver, and it looked as if all the sorrow in the world were raining down on her. Then her mother shook her head no.

No? Rasha was confused. *What does she mean, no?* But then the reason sunk in. If Rasha is to survive this place, she has to toughen up, and she can't toughen up if she's a sad sack puppy yelping for her mommy. Coach, Dale, and the other dogs have to believe that she's fearless. Her mother is trying to save her life, but that doesn't make this gesture hurt any less.

That was it. That was the last time her mother would make eye contact with her. It crushed her mother's heart, too. Letting go of her babies was always excruciating, but this was one more devastating blow.

Rasha crawled into her doghouse and sat quietly. She was so despondent, she could barely breathe. Unfortunately, a few months later it got worse.

The pups in her mother's next litter were all stillborn. Her body had given up after being forced to breed so many times. She couldn't fight any longer, and now that she couldn't breed, Coach had no more use for her. He ordered Dale to take Rasha's mom into the woods and shoot her.

When Rasha heard the news through the other dogs, she exploded and tore her doghouse to shreds. She wouldn't let Coach or Dale get anywhere near her for a week, but Chopper eventually calmed her down. He reminded Rasha that Coach would surely kill a dog who was too aggressive toward humans and that her mother wouldn't want her baby getting killed over her, so after some coaxing, Rasha eventually ceased growling at Coach and Dale. Dale then replaced her doghouse with another one just as shabby as the last.

But that all occurs months from now. Today, Rasha is sitting in her doghouse baking in the sun.

As Rasha sits there, she gets a whiff of whiskey and, sure enough, Dale has entered the yard. She can't stand that rank smell since it's so closely associated with a human she's seen do unspeakable harm to dogs. She's seen him beat dogs to death, shoot them in the head, and even drown them.

Soon after Dale enters the yard, Coach steps out of the back door. His wife, Jean, gives him a kiss on the cheek, but she doesn't dare cross the barrier of that door. Coach has told her that not only can't she attend the dog fights but that he also doesn't want her even stepping foot in "his yard." She respects his wishes and couldn't care less that he's running a dogfighting ring. She'd rather he do that than frequent the local bar hitting on other women like he did when they were first dating.

Coach is wearing his usual coaching garb. Today, it's matching shorts and a T-shirt with the school mascot: an eagle. In typical fashion, his .38 Special revolver sits in its holster on his belt. It's the same handgun he lends to Dale to shoot the unwanted dogs. Coach wears it out in the open everywhere he goes. He'd say that it's for protection, but when people step back or fall silent as he passes, his hint of a smile belies his power high. For the dogs, the gun has the opposite effect. It's a constant reminder of how powerless they are. Coach is the top dog out here—period.

"Which dog did you say, Coach?" Dale asks. Even though Dale is Coach's nephew, Coach insists that everyone call him by the job title on which he bases his entire life.

"That gray one with the white blaze on her face, Rasha," Coach says.

Rasha's stomach drops. *What do they want with me?!* But she knows. She's always known this day would come. And yet it still feels so sudden.

Rasha hides deeper in her doghouse. *If I don't come out, he can't make me fight.*

Dale walks over to Rasha's mound of dirt. He leans down to look into the doghouse. "Hey girl, where are you? Time for you to have some fun."

Rasha doesn't stir. She barely even breathes. *Please make him go away. Please!* Her stomach twists in knots.

"Rasha, get out here!" Dale hollers. "I'm not playing!"

Rasha remains hidden in her doghouse.

Chopper has stepped out of his shelter to see what the commotion is about. He sees the poor young dog resisting and remembers the terror he felt when he was dragged off to his first fight. "Youngin', I know you're scared, but these humans don't play around. If you don't come outta that shelter right now, they're gonna shoot you."

"I don't wanna fight, Chopper," Rasha says.

"None of us do, youngin'," Chopper says. "But if you don't, they're gonna kill you."

Dale tugs on Rasha's chain again, and Rasha keeps her paws firmly planted in the dirt.

"She's not coming out!" Dale yells over to his uncle.

Coach is standing over at Sadie's dirt mound unshackling her. "Then drag her out. Or do you want me to hold your little hand as you do it?"

Dale huffs and grabs the logging chain that leads into Rasha's doghouse. He tugs so hard, Rasha tumbles forward into the dirt. She digs her paws into the ground, attempting to steady herself.

Dale yanks harder on the chain, multiple times, shaking Rasha around by the neck. She coughs and gasps for breath.

Chopper calls into Rasha's doghouse with more desperation. "Rasha, I know you got some fight in you. I saw you bitin' at the humans when they were takin' away your siblings. This time, you're not fightin' for your family, you're fightin' for your *own* life."

Rasha sighs deeply. It's no use resisting. She'll have to think of another plan. She still has time before she'll be thrust into that pit.

Rasha crawls out low to the ground.

"Finally!" Dale says, frustrated. "What the hell is wrong with you?"

Rasha knows better than to bite Dale. She doesn't even want to. She wants to run away, but that's not an option. She looks up at Dale, full of fear. The urge to cry suddenly sweeps through her. *I don't want to fight. Why are they making me fight?*

The other dogs in the area have gone silent. They've all been through this, and from observing Rasha's personality over the past few months, she's going to lose this fight. This may be the last time they see her alive.

That's when Rasha notices that Sadie is being escorted to the shed by Coach. *I'm fighting Sadie?! But she's already been in multiple fights. She's more experienced than I am. Even if she hadn't, I don't want to fight her. I don't hate her.*

"I know what you're thinking, Rasha," Chopper says. "You're afraid of fighting Sadie, but she's not as tough as she acts. You don't gotta kill her, you just gotta prove to these humans you're willing to fight."

Before Rasha can ask Chopper what he means by that, Dale calls out to his uncle, who is almost at the shed. "These two dogs are always so damn chatty. You don't think she's in heat, do you?"

"I hope not," Coach laughs. "That's her father."

Rasha and Chopper stare at each other, shocked. Everything around them fades away.

My father?! Rasha isn't sure how to react. What a remarkable revelation at such an inopportune time. She'd assumed she'd never know who her father was, but she's known him most of her life without even realizing it.

Chopper feels heartsick. He always wondered what happened to his pups after he was forced to breed. Now the only daughter he's ever known is most likely about to die.

Dale pulls on Rasha's leash to lead her to the shed.

Chopper frantically jumps to the edge of his chain. "Fight, Rasha. I know you have a good heart and you don't want to hurt no other dogs, but no daughter of mine is dying in that pit. You got that? I want to see you again! Fight!"

Rasha drags her feet as she listens to Chopper, so Dale impatiently pulls on her leash. "Come on, girl. Get your game face on. You got a big fight ahead of you."

Rasha is so flustered she can't think of what to say to Chopper. There's so much to say that nothing comes out.

Dale continues to pull Rasha up the path to the shed. She drags her feet as she goes, delaying the inevitable. *Please don't make me do this! I'm not ready. I don't know how to fight. I don't want to fight. Think, Rasha. There must be a way out of this. Think.*

*   *   *

Dale pulls Rasha into the shed and shuts the door behind him. Light shines in through the cracks in the wood panels. Dust and dirt float through the air. A moldy smell attacks Rasha's sensitive nostrils.

In the middle of the room, thin wooden boards connect to make a circle. It's the pit. This is where so many dogs have suffered for so many years. Coach already has Sadie in one side of the pit behind a chalk line. Sadie sits on her haunches, at attention. Coach firmly grips the skin and fur of her neck with two hands. From the look in Sadie's eyes, if he weren't holding tight, she'd leap out of that pit toward Rasha and attack her right now.

Dale lifts Rasha over the side and plops her in the dirt inside the pit. Dale then grabs the fur around Rasha's neck and faces her toward Sadie.

Rasha's legs tremble and her heart pounds in her chest. She feels like she might faint. On the pit walls she sees scratch marks of all the dogs who tried to escape. She looks more closely and sees dark blood stains. She's so panicked, her skin feels like it's on fire.

"I don't want to fight you!" Rasha suddenly barks. She even surprises herself. It just bursts out.

Sadie calmly glares at Rasha. "They're only letting one of us out of here alive. It will not be you."

Rasha believes her. Everything about Sadie beams confidence and prowess, and everything about Rasha screams fear—her trembling paws, her jittery eyes. Rasha knows she can't beat Sadie in a fight. Sadie's eyes are filled with anger. *Why does she hate me so much? She doesn't even know me.*

"Listen to me, Sadie," Rasha pleads. "We can attack Coach and Dale and then run out of here... together. We don't have to fight."

"And who's going to open that door for us once we've killed these humans?" Sadie asks. "We'll starve to death in here."

"No, someone will come looking for them, and then when they open—"

"Enough!" Sadie growls. "There is no escape. Whoever loses they're going to kill, and I'm not dying today. But since you're so frightened, I'll make a deal with you. If you don't fight back, I'll kill you quick. But if you do, I'll still kill you, and I'll make you pay for it."

"Please, I didn't do anything—"

Dale yells over the two dogs as they bark at each other. "Listen to 'em. They're ready to go! Can we start?"

Rasha's heart is pounding so fast, she thinks it might explode through her chest. *No! I'm not ready!*

Coach gleefully howls into the air like a wolf. "I'm ready for a fight! On my count. Three... two... one!"

Coach and Dale let go of their respective dogs and Sadie barrels toward Rasha. Rasha doesn't even have time to react before Sadie slams into her, biting at Rasha's face.

"Stop!" Rasha yelps as Sadie repeatedly chews into her face and neck.

Rasha finally squirms out from her corner and rushes away from Sadie.

"Hold on!" Coach yells as he grabs Sadie.

Rasha cowers near the wall, her tail hidden between her legs. She looks at Coach and Dale pleadingly. *Why are you doing this to me?*

Dale grabs Rasha by the scruff and drags her behind the chalk line. "Coach, I think this one's cold. She didn't even run toward the middle."

"Patience, nephew," Coach says as he faces Sadie toward Rasha again from the opposite end of the pit. "I told you. Rasha comes from good stock. Both her parents are champions. That champion blood is coursing through her right now. It just needs a second to kick in."

"You're the boss," Dale shrugs. "But I think we gotta put this one to sleep."

Rasha stops breathing. *"Put this one to sleep."* She knows what that means—a bullet to the head. She hates Coach and Dale for forcing her to hurt another dog, for forcing that dog to hurt her. *This is it. Do you want to die or do you want to live? Those are the only two choices right now.*

Without warning, Rasha breaks free from Dale's grasp and charges straight toward Sadie. Before either Sadie or Coach can react, Rasha slams into Sadie and bites ferociously at her face. Sadie thrashes around on her back, but Rasha keeps biting so fast and with such force that Sadie isn't able to defend herself.

Coach quickly fumbles for the metal stick poking out of his pocket, slides it between Rasha's jaw and Sadie's face, and then pulls back on Rasha's head.

"Help me, idiot!" Coach yells at Dale.

Dale was stuck in a daze, staring at the two dogs, but suddenly he pops back into reality and grabs Rasha's two back legs, pulling her backward. Rasha finally stops biting, and Dale drags her through the dirt back to her side of the pit.

Dale gets a tight hold around her neck. "Whoo! Crap! We got a fighter here!"

"I told you!" Coach hollers with excitement. "Beast Dog Kennels, baby! Ain't no one better than me!"

Sadie shakes around, trying to loosen Coach's grip on her. "I'll kill you, Rasha! You faked being scared just so you could sneak attack me. You're a cheater!"

"I told you I didn't want to fight!" Rasha yells back. "They were going to kill me. I had to."

Coach strokes Sadie's head. "It's okay, girl. You'll get to fight again, just not this one. We got two future champions here. I don't want either one of you getting hurt."

Rasha looks at Dale and Coach, confused. *That's it?! I don't have to fight anymore today? Are they declaring me the winner? It was so fast. And Sadie gets to fight again, too? So they're not killing either of us?*

Rasha is in shock. She's filled with so many questions. That wasn't like any of the other fights she'd witnessed while sitting in that yard. The other fights lasted at least an hour and one dog was always killed afterward. *I really don't have to fight anymore today?* She doesn't want to get too hopeful, but she so desperately wants it to be true.

Coach looks over at Rasha. "Good job, girl. I knew you had that fighter instinct in you. I got plans for you. Don't you worry."

Dale lifts Rasha over the side of the pit, and she and Sadie are escorted by the humans back to the yard.

Sadie glares at the ground the whole way back to her chain. She doesn't want to make eye contact with the other dogs, knowing that Rasha got the better of her.

Chopper is beside himself with joy when Rasha comes into view. He jumps up and down on his chain. "Rasha, my little girl! You did it! I knew ya had it in ya!"

Chopper has no idea how much that comment stings. Rasha doesn't *want* to have the killer instinct inside her. She's incredibly ashamed, so she doesn't respond. She looks at the ground as well. The last thing she feels like doing is boasting.

She feels every dog staring at her. They can't believe it. She survived! That frightened dog who trembled throughout every fight in that shed actually lived to see another day, and it looks like she came out on top.

Coach and Dale attach Rasha and Sadie to their chains. Coach steps over to Rasha, pulls a treat out of his pocket and holds it up for her to take.

"Good job today, girl," Coach says. "You're gonna be a real killer. Even better, you're gonna earn me a lot of money."

Coach and Dale walk back into the house. Rasha spits out the treat. No matter how hungry she is for something so tasty, she doesn't want any gifts from that monster.

"Cheater!" Sadie yells out to the other dogs. "Watch out for this one. She cheats!"

"Not true!" Rasha pans from dog to dog, making eye contact so they know she's not lying. "I didn't want to fight, but she kept biting me. I had to defend myself. They were going to kill me if I didn't. What was I supposed to do?"

"You were supposed to fight with honor," Sadie hisses. She's standing as close to Rasha's dirt mound as her chain will let her. She's so angry, she's frothing at the mouth. "The rules are that you wait until the round starts and *then* you fight."

"Fight with honor?!" Rasha steps nearer to Sadie, although not as close as she could. She doesn't want to provoke her too much. "There's nothing honorable about these fights. They're forcing us to hurt one another. You heard them say that they were going to kill me. If I hadn't fought back, I wouldn't be here right now."

"Leave her alone, Sadie!" Chopper butts in. "You're just sore, because you ain't as tough as you want everyone to think."

"Wanna find out, old man?" Sadie sneers.

"Stop!" Rasha pleads. "This isn't who we are. We're not killers."

Other pit bulls watch the argument with unease. Despite the tension among all the dogs in the yard—for obvious reasons— they try to at least remain respectful of one another. They're all stuck in this hell together, so it doesn't make sense to take their frustrations out on one another. But in an instance like this, a bitter rivalry is inevitable. There's no use intervening, though. Of course, Rasha had no choice but to defend herself, and of course, Sadie feels humiliated. That's how life here works, and the truth is that both Rasha and Sadie could be dead in a month, so the other dogs have lost the will to mediate. They're also too busy anticipating the next time *they* have to fight.

Rasha picks up the treat that Coach gave her and tosses it into Sadie's area as a peace offering. "I promise you. I didn't want to fight. You must know that's true."

Sadie looks at the treat and scowls. She picks it up with her mouth and tosses it as far as she can. Another dog a few feet away leaps into the air and catches it, gobbling it up.

Sadie glares at Rasha, nostrils flaring. "One day I'm going to kill you. I don't know how, but if another dog doesn't kill you first, I promise you, *I* will."

Sadie turns to the other dogs in the area, glowering. "I'll kill *any* of you. You better hope they don't put me in the pit with you!"

With that, Sadie crawls into her barrel.

Rasha lowers her head.

"Don't pay her no mind, youngin'," Chopper says. "You survived like you had to. No shame in that."

But Rasha is riddled with guilt. She doesn't know how to respond to Chopper and doesn't have the energy anyway. She just curls up in her doghouse.

This day has punched her into submission. She licks the wounds on her face and neck that her tongue can reach. They sting with each lick.

She whimpers quietly as she tends to her wounds, hoping none of the other dogs can hear her.

What a disgusting experience. She attacked another dog. She never thought she was capable of something so horrendous.

How could I do that to another dog?... But what choice did I have? I tried not to bite Sadie too hard, but I had to make it look real. Like Chopper said, I did what I had to do to survive. And that's why I'm still alive.

Rasha pauses for a moment to let this sink in. *I'm alive.* This could have been her last day on Earth. Dale could have shot her in the head just like he did all those other dogs. But that didn't happen. Why? Because she betrayed her natural decency and hurt another dog.

No matter how much I rebelled against it, these humans have turned me into a fighter. What would I have done if they hadn't stopped me? Would I have hurt Sadie even more? Would I have killed her? Am I capable of such savagery?

In this moment, Rasha knows that everything has changed. *This is her life now. Fighting. Fighting to stay alive—no matter what. After what she did to Sadie, she's not sure of what brutality she's capable. *Is Coach right? Is there an evil lurking inside me?*

This thought stings more than any of her wounds. She may not have died in that pit, but she knows that every last ounce of her innocence did.

27

RASHA'S FIGHT, PART 4

LEARNING TO KILL

(ONE MONTH LATER)

RASHA'S HEART FEELS like it's going to explode from exhaustion. As part of her training, Coach and Dale have set her up in a contraption called a catmill—she's in a harness that's attached to a pole and she's made to run in circles. The machine is intended to build her endurance, and to give her an incentive to run, the humans have a rabbit trapped in a cage that dangles a foot in front of her the entire time.

The poor rabbit is petrified. Rasha tried to calm him down when she first started running, explaining that she's not actually able to catch him and therefore poses no threat, but he was too terrified to listen to reason. She doesn't blame him. Who wants to be chased by a predator as they lie stuck in a cage?

Coach and Dale are sitting on folding chairs drinking beer and whiskey, respectively, and enjoying every minute of the violent merry-go-round as if they were watching a football game.

It's been a month since Rasha's first fight. Chopper explained that her "fight" with Sadie was a test (the humans call it a "roll"). That's why it didn't last very long and Coach stopped it before either dog got too injured. He was simply trying to determine whether Rasha was game to fight. If she hadn't been, he would have had Dale kill her on the spot—no use in wasting time and money on a dog who doesn't have the urge to brawl. "Breed the best, bury the rest," as Coach always says.

Since Rasha passed that first test, she was forced to do one more "roll" with a different dog from the yard named Maxie. This time, the humans wanted to see whether she'd continue fighting despite being in pain. Since the fights are brutal, the humans want to make sure she won't quit even though she's being torn to shreds. Chopper was nice enough to tip her off to that fact, so Rasha fought it out despite severe gashes to her face and neck.

The fight lasted an hour—the longest, most gruesome hour of Rasha's life so far. She kept looking toward Dale and Coach to see whether they'd show her and Maxie mercy. *Haven't we chewed each other enough? With all the holes ripped into my skin and the blood gushing out of me, haven't I proved that I'm tough enough?* But Coach and Dale kept goading the two dogs. By the end, blood smeared the pit walls and both dogs were panting so heavily, they could barely lift their own bodies.

Luckily, that second "roll" was her last. Now, Rasha is being forced to train for a real fight—one in which she'll fight to the death. It will be against a dog from a different yard, and Coach and Dale will have a lot of money riding on it, so they'll expect big results from their budding champion.

The training has been grueling, as Chopper had warned. One day the humans will make Rasha run on a treadmill for an hour or so. Another day they'll have her lug around a heavy tire to build her jaw and leg strength. They also strengthen her jaw muscles by having her run up to a rope on a spring pole, latch onto it, and dangle. At the end of each day, Rasha is so fatigued, she crumbles to the dirt in her doghouse.

Sadie hasn't said a word to her since their fight. She refuses to even look in Rasha's direction. Rasha has decided not to bother her. She'd love to make amends, but Sadie's ego was hurt too deeply. Chopper assured Rasha that it was not personal.

"It's not you, youngin'," Chopper said. "We're all afraid of dying in that pit. Best way to stay alive is to make every dog think there's no way they could beat you. You just exposed that she's beatable, which means death in our world."

"But, as you said, the rolls aren't meant to be to the death. If all of us dogs worked together, we could just pretend to fight and trick the humans. Then none of us would actually get hurt."

"Maybe you could fake the first roll, but the second? No way. They'd know it wasn't real. They're expecting blood. And if they suspected you were both play fighting? Oh boy! They'd be right angry and you'd both be dead. No sir, it's every dog for himself or herself in that pit. That's just the way it's gotta be."

"So before you knew you were my father, why were you so nice to *me*?" Rasha asked. "What if they had made *us* fight?"

"Never would have happened," Chopper said. "They only match up males against males and females against females. Besides, there's no beatin' me. I've killed every dog I've fought."

Chopper pauses for a moment. He's so used to showing bravado as a survival instinct that it just slipped out. Deep down, though, every fight haunts him. Every single night he's bombarded by nightmares of murdering those dogs.

He whispers quietly to Rasha, hoping not too many other dogs hear. "I got no pleasure killing those dogs, Rasha. I just did what I had to do. I don't wanna give those humans the pleasure of seeing me die in that pit. You'll see. All those humans are cheering, hoping to see you die. It does something to you. You wanna live just to spite 'em. It's all you got."

Rasha is disquieted. Out of all the dogs, Chopper has been the nicest to her and yet he may be one of the most brutal killers in the yard. Not because he's heartless, but because that's what this place does to you. She went to sleep that night thinking. *I don't blame him for what he's done, but that's not me. I'm going to find another way. I just haven't figured it out yet.*

Rasha has only a few weeks left of training, so the pressure is on for her to figure it out. At this moment, though, she's focused on trying not to pass out as she runs full speed in circles.

The rabbit has gone quiet. He's just huddled at the far end of the cage, hiding his head in his front paws.

"Look at her run after that rabbit," Coach says proudly. "She'd give anything to rip him apart. You can't tell me these dogs aren't meant to fight. They're *bred* to fight. They love it."

"Hell yeah, they do," Dale says. He pulls out his flask and takes another swig of whiskey. "All these animal activists are idiots. Dog-fighting's just like boxing. We're just letting these dogs do what's natural to 'em."

"Let me tell you something, nephew," Coach says. "I love these dogs just like I love my football players. I *want* them to win. I don't wanna see them get hurt in that pit. I want them to kick that other dog's ass. But just like my players on the team, if they're a loser, they gotta get cut. Why do you think we won the state championship two years in a row? Because I'm a winner and I train winners. Period."

Dale gives his uncle a high five. "Hell yes, you do! Go Eagles!"

Rasha is irritated by their foolish banter. *Do you kill the players if they're not good enough, or do you just kick them off the team? Do you force them to bite one another to death, or do they just tackle one another? Chopper told me about your games. It's nothing like our fights. How dare you say you care about us? The hundreds of dogs buried in those woods are proof that you couldn't care* less.

"You know who's worse than the animal activist nuts?" Coach asks Dale but then answers before Dale has a chance to chime in. "Cops. Do you know that back in the 1860s when dogfighting was just beginning in America, it was mostly cops and firefighters running the operation?"

"What?!" Dale says. "No way."

"Look it up," Coach says. "Hypocrites. Then they act like *I'm* the criminal now. Do you remember how they raided my yard maybe ten years ago? Took all my damn dogs and killed 'em. If they really cared about the dogs, they wouldn'ta killed 'em. But I'm not worried about no cops. Hell, we both know I got at least two cops who come to the fights now."

Coach laughs and taps his beer bottle against Dale's whiskey flask.

"The cops said I couldn't own dogs for like a year. Did they ever come back to make sure I got no new dogs? No. Hell, they fined me like $500. I make ten times that on one fight—even more sometimes. And I make even more money selling dogs. I got this thing locked up, nephew."

Rasha can't take any more of this talk. She stops running in the catmill. Her heart pounds. She coughs from exhaustion.

"Hey, lazy ass," Dale yells. "Get back to running!"

"No, she's good," Coach says. "That's enough for today. We don't want our champion spraining a leg or something."

Dale walks over to Rasha, attaches her leash, and then takes her out of the harness as he detaches her from the pole. He looks over at the rabbit in the cage. His eyes light up. "Oh man, can I feed her the rabbit?"

Rasha freezes. Her stomach drops. *Feed me the rabbit?! No.*

"Yeah, she earned it." Coach laughs. "Man, you just love watching these dogs tear up them rabbits. I gotta buy so many bunnies 'cause of you."

Coach takes Rasha's leash as Dale steps over to the cage that holds the tiny, fearful rabbit. Rasha is in a panic. *I don't want to kill this rabbit. Can I just let him run away? Will Coach and Dale think I'm weak? Will they get angry if I don't kill him?*

Rasha is horrified: *I think I have to kill him.* The thought hits her hard and she feels like she'll vomit.

Dale picks up the rabbit by his ears. The furry little guy yelps. Dale holds the rabbit near Rasha's nose.

"You wanna eat him so bad, don't you?" Dale teases.

Rasha barks at the rabbit and growls. She's playing along, but her brain is going a million miles a minute trying to figure out how to get out of this one.

The rabbit kicks around, forcing Dale to lose his grip. The bunny plops on the ground and instantly darts away. "God dang it!"

The rabbit dashes across the grass toward the fence, and Coach lets go of Rasha's leash. "Go get her, girl!"

Rasha doesn't move. She doesn't want to do this.

"Go!" Dale yells.

Rasha jumps into a sprint toward the rabbit. The rabbit bangs into the fence. Unfortunately, there are no holes in the fence—that way people can't look in and see the dogfighting ring. But that means there's nowhere to go but underneath it. The rabbit immediately starts digging. Rasha runs up behind him. If only he could dig faster, but there's no way she can stall until he finishes a hole. It would look too suspicious.

"Hey!" Rasha hollers.

The rabbit freezes. His whole body is trembling.

"Listen, I don't have much time," Rasha says. "I'm not going to hurt you, but I have to make it look like I want to."

The rabbit just keeps shaking without turning around.

Rasha takes a deep breath. She has no idea if this will work, but she has to try something. She runs up to the rabbit, picks him up with her teeth as gently as she can, and begins shaking him back and forth. With one powerful swing, she hurls him up and over the fence.

Rasha stops moving and listens for the rabbit rustling on the other side. Nothing. *I killed him. Oh no... You thought throwing him would work?!... But what else could I do? I had to make his escape plausible.*

"Holy crap!" Dale yells. "Did you see that?!"

Coach laughs hysterically. "Oh man. Somebody's a little too excited. Man, she's not gonna win fights like that, but it'll entertain the hell out of everyone."

Rasha's heart sinks.

Just then, she hears rustling on the other side of the fence. "I'm okay!" a tiny voice says.

With that, the rabbit is heard scurrying off into the woods.

He's alive! Rasha is so relieved. *I don't have to be a killer. I just have to be clever.*

She steps back over to Coach and Dale with her tail between her legs, pretending to be embarrassed. *Idiots. You've never met a dog like me.*

28

PERSIMMON HAS BARELY eaten anything in the past few days. Twice a day, Dr. Misra brings her a plate of food and Persimmon just lets it sit in the cage until the vet decides to take it away.

The raccoon cries on and off throughout the day and night, hiding in her blanket even though it's uncomfortably hot and humid in the room. Derpoke, Laurel, and Lyric have left her alone to grieve, but they're all very concerned about her. She just lies there listlessly, staring at the wall.

Persimmon can't stop wondering what she could have done differently so that Bruiser would still be alive. The only thing she can think of is that she should have chewed off her own leg. It felt too grotesque at the time, but she'd much rather that than have any of her friends harmed.

I should have known that the team wouldn't leave me there. They're too loyal. From the start, they knew things wouldn't end well if they battled two giant humans who had guns—and yet they fought valiantly... How can The Enlighteners continue these missions? Either my friends get hurt and killed or other animals do. How do we win?

She feels like someone tore out her heart. She'd do anything to bring Bruiser back, but he's gone, and somehow she has to find a way to live with that. So far, it doesn't seem possible.

Derpoke is currently away from the house, sitting in the shade at the edge of the woods. He, too, is weighed down by depression. He misses Bruiser. He can't get the sound out of his head of Bruiser yelping as he was shot. Every time Derpoke closes his eyes, he sees his friend's bloody body lying in the leaves.

Derpoke wants to be with Persimmon. He's unaccustomed to not sleeping beside her at night. Being close to her always calms him. But she's not talking to anyone. He's worried she's upset at him over Bruiser's death—that maybe she blames him somehow. For now, he's giving her space. When she's ready, he knows she'll talk to him, and he has a lot to say about the future of The Enlighteners when she does.

Back in the house, Dr. Misra walks into the room and sees Laurel sitting by Persimmon's cage with Lyric huddled on the floor just below.

"You two are really fond of her, aren't you?" Dr. Misra says. She puts a plate of food in the other raccoon's and opossum's cages and then opens Persimmon's cage and puts in a plate of celery stalks that are smeared with peanut butter. Dr. Misra finally caught on that Persimmon refuses to eat other animals.

Dr. Misra looks in the cage at Persimmon, who is still hiding under the blanket. "Come on, peaches, you have to eat *something*. You need your energy." Dr. Misra sighs. "Don't give up. You're a trooper, I know it."

The vet looks at Laurel and Lyric. "I hate to say it, chickadees, but I wouldn't get too attached. I don't think our new guest is going to make it."

Dr. Misra walks out of the room, dejected.

Laurel steps over to the side of Persimmon's cage and tries to look at her under the blanket. "Persimmon, Dr. Misra is right. You should eat something. You need food to heal."

Persimmon remains quiet. Laurel wonders if she's asleep.

Laurel tries again. "Just eat one celery stalk. Please, I'm worried about you."

"I'm not hungry," Persimmon says quietly from inside the blanket.

"I don't think I've seen you eat at all in the past few days. It's not about being hungry, it's about surviving."

Surviving. Persimmon isn't so sure that's what she wants. She wants to fade away into darkness.

Persimmon pokes her head out of the blanket. She looks at Laurel with weary, sorrowful eyes. "You didn't know Bruiser, but if you did, you would have loved him. He had the kindest heart. His humans neglected him his whole life and then left him to starve to death in their backyard when they moved, but despite all that, he was so gentle with the whole team. Everywhere we went, he was always on alert to protect each of us from danger—no matter how formidable the attacker. I used to be so afraid of dogs with all my run-ins with them over food, but he helped me overcome my prejudice because he was so full of love."

Persimmon looks away from Laurel. She breathes in deeply, trying not to cry. "But now I'll never see him again. I just want to see him one more time. I want to thank him for risking his life to save mine. He deserved to be happy, Laurel. He was finally free and he deserved to be happy."

Tears stream down Persimmon's furry face. She hides her head under the blanket again.

Laurel puts her paw against Persimmon's cage. Her heart hurts for this dispirited raccoon. Laurel has suffered a devastating loss of her own, so she knows how debilitating it can be.

Laurel walks around to the front of Persimmon's cage and undoes the latch. She opens the door and steps inside. Laurel gently walks over to Persimmon and crawls under the blanket, snuggling up close to the heartbroken raccoon. Persimmon stops crying, taken off guard by this outpouring of affection.

Laurel puts her right paw around Persimmon's side and holds her tight. "It's okay to cry. I just don't want you doing it alone."

Persimmon takes a deep breath. She's barely breathed for days. Ever since she heard the news about Bruiser, she's wanted everyone to leave her alone. She's wanted to crawl into a dark hole and never come out. But now... feeling this kindhearted raccoon pressed against her, she realizes she desperately needed a hug. Her despair doesn't disappear, but for the first time, it lessens.

Persimmon knows that she will never heal from Bruiser's death, but this warm embrace from a raccoon she hardly knows reminds her that there will come a day when it won't weigh on her so heavily. So for now, she will focus on how comforting it feels to be held.

Persimmon closes her eyes, puts her paw on Laurel's paw, and then sleeps.

29

"PERSIMMON! DERPOKE!" CHLOE yells as she frantically runs after the hunter's pickup truck that's carrying away her two friends.

Chloe trips on a root and tumbles forward. She watches helplessly as the truck disappears down the dirt road.

Tucker rushes up to his partner. "Are you okay, sweet pea?"

"They're gone, Tucker," Chloe says. "They're gone... forever."

Gone. That's just a gentler way of saying dead. Chloe and Tucker cling to each other in shock. Three of their best friends are now dead or soon will be.

Chloe can't believe how horribly awry their plan went. *What were we thinking? We went from certain death for one team member to certain death for three. But it felt like it could work. The humans were supposed to be so taken off guard when we attacked that they wouldn't have time to react until we were too far away to do anything... The moment we saw those guns we should have rethought the plan. But it was too late. Everyone was already in place. What a catastrophe.*

In a daze, Chloe suddenly realizes she's staring right at Bruiser's body lying in the leaves. She quickly looks away and her eyes stop on the two frightened chickens, Hazel and Arden.

Chloe lets go of Tucker and dashes back over to the chickens. The birds are huddled together, shaking and hiding their heads in their wings. They've already been through so much tragedy in their lives, and just when they thought they were safe, this disaster occurs.

Chloe steps up to the two chickens, who are at least twice her size. She sits on her hind legs and gently caresses them with her front legs. "Everything's going to be okay. I'm here. Tucker's here."

"*We're* here." Aunty Adelaide shuffles over with Uncle Bennett by her side. Both raccoons look shaken and emotionally wiped out. Uncle Bennett stares at the forest floor, not saying a word. It still hasn't really sunk in that they just lost their niece, and they had such an affinity for Derpoke, it's as if they lost their nephew, too.

"We're going to take care of you," Chloe says to the two chickens, but they keep their heads tucked in their wings. This is too much for them to bear.

Chloe motions for Tucker to come cuddle with the birds. Aunty Adelaide steps over as well, and they hug the chickens as a group, keeping them safe in the center.

As Chloe sits there, it hits her: *At this very moment, Persimmon and Derpoke are most likely still alive. They're probably still in the back of that truck. If only we could fly after that vehicle, we could still save their lives.* Chloe sighs. *Instead, my dear friends are being driven to their deaths right now, and there's nothing we can do to stop it.*

That thought is so upsetting—the powerlessness of it all. She wants to scream at the top of her lungs—tear a hole in the ground—she's so angry. She wants to shake the forest floor until the cage with Persimmon and Derpoke in it gets tossed out of the truck, but it's hopeless. There is nothing she can do to stop their imminent deaths. She's just a little squirrel. In all her life, Chloe never felt so small.

*   *   *

Chloe and Tucker run through the leaves, deeply sniffing the forest floor. They've been following Nibbin's trail far into the woods for a day and a half. Aunty Adelaide and Uncle Bennett are back at their tree watching Hazel and Arden.

Chloe slowly stops sniffing the ground and halts. She sighs.

"What?" Tucker asks. "Did you lose Nibbin's scent? I still have it here."

"No," Chloe says dejectedly. She grinds her teeth anxiously. "This is hard to say… but I think we should stop our search."

"Huh?" Tucker walks over to Chloe. "You don't think we're going to find him?"

"I don't think he *wants* us to find him," Chloe says. "His path isn't accidental. It's deliberate. I think he's going back to live with the other minks."

Tucker nods.

"On top of that…" Chloe hesitates. "It worries me to think of Nibbin all alone in these woods, but the truth is, the longer we keep looking for him, the longer those chickens languish in those sheds."

Tucker's eyes widen. He knew they'd have to discuss the chicken rescue eventually. They've been so grief-stricken over Persimmon, Derpoke and Bruiser, and then so focused on searching for Nibbin, that they've avoided this subject. But it needed to be addressed at some point.

Chloe fidgets with the leaves below her paws. "I know that after losing so many friends it seems unreasonably dangerous to keep going, but thinking about the chickens trapped in those sheds weighs on me, pupsy. I also know that we're the only ones left in The Enlighteners, so it seems implausible to pull off this mission, but I can't walk away."

Tucker's expression gets more and more uneasy as Chloe reveals her intentions. He sits lower to the ground.

"Are you upset?" Chloe asks. She begins to ramble nervously. "We can talk about it more. I'm open to ideas. I know it's daunting with just the two of us. Daunting? Impossible even. Can you believe Hazel estimates that there are 60,000 chickens in those sheds? It's unbelievable. I know—"

"Yes," Tucker agrees. "We must move forward with the rescue."

Chloe stops chattering. "Really? You'll help me save the chickens?"

"I knew you'd want to," Tucker says. "I guess I've been dreading that you'd bring it up, but of course you're right. We can't leave them in those sheds. I just hope you have a plan figured out, because I have no idea how we could possibly pull this off."

Chloe kisses him all over his face. "Oh, pupsy. I'm so happy! Yes, I'm already working on a plan."

Chloe hugs him with her entire body—tail and all. "I love you for not giving up, you know that, right?"

"Well, we always said that we wanted a family. Now we will have 60,000 babies to raise."

Chloe smiles and squeezes Tucker even harder. The moment feels joyful, because it gives them something to believe in. Deep down, though, neither of them has any idea how they can achieve such an overwhelming feat. Are they foolish for not knowing when to give up, or are they brave for facing such insurmountable odds head-on? They've risked so much already, it's getting harder for them to tell the difference.

30

(PRESENT)

"YOU AND THE Enlighteners are sooo brave!" Laurel remarks.

She and Persimmon are lying down in Persimmon's cage, facing each other. They've talked through the night and into the morning, which has helped distract Persimmon from grieving over Bruiser. Persimmon even laughed a few times, which was a welcome feeling after being down for so long.

"It's not bravery driving us to rescue these animals. We see how much they're suffering and the only option is to help them. With what we've witnessed, how could we not?"

"But most animals, including humans, *don't* help them. Don't you dare downplay how courageous you are. Look, I'm a scaredy to the max, so I should know. Get this, you and I are raccoons, so I should be sleeping during the day, right? Instead, I'm so afraid of the dark that I switched my sleeping schedule to the night so I could hide in bed with Lyric and Dr. Misra. If that weren't bad enough, I burrow deep under the blanket, and if my feet are dangling outside the covers even the slightest, I freak out, thinking some monster is going to chew them off."

"A monster?" Persimmon laughs. "That's so odd. In the woods, we consider *humans* the monsters, but you're curled up in bed with one as protection."

"You have to get to know her better," Laurel says. "She is the best! And speaking of the best..." Laurel kicks Persimmon's rear feet excitedly. "I can't believe you and your friends are the ones who rescued those animals from the circus! Dr. Misra, Lyric, and I watched that on TV and we were amazed. It was like the most exciting thing I've ever seen in my life. Do you know they still haven't found any of the horses or goats? The circus left that town a while ago, and they basically gave up the search."

"Oh wow, that's wonderful! The last I heard they hadn't been re-captured, but I didn't realize that the humans decided to stop looking."

"Yep, we cheered every time a story came on the news about the rescue. All the reporters kept saying that it was animal rights activists—as in humans— that conducted the rescue, but it's so much more powerful that it was other nonhuman animals!"

Persimmon has no idea what a TV is or what reporters are, but she has a feeling that would take too long to explain, so she doesn't ask. "When our team rescued the minks, Vincent told us that humans had freed the minks from a nearby fur farm. I thought maybe that was a small group of humans and maybe even a one-time occurrence, but it sounds like there are more humans out there fighting on behalf of us other animals than I had imagined. I can't tell you how happy that makes me."

Persimmon's face has lit up. "That little boy, Gavin, saved both my life and Derpoke's by bringing us here, and then Dr. Misra revived me from the dead. You have no idea how significant that is. Our team has seen humans do unspeakable things to other animals. I was beginning to worry that humans were cruel by nature, but when I needed it the most, these two humans showed me otherwise."

Persimmon rolls onto her three legs as she gets more excited by this promising thought. "The question now is, how do we inspire *more* humans to care? I mean, even Dr. Misra, who, as you say, has devoted her life to healing other creatures, still eats some of us. So how do we encourage humans like her to care about all animals—the ones they eat, wear, and so on?"

Laurel bashfully turns away and clenches her jaw. "I can only imagine how awful you think I am for eating other animals."

"No," Persimmon answers quickly, smiling warmly. "I used to eat other animals, too."

"It never occurred to me to think about it from the fishes' perspective. I mean, I never killed a fish myself. I've been with Dr. Misra since I was a baby. She's always just given me a pile of meat and I've eaten it without a further thought. In the beginning, I didn't even realize it was another animal. Even when I found out, since I never saw that animal begging for her life as she was killed, I never understood how terrified the animals must be when they die—much less the pain they go through before and during their deaths."

"So, you've been here at Dr. Misra's house since you were a baby?"

Laurel stands up on her four legs. She hasn't told this story in a long time. She liked not having to think about it. "Yes, my mother and sister were hit by a car when I was very, very young, but my brother and I survived. A nice person found us alive in the road, sitting by our slain family and brought us to Dr. Misra's house. When we got old enough, Dr. Misra released us into the woods. My brother ran off, but I told him that I was done trying to survive in the woods. I ran right back to Dr. Misra's house. She then released me deeper into the woods, but I found my way back again. Sneaky me! The woods were super scary, and her house was always so cozy that I never wanted to leave it. She realized she couldn't get rid of me, so she let me stay, and I've been here ever since. It may sound odd to you, but I feel like Dr. Misra is my mother."

"Goodness gracious in heaven!" Dr. Misra steps into the room with Lyric at her feet and is shocked to find not only Persimmon's cage open but Laurel sitting inside the cage *with* Persimmon.

"What are you two scamps doing?" Dr. Misra rushes over to the cage. She quickly puts down the plates of food on the nearby table and places gloves on her hands. She holds up some fish to entice Laurel. "Laurel, you need to come out of there. She's a wild animal and can easily hurt you."

Laurel sits in the cage, not moving.

Dr. Misra puts the fish down and reaches into the cage toward Laurel. "Chickadee, you're gonna get yourself injured. Please step away from that raccoon."

Laurel bats away Dr. Misra's gloved hand. "We're fine. I'm not coming out!"

"Laurel," Dr. Misra scolds. "What has gotten into you?"

Lyric hops up and down trying to see what's going on. He loves all this drama and wants to be in on it. "Persimmon, Laurel, what are you two doing up there?"

Dr. Misra looks down at the rambunctious skunk. "Apparently, your sister has become a defiant teenager overnight."

Dr. Misra examines the two raccoons sitting calmly in the cage. Neither is showing any aggression toward the other. In fact, when she and Lyric entered the room, the two raccoons seemed like two kids having a slumber party.

Dr. Misra throws her hands up playfully. "I tell ya, I don't know who's in charge around here anymore. Me or all of you? What am I supposed to do, just leave all the cages open for every wild animal who prances in here?"

Dr. Misra looks directly at Persimmon and points her finger at her. "Okay fine, have your fun. But if I find any chewed-up shoes or poopy lying around, it's back in the cage. Got it?"

The vet plops the food dish in Persimmon's cage and places the plates in the other raccoon's and opossum's cages, too, although she closes those back up. She then leaves the room talking to herself. "When did this go from being a hospital to a hotel?"

Lyric stands on his hind legs with his mouth wide open. He shakes his tail at Persimmon and Laurel. "Troublemakers! You hit her glove, Laurel. Talk about sassy! What have you two been talking about all night?"

Persimmon and Laurel look down at Lyric through the cage. "Nothing," Laurel answers shyly. "Just talking."

"Why are you acting weird?" Lyric looks confused and then smirks. "Hold on, were you two making out?!"

"No!" Laurel yells at Lyric. "Go away. We're having a private conversation."

"What's 'making out'?" Persimmon asks.

"Oh my gosh, you were!" Lyric flops onto his side, rolling around. "Scandalous!"

Persimmon has an idea of what Lyric is suggesting and suddenly feels embarrassed. She thought it was all innocent, just two raccoons getting to know each other, but maybe there was something more going on. When Laurel put her paw around Persimmon, it felt more than comforting; it felt right.

Persimmon notices Laurel staring at her, but then she realizes Laurel is actually staring *past* her.

Persimmon turns around to see Derpoke leaning against the window screen. How long has he been there watching? She sees the mortified look on his face, and she has her answer. That's the look of someone whose heart has just broken into a million pieces.

31

PERSIMMON HOBBLES OUT of her cage and over to the window. As she nears the screen, Derpoke pulls away.

"What's going on?" Derpoke asks. There's a deep sadness in his voice.

Persimmon completely avoids the awkwardness of the moment. "Derpoke, hey! You haven't had a chance to properly meet my new friends, Laurel and Lyric. They're so silly. You're going to love them."

Laurel bounds over. "Hello there! You've been around, but I haven't had the pleasure of getting to know you."

"Hello, Derpoke!" Lyric jumps up and down, attempting to see over the table and out the window. "I'd come and say hi, but with these nails I'm a better digger than I am a climber."

Climbing also requires more energy than Lyric prefers to expend, but he keeps that part to himself.

"Hi," Derpoke says abruptly. His demeanor is cold, which is clear to the other three, causing a palpable discomfort. He turns to his raccoon friend. "Persimmon, can I speak with you alone?"

"Sure." Persimmon feels uneasy. She's pretty sure she knows what he's going to discuss, and she's worried that the conversation will get very uncomfortable very quickly.

Laurel leaps off the table, and she and Lyric trot toward the door.

As they exit, Lyric can be heard saying, "Somebody's crabby, right? Do you think he's always—"

"Shh," Laurel scolds him, realizing Persimmon and Derpoke can most likely still hear them.

The other raccoon and opossum are still in their cages watching the drama unfold. Derpoke peers at them with a perturbed expression, so the raccoon and opossum quickly look away and busy themselves so as not to seem like they're eavesdropping.

Now that Derpoke and Persimmon have some privacy, he asks, "How much longer before your wound heals?"

"Maybe another week."

"I've been doing a lot of thinking." Derpoke doesn't look Persimmon in the eye. "I was hoping when you're able to leave here, maybe we could go home."

"Back to Oak Tree Forest?!" Persimmon is caught off guard. This is not the conversation she thought they would have.

"Yes. With everything we've been through—everything *you've* been through—I think we have to be honest with ourselves. We tried our best to save other animals, but clearly we are in way over our heads."

"You want to quit the rescue missions altogether?!" Persimmon can't believe she's hearing this from Derpoke—her most loyal confidante. "I don't... how can... What about the chickens, Derpoke? They're counting on us to save them. How can we possibly leave them to be killed?"

Derpoke leans against the screen with his two front paws. He's been holding this in for so long it spurts out in a frenzy. "Persimmon, you almost died! *I* almost died. And Bruiser *did* die." Derpoke points at the bandage where Persimmon's leg once was. "Look at you. Your leg was chopped off. Your tail was shot off. If you keep doing these missions, pretty soon there won't be anything left of you."

Derpoke is practically frantic, so Persimmon does her best to calm him down. She leans on her two back legs to balance herself and gently puts her paw against the screen to rest on Derpoke's paw. "I hear what you're saying. I do not take any of this lightly. I miss Bruiser terribly and I know how lucky you and I both are to be alive. But you and I went into that shed together and saw the deplorable conditions. I can't leave those chickens like that. It would be *unforgivable* to leave them like that."

Derpoke leans his head against the screen and closes his eyes, feeling defeated. He sighs. "I can't lose you, Persimmon. I thought I'd lost you once. I can't go through that again. I don't understand, what has to happen to make you realize that we can't save all the other animals from humans?" Derpoke slumps against the windowsill— the weight of his sorrow too heavy to bear. "Do you have to die, Persimmon?"

Persimmon starts to answer him with some comforting words, but stops herself. She looks at her despondent friend crumpled against the screen. The summer sun shines brightly on the grass a few feet behind him. The loud chirping of various bugs fills the air. Leaves rustle in the wind. This beautiful calm reminds Persimmon of Oak Tree Forest. She, Derpoke, and Scraps used to have so much fun playing all night. She longs for that carefree time in their lives.

Persimmon moves her paw to rest where Derpoke's head is pressed against the screen. She caresses his fur.

"I miss Oak Tree Forest, too, Derpoke. I miss laughing with you and Scraps, climbing around the trees. I miss how joyful life felt. But we could go back to Oak Tree Forest right now and it wouldn't be the same. It wasn't as safe as we thought. That trap that I got stuck in? Humans put them all over the forest. We got lucky it didn't happen to us when we were younger. Those days weren't devoid of danger, my friend. We were just naïve then."

Persimmon continues to pat his fur. She hates seeing her sweet friend so forlorn. She wishes the screen weren't between them so she could scoop him up and cuddle with him. But that wouldn't help. What she has to say isn't comforting; it's upsetting. It's the truth.

"I know you don't want to hear this," Persimmon continues. "And it feels extreme to say, but if I die risking my life to save other animals, I am at peace with that."

Persimmon takes a breath. She's never been surer of her commitment to this cause. Coming so close to death didn't make her want to retreat; it made her want to fight harder. There are so few animals on her side fighting to free these other creatures, how could she possibly give up on them? This necessity to keep the missions going is clear to her, but she wants to make sure Derpoke understands why she can't quit.

"Derpoke, if I went back to playing in the woods knowing what I know, I would be just as bad as the humans committing these atrocities. I was able to feel cheerful in Oak Tree Forest because I was oblivious to the horrors happening to other animals all around me. I can't feel that happiness now—not with what I've seen and not until all other animals are free and safe."

Derpoke lifts his head. His eyes are wet with tears. "You can't feel happiness? You sure seemed happy with Laurel a few minutes ago, Persimmon."

Persimmon's heart sinks. It's as if Derpoke slapped her across the face. She looks away from him with her mouth open, at a loss for words.

Derpoke looks right at her. His melancholy twists to anger. "I get it. You can feel happy, just not with me."

Derpoke turns and slumps off the chair. He's uncoordinated, so he tumbles when he hits the ground. He stands back up and hobbles off the porch.

"Derpoke, where are you going?" Persimmon calls after.

Derpoke doesn't answer. He walks through the grass toward the woods.

Persimmon panics. She leans against the screen, tempted to rip through it to reach him. Derpoke seems so distraught, she's not sure what he'll do or if she'll ever see him again.

She yells out again, fearfully. "You're not going back to Oak Tree Forest by yourself, are you?"

Derpoke still doesn't answer. He stops at the edge of the woods, but doesn't turn around.

Persimmon leans her whole body against the window screen, almost popping it out of the frame. "Don't go! You're right. I lost my brother. I lost Bruiser. I don't want to lose you, too. Please, stay!"

Derpoke disappears into the forest.

Persimmon collapses onto the table. She feels drained. *What am I doing? My friends and family either leave me or get killed. Is Derpoke right? Am I leading us all into certain failure?... Giving up isn't the answer, though. Letting all these animals be tortured and killed is not an option... Of course it's not, but how do I lead us to victory?... What does victory even mean, though? It's impossible to save every animal from humans— our rescue missions have so far proved that—and yet we keep fighting and getting killed. So what am I supposed to do?*

Persimmon never felt more lost doing what she knows in her heart is right.

32

THE PIT BULL rescue is underway!

Rawly tugs at the strap on Rasha's collar and it finally comes loose. The heavy collar slides off her neck and lands in the dirt with a thud.

Rasha feels the weight of enslavement crash away from her. *I'm free!*

She sucks in a deep breath. All of a sudden, the air smells so fresh. For the first time in her life, she is in control of her own fate. Until this moment, Coach controlled everything—what she ate, when she ate, and how long she stayed chained up in the harsh weather. Worst of all, he forced her to brutalize other dogs. Now, though, all of that ends.

All over the yard, the same moment is playing out under the moonlight. Every dog is experiencing freedom for the first time, and it's the sweetest nectar they've ever tasted. They want to howl in celebration, but they know that they can't for fear of waking Coach, Dale, and Coach's wife, Jean.

"Thank you, Rawly," Rasha says as she licks his head. "I will always be grateful to you."

Rawly blushes under his fur. He loves these moments. There's nothing more gratifying than watching other creatures bask in the glow of freedom—especially when they never thought it possible.

"No need to thank me," Rawly says. "Anyone who comes across a place like this should want to get you out of here. I hate these humans for what they did to you."

"You and me both," Rasha says. "I have to go see my father. Thank you again."

Rawly smiles as Rasha rushes over to Chopper. Rawly is amazed at how far he's come in such a short time. Not too long ago he would have seen dogs like these as enemies. Now they're licking him on the head. Bruiser was a great ambassador and Rawly hopes to cross paths with him again. Sadly, Rawly has no idea that this will never come to pass.

Rasha sprints up to Chopper. His collar has already been removed, but he's still lying on the ground unable to walk because of his grave injuries. For the first time in both of their lives, Rasha is able to lick and nuzzle him. Finally being affectionate with her father is heartwarming, but the moment is overshadowed by the somber circumstances.

"Papa," Rasha says. "We're free!"

Without rising, Chopper licks her face. "We're free, youngin'. I never thought I'd live to see the day."

"The humans can't hurt us anymore," Rasha says. She wishes she could revel in this life-changing experience more, but now that she's closer to Chopper, she sees how serious his wounds are. It may be too late. Chopper may be Coach's last victim.

"We need to get you far away from this house, Papa," Rasha says. "Soon after we kill Coach, Dale, and Jean, I'm sure that other humans will swarm the yard. When that happens, we can't be anywhere near here. Are you able to walk?"

Chopper surveys the gashes covering his body. Moving will be excruciatingly painful, but if he wants to set foot outside this yard, he'll have to fight through it.

Chopper rolls onto his stomach, groaning loudly as the dirt crunches into his wounds. With all his might, he pushes his legs against the ground and attempts to lift his body. A sharp pain shoots through his left shoulder and he crumples to the dirt again.

"Dang it!" Chopper growls as he kicks at the dirt. "I been here my whole life, Rasha. Fighting. Killing. I don't wanna die here. I *can't* die here."

"You won't." Rasha licks his forehead. "I'm not leaving you. We'll do it at your pace."

Rasha tries not to get discouraged. Assuming that this raid goes well, Vincent revealed that The Dissidents would move on to freeing dogs in nearby fighting yards, and Rasha is holding out hope that she can reunite with her siblings—Afilia, Minton, Jax, and Remington.

Rasha knows it's a long shot. What are the chances that her siblings are even still alive much less held at a nearby yard? But now that she's finally free, anything feels possible.

Rasha hears a commotion among the dogs around them, so she looks up to see what the murmuring is about. Through the gate comes the first batch of dogs from the forest. They're carrying the carcasses of the dogs in their teeth. She knows about Vincent's plan, but seeing the battered bodies is still shocking.

She stands there, frozen with shame. *Are any of those dogs* my *victims?*

The yard fills with dogs carrying corpses of all the fallen dogs— ghosts of her victims come back to haunt her.

All the forced fights flash through her mind. All the violence. All the screaming for mercy. Every single fight was brutal, but that first fight plagues her the most.

33

RASHA'S FIGHT, PART 5

INTO THE PIT

(LESS THAN A YEAR AGO)

THE NIGHT HAS come: Rasha's first official fight.

She's been training for weeks, and Coach is eager to show off his new "killer." Rasha put on a good front that the training had toughened her up, but deep down, she's as gentle as ever, so she trembles as she sits in her shelter.

Rasha watches people stroll down the path and into the shed. She's seen this many times before, but everything feels different now that she's the one going into that pit.

She is repulsed to see the humans so cheerful. *I may die tonight, but for them, this is an entertaining night out. Are they really that devoid of compassion?* She already knows the answer to that question, though.

Rasha has seen a lot of these men attending other fights. The "dogmen," as they call themselves, are a tight-knit group. It's risky business fighting dogs, so they make certain that they vet everyone who attends.

Rasha watches as the visitors pay the entrance fee to the man guarding the shed door. Coach keeps this money as compensation for hosting the fight. It's one more way for him to get rich off this dubious operation.

In the past few weeks, on top of the training that Coach and Dale forced on Rasha, Chopper has given her some pointers on how to fight. Rasha felt disgusted learning techniques for hurting another dog, but she knew it would be foolish not to accept his help. Despite Chopper's aversion to this life they're forced to lead, he is a seasoned fighter and has learned tricks to throw off other dogs, as well as where to bite them for the most impact.

Even though Rasha is reluctant to fight, she's felt her aggression growing as this day has neared. At first she was alarmed—and ashamed—thinking that the training itself was making her meaner, but Chopper explained that the shots the humans had given her were filled with drugs, like steroids, that make even the nicest dogs vicious. *As always, at every turn, these humans are trying to coerce me into being a killer.* The drugs scare her even more than Coach's other training strategies, because the drugs change who she is from the inside—corrupting her mind, not just her body.

Of course, Coach is more than happy to defile Rasha's body as well. He recently knocked Rasha out with a sedative and ground her teeth with a sander to make them sharper. When Rasha awoke, she was furious. *They're deforming me to make me more lethal. Where does all this depravity end?*

She feels helpless. No matter how hard she resists being transformed into a monster, the humans surprise her with more and more devious tactics. She constantly reminds herself: *I am still me. They do not control me. They cannot change who I am as a dog.*

Tonight, as Rasha watches the degenerate humans enter the shed, she tries to stop quivering with fear. *I won't be able to properly defend myself if my paws are shaking.*

It's no use, though. It's impossible not to be riddled with anxiety. She's afraid of dying, but even more so, she's afraid of what she'll have to do to survive.

Chopper has warned her over and over—desperately—that she must go into this fight with a tough attitude. He doesn't want to hurt other dogs either—none of the dogs *wants* to fight—but he knows that if you go into a fight without cutthroat ferocity, then you'll end up chewed to pieces or with a bullet in your head—or both. He's gravely concerned that this will happen to Rasha, which is why he's done his best to train her with his most effective fighting techniques. Deep down, though, he knows that she is too kind for the fighting life. He would never reveal it to her, but he assumes that tonight will be the last night he will ever see her.

The parade of men entering the shed trickles to one or two stragglers when Rasha realizes: *They're all here. The fight's about to begin.*

Sure enough, Coach and Dale step out of the shed and into the grass toward Rasha. Her heart races even faster.

"Be strong, Rasha," Chopper says from behind her. "Follow the approach I taught you. You cannot lose."

Rasha is too nervous to look back at him or even respond.

Coach isn't wearing his usual clothing with the school eagle mascot on it. For the fights, he likes to make an impression with the other dogmen, so he's wearing a shirt and tie. Dale has a tie, too, but his shirt and pants are ill-fitting. Clearly Coach insisted his nephew dress up, and Dale threw on whatever he could find that resembled something formal.

The two men shine their flashlights toward Rasha.

"There she is!" Coach says. "There's our champion."

As the men approach, Sadie steps as far as she can toward Rasha. "You won't be able to cheat your way out of this one, Rasha."

"Shut up!" Chopper snarls at Sadie.

Sadie grins at Rasha and steps back to her doghouse door.

Rasha is shaken. She wants to yell at Sadie for being so pathetically spiteful, but she holds back. What's the use?

"Don't pay no attention to her, Rasha," Chopper says comfortingly. "You're the toughest fighter I know. Focus on *this* fight. Remember to keep calm and let the other dog lose from her uncontrolled temper."

Dale attaches the leash to Rasha's collar and escorts her toward the shed.

Chopper calls after her, overcome with emotion. "I love ya, Rasha. I believe in ya. There's nothin' wrong with defending yourself. Remember, you're not a killer. You're a survivor."

Rasha won't let herself off that easy, but this is no time to debate the issue. This is the time to say goodbye. No one has been as supportive and helpful to her survival as her father, so she wants him to know that.

"Thank you for everything, Papa," Rasha says. "I want—"

Dale yanks on Rasha's leash, choking her. "Do you two ever shut up?"

Rasha coughs from the collar strangling her. She can't get another word to come out. She then realizes that she's facing the shed. Panic sets in. The rickety building looms over her ominously. *That is where I'm going to die—only a few feet from where I spent my entire life.* She can feel herself walking toward the wooden structure, but she feels like she's in a dream watching herself from above.

After months of languishing on that chain, two intense test fights and weeks of grueling training, this is the moment. She is about to fight a dog she's never met. One of them will die tonight, and Rasha knows that she doesn't have it in her to kill. Which is why before every fight, she has desperately tried to conjure a clever plan to get out of it. *I'm a smart dog. I know I can come up with something. I need a moment to focus, though.* Unfortunately, time is running out.

*   *   *

Coach kicks open the shed door and Dale leads Rasha inside. Her nose is assaulted by a mixture of nauseating smells: sweat, cheap cologne, and pot.

A hush comes over the room. More than a dozen men are in the shed, and they're excited to see the new contender. The room pulses with malice.

Another female pit bull growls viciously in Rasha's direction.

Rasha jumps back. The young man holding the other dog on a chain tugs hard to keep the dog from attacking Rasha.

"Hold on, Viper," Marcus says. "You'll get your chance. Damn Coach, you sure you got the right dog? This one's about to pee herself."

All four of the young men standing near Viper laugh.

Rasha grimaces at Marcus's insulting comment. *It's easy to act tough when you're not the one who's about to fight for your life.*

Marcus and his friends are in their early twenties. He and one of his friends used to be on Coach's football team. They were a few years ahead of Dale at the same high school, although they certainly didn't hang out with him. In fact, if he hadn't been Coach's nephew, they would have picked on him just like they did his "loser" friends. Those memories aren't lost on Dale, so he's looking forward to seeing Rasha pummel their dog.

"Keep joking, Marcus," Coach says. "After Rasha gets through stomping your dog, maybe I'll whoop your ass, too."

"Ooooh!" All the men in the room laugh.

"Enough play time," Coach says. "Let's get this going."

Rasha hasn't made a sound since entering the room, unlike Viper, whose intimidating low rumble sounds like an engine about to explode.

As Dale leads Rasha through the shed, she peers at Viper. She wants to get a good look at who she's about to fight.

Viper has brown fur and bulging muscles on her legs and chest. *How did she get so strong? Even more important, how am I supposed to compete with her? If she knocks me down, I'll never be able to get back up.*

Viper's thick muscles aren't even her most intimidating feature—that would be her piercing white eyes. This brawny canine is a formidable opponent indeed. Rasha's biggest fear leading up to this fight had been harming another dog, but now the more immediate fear is being shred to pieces.

Dale stops Rasha in front of a scale and attaches her harness to a metal pole. Rasha is lifted off the ground and the two teams check her weight. They do the same with Viper. Both groups of men nod. As agreed upon, the dogs are of equal weight.

Dale lifts Rasha into a metal tub. Her heart is still racing, so she tries to calm herself by focusing on the process. *I remember this part. Chopper told me they'd wash me down.* Her father told her not only the best techniques for winning but also exactly what to expect when she was taken into the shed so she wouldn't be rattled. He explained that the humans wash each dog's fur in case one of the humans put any toxic substances on it. The chemicals sicken the other dog or deter the other dog from biting because of the fur's bad taste. Chopper said these dogfighting men are known to use all kinds of shady tricks to give their dogs an edge.

Dale walks over to Viper while Marcus steps over to Rasha. Each young man picks up a sponge from the tub, and Coach opens a bottle of liquid nearby. It's a mixture of warm cow's milk, baking soda, water, and vinegar. Coach pours the contents onto both dogs. The foul smell irritates Rasha's nose. Marcus and Dale wash their respective dogs with the sponges.

Rasha feels violated. *These humans grab us and handle us dogs like we're objects. I'm supposed to let him run his hands all over my body?*

Rasha isn't hateful by nature, but her disdain for humans grows stronger every time she's forced to interact with them.

A young man standing over Marcus says to him, "Make sure you wash her off real good."

"Chill, man," Marcus says. "This is Coach. He doesn't cheat. He's a legend. Probably the best dogman in this area."

"Probably?" Coach snaps back. "I am."

"You might be slipping, though, Coach. Look at this dog. Why are you bringing a sweet little puppy to a dog fight?"

Marcus's friends laugh.

"All right," Coach says. "Keep trash talking all you want, but we'll see what happens when they get in that pit."

"Oh we'll see what happens all right," Marcus retorts. "Your dog won't be looking so cute after Viper gets through with her."

Rasha ignores the men's cruel showboating. She's too busy staring at that pit, dreading the moment she'll be placed inside.

This whole time she has felt Viper glaring at her. That dog hasn't taken her eyes off her since she entered the room.

I don't think I'm gonna make it through this one. Look at her; she's pure muscle. And she seems so irate. With Sadie, I could tell her anger toward me was all for show, but this dog, she looks like she can't wait to dig her teeth into my flesh... Stop thinking like that. You're thinking like a coward. She's as afraid as you are. She's just better at hiding it. No dog wants to fight. She's just more determined to win than you are... How can I be determined to win?! I don't want to be here. I'm not vicious. These humans are vicious. They should be the ones fighting. Not us dogs.

Rasha's anger is boiling over, but she knows this is no time to dwell on her hatred toward these humans. Time is running out. She must come up with an escape plan. *I could fake being sick. Just fall over and start shaking... No, then they'd shoot me for being useless... I could tell Viper that I don't want to fight. We could turn on the humans and bite our way out of here... No, you fool. That didn't work with Sadie, so it certainly won't work with this dog you've never even met... Think. Come on. There has to be a way out of this.*

Rasha's nerves are clouding her judgment. She can barely breathe much less conjure up a clever getaway.

The men finish washing the dogs, and the dogs shake off the excess liquid.

Dale lifts Rasha over the wooden wall. As she's placed on the dirt, she suddenly feels very alone. She examines the scratch marks on the wall. *That dog is dead. That's what happens when you try to run away from this. That's me. Today, I will die.*

Coach crouches beside Rasha as Dale steps out of the pit.

"You got this, girl," Coach whispers. "You're a champion. When you're through with that dog, I don't wanna recognize her. You got it?"

Rasha feels sick. She tries her best to hide her shaking paws from Coach.

A man steps into the middle of the pit. He's a friend of both Coach and Marcus, and he'll be acting as referee.

The men in the room start shouting out bets to one another.

"$2,000 on Viper!"

"$3,000 on Viper!"

Everyone's betting on Viper. They see how robust she is and how she's growling ferociously at Rasha. They can't imagine puppy-dog-looking Rasha could win this one. Only Coach and Dale have $4,000 on Rasha, and even Dale is nervous about losing, although he hasn't said as much to Coach. He knows Coach would disown him if he showed doubt. If Coach is against one thing, it's thinking like a loser.

Each dog stands behind the white chalk line on her side of the pit. Viper keeps lunging and barking at Rasha.

"She's ready to go!" Marcus yells. "This one's ours, boys. Drinks are on me tonight!"

Rasha stares ahead. She doesn't look Viper in the eyes. She just keeps Viper in her peripheral vision in case she breaks free from Marcus's grip.

Everything in Rasha's body is telling her to run—to jump out of this pit. But there's only one way she's leaving this pit alive. There is no clever escape plan. There is only violence.

Rasha knows what she must do. For the first time since they met, she looks Viper directly in the eyes. Viper growls even louder. Rasha doesn't flinch. *Forgive me.*

"Both sides ready?" the referee asks.

Coach and Marcus nod. Rasha's paws are trembling so much, it feels like the ground is shaking.

"Face your dogs," the ref says. "Three... two... one... go!"

Rasha and Viper dart to the middle of the pit and slam into each other. Viper is so heavy and powerful that Rasha trips back into the dirt. Viper pounces on Rasha, biting down into her right shoulder.

The men shout with glee.

Rasha quickly bites at Viper's stomach, and the dog swivels to avoid the blow. Viper bites down hard on the back of Rasha's neck. Blood trickles onto Rasha's gray fur.

"Get up, Rasha!" Coach hollers.

Viper jumps on Rasha, bearing down heavily on Rasha's back as she bites harder and harder.

"It's over, baby!" A young man from Viper's side yells as he high fives another man. "This is gonna be a quick one!"

Marcus kneels beside the two dogs. "Kill her, Viper! Murder that bitch!"

"Fight out of it, Rasha!" Coach fumes.

Each bite stings worse than the last. Rasha feels like she is being stung by a thousand wasps over and over. Blood pours from the back of her neck onto the dirt.

Just then, Rasha twists around and chomps down onto Viper's throat. Viper tries to shake free, but Rasha holds on with a powerful grip.

"That's it, girl!" Coach yells. "Keep biting!"

Viper shakes her head and breaks free of Rasha's hold, stepping away from her for a moment. Rasha stands back up and faces Viper. She wants the fight to be over. Her neck hurts like hell. She doesn't want to fight anymore, but it's only just begun.

Viper lunges at Rasha again and their faces smack into each other. Each dog chews on the other dog's lip, nose, whatever they can bite into. Viper gets a hold of Rasha's ear and shreds the end off.

Rasha yelps.

"Oh, she got her good!" a young man calls out joyfully.

Each time a person shouts out something in celebration of Rasha's injuries, it angers her more. Her survival mode has kicked in. She just wants to get out of this alive. Her fatal flaw is that she's fighting defensively. She still doesn't want to hurt Viper. Meanwhile, Viper is aiming for the kill shots.

The fight goes on for a half hour, forty-five minutes—it feels endless. Both dogs are panting heavily. They're not attacking as swiftly. Their legs feel heavier. The pit walls are smeared with blood. The dirt is caked with it. Two of Rasha's teeth chipped when the dogs' mouths slammed together. Her neck is covered with bite marks. Her skin and fur are tattered. The dogs teeter when they stand.

Viper bites down hard on Rasha's left ear, which is already torn into strings of raw flesh. Rasha yelps and twists away.

"She turned!" the ref yells. "Back to your corners."

Coach and Marcus grab their dogs and pull them back to their corners. The fight has been broken up a few times. It's a short reprieve, but at least it's a break.

Rasha pants—she can hardly breathe.

"What the hell is wrong with you, Rasha?" Coach steams. "Kill her. Rip her damn throat out. Do you want a bullet in your head? I trained you better than this. My dogs are champions. You're not acting like a damn champion."

Rasha is burning with hatred. *What do you want from me?! My whole body is bitten to pieces. Why don't you get out there and fight, if you're so tough?*

"Both sides ready?" the referee asks.

Coach and Marcus nod. Rasha is the dog who turned away, so she'll be released first. If she doesn't run into the middle of the pit, she'll lose. She's tempted not to. She'll be shot in the head and this whole savage life will end. But there's something deep inside her that won't let her give up. *I want to live. I want to live.*

"Face your dogs. Three... two... one... go!"

Viper and Rasha rush to the center of the ring with all the energy they have left. Just before the two dogs bang into each other, Rasha ducks and clamps her jaw onto Viper's left front leg. Rasha shakes her head violently until she hears a loud crack.

Viper screeches in pain and falls onto the dirt.

Rasha stands over her, but doesn't attack further. Viper rolls around as she howls.

"It's over!" Coach yells as he hugs Dale. "I told you she was a killer. Did you see the power of that jaw?!"

Coach pats Rasha on the head and leads her back to their side of the pit. "Good job, girl! I knew you could do it."

Rasha sighs. It's finished. She survived. If no one were around, she'd cry.

"Hold on, hold on," Marcus says to the referee. "It ain't over."

"She's got a broken leg, Marcus," the ref explains.

"She ain't dead, though, right?" Marcus says. "She's still moving, right?"

"Uh…" The referee looks over at Coach.

"You're kidding," Coach says. He motions for Dale to restrain Rasha at their side of the pit and then walks over to the referee who's near the injured Viper. "Look at this dog. She can't even stand up."

Marcus steps up to Coach. "But she ain't dead. I'm not forfeiting. She can still fight. Let's go one more time. If she doesn't run to the center, then we'll call it. But she's a soldier. I know you fight fair, Coach. You don't want people saying you ended a fight early."

Coach grits his teeth. "I remember on that football field, I always told you never to give up—even if it's the fourth quarter and we're losing by three touchdowns. Maybe I taught you too well. Now you don't know when you've lost. But if you wanna play this out when your dog can't even walk, that's on you."

Rasha can't believe what she's hearing. *More?! What more can I do?* But she knows the answer to that. They want to see this dog murdered. This night doesn't end until one of these dogs isn't breathing. She was so close to finishing this fight, but there's no getting out so easily. Nothing about this life is easy.

Coach and Marcus crouch beside the dogs behind their chalk lines.

Rasha peers at Viper at the other side of the pit. For the first time, Viper's eyes don't have that venomous expression. She just looks like a scared dog. Rasha pities her.

Rasha lets out a long sigh and calls out to Viper, "I'm sorry."

Viper looks confused. She's never experienced compassion before, especially from a dog she's being forced to fight. Is this a trick? But Rasha looks so sincere. For a brief moment, Viper glimpses the kinder life she could have had. She doesn't want to fight. She never has. She wants to rest. She wants someone to mend her broken leg. She wants to be free. But soon, one of them will be dead, and despite her debilitating injury, Viper is determined that it will not be her. She *must* fight.

Rasha sees Viper's eyes turn back to icy rage. *She's still not giving up.* Rasha dreads what she has to do.

"Face your dogs," the referee says. "Three… two… one… go!"

Viper is let go first since the fight stopped because of her injury. She hobbles to the middle of the pit, growling, trying to intimidate, but it's tragic to see this mutilated dog attempt to be brave.

Coach lets go of Rasha. As Rasha nears her opponent, she pretends to bend down to attack Viper's good front leg. Viper leans down to protect her leg, which is exactly what Rasha wants. She leaps into the air, lands on the injured dog, and crunches down on the back of Viper's neck.

Rasha squeezes harder and harder until Viper finally yells out. "Please! I give up! Stop! You win!"

Rasha chews and chews on Viper's flesh, tearing deep gashes into her neck and head.

"Please!" Viper begs. "You win! Please, stop!"

Tears stream down Rasha's face. She wishes she was skilled enough to kill this dog quickly and put her out of her misery, but Rasha just keeps ripping into Viper's skin, hoping the humans will call the fight.

Viper squeals as Rasha continues her attack. A gaping hole in the back of Viper's neck will soon expose her bone.

Finally, the referee puts the breaking stick in Rasha's mouth and yanks her off of Viper. "That's it. Fight's over."

Marcus nods, but kicks the side of the pit. "Stupid dog!"

Coach runs up and leads Rasha to their side of the pit. "Future champion right here, baby! Watch out."

Dale pats Rasha on the head. "Good job, girl. You kicked that dog's ass."

Rasha crumbles to the dirt, spent emotionally and physically.

Coach walks over to Marcus. "Hey, no hard feelings. It was a hell of a fight."

"We're good," Marcus says.

"You want us to take care of your dog or do you want to do it?" Coach asks as he points to the .38 Special revolver in his holster.

"She embarrassed herself tonight," Marcus says. "Crying like a bitch. Forget the gun, let's give her a nice jolt."

Coach nods and turns to Dale. "Put Rasha on the operating table. I'll fix her up while you set up the shock treatment for Viper."

"You got it, Coach," Dale says. He walks over to pick up Rasha.

Rasha knows what the "shock treatment" is. Chopper told her. They'll shoot electricity through Viper's body. It's a painful way to go. *Hasn't she been through enough tonight?*

Rasha is riddled with guilt. Her face is covered with Viper's blood. She can taste it in her mouth. She looks at Viper, who is sprawled out on the ground with her tongue dangling out. Viper is panting heavily—her chest pounding up and down.

As Dale carries Rasha past Viper, Rasha wants to say something to her, but what can she say? She's already apologized. It almost seems disingenuous to belabor the point. She stares at the embattled dog, feeling sick with shame. She's hit with a realization that stings worse than any of her wounds: *I'm a killer.*

What disturbs Rasha the most is the inevitability of this moment. No matter how much she resisted being turned into a murderer, this was always going to be the outcome. The only way to stay alive in the dog-fighting world is to kill. She thought she was special somehow, that she could find a way to avoid it. But she's not. She's like all the other dogs out here—doing what they have to do to survive. So now the question is: how does she live with herself?

34

PERSIMMON STRAINS TO pull up her body with her good front leg. It used to be so easy to climb objects like this table leg, but now she feels like her body is made of bricks.

She's been going through rehabilitation all night, with Laurel and Lyric rooting her on—well, Laurel's been directing the physical therapy while Lyric lounges around watching.

Persimmon finally gives up, releases her grip and plops onto the ground.

Laurel rushes up to her. "Are you okay?"

"I'm wonderful." Persimmon sighs loudly. "I can barely climb a table. I should survive perfectly fine out in the forest."

"You're doing great," Laurel assures. "Right, Lyric?"

Lyric is daydreaming as he lies sprawled out on the rug. "What? Oh yes, amazing. Stupendous! Marvel—"

"She gets it." Laurel shakes her head. She turns back to Persimmon. "Why don't you take a break for a bit and then you can try again?"

Persimmon lies on her side and huffs. "I'm done for now. It's morning. I want to sleep. Besides, what's the point? I'll never be able to climb the same way again."

Laurel hunkers down beside Persimmon on the rug. "This isn't just about how hard it is to get around on three legs, is it? You're upset about Derpoke."

"He's been gone for days," Persimmon says. "He's never rushed off like that alone. He was so upset. What if he doesn't come back?"

"He'll come back. I saw the way he clung to you when you two arrived. That opossum is head over heels for you."

Persimmon hasn't heard the expression "head over heels" before, but she can infer Laurel's meaning. If only Laurel knew Derpoke was jealous of *her*, but Persimmon wouldn't dare reveal that. Persimmon isn't even sure how Laurel feels about her.

Persimmon changes the subject. "No, he's agitated that I still want to keep The Enlighteners' missions going. He thinks they're too dangerous."

"Well, from everything you've told me about these rescue operations, they do seem awfully dangerous..."

Persimmon shoots Laurel a stony look.

"Hold on." Laurel puts her paws up in surrender. "I know better than to try to talk you out of these missions, but maybe there's a way to do them that isn't so hazardous."

"I've been mulling over that very problem since the beginning of these missions, but so far everything I try goes awry. I'm open to suggestions, but for the chicken rescue, we're running out of time. Every day that I'm in this house is one day longer that the chickens are languishing in those disgusting sheds, and worse, it's one day closer to their deaths. I don't—"

"Excuse me! EXCUSE ME!"

A voice calls down from across the room. Persimmon and Laurel stop talking and look up at the cage near the door. Inside the cage is a little brown bat standing at attention and glaring at them. Thus far, they haven't interacted with him much because he's been recovering from a severe injury and he's mostly been resting. But today, he's wide awake and perturbed.

"Have you not noticed?" the bat continues. "It's morning. Time for quiet. Time for sleep. Thank you very much."

The bat crawls up the inside of the cage with his tiny feet, dangles himself upside down and wraps his wings around his body.

Persimmon and Laurel are intrigued by this critter, so they bounce over to the table and crawl up to his cage. Persimmon struggles to pull herself up, so Laurel lifts her. The two raccoons peer into the cage.

"Hello?" Laurel says. "My name is Laurel, and this is my friend Persimmon. Oh, and that's our other friend Lyric down there."

Lyric stands on his hind legs to get a better view of the bat.

Laurel continues. "We haven't had a chance to chat since you've been healing, so—"

"When the wings are closed, I'm closed for business," the bat says without opening his wings. "Come back some other time. Thank you very much."

Persimmon and Laurel look at each other. They shrug and step away from the cage. The bat peeks out of his wings and sees the two raccoons departing. He quickly flaps open his wings. "If you insist, I suppose I can converse briefly, but then I really must get some shut-eye."

Persimmon and Laurel turn back.

"The name is Senator Santiago. Pleased to make your acquaintance."

"Very nice to meet you," Laurel says. "You've been so out of it since you arrived, I'm interested to hear how you ended up in Dr. Misra's care."

"Ah yes, a silly mistake, really," Senator Santiago says. "A plethora of insects is always buzzing around those electric bug-zapper gadgets, so I tend to linger around them for meals. This time, unfortunately, I got a little too close—and zap! I got greedy. I am not proud of this."

"That sounds like an electric experience." Lyric grins really big and looks at everyone to see if they're laughing. No one is.

"Poor taste, sir," Senator Santiago says. "I don't see the humor in almost dying. Alert the doctor. I am ready to depart."

"Wait, he's sorry," Laurel says. She glares down at her friend and motions for him to apologize.

"Sorry, Santiago," Lyric says.

"It's *Senator* Santiago. I didn't spend all that time working my way up the ranks in the colony just to have a disrespectful skunk drop my title on a whim."

Lyric crouches, embarrassed.

"Hello?" Suddenly, a human voice is heard coming from the porch at the front door. None of the animals is close enough to the window to see who it is.

"Dr. Misra?" the voice continues. "Are you there?"

Persimmon, Laurel, Lyric, Senator Santiago, and the opossum all freeze in fear. Persimmon gets an eerie feeling. She recognizes this voice somehow. *Why does that voice sound so familiar?*

They hear Dr. Misra's footsteps heading toward the front door and then the front door opening.

"What a surprise!" Dr. Misra is heard saying. "So wonderful to see you, Gavin!"

Persimmon's heart skips a beat. *Gavin?! Oh my goodness, that's the little boy who set the trap. Why is he here? Is he coming to take me back?!*

35

PERSIMMON, LAUREL, LYRIC, Senator Santiago, and the opossum listen as Dr. Misra lets Gavin in. The boy's voice sends shivers throughout Persimmon's body. She must have heard him speaking when she was blacked out and she suddenly feels as if she's back in that trap with the metal clamp biting through her leg.

When Persimmon and her friends hear the two humans coming their way, she, Laurel, and Lyric rush to the other end of the room by the window. The three of them hide under the table in the darkness. If the boy tries to grab Persimmon, she is prepared to bite him and rip her way through that window screen regardless of whether her wound has healed.

Dr. Misra escorts the 11-year-old boy into the room and they stop at the doorway.

"Oh cool!" Gavin says. "A bat!"

Gavin reaches for the cage, and Senator Santiago instantly hops down from his perch and crouches into a ball at the bottom of the cage.

Dr. Misra stops the boy's hand. "Be gentle, dear. Remember, these are wild animals, so we don't want to upset them."

Gavin puts his hands in his pockets. "Yes, ma'am. Sorry. Where's the raccoon?"

The two humans survey the room and notice the two raccoons and skunk huddled under the table.

"There they are!" Gavin yells. "Aw, that sucks. They're hiding. Do you think they're scared of me?"

"Well, they're cautious around strangers, as they should be. Perhaps if we get some treats they'll come out to say hello."

Dr. Misra steps out of the room and Gavin follows.

"Should we make a run for it?" Lyric asks in a panic.

"No," Laurel says. "Dr. Misra wouldn't let him do anything to us. Persimmon, are you okay?"

Persimmon remains quiet. She feels a bit sick being confronted with this boy who played a major role in such a traumatic experience in her life. Part of her wants to run up and scratch the boy for what happened to Bruiser, but from the way Derpoke explained it, Gavin's father was the aggressor. That said, the boy still set the trap that started the tragic sequence of events, so she'd prefer never to see him again. And yet, here he is. *Why exactly is he here, though?*

Dr. Misra and Gavin walk back through the doorway, the vet carrying a plate of mangoes. Gavin sits down on the ground and the vet hands him the plate. The boy holds out a piece of mango.

"Come on, I got some tasty treats for ya!"

Lyric licks his lips. "Oh, what a cruel trick. Mangoes are my favorite."

"Lyric, don't even think about it." Laurel scolds. "That's the little boy who hurt Persimmon and her friends."

Lyric sighs and crouches again.

"Dang it," Gavin complains. "They don't like me." Gavin puts the mango back on the plate. "I can't believe the raccoon is out of its cage, though. That's so cool it's doing better!"

"We don't call animals 'it,' dear," Dr. Misra says. "She is a she, and yes, she's doing much better. In fact, I'll be taking those stitches out in a few days."

Persimmon perks up. *I can finally rescue the chickens! Hooray!*

"Are you gonna put it... I mean *her* back in the woods?" Gavin asks.

"Unfortunately, not," Dr. Misra says.

Persimmon gives Laurel a surprised look, but Laurel pats her on the back.

"Don't worry," Laurel says. "I'm good for my word. We'll sneak you out of here the moment those stitches are out."

Dr. Misra continues. "I can't release her back into the wild because she'd have too much trouble surviving in the woods with only three legs. She's still young enough to have babies, and if she tried to have them, she wouldn't be able to carry them or feed them properly, so they'd starve to death."

"Babies?!" Persimmon scoffs. "Who has time for babies when you're busy saving lives?"

"What happened to that possum I brought in with her?" Gavin asks.

"He's an opossum, not a possum," Dr. Misra says. "Both are marsupials, but possums live in places like Australia and New Zealand. To answer your question, I released him back into the woods since he didn't have any injuries. Although, that scamp keeps coming back here to snoop on my patients."

"Really?!" Gavin laughs. "I bet he does. He would not let that raccoon go. Do you think he wanted to eat her?"

"Oh no, I think they're friends."

Persimmon looks down at the ground sorrowfully. *My sweet Derpoke. I miss you so much.*

"I wish they'd let me pet them," Gavin says. "They look so fuzzy." Gavin looks up at Dr. Misra. "Do you think the raccoon hates me for setting that trap? I didn't mean to... I mean, I meant to, but I feel bad about it now."

Persimmon can't believe her ears. She knows the boy saved her life by bringing her and Derpoke to the vet's house, but she never understood why he did that. What a breath of fresh air to hear that he regrets setting the trap.

Gavin grins. "Oh boy, I finally told my dad I'm never going hunting again. Holy crap, did he get angry. That's about the angriest I've seen him. But I stood up to him. You would have been proud of me."

"I *am* proud of you, dear," Dr. Misra says. "That was brave of you. Your father's quite imposing."

"Yeah, he whooped me real good, but I didn't even flinch. I told him 'harder.'" Gavin laughs.

"Hmm." Dr. Misra pats the boy on his head. "If he gives you any more trouble about not going hunting, let me know. Got it?"

At that moment, Persimmon walks out from under the table and takes a few steps toward Gavin. Dr. Misra points for Gavin to check out the raccoon's approach. Gavin turns his head, and when he sees the raccoon making her way toward him, he brightens and whispers to Dr. Misra. "Oh my gosh!"

Gavin quickly picks up the piece of mango and holds it out for Persimmon. "That's right. It's for *you*."

"Persimmon, what are you doing?!" Laurel calls out. She's half tempted to rush out and pull the raccoon back to safety under the table.

"It's okay," Persimmon says. "Stay there."

Persimmon gets about a half foot from Gavin. She looks up at the boy. She still feels anger toward him for the pain he caused her and her friends. If it weren't for him and his father, Persimmon wouldn't be hobbling around on three legs, and more importantly, Bruiser would still be alive. But despite all that, she knows what she has to do. She just needs to find the courage to do it.

Persimmon looks Gavin in the eyes and says, "I forgive you."

She accepts the mango as a peace offering and eats it.

"Oh wow!" Gavin turns to Dr. Misra. "She likes it."

"I think you just made a new friend," Dr. Misra says.

Persimmon sighs. A colossal weight is lifted off her shoulders. She refuses to let hate consume her. *Our rescue missions are an important part of how we're going to save other animals from humans, but they're only a portion. This is the key. This is how we inspire humans to be more compassionate toward us. For all that they have made us other animals suffer, we have to forgive them.*

36

(TWO DAYS LATER)

"WHAAAAT?!" LYRIC IS aghast. He, Persimmon, and Laurel are sitting on the table near the cage where Persimmon sleeps. It's night, so the three are chatting like they usually do until the morning. This time, though, Lyric is in complete disbelief over what Laurel has just revealed. "You can't join The Enlighteners, Laurel! You'll die!"

"Relax," Laurel says. "I'm not joining them forever. I simply want to help the team on this one mission to rescue the chickens."

"But you heard what Persimmon said—many animals have been killed on these missions," Lyric says. "No offense, Persimmon."

Persimmon nods that she doesn't take offense.

"She's standing beside you on *three* legs," Lyric continues. "Is that not an indication of the danger involved?"

"Technically," Persimmon says. "I didn't injure myself on one of our missions. Getting stuck in that trap was a fluke."

"All the more to my point," Lyric responds. "You can just be walking around in the woods and get seriously maimed. The woods are filled with death traps! Don't leave, Laurel. We have everything we could ever want here at Dr. Misra's."

Lyric crawls on all fours toward Laurel. He takes hold of one of her paws and rubs it on his cheek. "Don't go. Don't go."

Laurel gently pats her friend's head. "Lyric, after everything Persimmon has told us about the chickens, I can't sit here in luxury. They need our help."

"Oh no," Lyric says. "You sound like *her*. You say 'luxury' like it's a bad thing." Lyric sits up and holds his plump belly for Persimmon to see. "Do you see this? I'm fat and I LOVE it. Have you ever seen a fat skunk out in the woods? No! You know why? Because we're all starving. How do you think I ended up here? I was running around all famished—practically skin and bones—and I ended up eating some poisoned food some idiot human left out for rats. I almost died! I could never, ever go back out there."

"No one is asking you to, Lyric," Laurel says.

Lyric flops onto the ground and flails around. "You're breaking up the family."

"Persimmon!" A familiar voice yells excitedly from the window.

Persimmon turns to see…

"Chloe!" Persimmon bolts for the window screen and just at that moment, Tucker, Aunty Adelaide, and Uncle Bennett climb into view as well. They all scrounge for space on the porch chair and press their paws against the screen with delight.

"Tucker! Aunty! Uncle!" Persimmon tears up and everyone starts crying.

Laurel, Lyric, Senator Santiago and the opossum and raccoon in the cages watch, startled by all the commotion.

"My dear niece," Aunty Adelaide says. "We thought you were dead. I can't believe you're actually alive!"

"How did you find me?" Persimmon asks.

"Derpoke told us!" Chloe says as she points to the opossum standing a few feet away on the porch.

"Derpoke!" Persimmon calls out. "I'm so happy to see you."

Derpoke half smiles. Persimmon can tell he's still hurt from their conversation a few days ago, but this isn't the time or place for her to discuss it with him.

"Derpoke told us the little boy who set the trap was the one who saved both of your lives and brought you here," Chloe says. "How amazing!"

"Even more amazing is that he came by the house the other day to see if I was recuperating," Persimmon says. "It sounds crazy after what happened with Bruiser, but he's actually a congenial kid. He even told Dr. Misra that he'll never hunt again."

"Wow!" Chloe, Tucker, Aunty Adelaide, Uncle Bennett, and Derpoke say in unison.

"And what about this Dr. Misra?" Uncle Bennett asks. "Derpoke said she saved your life, too."

"She's wonderful!" Persimmon says. "She dedicates her life to rescuing other animals just like we do. After all our horrendous run-ins with humans, we finally found two humans who are compassionate. That's a fantastic start."

A thought crosses Persimmon's mind. "Hey, where are the chickens, Hazel and Arden?"

The team members' expressions become serious. "Unfortunately, they're not doing so well physically," Chloe says. "Their health has been deteriorating, and we're not sure what the problem is. We'll tell you all about it in a moment, but first, we want to show you a surprise."

Persimmon's ears prick up.

Chloe continues. "After it seemed that you, Bruiser, and Derpoke had all been killed, Tucker and I were devastated. I suppose some might say that The Enlighteners were over, but Tucker and I felt strongly that all three of you would want us to keep going. We knew in our hearts that someone needed to rescue all those chickens and we knew we couldn't do it alone, so…"

Chloe turns to the dark forest and calls out proudly. "Enlighteners!"

Eyes appear among the bushes and trees. Then, out into the open, walk a few hundred deer, raccoons, squirrels, beavers, opossums, and skunks.

Persimmon is astounded.

"They heard the great Persimmon had been killed and came together from everywhere to finish what you started," Chloe says. "Now that we know you survived, they have come to fight by your side."

Persimmon is overjoyed. This is her dream. Hundreds of animals joining forces to save those in need. Rescuing every one of those 60,000 chickens will still be an uphill battle, but the team is so much closer to making that a reality. The Enlighteners are back together and stronger than ever.

37

PERSIMMON LIES ON her back on the table with surgical tools by her side as Dr. Misra carefully cuts out her stitches. The raccoon stares at the ceiling in a daze—the vet has slipped a sedative in Persimmon's fruit in case she gets feisty during the procedure.

Laurel, Lyric, and the opossum watch intently. Since it's early in the morning, Senator Santiago is asleep in his cage.

"You're such a good patient, aren't you, chickadee?" Dr. Misra baby talks to Persimmon as she works. "The best little patient in the world."

Dr. Misra pulls out the last stitch. "Success! See, that wasn't so bad."

Laurel sits quietly. She tries to suppress a frown, but she's sad to see Persimmon's visit at the house coming to an end. Getting to know this brave raccoon has been so magical, and even though Laurel said she wants to join The Enlighteners for the chicken rescue, she's scared of the danger. She'll never admit that to Persimmon, though.

Dr. Misra puts on gloves, gently lifts Persimmon and heads over to the cage. The raccoon looks up at the vet and then snuggles into her chest, clinging to her.

"Oh my goodness." Dr. Misra smiles. "Well, aren't you affectionate today."

The vet goes to put Persimmon in the cage, but the raccoon holds on.

"Dear, I'm just putting you to bed," Dr. Misra says. "You can rest in your blanky."

Persimmon continues to hang on. She's groggy, but she's able to get these words out. "Thank you for everything. You not only saved my life, you proved what I had hoped all along. That there are truly decent humans out there."

"Miss Chatterbox, huh?" Dr. Misra caresses Persimmon's back, softly running her fingers through her grayish-brown fur.

Lyric calls up to Persimmon from the floor. "You know she has no idea what you're saying, right?"

"Hush up," Laurel scolds. "Don't ruin this moment."

Lyric rolls his eyes and sprawls out on the carpet again.

Dr. Misra cradles Persimmon in her arms and begins to hum a tune that she makes up as she goes. "Welcome to the family, chickadee. You're gonna love it here, you'll see."

Never in Persimmon's life did she imagine she'd be cradled in a human's arms. It feels like a dream. *If only all humans were this kind, all would be well. Now that I've met Dr. Misra, I know it is possible... one day.*

Persimmon drifts into slumber. She must rest. Tonight, she and Laurel will meet up with The Enlighteners. Senator Santiago also offered his services as a military tactician, and Persimmon happily agreed to have him join them. They're all eager for the chicken rescue to officially commence.

Unfortunately, a shocking development awaits them—one that could derail the entire mission.

38

PERSIMMON AND LAUREL traverse the woods, going slowly so as not to strain Persimmon, who is still getting used to walking on just three legs. They left Dr. Misra's house hours ago—the moment the vet went to sleep—and are set to meet The Enlighteners closer to the farm where the chickens are held captive. They're almost at their destination.

Senator Santiago flies above. The bat hasn't flown in the open night sky in a while, so he's enjoying some aerial acrobatics while following the path of the two raccoons below.

Persimmon is used to chatting nonstop with Laurel, but Laurel has been unusually quiet since they began their journey.

"Are you okay?" Persimmon finally asks.

"Nervous, I guess," Laurel says.

Persimmon doesn't want to press too hard, but she also doesn't want Laurel bottling anything up. Persimmon pushes a little more. "Are you nervous about venturing so far from Dr. Misra's house or is it something else?"

"Yes, that's part of it," Laurel says. "But it's a combination of a lot of things. I haven't walked this deep in the woods in a very long time—you know, the whole 'the woods are a death trap' thing. I feel terrible that I didn't properly say goodbye to Dr. Misra, although

I know there's no way I could have. I feel bad that she'll wake up tomorrow and be worried sick about us. And of course, I feel guilty about leaving Lyric."

"I know," Persimmon says. "It's a lot to experience all at once. You're upending your entire life to join us on this mission. I can't tell you how grateful I am and how much you're needed."

Laurel stops walking, looks at Persimmon and smiles. "I want you to know—"

"Persimmon!" Chloe calls out. The energetic squirrel dashes toward the two raccoons. When she reaches them, Chloe gives Persimmon a big hug. "It's so good to see you! Whoops, I hope I didn't hurt you. I'm a little excited."

"Not at all," Persimmon says. "It's wonderful to see you, too!"

"Laurel, right?" Chloe asks. "Are you joining The Enlighteners?!" Chloe shakes her tail with glee.

"Yes, for this mission, I want to help," Laurel says.

"Oh wow!" Chloe hugs Laurel as well. "Come on, everyone's waiting for you."

"Before the team reconvenes, Chloe," Persimmon says. "I wanted to tell you something important."

Chloe faces Persimmon—her heart racing. *Is Persimmon angry that I kept The Enlighteners going without her?*

Persimmon rests her paw on Chloe's back and looks at her with confidence. "You should lead this mission."

Chloe falls silent and very still—something unusual for her. "But... *you're* the leader of The Enlighteners."

"Chloe, ever since I got injured, you've stepped up in such a major way. Not only were you courageous enough to continue the missions, but you also recruited an enormous team to join in. I have some ideas for this rescue, but you're in charge on this one. You're a great leader. I believe in you, and you should believe in yourself."

"You really think I can do it?"

"I *know* you can," Persimmon says.

Chloe hugs Persimmon again. "Wow, what a day! Come on, let's go see everyone!"

Persimmon, Laurel, and Senator Santiago follow Chloe as she leads them to the meeting area. Animals are everywhere: Deer sprint between bushes, beavers chew on tree trunks, skunks take turns crawling under brush, raccoons practice running as quickly as possible up and down trees, opossums take turns lifting one another onto their backs and so on. At first they seem to be playing, but they're really preparing for the massive rescue mission approaching.

The moment Persimmon walks into view, silence comes over the crowd. Everyone watches as she makes her way to a small clearing. Persimmon's breath is taken away as she realizes she's surrounded by hundreds of animals staring at her, waiting for her to say something. She wasn't prepared to give a speech. She's exhausted from hobbling on three legs for hours, but she knows that she must rise to the occasion.

Persimmon examines the crowd. "Look at how this team has grown. Apparently, I should die more often."

The animals chuckle.

"I see a lot of new faces here today, and even though I don't know you personally yet, I know you are all heroes. You know the dangers involved in these missions and yet here you are, ready to put your lives on the line to save other animals in need. I admire each and every one of you for that."

Persimmon slowly turns in a circle as she speaks so that she addresses everyone. "Before we embark on this undertaking to rescue the chickens, I want to make one important point: The goal of this mission is to save these birds. It is *not* to attack the humans holding them captive. I don't want any of you getting hurt, and also, I know this will come as a surprise to some of you, but not all humans are evil."

The crowd murmurs.

"I know it seems far-fetched. Most of us have had only horrific encounters with humans trying to harm—or even kill—us or someone we love, but I wouldn't be standing here today if it weren't for two humans who saved my life. One young boy—the very boy who set the trap that took my leg—carried me and my best friend, Derpoke, to safety after his father wanted to kill us. The other human was a woman who dedicates her life to rescuing animals who are injured. I would never have believed it if I hadn't been personally healed by her as I almost bled to death.

"Our job as members of The Enlighteners is not to fight against humans, but instead, to inspire more humans to be compassionate like those two. It feels like an impossible task, but we *will* do it. It is the only way that we will create true peace with humans."

Persimmon points to her squirrel friend who is standing a foot away from her. "Chloe has brought us all together for this important mission and she will lead the charge."

The team cheers, especially proud Tucker. Chloe blushes.

"Chloe will give you the details of the mission very soon, so I want to leave you with this: As I am sure she has told you, 60,000 chickens are trapped in those sheds. It's an overwhelming number to fathom, I know. Our team is the only thing—"

Just then, Persimmon sees the two chickens, Hazel and Arden. She perks up.

"Hazel! Arden!" Persimmon hollers happily. "As you may know, the team rescued these two chickens when we scoped out the farm. Come up here, you two."

Hazel and Arden flap their wings, but neither moves forward. Hazel begins to drag herself through the dirt to Persimmon, but Arden can't move at all. Persimmon suddenly notices that they're grotesquely obese, and the weight of their bodies is too much for their thin legs to bear. Their faces look haggard and sickly.

All the animals whimper at the distressing sight of these two birds struggling to move.

Persimmon's speech screeches to a halt. She rushes up to them. "Oh my goodness. You poor babies. What happened?!"

"The humans made us this way," Hazel says. "Because they want to eat us."

The humans made *them so big? How?* Persimmon is upset as she studies the two deformed chickens. *The poor babies look so broken. This is what humans will do to other animals just to satisfy their desire to eat them?*

Persimmon's blood starts to boil. She addresses the crowd with even stronger conviction. "These chickens, Hazel and Arden—*they* are who we are rescuing. Those sheds will be filled with thousands and thousands of birds suffering exactly like this. Our job is to save them. Are you ready?"

"Yes!" The resounding support of the team rings throughout the forest.

Persimmon nods to Chloe and the squirrel jumps into leader mode, explaining the final details for the chicken rescue.

Persimmon hugs the two chickens. She's glad to see The Enlighteners so revved about the rescue mission, which will commence in less than a day. They have to be enthusiastic to ensure the greatest possible success, which is why she wouldn't dare tell them how she really feels. *If these two chickens are this bad off when they've been out here in the clean air, eating properly and receiving excellent care, what will be the condition of the chickens still trapped in those filthy sheds? It pains me to think it, but what if we're too late?*

39

ELSIE THE KINDHEARTED, PART 4

(PRESENT)

DAY 34

ELSIE IS SURROUNDED by thousands of chickens lying pressed together on the grimy floor, moaning in pain. Every part of them aches—their joints throb from growing too large too fast, their skin is inflamed with boils and raw from lying in burning feces and urine. Most of them have plucked themselves bald in numerous spots from frustration, boredom, and insanity.

Dead birds line the shed floor. Every few days the farmer comes in and picks up who he can, but there are so many bodies that he doesn't get them all. Many of the birds are dying from organ failure. Their bodies are growing so unnaturally large that their organs can't keep up.

The shed is sweltering. Elsie's brain feels like it's going to boil in her skull. The summer sun bakes the metal roof, and too many bodies are mashed together without enough room to move around. The metal gate dividing the warehouse has been removed, but the chickens have ballooned to such a colossal size that it's still impossible to go an inch without banging into another chicken. Not that they can walk properly anyway. Their torsos are so heavy that their frail legs give way underneath and the birds spend most of their time sitting in the excrement-soaked litter that is brimming with bacteria and ammonia that singes their flesh.

Elsie hacks constantly from a respiratory infection that plagues the majority of the birds. Just like everyone else, she struggles to breathe because her body weight and other organs press down on her lungs. Her eyes burn incessantly. Her eyelids are red and swollen. Her body is disintegrating and there's nothing she can do to stop it.

Thirty-four days ago these birds rushed around as wide-eyed, chirping chicks, searching for freedom. They had just arrived in this world; they wanted to live. Now they sit quietly, overcome by excruciating pain, spending every minute hoping to die.

On this day, as on every day, Elsie sits with another chicken, comforting them in their final hours. This morning she sits with Sage. The farmer hasn't been in the shed for a few days, so chances are high that at any minute he'll barge through that door to commence his killing spree. Elsie was hoping Sage would die in the night, but she did not. Now her neck will be snapped in the most horrific manner and Elsie can't protect her.

Sage is resting her head on Elsie's side. They've been quiet for the past half hour, but Sage breaks the silence with labored breath. "I am ashamed to admit this, Elsie. I thought I would be brave when I died, but as the moment nears, I feel so afraid."

"Don't be ashamed," Elsie says. "The one who should be ashamed is the Giant. He stomps through here, acting all powerful as he preys on us helpless, tiny beings. *He's* the coward. *You* are brave."

"Do you think it will hurt when he snaps my neck?"

Elsie dreads this question. She's asked it every time by these poor birds and there's no comforting answer. The only thing she can think to answer is, "It will be quick. I've been witness to this moment many times, and it is quick."

It's not true. She's seen chickens convulse in the bucket. She can only imagine how long it takes them to die. But she can't say this to these chickens. That would be cruel. She has to give them *some* hope.

BOOM! BOOM! BOOM! The knock comes at the door. The moment has come. Sage jumps in fear.

Elsie puts her wing around Sage. "You are not alone. I am right here. I love you."

Elsie wishes she could pick up Sage and run away with her, but there's nowhere to run. Death is inevitable.

The farmer makes his way through the flock. So many chickens are dead and dying that he carries two white buckets with him. Sage shakes as Elsie holds her close. The man turns to the two birds and heads over.

Elsie steps back. She always feels so guilty at this moment, but she has to steer clear of the human or he might sweep her up too.

The farmer steps on Sage's torso and just as he's grabbing for her head, Sage bites down hard on his ring finger.

"Ow!" The farmer yells as he retracts his hand.

Sage looks over at Elsie. "Brave?"

Elsie replies proudly. "You are so brave."

The man angrily stomps on Sage and Elsie quickly looks away.

The farmer moves through the rest of the shed finishing his malicious routine and then exits.

Elsie despondently lowers her head. She's seen so many chickens murdered. She's not sure how much more she can take. *Where is Persimmon? We need someone to help us.*

Rumors have swirled about Persimmon and her team ever since it became clear that they most likely wouldn't return. Many of the chickens believe that Persimmon and Derpoke lied to them and that they took Hazel and Arden to eat them. Elsie refuses to believe this. She saw the kindness in Persimmon's eyes. She hadn't seen such kindness since she met Hop. *There's no way she deceived us. Maybe their plan to rescue us was discovered. Maybe the Giants stopped them and hurt them... I hope they're okay... They will come. They* have *to come or every single one of us will be killed and eaten. That can't possibly happen. It's too horrific to believe.*

She needs to see Hop. The two friends are a great comfort to each other after the farmer's traumatic visits. They spend most days and nights consoling dying birds, but when that becomes too much to bear, they console each other.

The shed is so crammed with birds that Elsie and Hop often have trouble finding each other, so they created a special chirp that helps them pinpoint the other's location. Elsie does her special chirp.

Elsie hears Hop chirp back. She politely pushes her way through the horde of chickens and finally comes upon her friend who is near the wall.

Hop looks just as despondent as Elsie. The chicken he was sitting with had his neck snapped and was carried off with all the other unfortunate birds. The experience hit Hop hard, as it always does. Sadness seems to drip from his feathers.

"The chicken I was just comforting... his skin had turned to mush," Hop says.

Elsie cringes. In the past few days they've seen a rise in a new sickness plaguing some chickens. A cut on a chicken's skin becomes infected and turns dark red or blue. Soon, the skin practically liquifies. The bird rots from the inside out. The disease is known to farmers as gangrenous dermatitis, but the chickens simply know it as a painful, gruesome death.

Elsie steps over to Hop. She puts her right wing around Hop's back. She dare not put her left wing around him; to do so would expose a shocking revelation: Two dark red lesions fester on her skin. She has survived thirty-four days in this vile place and she will not live past day thirty-five.

*   *   *

DAY 34, PART 2

Hours have passed. It's night. Elsie and Hop sit side by side in the soiled wood shavings. The shavings burn their raw flesh, but they're too fatigued to get up, and it hurts too much to move. Insects crawl through the grime, biting at their skin and eating the dead chickens throughout the shed.

Both chickens are emotionally spent. Talking feels laborious. It's just comforting being next to each other.

Every so often a bird bangs into them—or even tries walking *over* them—but they haven't the energy or willpower to reprimand each one. It's just part of life in the shed. There is no peace.

Elsie hasn't mentioned to Hop the wounds eating away under her wing. They sting… violently. She can almost feel the bacteria gnawing at her insides. Soon, Hop will catch on that she's in severe pain, but she's not sure how to bring it up. How do you tell someone that you're dying?

She knew this day would come. It was only a matter of time before one of them succumbed to the horrors of living on the farm. Elsie is glad it's her. She still dreams of Hop walking out the shed door to freedom. She'd hoped they'd do it together, but that dream has faded like so many others.

Hop starts to propel himself up. It's difficult to walk. His left leg is bent backward and it drags through the muck wherever he goes. He doesn't really walk; he heaves himself around.

"I guess I should look for anyone who's injured," Hop says. "It feels like that time."

"Stay with me a little longer," Elsie says.

Hop stops pushing himself up and sits back down. "Is Sage's death still haunting you? I'm sorry it was so upsetting."

Elsie nods. It was traumatic, but that's not it. *How do I tell him? How do I say goodbye?*

"I'm not well, Hop."

Hop turns to her. He doesn't breathe. "What do you mean?"

"I have some bruises under my wing," Elsie says. "The same bruises we keep seeing on so many chickens."

Hop gasps. He just spent a whole night with a chicken afflicted with this disease. The chicken was in such intense pain all night that he kept moaning about wanting to die. Not Elsie. He can't watch Elsie die this way.

"Are you sure?" Hop asks, clinging to some hope.

Elsie nods. She and Hop both know that chickens who have this disease die within a day. These will be their last hours together.

Hop feels like the whole room is spinning. He falls into his friend, laying his small head on her back.

Elsie coos. What a tremendous friend he has been. "I don't really know what's beyond this shed, Hop, but something tells me that no matter what it is, I was always meant to be in here with you."

Hop gets quiet. He's always been more fragile than Elsie—he's barely been able to hold it together watching all these chickens die such hideous deaths around him—but the thought of losing Elsie? This place has finally broken him.

The two friends sit there, distraught over what will soon come.

A loud squawking cuts into the mournful moment. Elsie and Hop jump back. They turn to see where the commotion is coming from, but it's too hard to see through the hordes of birds.

It sounds like a bird in distress. Elsie goes to get up, but a sharp pain shoots through her left side. She yelps in intense agony.

"Don't move," Hop says. He rubs his wing on her right side to soothe her.

The chicken in distress squawks more and more loudly, as if she's fighting for her life.

Hop looks at Elsie.

"Go," Elsie says. "It's okay. Someone needs your help."

Hop hesitates. How can he leave her in their last moments together?

"It's fine," Elsie assures. "She needs you more than me right now."

Hop sighs and nods. He hauls his broken body through the muck toward the sounds of distress.

Eventually, he comes upon a chicken who has crawled into a feeder and is now stuck between the metal bars. She thrashes around, trying to disentangle herself, but she's cracking bones in the process.

"It's okay," Hop says. "I'm here to help."

The chicken ceases thrashing. "I just wanted some food. No one would let me get food."

The chicken holds up her mangled wing. "It's broken. The Giant is going to kill me."

She's right. Hop knows full well that this chicken will be killed the next time the farmer comes around.

Just then, there is a loud creaking at the other end of the shed. The door is opening.

"The Giant's here!" the chicken screams.

The chickens scatter around in fear. Hop tries to lift himself up to see the door, but he can't see above them. Then he notices a dead chicken nearby. He feels awful about it, but he pulls himself on top of the chicken and looks deep into the shed toward the creaking. What he sees fills his heart with joy. It's the furry creature with that striking black mask: Persimmon!

40

FROM THE DOORWAY, Persimmon scans the shed. It's wall-to-wall chickens. At first it seems that the humans have added four times as many birds, but close observation reveals that the chickens have just ballooned to massive proportions.

"The night has come!" Persimmon yells excitedly. "We're breaking you free!"

The chickens stare at her, not reacting.

Persimmon continues, hoping to jolt them into action. "Anyone who can walk unassisted, follow the squirrels through the woods. They'll take you to safety."

The chickens still stare. Are they really allowed to just run out of here? Are they really not going to die a grisly death? It's such amazing news; it seems unreal.

"Come on!" Tucker stands at the front of a dozen squirrels who are waiting in the grass. "Follow us!"

At that very moment, the chickens hear birds from nearby sheds joyfully celebrating walking on grass for the first time. It finally hits the chickens in this shed: They're being rescued!

Chickens who can walk dart through the shed doors into the soft grass and follow the squirrels into the woods. Some cry as they take their first steps out of the foul building and into the fresh night air.

Laurel stands by Persimmon at the door. The two raccoons watch the chickens walk by. Dust and feces cake their wings; they're covered in blistered, red bald spots; their orange legs are twisted and deformed; and *this* is the healthiest of the flock. Persimmon's worst fears have been realized. This mission will be an uphill battle, and they've only just begun.

Not since her mother and sister were crushed by that car has Laurel seen such horror this close up. She feels queasy. Persimmon did her best to prepare Laurel, but until she was face to face with an animal whose skin has been ravaged by disease, she really had no idea how it would affect her. Laurel is overcome with sorrow. *What kind of monsters would do this to another living being?*

In the shed next door, Chloe has also already jumped into full gear, leading a team to rescue the chickens, and Derpoke is leading a team in the final shed farthest from the farmer's house.

Since Aunty Adelaide and Uncle Bennett know this part of the woods the best, they are stationed deep in the forest helping direct the chickens to safety.

Back in Persimmon's shed, a few thousand injured chickens drag themselves toward the door. These are the birds who can't walk but are still able to lug their bodies around with their wings.

"Phase two!" Persimmon calls out to the three dozen deer who are waiting by the door of the shed. They waited for all the chickens who could walk on their own to pass them, and now it's their turn to step in.

Persimmon turns to Laurel. "Ready?"

Laurel nods emphatically.

The two raccoons move through the shed, weaving between the chickens and calling out. "If you can't walk, it's okay. These deer will pick you up one by one and carry you to safety. Please leave them room to maneuver."

The deer swiftly begin taking turns picking up chickens with their mouths and placing them on their backs. Once they have a full load—about four or five chickens, depending on the size of the deer—they gallop into the woods in the direction that Tucker and the squirrels led the other chickens.

Persimmon's eyes already burn and she's barely been in the shed a few minutes. The dusty air hits her lungs and she begins to cough.

"Help me!" Chickens cry out as she passes them.

"We're here to rescue everyone," Persimmon assures. "Stay calm. The deer will get to you as soon as possible."

"Please, help us!" A chicken pleads with Persimmon as she runs by.

Persimmon stops and walks back over to the chicken.

"I can't walk," the chicken says with watering eyes. "I don't want to die in here."

Persimmon sits down and brushes the chicken's head with her front paw. "We're going to get you out of here. Those deer are coming one by one to carry each of you to a place where the humans—or as you know them, the Giants—can't hurt you."

Persimmon notices a chicken barely breathing in the grimy wood shavings. His face is smashed into the filth. The chickens in this area are so packed together that another chicken is sitting on his legs. If Persimmon weren't looking so closely, she'd think he was dead.

"He's my friend," the chicken says. "You'll take him, too, right?"

"Of course," Persimmon says. "We're rescuing everyone."

Persimmon looks back at the dying bird. She sees a dark red wound on his chest, but that's not what upsets her the most. Small insects are crawling into the wound and carrying out pieces of the chicken's flesh.

Persimmon gasps and looks away.

This is unfathomable! If only our team could rush them out of here faster, but there are so many of them, and not only can't the majority walk but their bodies have been destroyed. A distressing thought comes to Persimmon: *How many of them will survive once they've been taken to a safer location?*

Persimmon clenches her jaw. Since it was her leg injury that delayed the mission, she feels personally responsible for the extended agony these chickens have had to endure.

There's no time to feel guilty, though. Persimmon snaps out of her trance. "We'll get you and your friend out as quickly as possible, okay?"

"Thank you," the chicken says.

Persimmon runs around gaggles of chickens, relaying the plan. As she's running, she looks back and sees that Laurel has stopped in the middle of the shed. She's wiping her eyes and coughing. Persimmon rushes over to her.

"My eyes," Laurel says with tears pouring down her cheeks. "They burn so much."

"If you need to go outside, it's all right," Persimmon says. "Remember, we turned on that hose for problems just like this."

"No, no," Laurel protests. "I can do this. I want to go through the entire shed at least once before taking a break. These chickens don't get a break. I don't deserve one yet, either."

Persimmon looks at her to make sure she means it.

"I'm fine," Laurel says. "Don't let me hold up the mission."

Persimmon surveys the shed and sees that the deer have things under control, so she dashes out the front entryway and over to the shed next door. She watches Chloe as she directs chickens to line up in rows so the deer can pick them up as easily and efficiently as possible. *What a smart idea. Love that squirrel!*

Persimmon then darts over to the last shed on the left to check on Derpoke's progress. In Derpoke's shed, there are more raccoons, skunks and opossums helping out than deer. These smaller animals can carry only one chicken at a time, so this shed will take more time to clear out. This was by design, because Persimmon and Chloe felt that it was most important to clear out the shed nearest to the farmer's house first—the one Persimmon is overseeing—to minimize noise near the humans.

Persimmon sees a few young raccoons struggling to lift chickens onto their backs, so she walks over to them.

When one of the young raccoons sees Persimmon stepping up to him, he looks at the ground, ashamed. "I'm not strong enough."

"That's all right," Persimmon says. "You're doing great. Instead of carrying the chickens, why don't the four of you head to the back of each shed and inform all the chickens of the plan? It's getting a bit noisy in here, because the chickens are unsure what exactly is happening and getting worried they'll be left behind. The last thing we need is to wake the humans. It's a very important job. Can you do that?"

The young raccoons perk up. "Absolutely!"

The four raccoons split up and excitedly run through the shed calling out the plan for the mission.

A few feet away, Persimmon sees Derpoke helping a chicken onto a raccoon's back. She goes to say something to him when, out of nowhere, a loud squawking erupts behind her. Persimmon turns to see two chickens pecking each other next to an opossum.

"Stop!" the opossum pleads with the two chickens. "Please!"

Persimmon dashes up to the squabble. "Okay, okay. What's going on?"

The two chickens cease pecking each other.

"I was next!" one chickens hollers.

"No!" the other chicken yells. "I was sitting here waiting patiently and she pushed her way in front of me."

"Listen," Persimmon says, silencing the birds. "I know you're desperate to escape, but arguing will only slow down the process."

Persimmon calls out to the chickens within hearing distance. "We're here to save *all* of you, but we need your help to make that happen. Please, take turns and be patient. We'll get you out of here as quickly as possible."

Persimmon turns to the opossum. "Okay, what's your name?"

"Hanif," the opossum says.

"Hanif, you are wonderful," Persimmon says. "Thank you for all your help tonight. You can probably carry only one bird at a time, right?"

The opossum nods, so Persimmon points to one of the chickens. "Okay, you go first. Climb onto Hanif's back."

Hanif crouches and the chicken crawls onto his back with Persimmon's help. The opossum waddles off toward the shed door.

Then, Persimmon motions for a raccoon to come over. "Can we get your... Oh, Alister. Hello!"

It's Alister, the raccoon from Dr. Misra's house. He's missing an eye because a kid shot him with a BB gun, but Dr. Misra surgically sewed up the hole, and the area has healed up nicely.

A big grin forms on Alister's face; he's happy that Persimmon finally noticed he had joined the rescue effort. "You and Laurel kept talking about this mission so much that I had to check it out for myself. This is intense. I'm good with intense. How can I help?"

"Welcome!" Persimmon says. "I need you to carry this chicken."

"Great," Alister says. He turns to the bird. "Hop aboard, chicken."

Alister lowers himself for Persimmon to hoist the bird onto his back.

"Sorry for the trouble," the chicken says to Persimmon as she's being carried away. "Thank you!"

Persimmon sighs in relief. *As long as our team can keep solving all these small issues before they explode into larger ones, I think we can get these chickens out of here without a disaster. That's not too much to ask, right?*

41

IN CHLOE'S SHED she notices how much the chickens are struggling to crawl onto the backs of the smaller team members—the raccoons, opossums and skunks—so she dashes over to a young female deer. "Marigold, right?"

The deer looks at the small squirrel, surprised that she knows her name.

"You're risking your life for this mission; the least I can do is learn everyone's name, right?" Chloe beams. "I need you and one other deer to stay in the shed and lift the chickens onto the other team members' backs."

"Happy to help!" Marigold says.

Marigold calls a nearby deer over to her, and they begin gently hoisting chickens onto the backs of the raccoons, opossums and skunks. The rescue process speeds up instantly.

"Hooray! Did you see—" Chloe looks around for someone to celebrate with, wishing Tucker or Persimmon were there. They are not.

An opossum is walking by, so Chloe shakes her tail victoriously at the opossum. He stares at her, confused. "Did I do something wrong?"

"No," Chloe says. "I just… You're doing great. Keep up the good work!"

The opossum ambles over to a group of chickens.

Chloe runs back to the area where the team members are picking up the chickens and chips in lifting the chickens onto the animals' backs.

∗   ∗   ∗

Persimmon speeds through the grass along the exterior of the shed. When she gets to the far end, she calls up to the roof. "How's it going out here, Senator Santiago?"

Dangling upside down, the little brown bat turns his head toward the raccoon. "It's quiet. Just how we like it. See for yourself."

Persimmon peeks around the edge of the building to see the farmer's house. It's completely dark inside. How long will *that* last?

"How's the mission shaping up on your end?" Senator Santiago asks.

Persimmon shakes her head. "There are so many chickens, Senator Santiago. Most can't walk. There's only so many that we carry in one night. I'm concerned."

"You cannot ask more of yourself than your best. You will have saved more lives tonight than most have saved—or have even attempted to save—in an entire lifetime. That is a victory. See it as such."

Persimmon nods. It doesn't feel nearly good enough, but she can't argue with his logic.

"Thanks for keeping an eye on everything out here," Persimmon says. "I'll check on you later."

Persimmon rushes back to the end of the shed that faces the woods. *We still have hours before sunrise. Surely we can get these chickens to safety. If only we had more time. If only we had more team members. If only the humans hadn't put these chickens through this in the first place.*

Whenever Persimmon starts feeling disgust for humans' cruelty to other animals, she reminds herself of Dr. Misra and Gavin. *There is hope. Not all humans treat other animals like these chickens have been treated. There is kindness out there. We just have to keep searching for it.*

42

"HOP!" ELSIE CALLS out. Her dear friend is nowhere to be found in the mayhem around her. Chickens on all sides are pushing and scratching one another to escape to the other end of the shed. Elsie is getting trampled.

"Stop!" Elsie begs. "Please! Take turns. They're coming to help *all* of us."

The chickens don't listen. They frantically fight with anyone in the way of that door. Their efforts are useless, though. The door is a few hundred feet away and most of them can't walk properly, so they're flapping around wildly without really moving anywhere. Regardless of how futile their attempts are, this is their first chance to escape—and their last—so they refuse to give up.

Elsie chirps her special call for Hop. She listens for his response. She hears a quiet, distant chirp. She perks up. *I can do this. I can find him.*

Elsie musters the energy to slowly push herself through the mob of chickens. They scratch at her as she crawls by. A throbbing pain attacks Elsie's left side. *Ignore it. Keep going!*

"Elsie!" Hop calls out. He's pushing his way through the chickens in her direction. She can barely see him through the wall of feathers.

Finally, they crawl to each other. The wings of the birds around them smack Elsie and Hop in their faces as they talk.

"Thank goodness!" Hop says. "I was so worried I wouldn't be able to find you in all this chaos."

"Me too!" Elsie says. "Can you make it to the door?"

"Can *you*?!" Hop asks. "I thought you were in too much pain to move."

"I'm okay," Elsie says, hiding the agony she's in. "Let's get out of here."

Elsie and Hop drag themselves through the hoard of panicked chickens. Elsie whimpers in pain as she goes—the pain is so intense it feels like needles are stabbing into her side. It's so loud in the shed, though, that Hop can't hear how much his friend is struggling.

Unfortunately, the two companions don't make much headway with all the panicked chickens flapping around.

"Stop pushing!" a chicken yells at Hop. But then the chicken gets a good look at Hop, and his mood changes immediately. "It's *you*." The chicken notices Elsie, too. "Oh, and *you*!"

Hop and Elsie stare at him. Have they met this bird before? He seems to know them very well, but he doesn't look familiar at all.

The chicken turns to the bird next to him and attempts to quiet her down. "Hey! It's Elsie and Hop. Make way."

That chicken looks at Elsie and Hop and immediately recognizes them. She stops flapping her wings and moves to the side. To Elsie's and Hop's surprise, before they know it, bird after bird has stepped aside and made a pathway for the two friends to head to where The Enlighteners are carrying chickens away.

Elsie and Hop are incredibly moved by this gracious gesture. "Thank you," they call out as they drag themselves past the birds. "Thank you so much."

Ever since the chickens were tossed into this shed, they've seen these two loving birds comfort the least fortunate of their friends and family. They knew that these two were special—a gift to all of them. If any of the birds were unlucky enough to be stricken with an illness, they knew that they'd have someone to give them solace in their darkest moment. Their kindness did not go unnoticed, so now that all the other birds have a chance to help these two flee this shed, they're happy to oblige.

Hop drags himself forward and doesn't notice that his friend is moving more and more slowly behind him. Elsie groans as she attempts to fight through the pain. One more sharp burn shoots through her left side and she stops abruptly.

She lays her head on the wood shavings and whimpers. The chickens gather around her.

"Are you okay?" the chickens ask. Then they see the red lesions covering her raw skin. A gasp erupts through the crowd. She has The Disease—the one that devours flesh and kills in less than a day. They're shattered that such a kind-hearted chicken would meet such an ugly fate. Nothing that happens in this shed is fair, but this seems particularly cruel.

Hop turns around to see a mass of chickens, but he doesn't see his friend. "Elsie?"

He moves through the crowd. "Excuse me."

Finally, he gets to the center and sees his dear friend crumbled on the ground. He holds his breath. Is she dead?

Hop swiftly pulls himself next to her. "Elsie?!"

He sees that she's breathing, but she doesn't open her eyes.

"We're so close, Elsie. Don't give up. Please."

Elsie doesn't answer. The stinging in her left side is too severe. She can't move another inch and the door feels like miles from where she is. Freedom never felt so close and yet so very far away.

43

HOURS HAVE PASSED. Morning nears. Soon the sun will shine brightly over the farm and illuminate the massive rescue mission underway.

Each of The Enlighteners knows that time is running out, so they've sped up their efforts. They had already been working hard, though, so it's wearing them down.

Persimmon tried carrying a chicken herself, but she only got ten or so trees into the woods when she had to stop. Because Persimmon's right front leg is missing, the only way she can move around is to hop on her left front leg. But the chicken's weight was too much to manage with such a maneuver. The chicken kept almost falling off, so Persimmon was forced to stop and wait until another raccoon came by who could take the chicken the rest of the way.

Persimmon felt embarrassed, but mostly disappointed in herself. She used to be able to chip in more on all aspects of these missions, but now she feels like she can't pull her weight. *A true leader should be able to tackle any task or your worth to the team diminishes. These other animals need me to be at my best to save their lives, but I can't be.*

Right now, Persimmon is in her assigned shed, focusing on keeping the rescue running smoothly. She and Laurel are lifting chickens onto the backs of raccoons, opossums, and skunks.

Suddenly, a deer nearby collapses into the wood shavings, dropping four chickens off his back. Persimmon rushes over.

"Is everyone all right?" Persimmon asks.

The chickens nod. They're shaken up, but not injured.

"I'm sorry," the deer says.

He tries to stand up, but stumbles.

"Just rest a moment," Persimmon says as she caresses his face. "You're exhausted."

Persimmon scans the shed. "Laurel!"

Laurel darts over.

"I saw an empty plastic container outside near the hose," Persimmon says to her. "Can you fill that with water and bring it back here?"

"Of course!" Laurel runs out of the shed.

"I don't want to let the chickens down," the deer says mournfully.

"You're not," Persimmon says. "You've saved so many lives tonight—"

Suddenly, Senator Santiago flies in with lightning speed and shouts frantically. "Humans! The humans are coming!"

Persimmon's heart stops. *What?! Now? It's not morning yet. They* can't *be coming.*

Senator Santiago zooms through the air and out of the shed, off to the next building to warn the team in there.

Persimmon looks around the shed, paralyzed. A fourth of the room is still full of chickens—thousands and thousands of chickens. Now, all of them are going to die.

44

SIRENS! PERSIMMON, LAUREL, Chloe, the chickens, and all the other animals in and around the sheds hear them. The team heard the same sound when the humans in blue uniforms came and shot the elephants and tigers to death.

Persimmon looks around the shed at the massive flock of terrified, sickly chickens and then at her team members. The order that Persimmon is about to make will haunt her for the rest of her life, but there's no other way.

"Enlighteners, fall back!" Persimmon yells.

The deer, raccoons, opossums, and skunks stare at her. The plan was that if humans attacked, they had to retreat—it's the only way to ensure their safety, and it made sense at the time. But standing here with these dying birds, deciding to abandon them feels so wrong. How can they just walk away?

"Enlighteners, fall back... NOW!" Persimmon yells more forcefully.

One by one, the team members run out the door and into the woods. Team members with chickens on their backs carry the birds with them. Some deer pick up one or two more chickens to save their lives at the last moment, but the rest of the team scatters—the extra weight of a chicken might slow them down and make them easy prey for the humans.

"Don't leave us!" Chickens begin crying.

Chickens use their wings to drag themselves through the wood shavings toward the door. Their only hope is to heave themselves far into the woods where the humans can't find them.

Persimmon runs throughout the front of the shed, urging all team members to leave. "Go! Now! Your lives are in danger!"

In minutes, the shed is clear of any team members. Persimmon stops at the door and looks back. "We left a scent along the path," she yells to the chickens. "If you can, follow it to the meeting place. We'll be there waiting for you."

Persimmon feels sick, knowing that the promise of escape is hollow. These chickens can barely drag themselves to the door much less all the way to the meeting place. *They're all going to die—every one of them. How can we leave them?*

Persimmon knew from the beginning that The Enlighteners wouldn't be able to save all 60,000 chickens (thousands of them already died in the shed from disease, injuries, and more before the rescue even began), but she thought that they could at least save *more* than they are now. Too many things worked against the rescue effort, though. Most chickens could not walk on their own, the team members were worn ragged from running a mile into the woods carrying heavy birds, and the team wasn't able to work as many hours as Persimmon had hoped.

Now that time has run out, the team has only been able to save 1,500 chickens from this shed and around 2,000 from the others. That's a lot of lives saved, but in this moment, with all the birds flapping around desperately trying to escape, it looks like they've barely saved *any*.

Chickens haul their broken bodies on the ground toward Persimmon, screaming. "Don't leave!"

One frightened chicken crawls up to Persimmon and wraps his wings around her leg. "Please, help me!"

Persimmon is overcome with heartache, but steps back. She looks at all the helpless chickens crawling toward her and cries out from deep within. "I'm so sorry!"

Her apology is drowned out by their pleas for help, though.

No matter how much it hurts, she can't save them. She has to focus on protecting her team or else they'll lose their lives, too.

45

THE FARMER RUNS at full speed from the house toward the first shed. He has a flashlight in one hand and a shotgun in the other.

Suddenly, out of the night sky, a swarm of 200,000 bats torpedoes its way straight for the farmer. Senator Santiago leads the charge as they swirl around him, scratching and biting. The farmer shrieks and falls to the ground, dropping both his flashlight and his gun.

The man shakes around on the ground, howling in fear. He covers his face with his arms and crawls toward the house.

"Don't let up!" Senator Santiago yells to the other bats.

The swarm of little brown bats hovers overhead, with a few nosediving into the man's torso to scare him back into his home.

Two police cars skid into the dirt near the home.

"Battalion B, follow me!" Senator Santiago hollers.

Half the bats split from the group and zoom toward the police cars. They spin around the vehicles like a tornado, making it too hazardous for the officers inside to exit.

"We got them!" Senator Santiago yells. "Faster, troops! Faster!"

*   *   *

Persimmon sprints toward Chloe's shed, but she abruptly halts when she sees Laurel standing in the grass in a daze.

"Laurel, what are you doing?" Persimmon asks. "We're retreating to the meeting place."

"I'm waiting for *you*," Laurel says.

"I'll be there momentarily," Persimmon replies. "I have to make sure these other sheds are clear of team members."

"I'll come," Laurel says.

"No, you have…" Persimmon doesn't have time to argue. "Okay, hide at the edge of the woods. I'll be there shortly."

Persimmon goes to run away but stops herself. She feels bad being so curt with Laurel. "Thank you for waiting."

Laurel nods and then runs to the edge of the woods and plants herself down. She's not going one step further without Persimmon.

Deer, raccoons, squirrels, skunks, and opossums race into the woods out of Chloe's shed—some carrying chickens.

Inside, Chloe is directing chickens to hop onto the remaining team members' backs. As she rushes around, she trembles from being so upset. Chickens surround her and the team, squawking frantically and pushing to be next.

Persimmon scurries up to her. "Chloe, we have to evacuate."

"I know," Chloe says. "We just have to save a few more."

"We don't have time," Persimmon insists. "It's too dangerous. Tell your team to exit now."

Chloe looks at Persimmon, devastated. The rescue ended so abruptly. Her shed is still mostly full. She peers through the room at the desperate chickens staring at her, begging for her to save their lives. Then she looks at Persimmon with a pained expression. She can't. She can't bring herself to tell the chickens that they're being abandoned.

Persimmon nods. She understands. Decisions like this change you—they harden your heart. Persimmon does not wish that on this sweet-natured squirrel.

"It's all right." Persimmon hugs Chloe as she yells out. "Enlighteners, fall back! Now!"

The chickens scream and scrounge for the entryway.

"I'm sorry." Persimmon calls out to the chickens as she ushers Chloe and the rest of the team to the door.

Chloe and the other team members scramble into the woods as Persimmon runs over to Derpoke's shed. Derpoke's team has already cleared out. It's only chickens dragging themselves toward the door with Derpoke standing in the doorway calling out to them. "Follow the path into the woods. We left a scent leading to the meeting place. We'll be waiting for you."

Persimmon speeds over to her opossum friend. "I know how hard this is, Derpoke. I'm proud of you for clearing out your team."

Derpoke turns to her. "They're all going to die. This is horr—"

BANG! BANG! Shots ring out around the corner of the building in which Persimmon was originally stationed. Persimmon, Derpoke, and all the chickens in the shed jump in fear.

"Derpoke, go!" Persimmon yells. "The humans are coming!"

"What about *you*?!" Derpoke asks.

"I'll be there soon," Persimmon says. "I'm faster than you. Go!"

Derpoke waddles into the woods as quickly as he can.

Persimmon surveys the open area between the sheds and the forest. Frantic chickens drag themselves toward the woods. Any second now, humans with guns will come charging around the corner of that last building.

Before running to safety herself, though, Persimmon wants to make sure that every single Enlightener has cleared the area. Without hesitation, she runs directly toward the gunfire.

46

SENATOR SANTIAGO DARTS through the air, guiding all the little brown bats above the canopy of trees nearby. The police officers finally decided to be bold enough to open a window and shoot into the air, hoping to disperse the attacking aerial mammals. It worked. Luckily, no bats were shot, but Senator Santiago feels guilty he wasn't able to hold off the violent humans longer.

"I hope the team evacuated!" Senator Santiago says to himself as he flies to safety.

The four police officers jump out of their cars with their weapons drawn and bolt around the corner of the first shed. They're shocked to see thousands of injured chickens dragging themselves along the dirt and into the woods. The birds look like wounded soldiers scrounging for their lives right after a bloody battle.

"What in the hell?!" an officer says, his mouth agape.

Right then, they notice that in the middle of the flock of chickens is a three-legged raccoon.

"There's the culprit!" another officer yells.

Persimmon's heart races a million miles a minute. She quickly pivots and runs into the woods.

"Get that damn thing and shoot it," the officer says. "She's caused a lot of damage here."

Two of the officers split off and race after her.

Laurel is standing with a group of squirrels at the edge of the woods watching fearfully as Persimmon comes speeding toward them. "Go! Go!" Persimmon yells as she runs in their direction.

The squirrels' legs are shaking. They were stationed here to trick the humans into running in the opposite direction of the rest of the team and the chickens. It's a high-risk task, but they were brave enough to take it on. Now, though, they're joined by these two raccoons, and even worse, Persimmon is super slow because of her missing leg. How are they going to outrun these humans now?

Persimmon passes by Laurel and the squirrels, and they all dash into the brush.

The foliage is thick and the officers have to kick and rip their way through the vines and bushes to follow the sprinting critters.

The officers finally claw their way into a small clearing, and to their surprise they find a row of skunks with their bums facing the two men.

"Oh crap!" one officer yells just as the skunks synchronize spraying the humans.

The rotten stench fills the air. The men cough and wipe the yellow oil that's on their uniforms. "You gotta be kidding me!"

Right then, a large tree trunk crashes to the ground two feet to their right. "Holy crap, that was close."

Then another tree smashes against the forest floor right in front of them. The men jump backward. "What is going—"

Two more trees slam to the ground right in front of them.

"Retreat!" one of the officers yells.

The two men run back the way they came toward the farm.

When the humans are out of hearing distance, Laurel, the squirrels, and a small group of deer and beavers pop their heads out from behind the trees and cheer.

"We did it!" A beaver hugs a deer's leg next to him.

What the humans didn't see was that the deer took turns kicking down the weakened trunks in the direction of the unsuspecting officers, and that at the other end of the trunks are bite marks from crafty beavers.

Laurel is beaming. These humans won't be searching through these woods for a while, giving the team just the time they need to get the chickens as far away from this horrible farm as possible.

Laurel turns to hug Persimmon, but to her great shock, Persimmon has disappeared.

47

PERSIMMON HEAVES WITH all her might to pull open the door of the shed in which Derpoke's team was working—the farthest shed from the farmer's house. She's at the door that faces the human's home, which the team had left closed so as not to alert the humans.

"Come on! Please!" Persimmon uses every ounce of energy she has left to peel open the rusty metal door. She's dangling off the ground, pulling down on a lever with her good front paw while pushing with her back legs on the door frame.

She's breathing heavily from running around all night, and this tricky maneuver is proving nearly impossible.

Finally, the door gives. She drops to the ground and pushes the door open the rest of the way.

Inside, thousands of chickens are revealed, most of them sobbing. They turn to see the heroic raccoon standing in the doorway.

"Listen up!" Persimmon calls out. "There's still a chance to escape. If you can walk at all, the cornfield is only a few feet away just around this corner. As soon as we get a chance, a few team members will do their best to sneak into the field to carry you to safety. Good luck!"

Persimmon isn't sure if it will be safe for the team members to venture back to the farm during the day, but she wants to give these chickens as much of a chance to get out of here as possible.

Persimmon rushes through the dirt to the next shed. The sun is completely up now. Luckily, there are no humans in the vicinity, but she has no idea how long that will last. She lugs her heavy body up to the lever and pulls down, thrusting against the door frame with her back legs. She pants as she does it. She feels faint from exerting herself too much.

Finally, the door opens, but just barely. Persimmon falls to the ground. She lies there for a moment, trying to catch her breath. *Get up. These chickens will die if you don't fight through this.*

Just as Persimmon is about to push the door open, she hears human voices. She peers through the cracked door and sees that way at the other end, the humans are carrying chickens by their legs back into the shed. *No! I'm too late.*

Persimmon feels terrible, but she knows that she can't open the door to let any more chickens out of this shed. The humans will see her for sure, and then the chickens in the other buildings won't have a chance of escaping.

One more shed to go.

Persimmon runs through the dirt to the final building. She stumbles along the way. She's getting dizzy from exhaustion. *Come on! I don't care how tired you are, keep going!*

She crawls up the door of the final shed—the last chance to save any more chickens. She pulls on the lever and pushes with all her might to open the door. Thank goodness this one opens more easily.

She drops to the ground and peers through the crack. There are no humans in this one. In fact, the door has been closed at the other end.

Persimmon takes a few breaths and pushes the door open all the way.

The thousands of chickens stare at her, stunned. What an emotional roller coaster the past few hours have been. They started last night thinking they were doomed to a grisly death. Then, this team of peculiar-looking creatures comes and the chickens think that they are miraculously saved. Suddenly, they are thrown the devastating disappointment of the humans' arrival and abandonment by the team. After all that, this raccoon opens another door. What now?!

"There's a cornfield to the right," Persimmon calls out. "Get there however you can. We'll do everything—"

Persimmon stops talking. She sees a chicken far in the shed—a familiar face. It's Elsie. She's still in the shed. *Oh no! She didn't make it out.*

Persimmon is hit with a wave of guilt. This chicken was selfless enough to let another bird take her place when she had a chance at freedom, and now she's going to be left in here to be murdered?! *No. I will not let that happen.*

She rushes into the shed, weaving through the crowd of chickens. Finally, Persimmon makes her way to Elsie. She crouches to the ground. "Come on, crawl onto my back. I'm getting you out of here."

Elsie is stunned. "What about everyone else?"

"I'll do everything I can," Persimmon says. "But right now, it's your turn. Come on, we don't have much time."

"What about Hop?" Elsie asks.

Persimmon sees Hop sitting next to Elsie. Persimmon feels terrible that he didn't make it out, either. She sucks in a deep breath. *Oh goodness, I can't carry them both. The humans could come in here any moment. What am I going to—*

"I can drag alongside you," Hop says.

Persimmon sighs. *Thank goodness!* She inches closer to Elsie, and the chicken does her best to lug herself onto Persimmon. Unfortunately, it hurts so much that Elsie screams with every move. Hop pushes his back against Elsie to nudge her onto the raccoon. Finally, Elsie grabs hold of Persimmon's fur and braces to be carried.

With every ounce of energy Persimmon has left, she pushes herself off the ground.

"Take me next!" Chickens call out as Persimmon heaves forward.

Persimmon is too worn out to respond, though. She just keeps crawling forward through the filthy wood shavings. Using his wings, Hop drags himself alongside Persimmon and Elsie, excited to be moving toward that door again.

Persimmon hauls herself forward with Elsie's massive weight pushing down on her. Persimmon strains with every move. Her legs feel like they're on fire. *Come on! Fight through this!*

Persimmon's legs almost give way. Elsie sways on her back and almost falls off, but she rights herself. Persimmon keeps pushing through the grime, but her legs begin to shake. She hops one more time and then collapses to the ground. Elsie falls off and Persimmon's face is smashed into the urine-soaked wood shavings.

Persimmon rolls onto her side. She's panting heavily. Her body goes limp. She is defeated. "I can't save you," she cries out. "I'm so sorry."

Elsie drags herself over to Persimmon and gently rests her wing on the raccoon's side.

"You did everything you could," Elsie says. "It's okay."

Persimmon looks at Elsie. The raccoon was so busy trying to save Elsie that she didn't get a good look at her before. Elsie looks haggard and worn—so much worse than when Persimmon last saw her. Half her feathers are gone. In their place is raw, red skin and dark blue bruises. Her feathers are covered with dust and feces. Her eyes are weary. She wheezes as she breathes. This place has ravaged her. The thing that breaks Persimmon's heart the most, though, is that despite all this, as Elsie sits here looking at Persimmon, somehow, she still emits so much warmth.

"You saved so many of us tonight," Elsie says. "You're our hero."

Elsie and Hop lean against Persimmon and nestle their heads into her fur to comfort her. Everything goes silent for a moment. Just as Elsie and Hop did for so many chickens, they now comfort this despondent raccoon.

Persimmon would give anything—*her own life*—to scoop up every chicken within the walls of these sheds and carry them to safety, but it's impossible. Now she has to figure out how to let them go.

"Persimmon!" A voice calls out, breaking the silence.

Persimmon's eyes jolt open and she twists around to see Laurel maneuvering through the crowd of chickens toward them. Persimmon can't believe it.

"What are you doing here?!" Persimmon asks, bewildered.

"Looking for *you*," Laurel says. "I knew I'd find you here. You tell everyone else not to risk their lives, but here you are, by yourself, with all these humans running around."

"You shouldn't have—"

BAM! A chicken a few feet away bursts apart. Blood and muscle spray all over the chickens nearby.

"Damn it!" The farmer holds up his shotgun, cursing his bad aim.

Before Persimmon and Laurel can react, the man points the gun at Persimmon and pulls the trigger. Click. Nothing. The gun is empty.

"Run!" Persimmon yells at Laurel.

The two raccoons sprint toward the far door—the one they opened at the beginning of the rescue mission—but they're only halfway through the shed, so it's a few hundred feet away.

The farmer scrambles through his pockets. He can't find any more bullets and the raccoons are getting away. He curses again and starts running through the chickens, kicking at them to get out of his way as he heads straight for Persimmon and Laurel.

Just then, the far door opens and two police officers storm in.

"What's going on?" one officer asks.

They see the man running toward the raccoons, brandishing his gun.

Persimmon and Laurel screech to a halt. They're trapped—the police officers on one side and the angry farmer running toward them on the other.

Persimmon racks her brain. *What do we do?! Which way should we go?!*

That's when Elsie calls out as loudly as she can. "Protect the raccoons!"

As the farmer runs toward the middle of the shed, Elsie rolls right in front of him. The man kicks Elsie hard and she flies a few feet into the air and smacks onto the ground... dead.

Hop screeches—first in horror, then in anger. Immediately, the blood of every single chicken in that shed begins to boil. As the farmer charges forward, one by one, the other chickens roll toward the man, blocking his path to the two raccoons.

"Get out of my way, you idiots!" the man hollers as he kicks at the chickens.

Persimmon and Laurel see their chance. They run to the far-right wall and dart past the middle of the shed where the man is struggling to move forward with all these chickens throwing themselves as blockades.

Persimmon gets just past the middle of the shed and stops. She has a clear path to the door, but she can't. Not like this.

She turns to the farmer and shrieks, "Stop! Stop hurting them!"

Persimmon charges straight at the man, gnashing her teeth. "Stop it now!"

The man sees the raging raccoon barreling toward him and falls backward onto the ground. Persimmon runs a few feet from him. "Leave them alone, you murderer!"

"Get away!" The man shakes the barrel of his gun toward the raccoon to scare her away.

At the far end of the shed, one of the officers aims his gun at Persimmon.

"Got a shot?" the other officer asks.

"Not really," the officer says. "I don't want to hit that guy."

"Come on."

The two officers run toward the middle of the shed.

"Persimmon, come on!" Laurel hollers. "The other humans are coming!"

Persimmon glares at the farmer. "You don't treat other animals that way, you coward!"

She's never wanted to hurt a human so much in her life. She can feel the hate seething throughout her.

"Persimmon, please!" Laurel screams. She can't bear to watch Persimmon get shot to death right in front of her. She's already had to overcome watching her family get killed—she can't make it through something so traumatic again.

Persimmon digs her nails into the wood shavings in front of her. There's nothing else she can do. She turns around and rushes toward the door with Laurel following. A few moments later, they disappear outside.

The two officers make their way to the farmer, who is still cowering on the ground. "I lost thousands of dollars' worth of property tonight," he yells at the officers, "because you all couldn't do your jobs."

The officers frown and give each other a look.

The farmer continues yelling. "You're telling me you didn't have a clear shot of that vermin?"

"We're not exterminators, sir," one officer says with an eye roll.

They shake their heads and leisurely head back toward the far door. They're finished helping this ingrate.

One of the officers leans over and whispers to the other. "I'm not gonna lie, that was one badass raccoon."

The other officer laughs. "I hear that."

The farmer stands up and shakes the grime off his clothes. He stomps through the shed, cursing the whole way, and stops at the door that Persimmon and Laurel exited a few moments before. The officers have left the shed as well. He surveys the building, looking at all the chickens glowering at him. They're not afraid of him any longer. He may be giant, but they know that inside, he is truly small.

The farmer slams the door shut.

The shed is quiet for a moment. The chickens know that soon they will be killed—in fact, it's just a week away. It is certain now that they will never be rescued. But knowing that some of their dear friends made it out is a comfort. Those chickens will experience the joys of life beyond the shed—away from human tyranny.

In the center of the shed lies Elsie.

Hop drags himself through the litter and sits beside her. He's not sure what else to do. He just needs to be near her.

The other chickens crowd around Elsie as well. Hop's heart swells seeing so many birds mourning her death. A few birds snuggle in close, comforting him.

Hop isn't sure what's beyond the shed, but he wishes the rest of the world could see that within these walls are some of the kindest beings ever to grace the earth.

The Giants can trap us in these sheds and call us food, but that doesn't make it so. We feel sorrow when our friends are killed. We feel pain when we are kicked. We want to live. We deserve to live. No matter what the Giants say, we are not objects. We are not food.

I am Hop. This is Elsie. If only the Giants understood that, perhaps they would set us free.

Hop rests his head on Elsie's back and closes his eyes. *No one deserves what we endured in this shed. Not Elsie, not the other chickens, not me.*

48

RASHA'S FIGHT, PART 6

BREAKING POINT

I'M PREGNANT. RASHA knows for sure now. A mother knows these things.

It's been almost a year since Rasha's fight with Viper. She's been forced to fight two more dogs and she "won" both brawls. Coach was pleased because he thought she had turned into a vicious killer, but the truth is that Rasha just fought so hard because she wanted the fights to be over as soon as possible.

After all these bouts, Rasha is badly disfigured. Both ears are shredded. Her nose and face are so horribly chewed up that she's almost unrecognizable from that cute puppy she was not too long ago. It broke Chopper's heart to see his daughter mutilated, and it was even more distressing knowing that he couldn't help her.

Now that Rasha has "won" three fights, she is considered a champion in the dogfighting world. Since she's a champion, Coach can make a great deal of money from her offspring—just like he does from Chopper's—so Coach recently started using Rasha to produce puppies.

Breeding is a grotesque process. The female dogs are restrained with a device and then a male dog is forced to mount her. No matter how bad the fights were, this violation is worse. Rasha's hatred for Coach and Dale has reached a boiling point.

Becoming pregnant is the worst thing Rasha can imagine. *They're going to take my babies away. Coach is going to sell them to other sadistic humans who will force them to fight other dogs. They will get killed, or just as bad, become killers... like me.*

Tears swell in Rasha's eyes as she contemplates this horrifying future for her pups. Rasha saw how devastated Sadie was when Coach took her first group of puppies away. Sadie's been so filled with rage since Rasha met her that Rasha wasn't sure if Sadie had any kindness left in her. But this tragic experience left Sadie crying for days. Despite their contentious history, Rasha tried to comfort Sadie, but Sadie quickly snapped at her. So Rasha left her alone. Now Rasha dreads the same fate for her own puppies.

At that moment, Coach and Dale enter the yard through the side gate. Dale has a black pit bull on a leash. The dog looks to be four years old and his tail is between his legs as he walks. He looks surprisingly meek for a dog in the fighting world.

"This is some real amateur crap, Dale!" Coach yells as he stomps forward. "I can't believe you brought a stolen dog to the yard!"

"I'm sorry, Coach," Dale grovels. "It was stupid. I know that now. I thought you might find it funny."

"Funny?!" Coach hollers as they walk down the path to the area with the dogs on their chains. "You could blow up my whole operation. What the hell is funny about that?"

"Wait," Dale says. "What I mean is... As I told you, I was at the mall and I saw this couple I used to know in high school. They used to have this stupid animal rights club, and they would preach about how cruel it was to eat meat and all that crap. It made me so mad remembering that, so I wanted to teach them a lesson. I knew they'd had this pit bull for years. They'd treat him like their kid and crap. I thought it would be funny to take their dog and make him into a fighter. You know, because it would be ironic."

"Ironic? Do you even know what that means?" Coach grabs his own hair in frustration. "Boy, have you learned nothing working with me? Does it just go in one ear and out the other? Does it?!"

Coach pokes Dale in the side of his head as hard as he can.

"No." Dale rubs his head.

Rasha and the other dogs are listening in on this odd exchange. They always enjoy watching the callous Dale get chewed out by his uncle.

"I'm beginning to think I'm wasting my time mentoring you here at Beast Dog Kennels, Dale. Why do you think we train these dogs so hard starting when they're puppies? Why do you think we kill so many damn dogs after the rolls? Because, by nature, they're nanny dogs. They're wusses. They only become badass fighters because I'm the best at training them. Look over there at Rasha and Sadie. They got fire in their eyes. Now look at this wuss ass dog at your feet. Does *he* got that fire?"

Dale looks at the scared black pit bull whose ears are down. Dale lowers his head in shame. "Should I just shoot him then?"

Coach sees how dispirited his nephew is. He's spent a lot of time grooming Dale to take over the yard, so instead of completely discouraging him, Coach decides to make this into a teaching moment. "First off, did you check to see if he has a microchip or GPS tracker? The cops could be coming to my place right now."

"I'm on top of it," Dale says. "We found the microchip and already cut it out of his back. You taught me well."

"All right. Normally I don't like encouraging this type of thing, but I'm a businessman, so here's what we're gonna do. I'm busy right now prepping for Chopper's fight, so we'll keep this dog 'til next week. We'll do one roll. If he doesn't have any game, we'll get rid of him. If he does, we'll sell him to someone out of state. That way those activist kids don't find him. Maybe we can sell him as a package deal with a more experienced dog and make a little extra cash."

Dale lights up. It means a lot to him that his uncle respects him, so he's very pleased this turned out okay.

Coach motions to an empty spot in the yard by Rasha. "Chain him up with the other dogs. If we end up selling him, I'll have you handle the deal as a learning opportunity. But let me be clear, nephew, the next time you compromise my business, your little apprenticeship here is done. Got it?"

"Absolutely," Dale says. "It won't happen again."

Dale attaches the black pit bull to a chain. Rasha and the other dogs watch as the newcomer is stationed beside them. He crouches as flat as a pancake as if he's trying to melt into the ground to get away from Dale.

Dale points his finger in the dog's face. "Don't let me hear you whining no more. If I do, I'll put a muzzle on you and feed you to Chopper over there. Trust me, you don't wanna mess with *him*."

Dale follows Coach into the house. The black pit bull looks around at all the dogs. They look muscular, angry, and each looks capable of chewing him to pieces. He sprints into the wooden shelter and quietly starts whimpering to himself.

"Shut up in there!" Sadie barks at him.

Sadie's scolding just makes the pit bull cry louder.

"I said, shut up!" Sadie hollers.

"Leave him alone, Sadie," Rasha barks.

"Or what?" Sadie bares her teeth.

Rasha ignores her and steps toward the new pit bull's area as far as her chain will let her. She calls into the shelter. "Hello? I'm Rasha. We're friendly here. Well, everyone except Sadie."

The pit bull gets quiet.

"It's okay, you can come out," Rasha says. "What's your name?"

The black pit bull pokes his nose out of the shelter. "Finley. I don't want any trouble. I just want to go home."

Rasha sighs. This dog has no idea how hard life is about to get. She feels awful for him. She looks over at Chopper, who also looks concerned. He shakes his head, knowing that Finley won't last long here.

"Where was home?" Rasha asks.

Finley sticks his whole head out. "It was with my mom and dad, Maliq and Lucienne. I miss them so much."

Rasha continues making small talk to calm Finley down. "They sound like wonderful dogs."

"They're humans," Finley corrects.

"Humans?!" Sadie jumps in. "His parents are humans and they're nice? It sounds more like he got knocked too hard in the head by Dale."

Rasha ignores Sadie. She lies down so as not to seem too intimidating to Finley. "I don't understand. Your parents were humans? How is that possible?"

Finley lights up for the first time. He can't contain his joy when discussing Maliq and Lucienne. "They adopted me from a shelter. No one wanted to adopt me because I'm a pit bull. You know how humans are. They think we're all dangerous, but not Maliq and Lucienne. They knew I just wanted hugs. And they're always so full of hugs." Finley starts whimpering again. "I want to go home. When do I get to go home?"

Rasha knows the answer to that question, but she doesn't have the heart to say it. "You said the humans are nice? That seems so hard to believe. I've never met a kind human in my life."

"These ones are different. They're so nice that, unlike most humans, they don't even eat other animals."

"Huh." Rasha thinks about this for a moment. Compassionate humans. The concept is so foreign to her. And Finley even calls these humans his parents. *I wonder what his real parents would think about that.* Then she thinks about her own little pups on the way. *I bet his parents would rather be with him, but if they can't be, I guess they'd be happy that he was at least safe and loved.*

"I miss them so much," Finley says. "Do you think I'll ever see them again?"

"No!" Sadie blurts out. "Didn't you hear what Coach said? He's going to sell you to a human in another state. You better get ready to fight or you're gonna die."

Rasha runs toward Sadie and barks as close to her as she can get. "Shut up! Leave him alone. What is wrong with you? Don't you see he's scared?"

"He *should* be scared," Sadie barks back. She pulls on her chain, getting inches from where Rasha is standing. "And *you* should be, too. If this chain wasn't holding me back, you'd be dead already."

Rasha sits back down. She realizes how useless it is to let Sadie get to her. She shakes her head. "You're pathetic."

Sadie pulls harder on her chain to get as close to Rasha as she can. She pulls so hard that it chokes her. She coughs and steps back.

"You really don't get it, Sadie," Rasha says. "Everyone here sees through your act. You bark at all of us, trying to act tough, thinking that makes you look brave. That's not bravery. True bravery is staying kind in the face of all this evil."

"I'll show you who's brave!" Sadie glares at Rasha but doesn't move. Even she knows her threat is hollow.

"It's okay to be afraid," Rasha says. "Everything about this life is scary. Finley is allowed to be afraid, and the rest of us dogs should comfort him, because that's the right thing to do. Before Chopper found out that he was my father, he was kind to me. He's the toughest dog I know, but deep down he's the sweetest dog you'll ever meet."

Rasha looks over at Chopper and smiles. She turns back to Sadie. "Despite how mean you've been to me all this time, when Coach took away your puppies, I felt sad for you. For a brief moment, you let go of that tough persona and reacted honestly. I thought maybe there was hope for you, but I realize now that you're too cowardly to let yourself be vulnerable."

"Shut up!" Sadie fumes. "I'll kill you."

Rasha continues, unfazed by Sadie's threats. "It's not your fault you're like this. That's what this place does to us dogs. It makes us cruel so that we can survive. Which is the exact reason I won't let that happen to my puppies. They will not live this life."

Chopper cuts in, stunned. "You're pregnant?!"

He's as devastated by this news as Rasha. He doesn't want his grandkids suffering as fighters, either.

Rasha turns back to Chopper. She sighs deeply and nods. Chopper sees that desperate and determined look in her eyes. He's seen it before with other pregnant dogs.

"I know what you're planning to do, Rasha," Chopper says. "You're gonna fight Coach and Dale. It won't work. I've seen other mothers try it, and those humans find a way to trick them and take the puppies. Sometimes the mothers are killed in the tussle. I'll be chained up. I won't be able to protect you. I can't watch you die, Rasha."

Rasha looks at the grimy area in which she's been stuck most of her life—the piles of excrement staining the dirt, the splinter-filled shelter, the other scar-covered dogs. *This is no life for my babies. I'll fight to the death before I let those ruthless humans steal them.* It even crosses her mind to kill her pups as painlessly as possible to save them from the pit. She shudders. She'll do anything to spare them the life she's led.

This is it. This is her lowest moment. There comes a time when you can take no more. She thought she had reached that moment many times before, but now she knows *this* is the true breaking point. *If I die protecting my babies, I am at peace with that. I always thought I'd die in the pit, and for all the horrible things I've done to other dogs, maybe that's what I deserve. But I haven't. So I will protect them and die. That is how all this will end.*

But that is *not* how all this will end. Just when Rasha had given up all hope, the most miraculous thing occurs: One week later, a tiny, cunning mink steps up to her paws. He's the most daring creature she's ever encountered.

She sees that he's accompanied by an army of other minks, raccoons, and even a cat who despises humans just as much as she and the other dogs do. The mink presents a plan so bold that the hairs on the back of every dog in that yard stand on end. Not only will this army of dissidents free all the dogs on this property, but they're also going to murder the humans who have tortured them their entire lives. It's too good to be true and yet it will happen. The dogs have fantasized about this moment every miserable second of their miserable lives. Coach and Dale are going to die—very horrible and painful deaths. This is going to be wonderful.

49

THE TIME TO raid Coach's house is fast approaching.

The Dissidents speed around the yard, finishing last-minute prepa-
rations. Most of the pit bulls are freed from their chains, and the dog
carcasses from the woods have all been attached to the chains in their
place. The army won't burn the bodies until after the raid, though. That
would certainly alert the humans to their scheme.

Once the attack on the humans is finished, the army will need
to vacate the premises immediately. This fact is making Rasha very
anxious. Chopper is having immense difficulty moving on his own. He's
managed to stand up a few times, but then he can barely move an inch.

Leaving Chopper is obviously not an option, so Rasha is doing
everything she can to assist him in walking, but his injuries are too
debilitating.

"Are you ready to try getting up again, Papa?" Rasha asks Chopper.

Chopper lets out a deep breath as he lies on the ground. He
knows the urgency of the situation, but every time he moves, the pain
paralyzes him.

Finley stands on the other side of Chopper, waiting to help guide him along as well. After a week of witnessing what happens in this yard, Finley was certain he would die, so he couldn't be more grateful to be free.

Rasha's heart races a million miles a minute. She wanted to be deep in the forest by this point—partially because of Chopper's safety but also because of a secret she dare not tell anyone. She knows it's controversial because she even shocked herself when the thought came to her: *I don't want to kill these humans.*

When Vincent first proposed the idea a few hours ago, it excited her. These humans have done such horrific things to her and the other dogs that the idea of getting revenge felt exhilarating, but the more she thinks about it, the more her true, gentle nature seeps in.

I know Coach and Dale deserve to die for what they've done to us. And Jean deserves to die for knowing all along and doing nothing to stop it. I know that if they aren't killed, they'll just hurt more animals, but I don't want to kill anymore. My whole life I've been forced to hurt and murder other dogs, but I'm not a murderer. I know everyone here will think of me as a coward, but I can't do it. I just want to get as far away from this yard as possible and be free.

She considered admitting this to Chopper, but then she realized that she didn't have to. She could use the excuse that she had to get him to safety as a way of avoiding the attack on the humans. *It's sneaky, but I can't exactly be honest with the other dogs—not now at least. Everyone's so worked up about finally getting their revenge. If I told them, they'd be furious at me—maybe even turn on me. I would understand their anger, but I can't kill anymore. It's not who I am.*

Rasha sees Chopper struggling to stand up again, so she decides to try a different tactic. "Hold on a moment, Papa."

Rasha calls out to a brown female pit bull nearby. "You there, I need your help."

The dog, Basil, steps over to Rasha. "Sure. What can I do?"

"My father is gravely injured. We need to get him out of the yard before the raid on the house, in case any humans come rushing in here. Do you think you can help Finley and me carry him?"

Basil looks surprised.

Chopper cuts in. "Rasha, I don't want you all fussing over me."

"Hush up, Papa. This is the only way." Rasha turns back to Basil. "What do you say?"

"Let's give it a go. I just want to make sure I'll be back in time for the raid."

"Yes, absolutely."

Rasha, Finley, and Basil crouch near Chopper. "Papa, crawl onto our backs and we'll do the rest."

Just then, Sadie darts in front of Rasha, Finley, Basil, and Chopper and plants herself between them and the gate entrance.

"Where do you think *you're* going?" Sadie growls.

Rasha's a bit startled. For the first time, she had let her guard down. All the animals were being so gracious to one another. It felt like true harmony as she had always imagined, but then there's Sadie—bitter, vengeful Sadie.

"I'm taking my father to safety," Rasha explains. "As you can see, he can barely walk. Once we kill those humans, we'll have to run out of here. He'd get left behind and maybe killed by other humans."

"Once *we* kill the humans?" Sadie says. "So you're coming back?"

"Of course," Rasha says impatiently. "I just need to get my father a safe distance from the yard. Now step out of our way."

Sadie keeps her feet firmly in place and glares at Rasha. "You're not coming back. I know you, you coward. You're deserting us."

How does she know? Rasha's heart starts racing. A few minks, raccoons, and dogs have stopped to see what the row is about.

Sadie calls out to the growing crowd. "She's deserting us. She's going to run to safety while we risk our lives ridding the world of these humans."

Rasha's paws start trembling. That old feeling comes back—the panic before a fight. She feels sick to her stomach. *Will all these animals attack me for being a coward? Will they hurt my father and Finley, too?*

"Hey, let her go, Sadie," Maxie says. Rasha is surprised. Maxie is the dog she was forced to fight in her second "roll." To have this dog come to her defense means a great deal to Rasha.

"We've got enough soldiers here to kill three humans," Maxie continues. "Let her get her father to safety."

"Stay out of this," Sadie barks. "This is between me and the coward. We're going to determine once and for all who the real champion is."

Sadie glowers at Rasha. "What do you say, Rasha? Why don't we find out who the true champion is?"

"You fight her, you fight me," Chopper snarls.

"And me!" Finley says.

"Me too!" a few other dogs call out.

Sadie grits her teeth, realizing she's outnumbered.

"Shh!" Ember calls out to the growling dogs. "You'll wake the humans. You'll ruin the plan."

More minks, raccoons, and dogs have crowded around, sensing a fight.

"Okay, everyone," Rasha says, trying to whisper. "Thank you for your support, but there will be no fight. The fighting is over." Rasha looks at Sadie. "We don't have to hurt each other any longer. Don't you see that you're still thinking how the humans trained you to think? 'Champions?' Hurting another dog doesn't make you a champion. The humans have controlled us our entire lives. They made us think that we're enemies, but we're not. We're survivors. We did what we had to do to survive, but none of that matters now. We're free."

"Rasha is right," Vincent says as he parts his way through the crowd. He steps between Rasha, Finley, Basil, Chopper, and Sadie and looks around at all the dogs, raccoons, minks, and the cat. He faces Sadie to address her directly, but he's really talking to everyone.

"For the first time in your life, you are free, Sadie. Do you really want the first decision you make as a free dog to be just continuing to do what the humans forced you to do—to fight one another? No. Make your first act of freedom a defiant one. Every terrible thing that's happened in your life is because of humans—not one another. Save your hatred for them. Get revenge against the humans who did this to you. And not just to *you*, but to all dogs and to all us other animals."

Vincent turns his attention to the crowd that's encircling him. He's getting more animated as he speaks, scratching at the grass and dirt. "Humans have murdered countless minks, including my dear friends and family. A human sliced apart my brother right in front of me, and you know what The Dissidents and I did? We sliced apart *his* family. And we killed all his neighbors, too. We killed anyone who dared hurt one of my brethren!"

Vincent tears out a chunk of sod and slams it onto the ground.

"Humans are massacring us other animals by the billions. They must be stopped and the only way to stop them is to join forces and fight back."

Some of the animals hoot quietly in agreement.

Vincent looks at Rasha. "As of tonight, you are free dogs. No one will force you to fight any longer. If you want to walk through that gate right now, you are more than welcome to do so."

He looks back at the crowd of animals again. They are all enraptured by his speech. "But let me be clear. Our attacks may be surreptitious for now, but once the humans find out what we're doing, they will strike back with everything they've got—and every one of us knows how vicious they are. At some point, each and every one of us will have to make a choice to fight or perish. This is a war. We didn't start it, but we are going to end it."

Vincent points to different dogs, raccoons, and minks as he speaks. "I want you to rip them to shreds. Kill every human who crosses your path. *Then* you will be champions."

The crowd of animals scratches at the ground, too, ready for a battle.

Vincent licks his chipped tooth. "Together, we are an unstoppable force and the humans are our enemies. Let's go kill our enemies!"

Every animal can feel the fire burning deep within. All the anger they've stored up from years of abuse comes bubbling to the top, and they can't wait to take every ounce of it out on Coach, Dale, and his wife.

Vincent charges through the crowd and darts straight for the house, followed by a mass of angry animals.

Rasha, Finley, Basil, and Chopper watch the army as they speed away. Only Sadie is left standing across from the foursome. Sadie looks at the ground and huffs. She realizes how petty she has been. All those years of brainwashing sunk in so thoroughly, she wasn't able to see that her need to be the most dominant dog around was really just part of her subjugation. She feels ashamed for falling prey to it, but she's too proud to admit it now. Instead, she runs after the rest of the army toward the house. Better to take her fury out on the humans who did this to her.

Rasha, Chopper, and Finley look at one another. There's an unspoken understanding that they don't want to be part of what's about to happen in that house. Vincent's speech was rousing, but deep down they want a peaceful life—as they always have. That said, a part of them also knows it isn't possible to have peace with humans like Coach and Dale. So what's the solution? None of them has the answer. At this moment, they just want to get away from this place and never look back.

Rasha, Finley, and Basil crouch again and Chopper crawls onto their backs. It works. Slowly but surely, they make their way to the entrance gate. Freedom is only a few paces away.

50

A WAVE OF dogs, minks, raccoons, and one cat marches up to the back of Coach's house. No one makes a sound, but the collective rage is deafening. Vincent has a detailed plan, so they all know their roles. Now it's time to put it into place.

First, they must enter the home. Unlike all the other houses that The Dissidents have raided, Coach's house is like a fortress—every door and window is tightly locked. That poses a major problem because the safety of this mission hinges on a surprise attack. Without an easy entryway, getting in without waking the humans will be difficult.

Vincent and Rawly crawl up to a small window that leads to a bathroom on the first floor. Scraps, Drig, Linder, Dusty, and a few other raccoons follow, creating a line to the ground. The dozens of pit bulls stand ready at both the back and the front doors. When those doors open, they must be the first line of attack. They're hoping the raccoons open the doors quietly, but if their entry into the home awakens the humans, the pit bulls are ready to strike.

From the ground, a raccoon hands a sharp rock to the first raccoon holding onto the wall. That raccoon passes it to the next raccoon with his mouth, and soon the rock makes its way up to Rawly.

"Ready?" Vincent calls out to his soldiers.

A leader from each group stationed around the house calls back. "Ready!"

Vincent grins. This is it. The raid begins now.

Vincent looks over at the pit bulls positioned at the back door. He nods. Three dogs howl into the night air. Vincent turns to Rawly. "Now."

Rawly hits the sharp rock against the glass as hard as he can. It cracks the glass. He hits again and again. The dogs keep howling to mask the sound.

Each member of The Dissidents is tense, looking up at the windows to the bedrooms on the second floor. If those lights go on, things will get chaotic and dangerous very quickly.

Finally, Rawly smashes a hole wide enough to allow passage. Vincent motions for the dogs to stop howling, which they do immediately.

The lights do not go on. The humans are used to the dogs crying out in the night, so they have learned to sleep through it. The plan worked. They can now enter the home.

Rawly, Scraps, Drig, and the other raccoons quickly but carefully wriggle through the window, avoiding the shards of glass. Most of the pieces fell into the bathtub, so the raccoons hop over to the shower curtain and drop to the bathroom floor.

Right after, Vincent and other minks rush in through the window as well. It's as if the hull of a ship has been breached and the dark ocean water is quickly filling it up.

Stealthily, the raccoons divide into two groups, rushing to the front and back doors. At the back door, Drig stands firmly on all fours and Rawly jumps onto his back. Rawly stands on his hind legs and reaches for the doorknob. He's breathing heavily. This part of the mission is nothing like the missions he did with Persimmon. The dogs have already been rescued. They could all run away free now, but that wouldn't stop these humans from harming other dogs and most likely going on a hunt for these dogs. This mission is going one step further. Rawly understands why The Dissidents must kill these humans, but he still feels sick to his stomach. In a matter of minutes, these humans will be ripped to shreds and *he's* the one who's opening the door.

There's no turning back now. Rawly fidgets with the lock and turns the handle.

Dogs on the other side push, and sure enough, the door opens. Rawly and Drig quickly jump out of the way, and the room instantly fills with pit bulls. With light steps, they sprint up the stairs to the second floor. The air is filled with the ominous tapping of dogs' nails on hard wood.

The hallway is soon overtaken by a swarm of pit bulls. There are two bedrooms upstairs and two raccoons are stationed at each door to open them—Dusty and Linder at Dale's door and Rawly and Drig at Coach's door. Vincent sits on Sadie's back to lead the mission, but the rest of the raccoons and minks stand behind the dogs on the stairs and on the first floor. The minks and raccoons are only here for assistance. The dogs are the ones who were brutalized by these humans, so they're the ones who will end their lives.

The dogs listen attentively to the sounds on the other sides of those doors. The minks scoped out the bedrooms from the roof, so they know which bedroom contains Dale and which contains Coach and his wife. Now they must listen in to make sure the humans are still fast asleep. The Dissidents hear smooth, regular breathing. The humans are asleep all right.

The time to attack is now.

Vincent turns to the raccoons at the doors. He holds up his left paw. When he gives the signal, they will quietly open the doors simultaneously.

All the pit bulls brace to lunge. For their entire lives, they've fantasized about getting back at these humans for being so vicious to them and now the moment is finally here. There is no joy in it, though. They've never enjoyed killing. It's pure rage. Years of torment end tonight, and it all hinges on what happens in the next few minutes.

The dogs stare at Vincent's paw, anticipation rumbling inside. They're ready to charge at any moment.

Vincent looks at Dusty and Rawly and swiftly motions with his paw.

The two raccoons use both paws to turn their doorknobs. Dusty opens his door, but to Rawly's shock, his door won't budge. Rawly twists harder, but it still doesn't move. Coach's door is locked!

Rawly nervously looks down at Vincent. "What do we do?"

Vincent grits his teeth. This is disastrous. This door was their only way in. Minks already scoped out the window to Coach's bedroom and it's locked, too. They can't smash the window with rocks like they did the window downstairs. They'd never get it open before Coach woke up and either attacked them or called someone for help. Vincent is running out of ways to get on the other side of these walls and it is absolutely not an option to leave without fulfilling their mission. These dogs deserve to have their revenge.

There is really only one more option, and it's the most dangerous of all.

Vincent turns to his soldiers. "We'll have to lure these humans out."

51

VINCENT IS PERCHED on the windowsill at the end of the hall with Rawly and Ember by his side. The rest of the hall is filled with pit bulls—more eager than ever to bust into these bedrooms.

Sadie stands at attention, glaring at Coach's bedroom door. She wants to be the first to crunch down on his bones.

Scraps, Drig, Linder, and Dusty are stationed outside Coach's window on the roof so they can keep an eye on what Coach is doing inside the room. To get out onto the roof, the raccoons unlocked the hallway window and ripped out the screen. They did it as quietly as possible so as not to awaken Dale, whose bedroom door is already cracked open.

Vincent, normally unflappable, is agitated by the mission's turn of events. This is not at all what he had planned for this attack, and as he looks out at all his soldiers, he knows that everyone's lives are in grave danger. So many things could go wrong—Coach could call the police, Coach could refuse to open the door. Each scenario leads to dire consequences. But what actually happens, no one sees coming.

Vincent holds up his paw. The Dissidents go deathly still. This is it.

With a swift scratch at the air, Vincent signals for the attack to begin. Immediately, a dozen pit bulls charge into Dale's bedroom. Dale screeches in terror, and then a violent banging is heard as he shakes to break free from the dogs ripping him to pieces.

Through the window, Scraps sees Coach hop out of bed so the raccoon yells to Vincent and the dogs. "He's up!"

Coach looks around for a moment, disoriented. Then he realizes that his nephew is screaming for his life.

"Dale?!" Coach shouts.

Coach runs back to his bed, reaches under his pillow, and sprints toward the door.

Scraps sees the shiny metal object in Coach's hand, but he can't tell what it is until it's too late.

Coach swings open the door and the dogs burst into the room.

BAM! Coach unloads his .38 Special at the lunging dogs. The bullet shoots through the chest of one of the dogs, Vladimir. He yelps as he falls to the ground. Jean screams at the top of her lungs as the room fills with pit bulls jumping onto her husband.

The attacking pit bulls chomp down into Coach's legs and feet. Sadie grabs a hold of Coach's calf with her powerful jaw. The man points the gun at her head, but just at that moment, Maxie bites into his thigh and Coach shoots Maxie in the shoulder instead. Maxie howls and drags herself to the other side of the room.

Seeing no way of avoiding the deadly weapon, Sadie and the other dogs retreat for the door.

Back in the hallway, Vincent runs straight toward the bedroom. Everyone else is running *away* from the gunfire, but Vincent runs straight *for it*. He knows what's coming next. Coach is going to slam that door shut and then they'll never be able to get inside again.

Rawly, Scraps, Drig, and Ember see Vincent sprinting toward the door and instinctively rush after him. He must have a plan, right?

Coach shoots at the door as the dogs dash out of the room. Fortunately, this bullet doesn't hit any of the fleeing canines. The room is officially cleared of attacking dogs except Maxie and Vladimir, who are wounded, so Coach sees his moment. Though blood pours out of his legs and feet, he pushes himself up and hobbles toward the door. Just before he closes it, Vincent, Rawly, Scraps, Drig, and Ember bolt into the room.

"What the hell?!" Coach gasps as the small critters scamper past his feet.

Instead of firing his weapon again, he pushes his shoulder into the door and slams it shut. He twists the lock.

Vincent, Rawly, Scraps, Drig, and Ember dart under the bed, sending Jean into another screaming fit.

"There's more! They're under the bed. Shoot 'em!"

"Shut up, woman!" Coach yells. "They're just rats and raccoons. I'm not wasting bullets on 'em."

All the other Dissidents hide in the hallway, not sure what to do next. Some of them saw Vincent and his daring companions rush into the bedroom, but there's no way of getting in there to help them.

"Dale?" Coach yells through the door. "Are you okay, nephew?"

No answer.

Jean grabs for her cellphone on her nightstand. Her hands are shaking, so she fumbles to unlock it and dial.

"What are you doing?" Coach yells.

"I'm calling the cops," Jean says through tears.

Coach staggers over to the bed and hits the phone out of her hands. "You can't call the damn cops. They'll see the whole setup in the backyard—the shed, the pit, all the pit bulls. Are you trying to get me sent to jail?"

"You're all bit up," Jean says. "What are we supposed to do, just sit here?"

"Will you shut up for a second?" Coach yells as he falls back onto the bed. "I need to think."

Blood pours out of the wounds on his legs and feet. His right foot is missing some toes. His pajamas are tattered, and the high school eagle mascot on his shirt is smeared red. He breathes heavily as he holds the gun by his side.

The two dogs who were shot, Maxie and Vladimir, whimper as they sit curled up together in the corner.

"You two shut up or I'll put another bullet in you. I feed you. I take care of you and *this* is how you repay me?!"

The dogs quiet down and curl up even tighter.

From under the bed, Vincent calls out toward the door. "Everyone keep clear of the hallway. We have no idea if he'll start shooting again."

Sadie and the other pit bulls are packed together, filling the stairs and spilling onto the first floor. Some of them are stained with Dale's blood. One human down, two to go. They were so close to getting Coach, but now, who knows what will happen?

Sadie curses herself. *I had him. What a weakling I am. I saw the gun and I ran. I could have made his throat, but instead I ran.*

Vincent turns to Rawly, Scraps, Drig, and Ember, who are huddled at the far end of the bed near the wall. They're trying to be brave, but they're shaking in fear.

"Impressive," Vincent whispers. "You all heard that gun going off and you *still* ran in here. That's what makes you Dissidents. And that's why together we will ensure that neither of these humans leaves this room alive."

The group stares at Vincent. They want to believe they made the right choice by running in here, but sitting above them is an irate human with a loaded gun, who will have no problem shooting any one of them if they step out from under this bed.

Coach is lost in thought. Jean cries to herself on the bed beside him. She has her legs pulled up to her chest with the covers wrapped around her.

"Who the hell would sic my own dogs on me?" Coach mumbles to himself.

An idea pops into Coach's head and he sighs loudly. Jean jumps at the sound.

"It's okay." Coach pats her on the leg and whispers. "I get it now. It's gotta be Maxwell who set this whole thing up. Chopper beat his dog tonight at the fight. I knew that idiot Maxwell would be sore about it, but I didn't think he'd take it *this* far. Don't worry, babe. I got this."

Coach calls toward the door. "Maxwell, is that you? Hey man, Chopper won that fight fair and square. I told you he was a good fighter. How about this? We can resolve this like men. We'll do a rematch. When Chopper heals, he can fight again. Or maybe instead I'll offer up my best fighting dog, Rasha. I'll double the purse. What do you say?"

No answer. As Coach talks, he pats the blanket on some of his wounds, trying to stop the blood.

"Just let me know that Dale is okay. I wanna hear his voice."

Still no answer. Coach hits his fist on the bed. "Maxwell, damn it! Answer me! If you hurt my nephew, I swear to God, I'll murder your entire family and feed them to your dogs."

Jean cries louder. Coach puts his arm around his wife and rubs her back. "It's okay, baby. We're gonna get out of this just fine. Maxwell's just angry his dog lost the fight, so he's trying to send a message. Isn't that right, Maxwell?"

At the top of the stairs, the dogs rustle behind Sadie. She turns to see the pit bulls squeezing to make room for none other than Rasha. Sadie is equally stunned and annoyed to see her. *She shows up now? After we've already been attacked by Coach?*

Rasha makes her way beside Sadie but doesn't say anything. She's still surprised that she's here herself. Rasha had made up her mind to stay out of this fight. She, Basil, and Finley escorted Chopper to safety in the woods, and just as they were settling down to give Chopper a short rest, they heard the gun shots back at the house. At the sound of those shots, guilt overcame Rasha. In her heart, killing feels wrong and putting her babies at risk feels wrong, but isn't abandoning her pack also wrong? And when her pups grow up, wouldn't they be disappointed that their mother was a deserter?

She realized that no matter how much she wanted to put fighting behind her, she would have to join this one last brawl. So she and Basil ran as fast as they could to the house, and the other dogs ushered Rasha to the front of the line, knowing that she's the best fighter in the yard.

Sadie knows why Rasha is here, so she turns to her and growls. "Stay out of my way. *I'm* killing Coach."

Rasha nods. She's just here to help keep the other dogs safe. She's fine letting someone else do the killing.

Vincent calls out from inside the bedroom. "Sadie, are you out there?"

"Yes," Sadie says. "Tell us what you need. We're ready to attack."

"I'm here, too, Vincent," Rasha says.

Vincent perks up. He's happy to hear Rasha has joined the fight. "Perfect. We'll get that door open soon, but before we do, I need to know how many bullets that gun holds."

"I've seen him kill countless dogs with that gun," Rasha exclaims. "It has six bullets."

Vincent licks his chipped tooth. He has a new scheme worked out and that information was the missing key. "He fired the gun three times, which means he has three shots left. Everyone listen up!"

The dogs on the stairs and the soldiers under the bed stand at attention. Coach is still blathering away through the door at Maxwell and has no idea that a plot is brewing right under his feet.

"Here's the plan," Vincent declares. "I'm going to get this human to fire that gun three more times and when I do, I need you..." He looks at Rawly and Drig. "...to run out as fast as you can to open that door."

"What do you mean you're going to get him to 'fire that gun'?" Rawly asks. "Are you planning to get him to shoot at *you*?"

"Don't worry," Vincent says. "I can handle this human. The important thing is that no one except me runs out from the safety of this bed until that gun is empty. If you do, you're liable to get me or yourself killed. Got it?"

"Vincent," Rawly protests. "I don't—"

"The decision is made. That is the plan." Vincent then calls to the dogs in the hall. "Did everyone out there hear that? After those three bullets go off, run to that door and get ready to lunge in here and kill these vile humans."

"Yes!" The dogs cheer. They feel empowered again. Excitement fills the hallway.

Rasha feels that nausea she always gets before a fight. She has a bad feeling about this.

Vincent continues his rallying cry. "I want all of you in that hallway to make a lot of noise. Humans get easily disoriented with noise."

Vincent scratches his nails into the bed frame, sending chills down the spines of Coach and Jean. "Mark my words, Dissidents, you will have your revenge tonight!"

The Dissidents in the house begin to chant. "Coach is dead! Coach is dead!"

Coach and Jean look at each other as the house fills with the loud barking of dogs and hissing of raccoons and minks.

"Hey, shut up out there!" Coach hollers. "I'll shoot all of you dead. I got no problem getting new dogs!"

"Coach is dead! Coach is dead!" The ominous chanting continues.

Coach is distracted, so Vincent jumps into action. The mink crawls into the covers and scratches at Jean's leg. Jean screeches and throws the blanket on the floor. "Shoot it! Shoot it!"

Caught up in the moment, Coach shoots at the blanket, not realizing Vincent is already back under the bed. One bullet!

Vincent runs up the back of the bed and onto the mattress, biting at Jean's back. She leaps out of the bed and sprints across the room. Coach swings his fist at Vincent, but the mink bounds out of the way just in time. Coach reaches for the tiny creature, but when he sees Jean fumbling with the lock on the door, he rushes to the door instead.

Before Jean can undo the lock, Coach grabs a hold of her and throws her back onto the bed. "You idiot! Are you trying to get us eaten alive?! Those dogs out there are trained killers."

Jean cries and hollers unintelligibly. She can't take any more of this madness.

Vincent capitalizes on Coach's distraction again by crawling up the man's leg and biting into the wound on his thigh. Coach grabs at the mink but misses, and Vincent climbs up his back toward his head. Coach reaches behind him to seize the mink when the gun accidentally goes off and shoots into the air by the man's ear. Two bullets!

Coach drops the weapon on the ground and falls to his knees. He clutches his ear in pain. Vincent's ears are ringing, too, but luckily he had jumped onto the bed just in time, so the gun wasn't too close to his head. Seeing the mink jumping toward her, Jean rolls over onto the floor and curls up in a ball by the wall.

Rawly sees his chance. He grasps the gun with his teeth and pulls it under the bed.

Coach notices the raccoon stealing his gun, so he grabs the bed frame. With one mighty pull, he lifts the bed off the ground and throws it into the wall. Rawly, Scraps, Drig, and Ember are revealed. They scatter immediately.

Scraps and Drig run for the door while Rawly rushes toward an open closet with the gun in his mouth. Ember runs behind Rawly, twists around and hisses at Coach.

Coach is stunned for a moment at the gall of this tiny being, but then charges toward her. Vincent catches up and the two minks run circles around the man's legs, trying to slow him down. Coach kicks at them. "Get out of my damn way, vermin!"

Drig slides into the door and stands on his four legs. Scraps quickly hops onto the raccoon's back and reaches for the doorknob. It's just out of his reach, so he jumps up and swings on the doorknob, trying to twist the lock open with his teeth.

Coach swings his foot at Ember, landing a blow. She hurls into the wall and hits it with a thud. Her body lands on the ground.

"I'll kill you!" Vincent screams as he leaps onto Coach's leg and digs his nails and teeth deep into Coach's skin.

Coach yells, but as he goes to grab for Vincent, he steps down on his foot with the missing toes. Pain shoots up Coach's leg and he trips into the closet, disappearing along with Vincent. Somewhere in that darkness, Rawly is covering the gun with his body and now Coach has fallen right beside him.

Scraps finally undoes the lock and swings his body to open the door. The room fills with infuriated pit bulls.

Jean shrieks as five dogs swarm on top of her, violently yanking her apart.

Rasha, Sadie, and the other dogs rush toward the closet. The gun still hasn't gone off a third time. They hesitate. Rasha looks over at Sadie, but Sadie doesn't move.

Without another moment's hesitation, Rasha charges into the closet. The rest of the dogs listen in horror to a loud tussle inside. Should they run in? Will they get in Rasha's way? Will they get shot themselves?

BAM! The gun goes off a third time.

The room goes silent. Sadie begins to lead the rest of the pit bulls toward the closet when Rasha comes bounding out, dragging Coach with her teeth deep in his shoulder. Coach shakes around, screaming with Vincent hopping on his stomach, chewing at him and digging holes into the man's skin.

"Die, human! Die!" Vincent fumes.

Rasha pulls Coach to the middle of the room and lets go. Vincent looks around at the pit bulls circling the human. They've got this from here. He jumps onto the ground and runs to check on Ember.

Rasha steps back from Coach and motions to the other dogs. "He's all yours."

Coach sits up, bleeding from multiple wounds. He peers around at the pack of pit bulls growling viciously. "Sadie, Krait, stand down. What the hell has gotten into you? Stand down, I said."

Sadie gets right in his face, growling so deeply, her body rumbles. Coach feels her hot breath on his skin.

"You ungrateful animals," Coach says.

The dogs give one another satisfied looks. The moment. It's finally here. Revenge.

In a flash of rage, the dozens of dogs lunge at Coach and rip every muscle from his bones.

The bodies of Coach and his wife are so badly mangled, no one would be able to tell that they had been human.

Rasha stands against the wall. She looks away from the slaughter, but she can hear every scream and bite. The sickness in her stomach doesn't dissipate. A part of her feels relieved. *We're free. Coach will never harm another dog.* But another part of her wants to run away, wishes she hadn't felt compelled to come back to the house to help. *This is the end, right? This is the last time that I'll ever have to kill... right?*

Rasha reopens her eyes, but she's startled by what she sees in front of her. There's a mirror on the open closet door, and for the first time in her life, she gets a clear view of her own reflection. She sees the shredded flaps of skin—all that's left of her ears. She sees the chewed-up flesh on her snout—all that remains of her nose. Her face has been so thoroughly bitten apart that it's difficult to look at herself. The pain that she has endured is right there on her face for everyone to see. She quickly looks away. *I'm hideous.*

Anguish bubbles inside her. She's unable to stifle her emotions any longer. She closes her eyes and lets out a loud, pained howl.

All the pit bulls stop what they're doing and join in. Coach and Dale used to reprimand them when they made any noise, but now they don't have to answer to anyone. Their cries are filled with heartbreak over everything they've been put through in their lives, but there's also a hint of joy. Coach is dead. Never again will they be enslaved by humans. And it is up to them to ensure that no other animals are subjected to the same cruelty.

The Dissidents ignited in the dogs a passion for justice. Together, they will stop at nothing to achieve it—so help the humans who get in their way.

52

"RAWLY!" SCRAPS DASHES across the bedroom through the pit bulls. Drig follows right behind him.

The two raccoons finally push their way to the closet door and peer inside, looking for their friend. They see the gun lying in the middle of the floor. Then they see Rawly's furry tail.

"Rawly, are you okay?" Scraps runs over to his friend, fearing the worst.

Rawly isn't moving. He's staring into the darkness of the closet.

Scraps shakes his leg. "Are you shot?"

Rawly looks at his small companion, glassy-eyed. He shakes his head no.

Scraps and Drig let out a sigh of relief.

"Thank goodness!" Scraps says. "Come on, let's get out of here."

Rawly doesn't move. He can't get his mouth to form words. When that human fell right beside him and wrestled the gun out from under him, he thought he was going to die. In the same instant, he felt ashamed that he had let the human pull the gun from his grip, possibly allowing the man to kill one of the other Dissidents. But then Rasha overtook Coach, and he accidentally pulled the trigger, luckily missing everyone in that closet.

That near-death experience shook Rawly to the core. It changed him somehow.

Scraps gives Rawly a big hug. "You're a hero! That was so amazing how you took that human's gun. Amazing!"

Rawly nods. He can't quite match the small raccoon's enthusiasm at this moment, but he's starting to come out of his daze and realize the impact of his courageous feat.

"I guess I *am* a hero. You two were able to open that door?"

Scraps and Drig nod proudly.

"Then you're heroes, too," Rawly says. He taps his paws against theirs in celebration. "Come on, let's get out of here. I need some fresh air."

The three raccoons make their way through the pit bulls, avoiding the bloody mess in the center of the room. A foul stench fills the air, and most of the pit bulls have scattered outside for the final stage of the plan.

Across the room, Vincent, Rasha, and Ember stand beside the ailing Maxie. Thankfully, Ember was not injured from Coach's attack. She was merely knocked out from hitting the wall.

Unfortunately, Vladimir has already succumbed to his wound. Maxie is still curled up beside him, bleeding from her shoulder. She's beginning to feel lightheaded.

"I'm sorry, Maxie," Vincent laments. "You deserved to enjoy your freedom. I had no idea humans slept with guns in their beds."

"It's okay, Vincent," Maxie musters. "We're free. We never thought this day would come."

"What can we do for you, Maxie?" Rasha asks.

"I don't want to die in this room," Maxie sighs. "Can you help me to the forest? My whole life I stared at those trees as I was chained to that ground. I always wanted to go for a walk in the forest."

Vincent knows exactly how she feels. He and his cagemates at the fur farm daydreamed about escaping into the woods all the time. It was such a cruel tease to have freedom so close that you could taste it.

"We'll make it happen, Maxie," Vincent says as he looks to Rasha.

Rasha just went through an exhausting experience carrying Chopper through the woods. She's fatigued and concerned that she doesn't have the energy to do the trek again, but she's determined to make Maxie's wish come true.

Rasha steps beside Maxie as the dog attempts to stand. Maxie wobbles. Then Sadie rushes over and stands on the other side of Maxie to keep her balanced.

Rasha and Maxie look at Sadie with surprised expressions.

"That bullet was meant for me," Sadie says. "Let's get you to the woods."

Rasha and Sadie escort Maxie through the bedroom door into the hall.

Vincent turns to the remaining dogs in the room. "You know the plan, everyone. Get whatever items humans would steal if they were robbing someone. After that, we'll move onto Maxwell's house. I imagine those dogs imprisoned in that yard are in just as bad shape as you were here. Before dawn, they will be freed too."

With their teeth, the dogs grab Coach's wallet, Jean's purse, and Coach's gun.

Vincent nods in approval as they vacate the room. He and Ember are the only ones left. He peers at Vladimir's body in the corner.

"Tonight was tricky," Vincent says. "The unexpected circumstances cost the lives of two Dissidents."

"Two?" Ember asks.

"Maxie. She won't survive that bullet wound." Vincent digs his nails into the wood floor. "Nothing like this will ever happen again. If any of the bedroom doors are locked at the next house, we'll stampede through the windows and crush those humans before they even think about grabbing for a weapon."

"Don't focus on the past," Ember says. She steps in front of Vincent, blocking his view of the dead dog. "What's done is done. We still have a long night ahead."

Just then, Apricot saunters into the room. She looks surprised when she sees the two minks standing face to face. "Oh, excuse me. I didn't realize something intimate was going on. I can leave you two alone."

Vincent is confused. A pile of muscle and bones lies to his right and a dead dog to his left. Intimacy was the last thing on his mind, but he knows very little about cats, so he just assumes they have odd mating habits.

"You're fine," Vincent says. "Did you need something?"

Apricot tiptoes closer to them, eyeing the bloody mess in the middle of the room. "I've never seen such large prey killed before. I was curious to see the outcome. I know, it sounds macabre, but right now around 50 dead dogs are being lit on fire in the yard, so a lot of morbid stuff is going on tonight."

"Ah, they've begun." Vincent rushes over to the window and crawls up to the windowsill. He surveys the backyard. Dog carcasses have been placed at each station with collars around their necks and a few corpses are already burning.

"Good, the raccoons are right on schedule. I'll leave a few Dissidents behind to make sure the bodies burn enough to mask the months of decomposition while the rest of us trek to the next location. We'll have disappeared into the woods long before humans discover what we've done here."

Ember climbs up to the window to get a better look while Apricot stands on her hind legs alongside her.

"I have to ask before we go," Apricot says. "I saw some dogs carrying items from this house into the forest. I'm assuming that's part of the plan and not just a few thieves looking for extra cash and lipstick, right?"

"You assumed correctly," Vincent says. "Humans are lazy. They always look for the answer that creates the least work for them. They'll assume that the humans from Coach's yard and Maxwell's yard killed one another over some dispute about a dog fight. We'll plant the stolen items from Coach's house at Maxwell's house to further sell that theory."

"Ooh, so mischievous." Apricot's eyes widen. "I approve. My favorite part is that the humans have no idea about all this scheming."

Vincent watches as the raccoons pour gasoline onto more bodies and light the matches. "Humans are so arrogant. They think that they can enslave and abuse us other animals without retaliation. I can't wait to see the looks on their faces when they find out the truth. Of course by then everything and everyone they ever loved will be gone or dying."

Vincent hops down to the ground with Ember following.

As Apricot watches the two minks leave the room, her own humans, the Kojimas, cross her mind. She imagines the shocking scenario of a horde of dogs and minks tearing *them* apart. *They may have attended the circus without caring about how those creatures were abused, but they're not as bad as the humans in* this *place. Surely I could convince Vincent to leave them alone, right?*

Apricot tries to shake the Kojimas out of her mind. She looks at the bloody pile of human remains, attempting to enjoy the thought of attacking such large prey. But the faces of her human family keep popping back into her head.

Apricot huffs. *What a nuisance. This was supposed to be fun coming up here and scoping out the kill, but now it's soured.*

With that, she steps out the door and doesn't look back. She's not sure how to feel about Vincent's ultimate goal, but she does know one thing for sure—having a conscience sure is tiresome.

53

MAXIE HAS COLLAPSED in the backyard near the doorway. Rasha and Sadie stand beside her, attempting to get her back on her feet.

"I can't," Maxie says. She's lightheaded and fading. "I need to rest."

Maxie lays her head in the dirt. She closes her eyes. "I guess I wasn't meant to leave this yard."

Rasha looks out over the property with the carcasses in flames. It saddens her to think that Maxie will end up just one more corpse lying in the dirt. She's so close to escaping. It can't end this way.

"I'll be right back." Rasha rushes back into the house and up the stairs. She barrels into Dale's room and is happy to find a blanket draped over a rocking chair. She grabs the blanket and darts back down the steps.

"Here," Rasha says. "Roll onto this. We'll do the rest."

Maxie scooches onto the blanket and lies down. She closes her eyes again. She's so tired.

Rasha looks over at Sadie. "Ready?"

Sadie nods.

The two pit bulls grip the blanket with their teeth and drag Maxie toward the entrance gate. Rasha and Sadie struggle the whole way, because, like all the dogs, Maxie was fed and trained to be pure muscle.

Finally, the two dogs manage to pull Maxie through the gate and around the fence into the forest. Maxie opens her eyes and looks up at the trees. She smiles and takes a deep breath.

"Oh wow, look at this. It's as gorgeous as I imagined."

Rasha and Sadie pull Maxie past the graves of the fallen dogs, deeper into the woods. Maxie breathes in the fresh air. She watches the trees rustle in the breeze with wonder.

"Thank you for this, ladies. This is the best moment of my life."

Rasha's heart sinks as she pulls the blanket. *The best moment of her life? She's finally free and instead of enjoying years of much-deserved liberty, she's dying.* Rasha didn't think it was possible, but her hatred for Coach deepens.

Rasha stops pulling the blanket for a moment. Sadie does, too. They both need a break.

"You're free, Maxie," Rasha says. "We all are. None of us ever thought we'd see the day. It *is* a great moment."

"Yes, but not just that. This is the best moment of my life, because we're all together—working together."

Rasha and Sadie give each other a look. They certainly never thought that possible with all the bad blood between them.

"From the moment we're born, those humans try to make us think that, by nature, we're vicious fighters," Maxie says. "I even started to believe them after what I did in those fights. But we're not. We're full of love. I wanted so much for that to be true. And now I know it is."

Rasha and Sadie sit down on the blanket beside Maxie. They curl up next to the injured dog and Maxie is filled with warmth. She'd been locked on that chain, devoid of affection, most of her life. This reminds her of being snuggled up to her siblings and her mother when she was a puppy.

The three pit bulls talk as if they were childhood friends reuniting as adults. Soon Maxie is too fatigued to chat, but she smiles and listens to Rasha and Sadie. After a while, the two dogs notice that Maxie is no longer breathing. They get quiet. The sounds of the forest are heightened. Insects chirping and buzzing. Leaves rustling in the wind.

They're free. It's so surreal. They, too, had daydreamed about hiking in these woods. It seemed an impossible feat. They had traveled in a vehicle when Coach and Dale took them to fights on other properties, but they were in a crate until the fight itself. Now, for the first time, they are actually able to roam wherever they'd like.

It's bittersweet, though. Their first moments of freedom are tarnished by the death of their companion. But, as Maxie said, how beautiful it is to at least experience these moments of harmony together.

Rasha looks fondly at Sadie and Maxie by her side. *We're not evil. I am not evil. Coach was wrong.*

Despite everything those humans did to try to make her a killer, it didn't work. It couldn't work, because deep down she was always kind. This is the most important revelation of Rasha's life. She can now begin to heal.

54

DR. MISRA STANDS at her kitchen counter chopping mangoes. It's early morning and time to feed everyone. Lyric is at her feet, impatiently clawing at her shoes.

"Mangoes!" Lyric cheers.

"Lyric, what did we discuss about patience?" Dr. Misra gently chides.

Lyric stops scratching and lies on the floor, but his black-and-white tail still flops back and forth ecstatically. With mangoes coming his way, she can't possibly expect him to sit still.

Lyric hears the plastic of the pet door flap open. He twists around and peers down the hallway to the front door. To his great delight, Persimmon and Laurel bound toward him.

"Laurel! Persimmon!" Lyric rushes in their direction.

The two raccoons cuddle up to him and the three hold their embrace.

Dr. Misra instantly stops cutting the mangoes and swoops down to hug the three animals.

"My chickadees!" Dr. Misra says. "I was so worried. Where have you been?"

Dr. Misra sits on the ground, and the two raccoons crawl into her lap, nuzzling up to her. The vet kisses Persimmon and Laurel on their furry heads.

Dr. Misra notices the dirt from the two raccoons marking up her pants and shirt. "Goodness gracious, you're filthy. What have you two scamps been doing?"

Persimmon and Laurel jump out of Dr. Misra's lap and run down the hall. They stop halfway and turn to see if she's following.

"Where are you going now?" Dr. Misra asks.

"Come on! Follow us!" Persimmon says as she moves closer to the door.

Dr. Misra catches on that the two raccoons want her to follow them, so she walks down the hall. Persimmon and Laurel then jump through the pet door.

"What has gotten into you?" Dr. Misra steps down the hall with Lyric following.

She opens the door and is absolutely shocked by the sight before her. There, in her front yard, are 3,500 chickens spilling into the forest. She can't believe her eyes. At first she just looks back and forth at all the chickens with her mouth agape.

The thousands of chickens sit and stare right back at the vet. The only humans they've ever known have all hurt them terribly, so it took a lot of convincing from The Enlighteners that not all humans are menacing. Now that they see Dr. Misra in person, though, she already feels different from those other humans.

Dr. Misra looks down at the chickens on the porch. In front, Persimmon is standing with Hazel, Arden, and a third chicken. The raccoon escorts the third chicken up to the vet. The chicken has a broken wing.

"She's hurt," Persimmon says. "She needs you to heal her like you did me."

Dr. Misra kneels down. She's confused by this little raccoon's chattering.

"Where did all these chickens come from?" The vet thinks for a moment. "Wait, did they come from the Miller broiler chicken farm up the road?"

Dr. Misra looks more closely at the chickens around her on the porch. She sees the featherless spots on their backs and bellies. She sees their raw skin with boils. She sees how haggard they look. "My goodness, they did!"

The vet looks at the two raccoons, her eyes popped wide open. "Oh my, what did you two do?! Isaac is going to have my head for this."

"They need your help!" Persimmon insists. She's getting frustrated that Dr. Misra doesn't understand why the team has brought the chickens to her. This language barrier is maddening.

Persimmon looks back at the flock of chickens sitting in the grass and dirt. She notices one bird in particular at the bottom of the steps. He's hunched over, his breathing is labored and his legs are misshapen. He's clearly nearing death.

"Laurel," Persimmon says. "Can you help me lift that chicken?"

The chickens on the steps make a pathway for Persimmon and Laurel to crawl to the bottom of the steps. Then Persimmon helps push the ailing chicken onto Laurel's back. Laurel carries the chicken up the stairs and onto the porch. She crouches and Persimmon gently helps the chicken onto the ground in front of Dr. Misra.

"He's dying!" Persimmon says. She's getting a little more frantic. She's brought these poor chickens all this way, promising them that this human will save them, and she's terrified of letting them down. "Please, you have to help him!"

Dr. Misra caresses the feeble chicken on his head. He looks awful. His skin is covered with boils and his legs are twisted underneath him. "You poor baby. What happened to you?"

The vet looks up at all the sickly chickens filling her porch and lawn. Most aren't much better off than this chicken before her. It finally clicks. She looks at Persimmon and Laurel. "You want me to *heal* them? Is that why you brought them here?"

"Yes! Yes!" Persimmon and Laurel hug each other. Finally, she gets it!

"That's so beautiful." Dr. Misra says. "Bless your little hearts."

Dr. Misra takes in a deep breath. How can she possibly help all these chickens by herself? How long before Isaac Miller comes searching for "his" chickens and finds them strewn out on her lawn? She has to act fast and she can't do it alone.

55

DR. MISRA'S HOUSE is full of activity all morning. She immediately called a friend of hers, Niabi, who runs a farmed animal sanctuary, and that friend called all the animal rescuers she knows. They all rushed to the vet's house to chip in and get the chickens off to safer locations.

Persimmon, Laurel, Derpoke, Chloe, Tucker, Aunty Adelaide, Uncle Bennett, Lyric, Senator Santiago and some of his bat troops, Alister (the raccoon who is missing an eye), Marigold (the young female deer who helped Chloe during the chicken rescue), and the squirrels, raccoons, deer, beavers, skunks, and opossums watch in amazement from the woods as the humans work diligently to gently carry the chickens into trucks and cars. It's a heartwarming sight to see so many humans coming together to save other animals. This is a dream come true for the team.

The good news is that by late afternoon around 1,500 birds, including Hazel and Arden, have been driven away to various locations where they'll be treated with kindness for the rest of their days. They'll have clean straw bedding, nutritious food, and veterinary care that they so desperately need. Some won't survive the journey, but at least they will have spent the last few hours of their lives surrounded by loving humans—finally free from the filth of the sheds.

The bad news is that 2,000 chickens are still sitting on Dr. Misra's front yard and in the forest surrounding her house. Niabi's crew was the final truck to leave, and now Dr. Misra and Niabi are left surveying the remaining birds—both women have distressed looks on their faces.

"There's too many of them," Niabi says. "I called everyone I know in the area who can house chickens, and we all took as many as we could—*more* than we could. What are we going to do with the rest of these birds?"

"I wish I could keep them here, but I don't have a place for them," Dr. Misra says. "Besides, it's too close to the Miller farm. He might come snooping around, and if he finds them here, I could be in a heap of trouble."

Persimmon overhears this conversation. She had a feeling this number of chickens would prove too many for the humans to rescue, so she had the team waiting in the wings for this moment.

"Enlighteners," Persimmon calls out. "Let's move them out!"

All the team members jump into action, picking up chickens and carrying them into the forest. They will split the chickens into smaller groups deeper in the woods and various team members will watch over them. Persimmon made sure to consult with the chickens first so that they could be stationed with friends and family, but she didn't want too many chickens kept in one place. First, she was worried that finding them would be too easy for the farmer and other humans that way. Second, if predators like coyotes or mountain lions came across the chickens, protecting the birds in smaller groups would be easier for team members.

Overall, Persimmon knows that the chickens taken in by the humans have a better chance at survival, but this is the best that she could do and the chickens are just grateful to be liberated from the shed.

Dr. Misra and Niabi watch in amazement as all these different forest creatures join in on the rescue. These ladies have been rescuing animals for years, but they've never seen anything as wondrous as this.

By night, all the chickens have been escorted to their new homes in the forest, and Dr. Misra said her goodbyes to Niabi. Now Dr. Misra is raking up the feathers on her lawn as best she can and hosing down the grass. She wants to rid her home of evidence in case the farmer—or possibly even the police—comes searching for the chickens. It works. Besides a few stray feathers that will hopefully blow away in the wind and some feces that will hopefully blend into the dirt and grass, no one would know that a few thousand chickens had just been perched on her front yard.

After cleaning up the mess, Dr. Misra plunks herself down on the steps of the front porch. She is tuckered out from the unexpectedly eventful day.

Now that all the other humans have left, Persimmon, Laurel, and Lyric trot over to Dr. Misra.

"Well, well, well." Dr. Misra smiles. "Nice of you three to show up after all the hard work is done."

Lyric snuggles up to Dr. Misra's side. "Remarkable! Bravo!"

Laurel crawls into Dr. Misra's lap. "You're a hero!"

Dr. Misra almost falls back from the onslaught. "Goodness gracious. Apparently you're pleased."

Persimmon sits near the bottom step and looks up at Dr. Misra. "I'd always hoped to meet a human like you. You are extraordinary."

Persimmon hugs Dr. Misra's leg. The vet caresses the top of her furry head.

"Things have gotten a lot more exciting since you showed up, chickadee," Dr. Misra says. "Perhaps it's about time I gave you a name since you're such a big part of our lives now, eh? How about Captain

Courageous? No. Don't get me wrong, you *are* heroic, but it needs to be simpler."

After hearing that, Lyric leaps up the stairs and disappears into the house. Dr. Misra, Persimmon and Laurel are surprised by his sudden departure. A few moments later, he comes bounding through the pet door with a persimmon in his mouth. He excitedly drops it at Dr. Misra's feet.

"Ta da!" Lyric says.

Persimmon and Laurel smile at how savvy he is.

"Now Lyric," Dr. Misra says. "I just gave you all those mangoes earlier. Must you always be so obsessed with eating?"

"No," Lyric protests. He pushes the persimmon closer to Dr. Misra. "That's her *name*, silly."

"Okay, okay," Dr. Misra says. "We'll share it."

Dr. Misra takes out a pocketknife and cuts a few slices for herself, Persimmon, Laurel, and Lyric.

"It was a valiant effort, Lyric," Persimmon says as she munches on the fruit. "Is it just me or does it feel odd to eat food that bears my name?"

Dr. Misra watches the trio chew on the fruit. "Huh. Persimmon. You know, that's actually a pretty name. What do you all think?"

The two raccoons and skunk look at one another and dance happily.

Dr. Misra sees the critters perk up. "Okay, it's settled. Persimmon it is. It's fitting for my little vegetarian anyway."

Dr. Misra looks out over her yard. She sees a white feather blowing through the grass and sighs. "Those poor chickens. In all my years as a vet, I've seen some gruesome sights, but these chickens may have had it the worst. I don't... They looked so sickly and beaten up."

Persimmon and Laurel stop eating and look up at Dr. Misra. It's comforting to see her so moved by the chickens' suffering.

"Those are the same chickens I eat, aren't they? I have a chicken in the refrigerator right now. I don't... I mean, why..."

Persimmon puts down her slice of fruit. She's watching a miracle. Right before her eyes, Dr. Misra's compassion is awakening. Persimmon can barely stop herself from jumping up and down. *Yes, that's it. You're getting there.*

Dr. Misra looks down at the raccoon who is staring back up at her. "I feel so bad, you know? I could never hurt any of those chickens myself. I wouldn't dream of killing them and then eating them, and yet... there's that body in my fridge as I speak. Am I a bad person, Persimmon?"

Persimmon clutches Dr. Misra's hand. "No, you were just following what you had been taught to do your whole life. I did the same thing."

Dr. Misra smiles. She can't help it with this raccoon chattering at her.

"You are so cute, you know that, Persimmon? Should I follow your lead—no more eating animals?"

Persimmon is so overjoyed that she jumps onto Dr. Misra's lap and rolls around. "Yes! Yes! You get it!"

Laurel hops into Dr. Misra's lap to join in on the fun. Both raccoons roll around taking turns hugging and licking the vet.

"Oh my goodness!" Dr. Misra falls onto her back on the porch. "You nutballs!"

Lyric thinks about joining in, but instead he sees the rest of the persimmon lying on the step and he quickly snatches that up and shoves as much of it into his mouth as he can fit.

"Okay, okay!" Dr. Misra sits up. "Enough fun. Your paws are sticky. I need some rest after this long day. You're welcome to join me... or to go rescue another barnful of chickens. Knowing you, you'll do the latter, of course."

Dr. Misra opens the door and steps inside.

Persimmon turns to Laurel and Lyric with a giant smile beaming across her face. "Amazing, right?"

"Epic," Laurel says. "I told you she was compassionate. She just needed a little nudge."

"Do you know how huge this is?" Persimmon says. "First Gavin stops hunting and now Dr. Misra says she'll stop eating other animals. That's genuine progress. Our efforts are working!"

Persimmon's mind starts swirling with ideas. She was so focused on rescuing the chickens that she forgot about ways to enlighten humans during her rescue. "I got it!" she suddenly blurts out.

"Got what?" Laurel says.

"A way to reach humans through our latest rescue," Persimmon says. "Dr. Misra was moved to care more about the chickens after seeing how much they'd suffered, so maybe we can do the same with other people. Here's my idea: Sadly, some of the chickens died while making the trek to Dr. Misra's house. Instead of just burying them, we should take them to the humans' houses and lay the bodies on the doorsteps. I'm not saying the humans will immediately stop eating other animals, but maybe seeing how battered the chickens' bodies are will plant a seed of compassion."

Lyric grimaces at the thought of such a grisly sight, but Laurel nods. "A little gross, but it's a smart plan. You know what we should do to emphasize the point? We should put the chickens' bodies on plates. That way it will show the humans how the chickens really look before they eat them."

Persimmon's eyes light up. "Oh wow! Clever." She peers out into the woods. "I can't wait to tell everyone."

"Oh." Laurel's smile drifts away to a frown. "I guess you're gonna leave now?"

Persimmon is at a loss for words. She's been enjoying Laurel's company for weeks now. Whenever Laurel is around she feels happier—

even with all the drama during that time. She knew she'd have to say goodbye eventually, but now that the moment is here, it feels so sudden. "I don't have to leave right now, but at some point, the team will start to wonder where I am. I told them I'd meet them at the resting spot soon."

"Yes, of course…" Laurel doesn't look Persimmon in the eyes. She's clearly nervous. "Rescuing those chickens was so… it made me feel so helpful. It was scary, of course. I mean, I always thought I was brave until I had a gun pointed at me. Well, I *am* brave, but what I—"

"She wants to join The Enlighteners," Lyric exclaims. "Will you let her on the team or not?"

"Lyric!" Laurel yells. She tosses a piece of uneaten fruit at him.

Lyric dodges the fruit. "What? I'm helping. You're blabbing on, just like you always do when you're nervous."

Laurel turns back to Persimmon and stands up straight, attempting to regain her composure. "As I was saying, this whole experience has changed—"

"Yes, of course you can join The Enlighteners!" Persimmon cuts in, hugging Laurel. "We'd be honored to have you on our team."

"Oh, hooray!" Laurel hugs Persimmon back.

Lyric rolls his eyes and walks toward the pet door.

"Lyric, wait!" Laurel calls after him. "You're not going to say goodbye?"

"I already said goodbye," Lyric says. "Remember when you went off to the rescue mission in the first place? I knew right then that you were leaving for good. Why do you think I cried so much?"

"Because you're dramatic," Laurel says.

Lyric nods. He can't argue with that.

"I wasn't sure I wanted to join the team at that point, though," Laurel says. "How did you know?"

"I've seen the way you two snuggle. When you find that, you'd be a fool to let it go."

Laurel blushes. She walks over to the skunk and wraps her front legs around him. "I love you! I love you! I love you, my brother!"

Laurel pulls the purple collar off her neck and hands it to Lyric. "This way you won't forget me."

"I'll never forget you, Laurel," Lyric says. "Keep it. That way *you* never forget that you always have a home."

Laurel puts the purple collar back around her neck. "I promise we'll visit. Aren't you excited to see what species of animal we bring back next time?!"

Lyric shrugs. "Only if they're skunks. It was nice seeing some other skunks after so long."

Persimmon and Lyric say their goodbyes and Lyric walks into the house. Just before Persimmon and Laurel disappear into the forest, Laurel turns to look at Dr. Misra's house one more time. After her traumatic experience as a baby losing her mother and sibling, she thought that this place would be her home for the rest of her life. Why venture into the dangerous forest when she has everything she needs here?

But Persimmon's passion for saving other animals is inspiring— enough to give up comfort and safety. She never officially said goodbye to Dr. Misra, but that's because she doesn't consider it a farewell. She'll visit again. It will be her vacation home, she muses to herself. Laurel skips into the woods. She is officially an Enlightener!

56

RASHA SITS BESIDE Chopper among the trees. She licks his wounds as he goes in and out of consciousness. The sunlight during the day seemed to help warm him—even heal him a bit—and at times he even awakens and seems peaceful resting in the leaves without a heavy chain around his neck. But Rasha can't help but feel heartbroken that she's watching her father slowly dying.

It's night now. Finley is curled up nearby watching Rasha's tireless efforts to bring Chopper back to health. Rasha, Finley, and Basil pulled Chopper farther into the woods with the blanket Rasha and Sadie used to carry Maxie, so at least he has something comfortable to lie on.

The rest of The Dissidents are strewn about the woods in the vicinity. Everyone is exhausted after traveling deep into the forest as far away as possible from the two properties they just raided to rescue the dogs.

The second rescue mission was a great success, and The Dissidents have added another 50 pit bulls to the army. All the dogs are getting along well, commiserating over their shared violent histories.

Vincent is confident that whenever people come across the homes with all the human and canine remains, they'll fall for all the clues that The Dissidents left behind. What person would assume that a group of escaped minks led a team of raccoons and dogs to exact revenge on some savage humans?

Vincent has plans to raid all the dogfighting yards they can find in the area over the next week, and then he'll have built up his army with enough powerful and protective dogs to move to the next, more ambitious part of his plan.

While the other Dissidents rest, Vincent goes over his ideas with Ember, Sadie, Krait, and a few other loyal members. He doesn't tell them everything—just the aspects that he'll need their help to accomplish.

Rawly has no idea that this secret meeting is taking place, or he would certainly expect to be part of it. Instead, he's sleeping alongside Drig, Linder, Dusty, Scraps, and Apricot. Rawly didn't reveal to his friends that his experience in the closet had rattled him. He went along with the second mission like he was completely fine. He was glad, though, that the dogs took care of the humans in the second house quickly and without him in the room. He wasn't sure his nerves could take another harrowing incident so soon.

For now, Rawly and the rest of the group are fast asleep—everyone, that is, except Scraps. The young raccoon can't get the image of all those dogs' bodies burning out of his head. It seemed so gory but also so clever. It thrills him to think that The Dissidents tricked the humans.

He also can't believe that he was one of the raccoons who helped light the fires. *Persimmon would have a heart attack if she knew I had been that close to fire.* He grins. He enjoys that feeling of independence—of being more grown up.

As Scraps starts to drift into slumber, he hears rustling in the forest a few feet away. He pops up, which startles the sleeping Apricot. She yowls and leaps into the air, awakening Rawly, Drig, Dusty, and Linder.

"What's going on?!" Rawly asks.

"There's someone out there," Scraps whispers.

The rustling comes again—only closer. The crew ready their claws.

"Scraps?" a tiny voice calls out.

Scraps knows who it is immediately. "Nibbin?"

Scraps sprints a few feet forward to find Nibbin trembling. The young mink inches back with every step Scraps moves toward him. "Nibbin, it's me. What's wrong?"

"Don't be angry at me." Nibbin starts to cry.

The raccoon's heart is racing. "Nibbin, what is going on? Is everyone okay?"

"Persimmon, Derpoke, Bruiser..." Nibbin is breathing so hard that he looks ready to faint. "They're dead. They're all dead."

Everything in the world around Scraps fades away—the trees, the leaves, his friends. The darkness seems to thicken around him. His brain can't compute such horrific news. Three of the closest animals in the world to him—all dead?

Rawly rushes closer to Nibbin. "What did you say?!"

Nibbin twists around and dashes a few trees away.

"Nibbin, stop!" Rawly shouts. "Tell us what happened. What do you mean 'they're all dead'?"

"Don't be angry at me," Nibbin says.

Rawly, Drig, Linder, Dusty, and Apricot move toward Nibbin, getting frustrated with his erratic behavior.

"Nibbin, we're your friends," Rawly says. "We're not going to be angry at you. Tell us what happened."

Scraps doesn't move. He's within hearing distance, but he can't move.

"Persimmon got stuck in a trap. We tried to get her out, but we couldn't. She lost too much blood. She died."

The group gasps.

"A hunter came with his son," Nibbin continues. "He shot Bruiser and carried away Persimmon's body. Derpoke wouldn't let go of her, so he took Derpoke and said he was going to eat him. The humans killed them all. I miss Persimmon! I miss them so much!"

Nibbin crumbles into the leaves. The team is silent. They can't believe that their three friends died such gruesome deaths.

Behind them, Scraps is lying on the ground, weeping. Rawly and Apricot step over to the raccoon and wrap their paws around him.

Nibbin is bawling, too, so Drig picks up the small mink and holds him. Nibbin has felt so guilty about the whole incident, and he's been wandering in the woods for two weeks looking for Vincent's troops. He didn't realize Scraps, Rawly, and all his old teammates would be with them, though. He was trying to rejoin the other minks and hopefully never have anyone find out about his involvement in the deaths of his friends. But then he saw Scraps and he felt compelled to reveal the truth. Well, not the entire truth. He neglected to mention that the reason Persimmon got stuck in the trap in the first place was because she was saving *him*, but he fears everyone will hate him if they know what really happened.

If only Nibbin understood the new trouble he had caused by inaccurately reporting who had perished. He might never have said a word. But it's too late now. The wheels have been set in motion.

57

SCRAPS SOBS UNCONTROLLABLY inside a tree trunk. Apricot sits 60 feet below at the base. The despondent raccoon asked to be alone so she is giving him his space, but she wants to be close in case he needs anything.

Rawly went off with Drig, Dusty, Linder, and Nibbin to break the news to Vincent about Persimmon, Derpoke, and Bruiser. Vincent was infuriated. He practically tore a tree down with his own claws. He wouldn't be free if it weren't for Persimmon, and he had always hoped she'd come to her senses and join his army. That said, he's not surprised by her demise. He suspected that humans would eventually kill her if she kept trying to make peace with them. This simply confirms what he already knew—humans must be eradicated.

Instead of venturing straight back to Scraps, Rawly decided to have a meeting with his raccoon crew and Nibbin. He wanted more information from the mink about exactly what happened with his friends' murders, and he was sure the gory details would upset Scraps.

While they conduct their meeting, Apricot still sits quietly by the tree where Scraps is hiding. She licks her paws incessantly out of stress but stops abruptly when she hears rustling in the leaves ahead of her. She looks up to see Vincent heading toward her. He's accompanied by Sadie, Krait, and another pit bull, Grigor, who was rescued from the second dogfighting yard. Vincent is so much smaller than these three muscular dogs, but with his stern expression, he's still the most foreboding of the four.

"I heard about your friends, Apricot," Vincent says. "The news saddens me deeply."

"I'm worried about Scraps," Apricot replies. "Persimmon, Derpoke, and Bruiser meant everything to him."

"That's why I'm here," Vincent says. "I, too, lost close family and friends. I thought perhaps I could console him."

Apricot looks high up in the tree. "Hope you like climbing."

Minks are excellent climbers, so Vincent ascends the tree with ease. When he reaches the hole where Scraps is hiding, he perches on a branch outside so as not to invade the grieving raccoon's space.

Scraps stops crying for a moment, realizing Vincent is there. "I guess you heard."

"I did," Vincent says. "It's a travesty. They were all great heroes. I owe my life to them, as well as to you. I know it can't compare to how you are feeling, but I am devastated."

Scraps wipes his eyes, but the tears keep coming. "I wish she were here right now. I wish this were all a dream."

Scraps sits with his head held low.

Vincent steps into the tree and crouches beside the raccoon. They're about the same size. "I rarely ever talk about this, Scraps, but I've lost family members, too. My brother Frestin..." Vincent cringes. He so rarely ever says his name, it hurts to get it out. "He was skinned alive right in front of me by a vile human."

Vincent thinks about his brother covered in blood with his skin yanked off, still alive in the pile of carcasses.

"Every day that image of my brother haunts me. How helpless I felt as he was murdered. The fury and heartache I felt that day is just as powerful today. Nothing will ever heal that wound, Scraps. But…"

Vincent pauses. He moves to face Scraps. "There was one thing that brought me some solace."

Scraps looks Vincent in the eyes. He wants so much to feel better.

"Revenge," Vincent hisses.

The hair stands up on the back of the young raccoon's neck. Revenge? This hadn't even occurred to him.

"You can't bring back your sister and friends, Scraps, but you *can* make that man and his son suffer for what they did to them. That's what I did to the Petersons. My mink friends tore apart the Petersons' flesh while they were sleeping. Knowing that those repugnant humans died such agonizing deaths brings me so much relief."

Scraps isn't crying any longer. He's stunned—and mesmerized—by Vincent's proposal. He doesn't feel happy, but the hope of vengeance hurts less than despair.

"At the bottom of that tree are three pit bulls," Vincent continues. "Three of the most powerful soldiers in The Dissidents, and they've agreed to help you avenge your sister and your friends. What do you say?"

Scraps's heart pounds in his chest. He takes a deep breath. "Yes."

58

RAWLY, DRIG, DUSTY, and Linder have been plotting for hours what to do about the deaths of Persimmon, Derpoke, and Bruiser. After being grilled for what felt like forever, Nibbin was exhausted, so he left to find a place to rest and the raccoon crew continued their discussions. Finally, they came up with a plan and decided to share it with Vincent.

Rawly and his crew find Vincent, Ember, a few pit bulls, and some minks deep in discussion in the hole of a giant tree that fell down in the last major storm. The roots of the tree dangle in the background covered in spider webs.

"Vincent," Rawly says as he walks over to the group. It suddenly hits him that they're clearly having an important meeting to which he was not invited. "You were probably looking for me to be part of this meeting, so I apologize that we were off on our own. We had a lot to discuss. I want to share our ideas with you."

"Mmm," Vincent murmurs, only slightly interested. This is the second time tonight that Rawly has interrupted Vincent's meeting, so the mink is getting a bit perturbed. Vincent wants to focus right now. A great deal of strategizing is needed for what he has planned next for The Dissidents.

Rawly doesn't notice Vincent's disinterest. "We have two friends, Chloe and Tucker, who you probably remember, that we want to find. Maybe we can convince them to join The Dissidents. Then, we thought we'd search for Derpoke. Chances that he's still alive are slim, but maybe the humans kept him in a cage somewhere. If they plan to eat him, maybe they're fattening him up first. It sounds far-fetched—and gross—but we're trying to be optimistic."

"Sounds like a good plan," Vincent says in a rush. "I hope you find your friends, and of course, they are welcome to join The Dissidents."

Vincent turns back around to continue discussions with his army. Rawly is disappointed. He was hoping Vincent might push back, saying that he couldn't lose so many vital soldiers at such a critical time.

"I mean," Rawly speaks up. "I know it will be tough not having us around as you plan the next mission, so if you need one or two of us to stay, we can."

"We'll be fine," Vincent says. "I understand the importance of reuniting with your old Uncaged Alliance members. You can rejoin us after you've done so."

"Okay. We'll get Scraps and Apricot and be on our way then."

As Rawly, Drig, Linder, and Dusty begin to walk away, Vincent calls out. "Actually, Scraps and Apricot have gone off on their own mission."

"They have?" Rawly asks. "What *type* of mission?"

"Scraps decided that he wanted to dispose of the humans who killed your friends."

Rawly and his crew almost fall over.

"He what?!" Rawly asks. "He's going to kill them?"

"Yes," Vincent replies calmly. "He's fine. I sent three of the fiercest dogs from The Dissidents to help him. He's completely safe with their protection."

"I don't understand," Rawly says. "You just let him go? He's only a child. He could get killed."

Vincent grits his teeth. He doesn't like being questioned. "Better to die defending someone you love than to go the rest of your life regretting that you let their killer go free. Isn't that what drove you to release those tigers, Rawly—killing all those humans for what they did to Claudette and Fisher? And yet you judge others for wanting to do the same?"

The pit bulls and minks move in closer to Rawly and his crew. Things are getting tense and they want to protect their leader.

Rawly eyes the formidable creatures, but he continues his rant. "But Scraps isn't a fighter like me, Vincent. He's a sweet, young raccoon and he's devastated. Persimmon wasn't just a sister to him. She was basically his mother. He'd known Derpoke his entire life, and he and Bruiser were inseparable. Who knows what he'll try to do in the state he's in? You might have just sent him to his death."

Vincent scrapes his nails through the dirt. He's trying to contain his anger, but his patience is wearing thin. "I told you already and I will not repeat it again. I sent three of the best warriors from The Dissidents. I need their help here as I plan the next mission, but instead, I asked them to protect Scraps. He isn't going to die. He's going to get vengeance."

Vincent steps closer to Rawly. The pit bulls and minks follow. "After all Persimmon did for us other animals, Rawly, she deserves to be avenged. As her brother, Scraps deserves to be the one to do it. No one—not you, not me—should get in the way of that. Persimmon, Derpoke, and Bruiser were your friends, too. I think the question you should be asking yourself is… don't you want to help him?"

Rawly is speechless. The question embarrasses him. He realizes that a true Dissident would have conjured the plan to rid the world of these barbaric humans the moment he had heard about his friends' murders. He and his raccoon crew did think about defending themselves against the humans if they were able to locate Derpoke alive, but they didn't concoct a plan to attack the humans. There's been so much bloodshed lately; Rawly was simply focused on rescuing his friends.

But he can't admit that to Vincent. Clearly the mink already doesn't see him as a leader in The Dissidents or he would have been invited to whatever planning session Vincent is holding right now. This is a chance to prove to Vincent that he's indispensable to The Dissidents.

"Of course, we'll join Scraps," Rawly says.

"You'll want to leave now then," Vincent says. "They left hours ago with Nibbin leading the way. Apparently, the location is about a week away, so perhaps you'll be able to catch up with them before they reach their destination. I wish you all well."

With that, Vincent and his conspirators head back to the hole by the tree roots.

Rawly turns to Drig, Linder, and Dusty. "Come on, let's find Scraps."

59

PERSIMMON LETS OUT a big yawn as she awakens. It's twilight. Everything around her is purplish blue. She peers at Laurel, who is curled up beside her still asleep. Persimmon usually sleeps in a fallen tree, but on Laurel's request, they slept out in the open in a comfortable patch of thick grass. Their fur is still warm from the sun shining on them throughout the day.

The past few weeks have been so tumultuous that they almost broke Persimmon, which is why she's spent the past few days just resting. Finally, she feels relaxed. The rescue of the chickens was as much of a success as she could make it. The team saved thousands of chickens' lives and no one from The Enlighteners was injured. And, of course, now she has Laurel by her side, which makes everything in life brighter.

Persimmon was also pleased with her plan to reach out to humans after the chicken rescue. The morning after the mission, Persimmon, Laurel, and Chloe, along with a few deer and raccoons, snuck over to a nearby neighborhood and placed the bodies of two dozen chickens on plates outside humans' front doors—the team "borrowed" the plates from Dr. Misra's house. Persimmon and her crew then hid in trees and bushes to see people's reactions.

People were just starting their days, getting ready to head to work, when they opened their doors to a massive shock. There, lying right in front of them were the dead bodies covered in boils, disease, and wounds. All the humans gasped—some screamed. They had heard about the raid of the chicken farm on the news, so they understood that this was a message from some animal activists. Some people were annoyed and tossed the bodies in the trash, but Persimmon could tell that a few were moved by the sight (it's difficult not to feel a hint of guilt when confronted with the entire bruised body of an animal you normally eat).

There's no way for Persimmon to know how much of an effect this outreach had on those humans, but she feels confident that it planted a seed. If humans are never confronted by the horrors of their choice to exploit other animals, why would they stop?

After that excursion, The Enlighteners came to this spot in the woods for a well-earned break.

Right now, the rest of the team, including a few hundred chickens, is scattered throughout the nearby woods. As was planned, the rest of the chickens are dispersed in groups with other animals deeper in the woods.

Persimmon told the team that they should take a few weeks off to rest before jumping into their next mission. Some of the new members ventured back to be with their herds and packs, but they told Persimmon that whenever she started her next mission she should send Senator Santiago to find them.

Derpoke, Chloe, and Tucker are, of course, staying with Persimmon, and The Enlighteners now have a few new dedicated members: Senator Santiago and a dozen-bat battalion, Marigold (the young female deer who helped Chloe during the chicken rescue), Alister (the raccoon who is missing an eye), and some of the squirrels, deer, skunks, raccoons, beavers, and opossums.

Aunty Adelaide and Uncle Bennett were impressed by the outcome of the rescue mission, but the life of an Enlightener is far more eventful than they can bear. They'll stay in the safety of their tree. Their farewell to Persimmon and her team was emotional. Despite their early concerns with her missions, they are incredibly proud of their niece for what she has accomplished.

Persimmon smiles to herself as she gazes at the sleeping Laurel. Everything feels calm. She always feels this way when she's snuggled up to Laurel. Most of the time, Persimmon is overburdened by the enormity of trying to rescue the countless suffering animals. She's also plagued with an ever-present sorrow over the friends she's lost and the animals she wasn't able to rescue. But in Laurel's embrace, all this fades away. Life is serene. It feels as if somehow everything is going to be okay.

Laurel stretches out her legs as she rustles from her slumber.

"Wake up, sleepy," Persimmon says.

"You're already awake?" Laurel says without opening her eyes.

"Yep. I was thinking."

"That's so out of character for you," Laurel grins. "Let me guess. You were thinking about how you're going to save all the animals of the world."

"No, I'm following your advice not to ponder that while we relax."

"Hmm. Sounds like the sage advice of a very smart raccoon."

"A genius, in fact." Persimmon runs her paw through Laurel's fur. "I was just thinking about how marvelous it feels to be happy."

"Ha. Well, it's nice to see you relaxed. When I first met you, I thought, 'This raccoon is intense.' But I understand now that you had the weight of thousands of lives depending on you. That will make anyone intense."

Laurel stretches out her legs again and yawns. "This last week has been really nice, but I have to admit, that night when Dr. Misra was cradling you, a part of me wished that would be our life together. You, me, Lyric, and Dr. Misra living in peace and being happy."

"I understand. After having only two weeks of that life, I see how easy it would be to get used to it. You can go to sleep without worrying a predator might sneak up and attack you. The only human around is kind to us. You get food given to you multiple times a day. Everything is easier."

"If only you weren't so compassionate. Life could be so tranquil." Laurel grins and sits up to face Persimmon. "Promise me that one day we'll go back to Dr. Misra's house. We'll curl up on the couch by Dr. Misra and Lyric and have a movie night again."

After Persimmon was permitted to roam Dr. Misra's house freely, Laurel and Lyric introduced her to television and movies. Persimmon had seen televisions and computers in people's homes before, but she never understood what the humans were watching. Laurel did her best to explain them to her, and eventually they all nestled together on the couch.

Laurel hops in place, unable to contain her delight. "Next movie on my list is one of my favorites: *Titanic*!"

"What's that about?"

"It's about two people who fall in love on a boat that sinks. It's so sad. It's wonderful."

"Why would you want to watch something sad?"

"It's sad in a good way. And so romantic. You'll love it! Trust me."

Persimmon can't help but smile. Laurel looks so cute getting so excited about this movie.

The two raccoons lock eyes. They get quiet for a moment. It's sweet and awkward. Laurel looks away, feeling shy. That's when she notices someone staring at them from between some bushes off in the distance.

Persimmon turns around. "What?"

"You-know-who is spying on us," Laurel says.

"Derpoke?" Persimmon says. "Oh, poor Derpoke. I keep trying to talk to him, but he's been so distant lately. Give me a minute."

Persimmon trots through the grass over to a group of bushes. She sees Derpoke crouched in a ball attempting to hide.

"Derpoke?" Persimmon calls.

Derpoke stays very still, hoping she doesn't see him.

Persimmon crawls through the bushes and sits beside Derpoke. He looks up at her. She smiles. "Hello, my long-lost friend."

"In case you think I was gawking at you like a weirdo, I wasn't," Derpoke says. "I was coming to talk to you, but then I saw that you were with…" Derpoke can't bring himself to say Laurel's name. "… her, so I decided to wait until you were available. That's all."

"You can always come talk to me. You don't have to wait. I've been wanting to chat with you for days, but you keep finding reasons to walk away."

Derpoke looks down at the grass. "You're always with *her*. I'd prefer to talk to you alone."

Persimmon sighs. "Derpoke, I miss you. I know Laurel and I have gotten close and that upsets you, but I don't want that to come between us."

Derpoke still doesn't look at Persimmon. He fidgets with the grass under his toes. "It's hard for me to be around you two. The way you look at her… I always wanted you to look at *me* that way."

Persimmon moves closer to Derpoke, hoping he'll look at her. He does not. "Do you know that you're my favorite animal out of everyone? Always have been. Always will be."

Derpoke is silent. He rests his head on his paws.

"I'm serious. I love Scraps dearly. I love everyone in The Enlighteners, and I'm enjoying getting to know Laurel, but no one compares to you. You and I have a special bond. You are my heart."

Derpoke finally looks at her. He wants to believe it. Even if she doesn't love him, he wants to believe that he's still special to her.

Persimmon smiles warmly and puts her paw on his.

Suddenly there's a commotion off in the distance. The Enlighteners are yelling and shouting, but Persimmon can't make out what everyone is saying. She sniffs the air. Her curious expression melts into terror. She turns to Derpoke. "Wolves!"

*   *   *

Persimmon quickly pushes her head through the brush and yells to Laurel. "Run up that tree! Hide!"

"What's happening?" Laurel asks.

"Just do it!" Persimmon shouts. She rushes back to Derpoke. "The wolves must have been attracted by the smell of the chickens. They're too close. We can't run. They'll see us. Just stay very still."

Persimmon puts her body around Derpoke and lies as motionless as possible.

There's rustling in the grass near them. Two wolves saunter through the brush near Persimmon and Derpoke.

One of them looks at Persimmon. Without hesitation, Persimmon puts her body in front of Derpoke to shield him. "Please, we're friends. Don't kill us!"

The wolf continues walking past the two smaller animals without saying a word. Then two dozen more wolves amble by. All of them gaze at the terrified Persimmon and Derpoke, but they just keep walking.

Persimmon and Derpoke tremble in place, confused and terrified.

Finally, all the wolves pass by. Persimmon whispers to her opossum friend. "Come. We need to get in a tree. Maybe they'll circle back around."

Persimmon and Derpoke quickly but quietly crawl through the brush toward a tall tree. Just then, a group of skunks treks past the two friends.

Persimmon is flummoxed. "Be careful," she whispers. "There are wolves nearby."

A young skunk stops. "Yes, we know. We're following them. Haven't you heard? All the animals of the forest are having a meeting. An army is forming to defend us against humans."

"You mean The Enlighteners?" Persimmon asks quizzically. "That's us."

"No, I've heard of you, too," the skunk says. "This is another group: The Dissidents."

"The Dissidents?" Persimmon thinks about it for a moment. She looks at Derpoke. "Rawly," both of them say at the same time.

Rawly said that he would take on humans, but starting an army? Persimmon can't believe it. It feels grander than something he could accomplish.

Persimmon turns to the skunk. "Rawly is a raccoon who used to be part of our team. I didn't realize he had it in him to assemble an entire army, though."

"Never heard of him," the skunk says. "The leader of The Dissidents isn't a raccoon. He's a mink named Vincent."

Persimmon and Derpoke are stunned—and yet not surprised at all. Of course it's Vincent. He's the most cunning animal they know.

"Excuse me," the skunk says. "I have to catch up with my family. Follow our scent. You'll want to be part of this meeting."

The skunk rushes off.

Persimmon turns to Derpoke. They exchange a concerned look. They both thought they were about to be eaten by a pack of wolves, but somehow this news feels more ominous.

Persimmon hasn't thought about Vincent in a while, but she gets a sick feeling in her stomach. If Rawly had been assembling this army, she would have been worried that he'd make a mess of the operation and get a bunch of animals hurt in the process. But if Vincent is running it, he's quite capable of succeeding. The question is: what exactly is he planning?

60

"THAT'S HIM," NIBBIN says.

Scraps, Nibbin, Apricot, Sadie, Krait, and Grigor crouch low to the ground in the woods. There's a clearing in front of them with a house to the far right and three men sitting on logs by a fire. A few feet behind the humans is a small shed with a pickup truck next to it. Empty beer cans litter the ground beside the men. Gavin's father, Rick, is wearing the same camo hat and pants he wore on that fateful day.

"Are you sure?" Scraps asks. "I need you to be sure."

"Positive," Nibbin says. His voice is heavy. You don't forget the face of the man who killed three of your best friends.

Scraps nods. He grits his teeth. He's never felt more hatred toward a human in his life. He surveys the area around the humans. "There are no visible weapons. We attack now. They'll have no idea what hit them."

"Agreed," Sadie says. "Let's circle around to the other side and attack from behind."

Just before the team moves, Nibbin sheepishly speaks up. "Scraps? Those two humans sitting by that man weren't there when Persimmon, Bruiser, and Derpoke were killed."

"Do you see that truck behind them?" Scraps says. "A whole row of dead squirrels is dangling off the side."

Nibbin hadn't noticed. He was too busy staring at the hunter. The last time he saw him was one of the worst days of his life.

"These humans are monsters, Nibbin," Scraps says. "They must be stopped."

Scraps quietly but briskly darts into the woods with the dogs and Nibbin following. Apricot is stunned by how fast all this is moving. She's never seen Scraps like this before—taking charge, filled with rage. She's not sure if she's impressed by his newfound boldness or saddened that his playful innocence has all but disappeared.

$$* \quad * \quad *$$

Rick and his two hunting buddies sip their beers, chatting. The fire is the only light around, and the orange glow flickers on their faces and glimmers on the trees at the edge of the forest.

The men are so inebriated that they teeter on their logs as they talk. Rick laughs heartily as he finishes a story about Gavin. "Then I whooped him 'til he couldn't walk the next day."

Another man with a large belly grins. "Knowing your son, he probably liked a good spanking on the butt. 'Oh, hit me again, Daddy.'"

The third, lankier man laughs so hard that he falls off his log.

Rick kicks dirt at the larger man. "Shut up, Davis! I'll whoop you, too."

Davis and the lanky man continue to laugh.

At that moment, Apricot prances out from the woods and stops on the other side of the fire. The three men stare at her with bewilderment.

Davis looks at the beer can in his hand. "What's in this stuff? Am I hallucinatin' or did a cat just appear out of the woods? Is he yours, Rick?"

"She, you idiot!" Apricot chides.

Rick picks up an empty can and tosses it at the orange tabby. "No, she ain't mine. Get the hell outta here, vermin!"

Apricot gracefully dodges the can and hisses at them. "Three... two... one..."

Right then, Sadie, Krait, and Grigor pounce on the backs of the three men. Davis falls forward into the fire and screeches. His clothes and hair light up instantly. He hops up and trips on the log, falling face forward onto a rock. He continues to burn as he lies there motionless.

Krait chews at the lanky man's throat. Blood spews from the man's neck, so Krait and Grigor turn their attention to Rick.

Sadie has pinned Rick to the ground, but she hasn't gone for the kill shot yet. She's waiting for Scraps to get a turn at him. Krait and Grigor chomp down into the man's arms as he hollers. All three pit bulls put their weight on Rick as Scraps runs up to the man's head and scratches at his eyes, nose, and mouth.

After Scraps has had his fill, he steps back. "Finish him."

Sadie clamps down on Rick's throat with her mighty jaw and rips out a massive chunk. The man grabs his neck and starts crawling toward the woods. Scraps and his crew watch the man pull himself a few feet and then stop. He bleeds out in seconds.

Nibbin is hiding in the woods with his eyes shut and his ears covered. He wishes he were curled up in a fallen tree beside Persimmon far away from here, but he knows that's not possible.

Scraps and the three dogs are caked in blood. They turn their attention to the small shed near the truck. Apricot joins them as the five animals sprint to the shed door and Scraps hops onto Sadie's back to undo the latch.

When Scraps pulls open the door, they are faced with a house of horrors. Inside, heads of animals line the walls—deer and even a bear. A lamp made out of a deer's skull and antlers sits on a table. Two rabbits dangle by their legs from the ceiling. Blood still drips from the rabbits' fur onto the floor, which is already stained red. Knives lie strewn on the table, and a rack of guns looms on one wall. This shed was built by a mass murderer.

There is no sign of Derpoke or Persimmon. Scraps's great fear was that he'd see Persimmon's or Derpoke's body cut open or maybe Persimmon's fur laid out, ready to be made into a cap. His mind speeds through a thousand gory thoughts.

She didn't have a tail. They probably just threw out her body. One of those guns was probably used to kill Bruiser. One of those knives was probably used to gut Derpoke.

With each thought, a fire burns even greater inside Scraps.

"Do you see your sister or friend?" Sadie asks.

"No," Scraps replies.

"Should we drag the human remains into the woods?" Sadie asks. "Maybe bury them so it's harder for the humans to find them?"

"Soon," Scraps says. He turns to the house. "But we're not done yet."

61

PERSIMMON AND THE other Enlighteners (Laurel, Derpoke, Chloe, Tucker, Marigold, Alister, Senator Santiago, and the other new team members) can't believe their eyes. They're walking through the woods and they've come upon a massive herd of animals—thousands and thousands of creatures of all kinds. Some are the same as those in The Enlighteners, but there are also so many more: minks, wolves, bears, foxes, mountain lions, dogs, cats, porcupines, turtles, frogs, snakes, elk, lizards, mice, rats, rabbits, chipmunks, coyotes, owls, crows, sparrows, and more.

Never could The Enlighteners have imagined that all these animals would congregate, but here they are getting along perfectly fine—and clearly getting up to something.

As The Enlighteners make their way through the animals, a great deal of whispering surrounds them. It starts with the minks The Enlighteners rescued from the Peterson fur farm. They recognize some of the team, especially Persimmon—the raccoon without a tail and now without a leg who started this whole revolution. She's alive! The minks spread the shocking and thrilling news to the other animals.

Persimmon and The Enlighteners feel uncomfortable when they realize that thousands of animals are staring at them and murmuring.

A black mink finally walks up to Persimmon. "Persimmon? Is that really you?"

"Yes," Persimmon says. "Do I know—"

"Oh my gosh!" the mink yells. "She's alive!"

"She's alive!" rings throughout the thousands of animals.

Persimmon and The Enlighteners crouch down, overwhelmed.

"What is happening?" Persimmon turns to Laurel and Derpoke.

"Whoa!" Laurel is beaming. "You're a celebrity. Does this happen everywhere you go?"

Persimmon shakes her head no.

Minks from the Peterson fur farm push their way to the front of the crowd. They touch Persimmon's fur to make sure she's real. "We're so happy you're alive! We thought you were dead."

The black mink turns to Derpoke. "Aren't you the opossum from the rescue, too? You're also alive?!"

Derpoke looks at Persimmon, stunned.

It suddenly dawns on Persimmon what all the fuss is about. "You must have heard about the trap. No, I survived. Minus a leg, but I'm okay. How did you hear about that?"

In the distance, animals shuffle to the side to create a path for Vincent as he hurries through them.

Vincent stops in front of Persimmon, mouth agape. "I can't believe… It's true! You're really alive."

Vincent isn't much of a hugger, but he can't control himself. He wraps his front legs around her neck. Vincent then pats Derpoke on the back. "And you're alive, too, Derpoke. Incredible!"

Persimmon is surprised by his unusual show of affection. "Yes, we're okay. What is happening? How do you know about the trap?"

"Come, Persimmon!" Vincent says, waving for her to follow him. "There's so much to tell you."

Persimmon looks around at all the animals staring at her. *I bet there is.*

*   *   *

Vincent takes Persimmon to the fallen tree where he conducts all his meetings. The roots with the spider webs dangle in the background. Most of the other Dissidents steer clear of this area to give Vincent space as he conjures up secret plans for the missions. Only Ember and a few minks and pit bulls are nearby.

At first, Vincent just stares at Persimmon. He feels like he's looking at a ghost.

"You'll have to forgive me," Vincent says. "I am in awe that you're standing right in front of me alive."

"I understand." Persimmon laughs. "I feel bad for Nibbin. He must have felt awful thinking he was responsible for my death, and for Derpoke's and Bruiser's. He ran off from the team, so he wasn't there when the other members found out that Derpoke and I had, in fact, survived. I should have known he'd attempt to rejoin you and the other minks. Where is he now?"

Vincent isn't sure how much of the truth he should reveal. According to Rawly, Persimmon doesn't even know that Rawly, her brother, and the others left The Uncaged Alliance to join The Dissidents. It certainly isn't a good start to Vincent's reunion with Persimmon to mention that her brother and her friends went off on a possibly fatal mission with Vincent's encouragement, so Vincent decides to be discreet.

"Nibbin is with a subgroup scoping out our next rescue mission." Vincent quickly changes the subject before she asks any more questions about Nibbin's whereabouts. "I'm sorry to hear that Bruiser was, in fact, killed. It's a tragedy. Before I met him, my only experience with dogs was Mando and Diablo, so I despised all canines. But Bruiser's kindness showed me that not all dogs are vicious. He will be greatly missed."

"Yes, I miss him every day," Persimmon says with a sigh. It's still hard to believe that she'll never see him again.

Vincent sees that Persimmon's spirits are dimmed, so he continues to another topic. "Speaking of which, you may have noticed that a few hundred dogs have joined The Dissidents."

"I have," Persimmon says. "Most look to be of the same breed, in fact."

"Astute observation," Vincent says. "They're all from the same type of abusive background. Over the past few weeks, The Dissidents and I rescued dogs from six different properties. The humans raise these dogs to fight one another to the death, and as disgusting as it sounds, the humans do this for fun. People gather in crowds and cheer as the dogs tear each other apart. Humans never cease to amaze me with how depraved they can be."

"Oh my goodness, that's awful! I'm so glad you rescued them. How did the missions go? Clearly you have a big enough team to raid the properties."

"We think of ourselves as more of an *army* than a *team*, but yes, the missions were an incredible success and now we're moving to the next phase of our plan. All the animals you saw out there have joined us only in the past week because we need as much help as we can get to pull it off."

"Ah, so what's the next phase of your plan?"

"We'll get to that in a moment. First, I want to ask how The Uncaged Alliance fared? I see you have some new members as well."

"To start, we changed our name to The Enlighteners. It's more fitting for our goals as a team. But yes, we do have some wonderful new members. We haven't been able to pull off as many missions as you, though. We had a major setback when I almost lost my life in that trap, but despite that, we have conducted two more missions since the fur farm. One was at a circus. I'm not sure if you know what that is."

"Actually, your rescue effort at the circus was the talk of the forest a while back. I heard it erupted into violence, but I applaud your boldness. What an audacious move to conduct a mission in the middle of the city."

"Hmm," Persimmon lowers her head. "It got... we did everything we could. We rescued some animals, but it did get chaotic. We just had too many factors working against us."

Vincent can tell Persimmon feels ashamed about the outcome. He decides not to belabor her over it. "You said you conducted a second rescue effort?"

"Yes." Persimmon brightens up. "It was much more successful. We rescued thousands of chickens who were going to be killed by humans for food."

"Chickens. I've heard of them. They're birds, right? Congratulations on freeing them."

Vincent can't help but look at the place where Persimmon's leg once was. "I don't mean to be rude, but I have to ask: How did you survive the trap?"

"I should be dead," Persimmon says. "That's the most miraculous thing I want to share with you, Vincent. *Humans* saved me."

"Humans?!" Vincent can't believe his ears. Neither can Ember, the minks, and the dogs. They lean in more closely.

"Yes!" Persimmon says. "Nibbin probably mentioned that a boy and his father set the trap, and when they came to get me, my loyal team tried to rescue me. Sadly, that's when the man shot Bruiser. But what happened next is one of the biggest surprises of my life. The father took Derpoke and me back to his home where he was surely going to kill us, but the boy, Gavin, was so upset by Bruiser's death that he snuck Derpoke and me away to protect us from his father. That act of kindness saved our lives!"

Vincent's heart skips a beat. *The boy* saved *her?!* A pang of guilt runs through Vincent. *That boy could already be dead, and I'm the one who encouraged it. Of course, Scraps could also be dead if the mission went awry.* Now he certainly won't be telling Persimmon what her brother is doing.

"The next miracle, Vincent, is that Gavin took us to a human, Dr. Misra, who devotes her life to rescuing and healing other animals. Exactly what she did to stop the bleeding is beyond my comprehension, but somehow she healed me. On top of that, Dr. Misra and Gavin are incredibly sweet. I know you are leery of humans, which you have every right to be, but these two showed me that there are some decent humans out there."

Vincent looks away from Persimmon in disbelief. He stares at the spiders walking around on their webs. *Kind humans? And they're the ones who saved Persimmon and Derpoke? It sounds too fantastical to be true.*

Vincent turns back to Persimmon. "This is just so… Every single human I've ever encountered is downright depraved. This is hard to believe."

"I understand, but don't forget, you're the one who told me that you'd heard humans had freed minks at another fur farm. There are some honorable humans out there, Vincent. We just have to keep looking for them."

Vincent stands up straighter. "My goal right now is to rescue as many animals as possible. I don't have time to search for a few honorable humans. What would be the purpose anyway?"

Persimmon steps closer to Vincent. "Don't you see? Humans like Dr. Misra and Gavin are the key. They're the ones who will help us make peace with *all* humans."

"Are you serious?!" Vincent scoffs. "With everything you've seen humans do to us other animals, do you seriously think that we can make peace with them?"

"We *have* to make peace. What's the other option—wage war? Please tell me that's not the next phase of your plan."

Now, Vincent steps closer to Persimmon. He digs his nails into the dirt. "The war began thousands of years ago, Persimmon. Trust me. I've done my research. I've spoken to countless animals since I escaped that cage at the fur farm. Humans have been exploiting us, torturing us, murdering us for a very long time. They've done gruesome things to us that you won't even believe—that you won't *want* to believe. The thing is, we other animals are losing so badly that we can't even see the war for what it is. It's genocide. Humans think they can do whatever they want to us, as if the whole purpose of our existence is to serve their needs."

Vincent angrily kicks dirt behind him. "That ends now. We're fighting back."

"Vincent," Persimmon sighs. "What are you saying, exactly? Are you just going to go around murdering every human you see? How does that make you any better than them?"

Things are getting tense. Vincent doesn't like being questioned, especially when his troops are watching. He motions for Ember, the minks, and the pit bulls to leave the area. They do. Vincent steps toward the roots of the tree for more privacy. Persimmon follows.

"You're not understanding, Persimmon. You believe I'm doing this out of revenge. As if I'm taking my anger toward the Petersons out on all other humans. That's not it at all. Humans are sadistic by nature. Why else would they get enjoyment from watching other animals chew each other to death? Why else would they slash our throats and not care when they hear us screaming in pain? You can't reason with someone like that. They don't care if we suffer. They *enjoy* it when we suffer. I wish there could be peace. I worry about how many more animals will die when we fight back, but I told you, I've done research. I've spoken to many creatures about this. History has proved that as long as humans are around, there cannot be peace. Think about it: Why does one species get to annihilate all the rest of us? By exterminating humans, we're defending ourselves from extinction."

Vincent is so sure of this. That's what makes Persimmon's fur stand on end. That, and the fact that he's making some reasonable points. She knows all too well how demented some humans can be. If she's going to convince Vincent not to move forward with this war, she'll have to tackle the debate from another angle.

"Vincent, let's put aside the fact that it's wrong to go around murdering humans. You must know that you can't win a war against them. They're so much more powerful than we are. They have so many weapons. I've been doing research myself. Humans have an uncanny talent for creating deadly weapons. If nothing else, it's not strategic to think that we can overpower them with just our claws and teeth."

"I am aware of their weapons and I have ideas about how to deal with them. Let me ask you this, Persimmon: What is *your* solution—to reason with them? Do you really think you can reason with depraved humans like the Petersons—humans that show no emotion as they skin other animals alive?"

"You're right. Humans like that are sick, and that's why we shouldn't start with them. We start with humans that already show an affinity for us other animals. Some humans consider dogs and cats part of their family. Surely, we can convince them that you and I, cows, chickens, and other animals are no different than their beloved dogs and cats."

"How do you convince them? Humans aren't even intelligent enough to understand what we're saying."

"Yes, communication is an incredible challenge, but here's the most promising news yet: I was able to convince Dr. Misra to stop eating other animals. After she saw how much the chickens were suffering, she said that she would stop eating them. How wonderful is that? She's proof that it can be done."

"Wow, one human. What a victory. And while you took the time to convince that *one* human, millions—maybe billions—of other animals were slaughtered around the world. Do you even know what the world is?"

Persimmon had discussed the concept of the world with Laurel, but it was confusing. At the very least, she understands that the forest where she grew up is only one minuscule portion of their habitat. "I learned about the world as much as I could. I plan to learn more."

"All you need to understand right now is that everywhere—*everywhere*—humans murder us other animals by the billions."

Persimmon is annoyed by how smug Vincent is getting, so she throws this at him: "If you've got this all figured out, before you condemn humans for being so irredeemably evil, how about the fact that some of those animals out there in your Dissidents are predators? Wolves, mountain lions, MINKS. You all eat other animals, too."

"All the animals in The Dissidents who are not carnivores do not eat other animals. I was inspired by your great leadership to adopt that rule. But I will admit that the rest of us who are carnivores still eat other animals. That said, we've made a truce. Until we get rid of the humans, we're only eating scraps from humans' trash, animals who died naturally or the remains of humans. Once the war is over, we'll return to our old ways, because we're carnivores and we need to eat other animals to survive. As you know, though, humans are not carnivores. They have a choice to be compassionate or to kill. They *choose* to kill. And killing other animals to eat them is only one of countless issues. Do I really need to list all the sadistic ways that humans exploit and torture us? The crimes that humans commit against other animals far outweigh what the rest of us do to one another. They poison our rivers. They destroy our habitat. Did you know that humans toss giant nets into the oceans and just round up whichever creatures happen to be swimming there? They don't even eat all of them. They throw the ones they don't want in the garbage, or they cut off their fins and toss the animals back into the water to drown. What other creature kills animals with so little regard? I truly don't think you understand the scale of their crimes."

Persimmon is stunned. Vincent has clearly done a lot more research than she has. She barely knows anything about the ocean other than that it's much larger than any lake she's ever seen. She feels overwhelmed. How can she convince billions of humans to be more compassionate? She can't even speak to them, and while she knows that a small number of humans are fighting to protect other animals, the majority of humans clearly don't listen to those human allies. So why would they listen to a tiny raccoon?

Vincent continues. He sees that Persimmon is speechless. Maybe he's finally getting through to her. "You saw all those animals out there who have come to join The Dissidents, Persimmon. How many soldiers do you have in The Enlighteners? Not nearly as many. And why do you think that is? Because word got out that The Dissidents are finally fighting back against the humans and that's exactly what these animals want."

"Of course that's what they want. They've spent their lives being tormented by humans and watching helplessly as humans murdered their families and friends. They have every right to be angry. That's why it's always easier to get followers with promises of war than it is with promises of peace. But don't be fooled. Deep down, below all that anger, what all those animals really want is freedom and peace. You don't stop violence with more violence. You stop it with kindness and understanding. That is what will create long-lasting harmony among all species."

Persimmon looks Vincent in the eye. How can he not agree with her? "Humans are capable of compassion, Vincent. The fact that I'm standing here alive is proof. I'm telling you, killing humans is not the answer."

"No?" Vincent grins. He sits down beside Persimmon. He's been waiting a long time to tell her this shocking news, and this is the perfect moment. "Persimmon, I'm going to tell you something that will change your entire perspective on these missions. Are you ready?"

Persimmon braces herself. This cunning mink always has something devious up his sleeve. What now?

"You mentioned that the rescue of those chickens was a success. So am I to assume that no one was hurt during the mission?"

"No one in The Enlighteners was injured. I made sure of that."

"By the way you phrased that, it would seem *someone* was hurt then. Am I right?"

Persimmon senses that he's setting a trap, but she's not one for lying. If she's going to win this debate, it will be with honesty. "We did our best to rescue the chickens, but there were too many of them. Humans rushed at us before we could rescue all the chickens."

"Uh-huh. And there were mass casualties during your rescue effort at the circus as well, correct?"

Persimmon lowers her head. "Yes. As I said, things went awry. The creatures were too big. I knew from the beginn—"

"Yes, I'm sure you did everything you could. And I also know that your first mission with the calves ended with every single one of them being slaughtered. Conversely though, when you rescued us minks, the mission was a great success, right? No casualties?"

"Well, some of the minks were already injured in the cages when we arrived, but eventually we rescued everyone. Clearly you have a point to all this, Vincent, so just make it."

"All your rescue missions have been thwarted by humans except when you rescued us minks. Every single one of us made it out safely, because the Petersons didn't come running out and attack us. And the only reason for that is because they were already dead."

Persimmon doesn't say a word. She knows Vincent is crafty, but she did not see *that* coming.

Vincent stares at Persimmon, watching her shocked reaction with great interest. "While you and I were outside releasing the minks from their prisons in the yard, I had another team of minks, led by my brother Trenton, go to the house and kill the Petersons in their sleep."

"I knew you were up to something." Persimmon shakes her head. "I didn't know it was this, but I knew you were up to something that night."

"Of course we were. You don't put your soldiers' lives at risk by hoping the humans don't wake up. Do you really think we were that quiet that we didn't wake a house full of humans? No, with all that commotion right outside their windows, the Petersons surely would have arisen. And you know what they would have done? They would have murdered all your friends and then recaptured all the minks just so they could murder *us* one day. Humans are malicious, Persimmon. Not every single one of them, but most of them. To think that humans will give us our freedom if we ask nicely enough is naïve. We have to fight for it."

Persimmon shakes her head. This mink is getting on her last nerve. She steps to the edge of the hole and points over the rim. "All those animals out there are gathered here because they believe that you can save them. If you wage war against humans, it won't end with all of them alive. Humans will shoot them into a million pieces. How will you feel then? How will you feel when you lead all of them to their deaths?"

Vincent grits his teeth. That rankles him to no end. *How dare she suggest that I'm leading them to their deaths.* He charges forward and gets in her face. "Really? You of all animals dare say that? How many of your friends have died following *you*?"

That stings. Persimmon instantly thinks of Bruiser, Claudette, Fisher, and all the animals she couldn't save—Gilby, Nayana, Elsie, and so many more.

"Every time I see you, Persimmon, humans have chopped off another one of your body parts. You really think humans want peace? They want to gut you and wear your fur as a hat. After everything you've been through, how can you still defend them?"

Persimmon shakes her head disappointedly, realizing that nothing she says will get through to this mink. "You know what the saddest thing is? With all these animals gathered, if we worked together, we might actually be able to save ourselves."

Persimmon steps out of the hole.

Vincent stares at the spot where she was just standing. He regrets being so harsh. She's right about that, which is why he was hoping she'd join The Dissidents, but that will never be. He hates how cutting things got between them. He truly does respect her. He also finds it disconcerting that she'd think he would risk the lives of The Dissidents so carelessly. Vincent doesn't want things to end on such a sour note.

He climbs to the top of the hole and searches for Persimmon. He sees her making her way through the crowd of animals. "Persimmon! Wait."

Persimmon stops and turns around.

Vincent takes a deep breath to calm his temper and steps over to her. "Do you really think my plan is so cavalier as to have The Dissidents run around, biting and scratching all the humans to death?"

Persimmon's not sure what to say.

"Come on," Vincent says. "You know I'm cleverer than that. And I would never put my soldiers at risk so irresponsibly."

Vincent proudly looks around at his powerful troops. He looks back at Persimmon and pronounces, "I'm not building this army to fight all the humans. I'm building it to fight all the humans that are left."

"What does *that* mean?" Persimmon asks, mouth agape.

Vincent licks his chipped tooth and grins. "The day you join The Dissidents, we'll discuss my tactics, but for now, I want you to know that I do believe you that there are some decent humans out there. Regarding that, a dog named Chopper was seriously injured in a fight. Maybe that human, Dr. Misra, who saved you, can help him."

Persimmon is surprised by Vincent's sudden change in demeanor. "Yes. Maybe. Hopefully."

"Good." Vincent turns to Basil—the brown female pit bull who helped Rasha and Finley carry Chopper into the woods. "Basil, can you take Persimmon to see Chopper?"

"Of course," Basil says. "Follow me."

Persimmon and Basil walk off together.

Persimmon and Vincent leave their dispute feeling empty and dissatisfied. They wanted so much to persuade the other to understand their point of view, fearing that if they did not, it would lead to the imminent death of so many animals, including each other.

If only they both knew the dangers that lay ahead; their conversation would have gone very differently.

62

RAWLY AND DRIG race through the woods, panting. They've been tracking Scraps and his group for days and barely sleeping for fear of not catching up to them in time. Dusty and Linder couldn't keep up, so they are almost a day behind.

Finally, Rawly sees the glow of a fire off in the distance. Raccoon tracks lead directly to it. "That must be it!"

Rawly and Drig quicken their pace. They make it to the edge of the woods and are shocked to see three bloody bodies strewn on the lawn, one of which is covered in flames.

"Oh no!" Rawly says. "We're too late."

Rawly notices Nibbin, who is hiding in the brush with his eyes and ears shut. He rushes up to the mink, and Nibbin shrieks when the raccoon touches him. "It's me, Nibbin. Are you okay?"

Nibbin nods, but doesn't say a word.

"Where is Scraps?"

Suddenly, screams are heard from inside the house. People are howling, begging for their lives. "No! Oh God, no!"

Rawly and Drig sprint toward the screaming. Rawly stops when he notices that Nibbin is not following.

"Nibbin, come on!"

Nibbin cowers in the brush.

"I need your help, Nibbin." Rawly begs. "Please!"

The screeching in the house gets louder and more frantic.

Nibbin sucks in a deep breath and runs with Rawly and Drig up to the house. A hole is torn in the screen. The screams become more distinctive—a woman and a young boy bellowing in pain as dogs growl and chew.

Rawly, Drig, and Nibbin jump through the screen and dash up the stairs. At the top, they twist around the corner and speed into the bedroom.

Inside, to their horror, they see Sadie, Krait, and Grigor ripping their teeth into a woman's back as she covers Gavin with her body. The boy has a large knife in his right hand, which he swings at the attacking dogs. "Get away! Leave us alone!"

"Stop!" Rawly yells at the dogs. "Stop!"

Scraps and Apricot, who are planted near the doorway, are stunned to turn and see Rawly, Drig, and Nibbin standing there.

"Stop!" Rawly shouts again.

The dogs are so frenzied that they keep chewing at the woman's flesh, trying to pull her away from the boy.

Rawly knows what he has to do. He runs through the room, gets right next to Sadie and waves his paws, signaling her to stop biting the mother. Gavin swings the knife at the charging raccoon, not realizing Rawly is there to protect him.

Rawly dodges the knife and grabs Sadie's tail to get her attention. The pit bull swings around and rams Rawly away with her head.

Scraps is horrified to see his friend thrown into the wall. "Stop! Stop!"

The three dogs cease biting and step back toward Scraps.

"What's going on?" Sadie asks, breathing heavily, her eyes darting around; she fears they're being attacked from behind.

The mother's back is ripped apart. One of her feet is chewed like a bloody toy. But she's still alive. She covers her son with her arms, and they both weep in the corner.

"Mommy! Mommy!" Gavin repeats over and over. His hand shakes uncontrollably as he holds up the knife, attempting to be threatening.

Rawly stands up and limps over between the humans and the pit bulls. His loyal friend Drig steps over by his side—if Rawly is going to be attacked, then so is he.

A chill runs down Rawly's spine when he sees that Scraps and the dogs are covered in blood. Sweet, playful Scraps covered in blood. It feels like a nightmare.

"Don't do this," Rawly says. "Nibbin, tell them what you told me about the boy and Bruiser."

Scraps, Apricot, and the dogs turn to look at the small mink.

"The boy didn't want to shoot Bruiser," Nibbin whispers, afraid if he talks any louder he'll upset everyone even more than he already has. "His father kept yelling at him to shoot Bruiser, but he cried and said no."

"See," Rawly says. "The boy didn't want to hurt Persimmon, Derpoke, and Bruiser. His father did. His father is the sadistic one."

Scraps defiantly stands up taller. "Nibbin told me that the boy was the one who set the trap that killed Persimmon, Rawly. How can he not be guilty of killing her?"

"I understand," Rawly says. One of his paws was injured when Sadie threw him, so he's standing on three legs and holding the fourth limp. "But the boy was only doing what his father taught him to do. He was being raised to be evil, but when his dad tried to bully him into shooting Bruiser, he refused. That tells me that he's capable of decency despite his violent upbringing. Look at him. He's just a child."

"I've seen humans burn puppies alive," Sadie growls. "They couldn't care less about us other animals—no matter what age we are. Look around the room. There are dead body parts everywhere and you dare call this human innocent?"

Scraps and the whole crew examine the boy's bedroom. A rabbit foot sits on the nightstand. Two hats made out of raccoon fur and another raccoon tail dangle off Gavin's backpack.

"For all we know, that hat over there is Scraps's sister," Sadie says.

Scraps knows it is not because the tail is intact, but it disturbs him to see the fur of raccoons used as a trivial accessory. "He's a murderer, Rawly. There's no defending him."

The pit bulls brace to attack again.

"Scraps, wait," Rawly says. He limps closer to the raccoon. "Please. This isn't you. You're not a killer. I know you're filled with anger over the deaths of Persimmon, Derpoke, and Bruiser—*I* am too—but killing this boy and his mother doesn't resolve that. You already killed the father. It's finished."

Sadie gets in Rawly's face. "He has every right to get revenge, and you have no right to take that away from him."

Rawly cringes, fearing the wrath of this powerful dog. Drig steps over and bares his teeth, prompting Krait and Grigor to bare their teeth at the raccoons.

Apricot's fur stands on end. "Surely we can settle this without turning on one another."

"She's right," Scraps says, holding up his paw to halt the dogs. "Like Vincent said, the humans are our enemies; not each other."

"We're not standing down until they do," Sadie growls.

Rawly steps back and nudges Drig to do the same. "We didn't come here to brawl with you, Sadie. We respect you. You know that. For one second, though, think about this from the boy's perspective. The way Coach abused you and tried to make you and the other dogs into killers, this boy's father did the same to him."

Sadie, Krait, and Grigor think about this for a moment. The idea of a human being kind is so foreign to them. Even worse, this boy's room is filled with evidence that he is, in fact, a murderer. That said, the concept of the boy as a victim resonates.

The pit bulls examine Gavin. He may be holding a knife, but he still feels harmless. Tears stream down his face as he clings to his mother. His father looked like a murderer, but this frightened boy in his dinosaur pajamas does not. All at once and unexpectedly, the dogs are conflicted.

"What about Claudette and Fisher, Rawly?" Scraps asks. "Getting revenge didn't bring them back, but you felt relief knowing those humans got what was coming to them."

Rawly nods, not sure how to respond. He looks back at the boy and his mother cowering in the corner. *What am I doing? This boy did take part in killing my friends, and his mother must know that he and his father are killers... But brutalizing them in retaliation feels so far off from why we started these rescue missions.*

Then it hits Rawly. He didn't come running all this way just to fight for the life of this boy and his mother; he's fighting for Scraps. He promised Persimmon that he'd take care of her little brother. Stopping Scraps from committing such a violent act is certainly part of that.

"What I did was wrong, Scraps." Rawly surprises himself when these words come out. At the time, making those humans pay for murdering Claudette and Fisher felt justified, but if this is what it wrought—corrupting such a sweet raccoon as Scraps—maybe he made a mistake.

"Persimmon was right. By letting those tigers free, I killed some innocent humans. Some of the humans deserved to die, but not all of them, and I have to live with that. Claudette was so loving and Fisher had a good heart too. They wouldn't have wanted me to do that just as Persimmon wouldn't want *you* to do *this*."

Scraps thinks about Persimmon. He remembers curling up beside her every night as they slept. How she saved his life after their mother abandoned him. Every memory he has, Persimmon was there—watching over him, doting on him, taking care of him. She used to kiss his ears. He loved that. No matter what she was eating, she'd always share it with him. She was brave and smart and so full of love, and he'll never, ever see her again.

Then there's Derpoke. He was there from the beginning, too. He was like a father to Scraps. He always griped when Persimmon and Scraps wanted to go on a dangerous adventure, but then he'd always admit how fun it was afterward. Derpoke made complaining endearing. He was sensitive and intelligent and so full of love, and now Scraps will never, ever see him again, either.

Then, of course, there's Bruiser. Scraps marveled every day that he was so close to such a towering canine, but Bruiser was so gentle with him—like Scraps was a butterfly. Bruiser instantly became his best friend. They had so much fun together—goodness gracious, did they have fun jumping around and biting each other. He was loyal and playful and so full of love, and Scraps will never, ever see him again.

Scraps peers at the boy and his mother. Gavin's pajamas are smeared with his mother's blood. Rawly is right. Persimmon would be devastated that her little brother was terrorizing these humans. But Persimmon isn't here. She gave humans too much credit. This boy looks innocent now, but wait until he's an adult; then he'll have walls covered with the heads of other animals as trophies just like his father. This boy is a murderer. There's no other way to see it.

Scraps turns to the pit bulls. "Kill them."

Sadie, Krait, and Grigor barrel through Rawly and Drig, knocking the raccoons off their feet. Gavin and his mother shriek as the dogs rush toward them. Krait and Grigor grab the mother by the legs and drag her across the floor. Gavin holds onto her and swings his knife, but he falls forward onto the ground, dropping the weapon. Sadie pounces on him, and minutes later the two humans are dead.

The room goes quiet. Rawly feels sick. He slumps over. *What have we done?*

Apricot and Nibbin have hidden under the nightstand. They feel sick, too. Killing Coach felt justified. Killing the hunters felt justified. But this... this feels wrong.

Rawly turns around and looks at Scraps. He wants to yell at him. *He didn't have to kill them! This is going too far.* But then Rawly sees that Scraps is shaking and that he's soiled himself out of fright.

Scraps notices Rawly staring at him. Tears well up in the young raccoon's eyes. "I just want Persimmon back."

"I know, Scraps," Rawly says. "I know."

Rawly can't believe that things have taken such a dark turn. Up until now, he thought of himself and The Dissidents as heroes, but tonight does not feel heroic.

He looks around at Scraps, Sadie, Krait, Grigor, Apricot, and Nibbin. None of them looks joyful. This wasn't a victory. They all look hurt and confused.

This isn't who we are, Rawly muses. *We're not vicious killers.*

He's right. He's absolutely right, but then the truth crashes through him. *But maybe this is who we've become. The humans have finally pushed us too far. There's no going back now—and it only gets worse from here.*

63

PERSIMMON AND BASIL make their way through the thousands of animals gathered throughout the forest. They soon come upon The Enlighteners, who are mingling with the various creatures—the team is especially excited to talk to species they've never interacted with before.

Laurel sees the distress on Persimmon's face. "Are you okay, Persimmon?"

"I'm fine." Persimmon attempts a smile but is clearly rattled by her conversation with Vincent. She sees Chloe talking to a mountain lion a few feet away. "Chloe? Can I speak to you for a moment?"

Persimmon addresses Laurel, Derpoke, and Chloe, who are standing in front of her. "Can the three of you help me with something? This is Basil. She's going to take us to an injured dog who needs our help."

Persimmon's three loyal friends nod and then follow her and Basil through the crowded forest to a quieter spot. There sits Rasha and Finley with Chopper, who is sleeping on a blanket.

"Rasha," Basil says. "This is Persimmon. She may be able to help Chopper."

For the first time in a long time, Rasha and Finley perk up. Things have felt so hopeless lately. They've spent the past week sitting beside

Chopper, watching him slowly die, and on top of that, Rasha is disappointed that she didn't find any of her other family members (Minton, Remington, Jax, and Afilia) at the other dogfighting yards. With everything feeling so dour, it's astounding to think that Chopper may still have a chance at survival.

That's when Persimmon sees Rasha's face—her horrifically mangled face. All the pain that this pit bull has endured is exposed right there in her shredded ears, chipped teeth, and chewed-up nose. Persimmon can almost feel the bite marks as if she had been there herself. *What kind of ruthless human could do this to another animal?*

Persimmon is instantly reminded of Gilby. She felt the same overwhelming urge to save that innocent calf as she feels to save Rasha. Persimmon knows that Dr. Misra will do everything in her power to bring Chopper back to health, and even if she can't, it brings Persimmon some comfort to think about how much Rasha and Finley will appreciate Dr. Misra's efforts. They've never known a human to be kind, but they'll see it with their own eyes.

We'll heal one another. Vincent is too short-sighted. It is possible to make peace with humans. We simply have to heal one another, one by one.

Persimmon jumps into leadership mode. She coordinates a few deer from The Enlighteners to carry Chopper to Dr. Misra's house. The journey will be long, so Persimmon is anxious that Chopper may not make it, but at least there's still some hope.

Before Persimmon leaves, she asks Chloe to guide The Enlighteners back to the place in the woods where the team was relaxing. She plans to reconnect with them once she and her crew safely escort Chopper and the dogs to Dr. Misra. After that, they'll move forward with their next mission.

Persimmon hikes alongside the deer, who are carrying Chopper. Rasha, Finley, Laurel, Derpoke, and Basil follow (Basil decided to join The Enlighteners for this mission). They hike 30 trees into the woods when they are stopped in their tracks by the sight of Scraps, Rawly, and their crew.

Persimmon lights up. Scraps does not. All the air collapses out of his lungs.

At that same moment, Vincent is gathered with his officials in the hole of the fallen tree. His face is lit with rage as he reveals the violent details of the next stage of his plan.

The officials' paws shake as they listen—partly out of fear and partly because the moment is finally here. The Massacre is about to begin— only this time it will be of humans.

END OF BOOK TWO

Thank you so much for reading *Vincent and The Dissidents*!

If you enjoyed the book, please leave a review on
Amazon, Goodreads, and wherever else you order books.
Five-star reviews are a great way to encourage others to read
The Enlightenment Adventures.

Also, visit Christopher-Locke.com to sign up for my newsletter.
That way you'll be the first to know when Book Three is published!

ACKNOWLEDGEMENTS

My wife, Jaya, it means the world to me that you adore these novels and characters so immensely. It's been quite the journey as I've written and published this series over the last few years (one more to go!), and I couldn't have accomplished it without your love and support.

Dad, Mom, Mike, Beth, Marina, Arun, RoseMarie, Chris, Mena, Sunny, Michael, Mickayla, Katelyn, Phil, Tigg, Myka, not only are you my family but you're also my friends. Thank you for your words of encouragement as I wrote this series!

Tin Tin, Midge, Tamarind, Cupcake, Rascal, and Cedar, I am proud to be your father and uncle. Everyone needs a little cute in their life, and you all provide that in abundance!

L.A. Watson, you did it again! Another cover that is a masterpiece!

Chrystal Ferber, Lisa Winebarger, John Goodwin, Mike Wolf, and Melanie Piazza, each of you are heroes for dedicating your lives to helping animals! Thank you for taking the time to answer my plethora of questions as I did research for the novel.

A very special thank you to the following people who generously supported my crowdfunding campaignto publish this novel. I am genuinely moved that you helped me follow my dreams:

Gina Ann, Jaya Bhumitra, Erin Browne and Chris Bledsoe Cort Cunningham, Dad, Bryan Ebert, Hannah Miriam Jaag, Mark Meunier, Thomas Negron, Kim Phan, LaVonne Vashon, Hannah Elizabeth Williams

www.ingramcontent.com/pod-product-compliance
Lightning Source LLC
Chambersburg PA
CBHW031131120726
47905CB00006B/1644